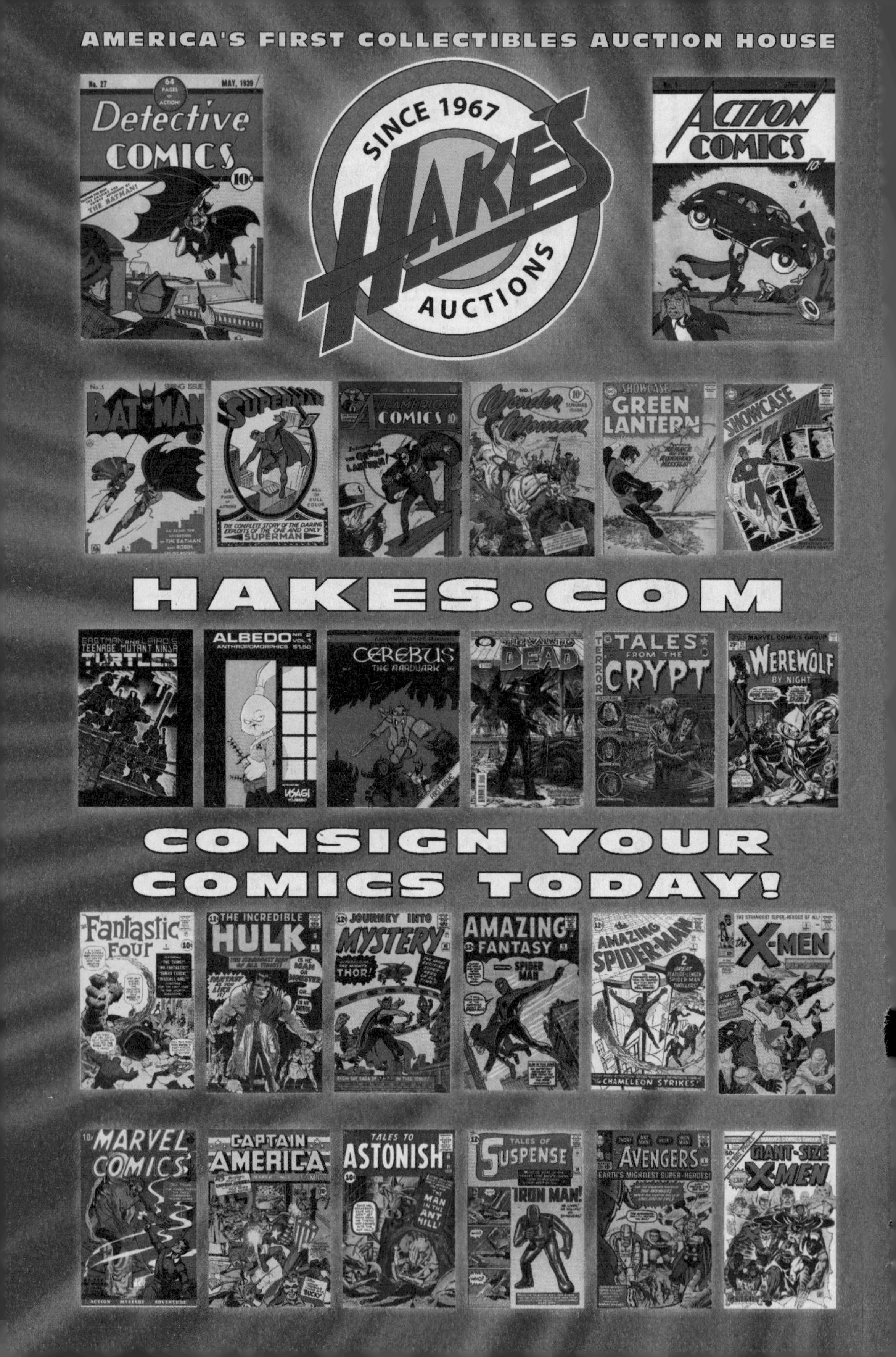
AMERICA'S FIRST COLLECTIBLES AUCTION HOUSE
SINCE 1967
HAKE'S
AUCTIONS
HAKES.COM
CONSIGN YOUR COMICS TODAY!

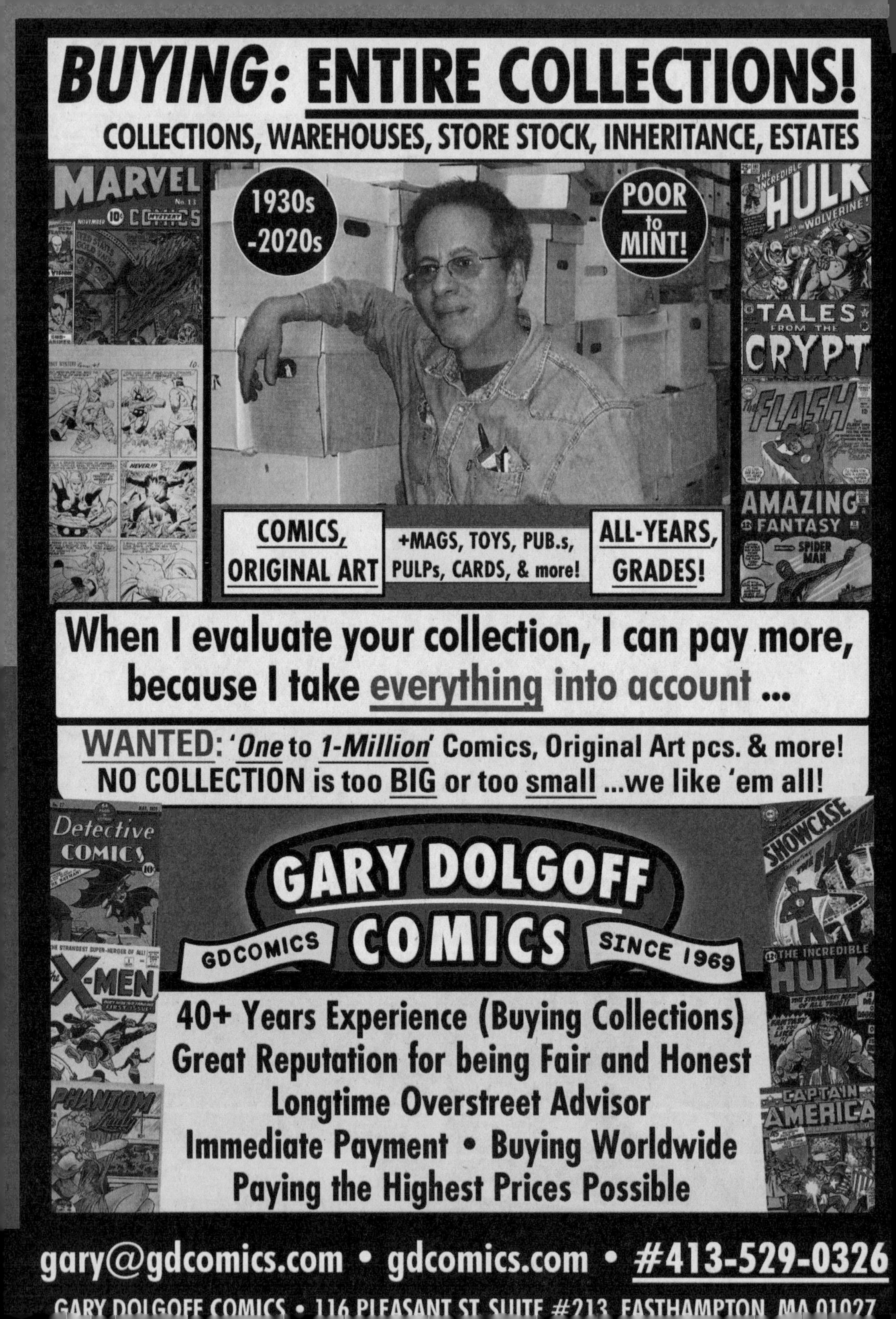
BUYING: ENTIRE COLLECTIONS!
COLLECTIONS, WAREHOUSES, STORE STOCK, INHERITANCE, ESTATES
1930s -2020s
POOR to MINT!
COMICS, ORIGINAL ART
+MAGS, TOYS, PUB.s, PULPs, CARDS, & more!
ALL-YEARS, GRADES!
When I evaluate your collection, I can pay more, because I take everything into account ...
WANTED: 'One to 1-Million' Comics, Original Art pcs. & more!
NO COLLECTION is too BIG or too small ...we like 'em all!
GARY DOLGOFF COMICS
GDCOMICS
SINCE 1969
40+ Years Experience (Buying Collections)
Great Reputation for being Fair and Honest
Longtime Overstreet Advisor
Immediate Payment • Buying Worldwide
Paying the Highest Prices Possible
gary@gdcomics.com • gdcomics.com • #413-529-0326
GARY DOLGOFF COMICS • 116 PLEASANT ST. SUITE #213, EASTHAMPTON, MA 01027

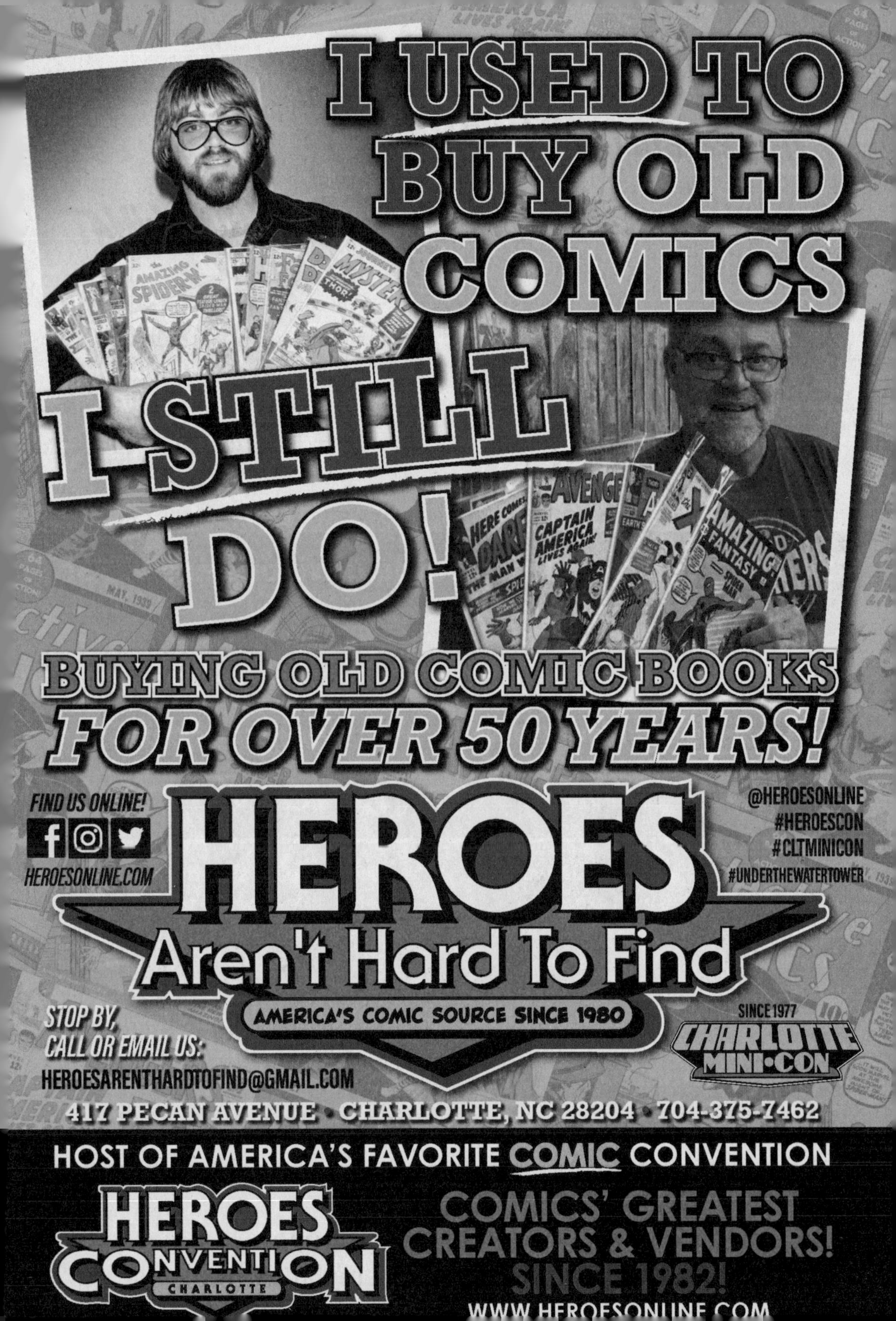

I USED TO BUY OLD COMICS
I STILL DO!
BUYING OLD COMIC BOOKS FOR OVER 50 YEARS!
FIND US ONLINE!
HEROESONLINE.COM
@HEROESONLINE
#HEROESCON
#CLTMINICON
#UNDERTHEWATERTOWER
HEROES Aren't Hard To Find
AMERICA'S COMIC SOURCE SINCE 1980
STOP BY, CALL OR EMAIL US:
HEROESARENTHARDTOFIND@GMAIL.COM
SINCE 1977
CHARLOTTE MINI-CON
417 PECAN AVENUE · CHARLOTTE, NC 28204 · 704-375-7462
HOST OF AMERICA'S FAVORITE COMIC CONVENTION
HEROES CONVENTION CHARLOTTE
COMICS' GREATEST CREATORS & VENDORS! SINCE 1982!
WWW.HEROESONLINE.COM

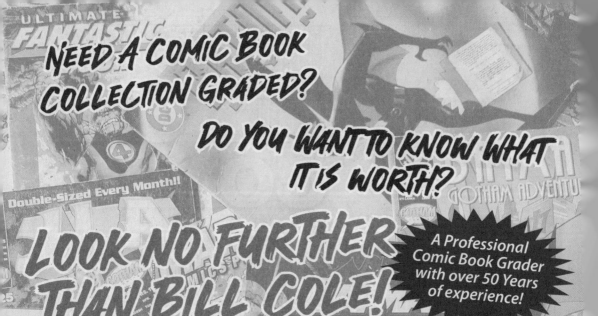

STEPHEN A. GEPPI PRESENTS

THE OVERSTREET COMIC BOOK PRICE GUIDE TO

LOST UNIVERSES

2ND EDITION

BY ROBERT M. OVERSTREET
& J.C. VAUGHN

C.C. BECK + SCOTT BRADEN + PAUL CASTIGLIA
WILLIAM M. COLE + BOB HARRISON
RIK OFFENBERGER + AMANDA SHERIFF + J.C. WASHBURN
CONTRIBUTING WRITERS

MARK HUESMAN + AMANDA SHERIFF
EDITORS

YOLANDA RAMIREZ
PRICING EDITOR

MARK HUESMAN + DAWN GUZZO
LAYOUT & DESIGN

JASON C. ODOM + SHAWN SIPPEL
PROOFING & EDITORIAL ASSISTANCE

SPECIAL THANKS TO

MIKE BARON + DIEGO BERNARD + MIKE BOLLINGER + COMICLINK + MARK DAVIS + JOSH DECK
CECI DE LA CRUZ + DIAMOND COMIC DISTRIBUTORS + GARY DOLGOFF + SHELTON DRUM + JACKIE ESTRADA
JOSH GEPPI + MIKE GOLD + GENE GONZALES + BUTCH GUICE + HAKE'S AUCTIONS + HERITAGE AUCTIONS
JIM HOLLISTER + JAYJAY JACKSON + JOSEPH A. JAMES + NICK KATRADIS + MINDY LOPKIN + ROLAND MANN
TOM MASON + BRIAN MILLER + MYCOMICSHOP.COM + JOSH NATHANSON + DAVE OLBRICH
BRIAN PULIDO + CONAN SAUNDERS + NILE SCALA + JIM SHOOTER + SHAWN SIPPEL + KARLA SOUTHERN
DOUG SULIPA + TIMOTHY TRUMAN + BILLY TUCCI + ALEX WINTER

GEMSTONE PUBLISHING • HUNT VALLEY, MARYLAND
WWW.GEMSTONEPUB.COM

For information, write to: Gemstone Publishing, 10150 York Rd., Suite 300,
Hunt Valley, MD 21030 or email feedback@gemstonepub.com

Spider-Man 2099 Hardcover Edition ISBN: 978-1-60360-612-7
Spider-Man 2099 Soft Cover Edition ISBN: 978-1-60360-611-0

Lady Death Hardcover Edition ISBN: 978-1-60360-616-5
Lady Death Soft Cover Edition ISBN: 978-1-60360-613-4

Scout Hardcover Edition ISBN: 978-1-60360-618-9
Scout Soft Cover Edition ISBN: 978-1-60360-617-2

Printed in Canada

First Edition: June 2024

GEMSTONE PUBLISHING

STEVE GEPPI
CHIEF EXECUTIVE OFFICER

J.C. VAUGHN
PRESIDENT

ROBERT M. OVERSTREET
PUBLISHER

MARK HUESMAN
EDITOR - PRINT

AMANDA SHERIFF
EDITOR - DIGITAL

YOLANDA RAMIREZ
PRICING EDITOR

SHAWN SIPPEL
DIGITAL STRATEGY DIRECTOR

TOM GAREY
KATHY WEAVER
BRETT CANBY
ANGELA PHILLIPS-MILLS
ACCOUNTING SERVICES

WWW.GEMSTONEPUB.COM

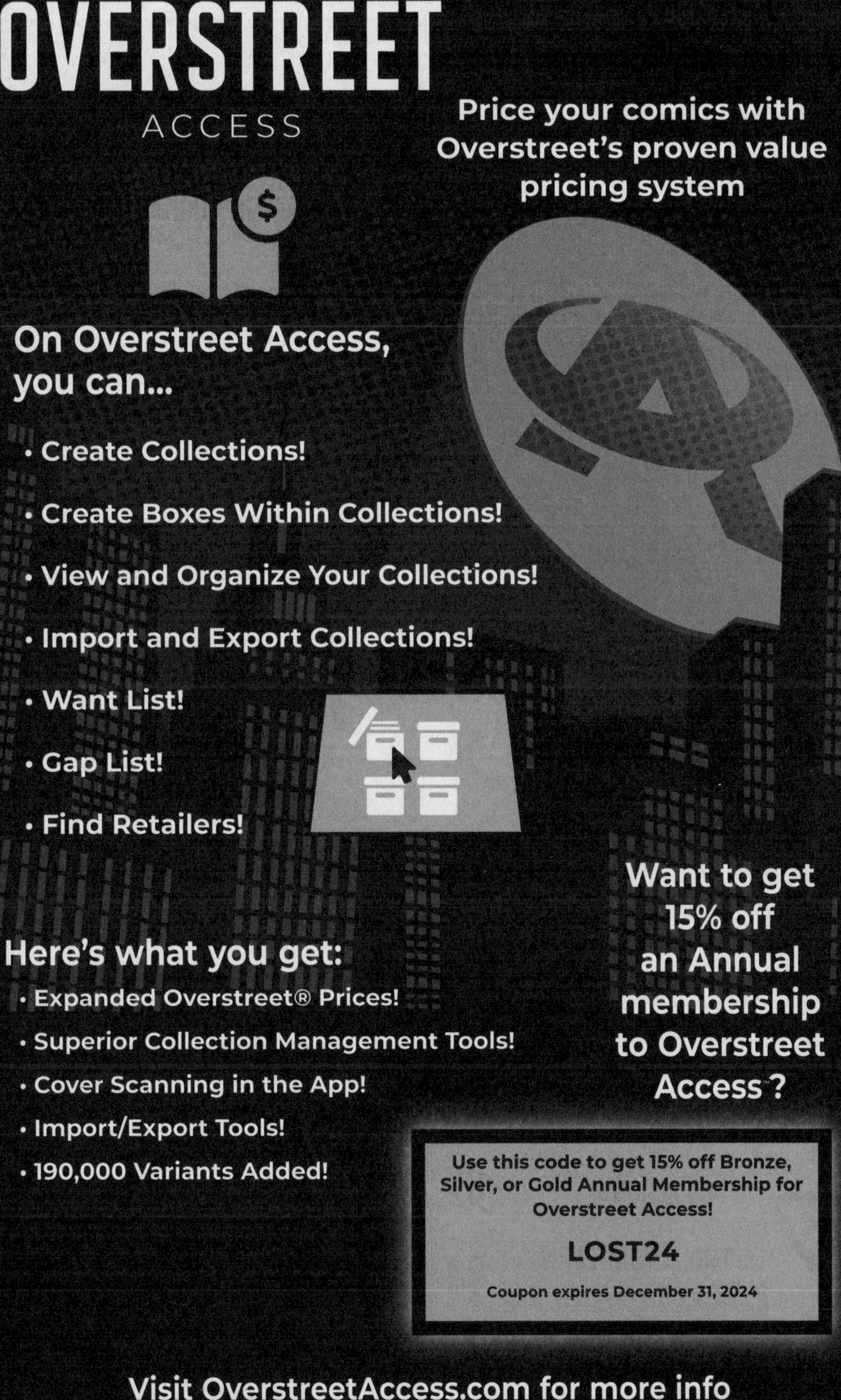
OVERSTREET
ACCESS
Price your comics with Overstreet's proven value pricing system
On Overstreet Access, you can...
• Create Collections!
• Create Boxes Within Collections!
• View and Organize Your Collections!
• Import and Export Collections!
• Want List!
• Gap List!
• Find Retailers!
Here's what you get:
• Expanded Overstreet® Prices!
• Superior Collection Management Tools!
• Cover Scanning in the App!
• Import/Export Tools!
• 190,000 Variants Added!
Want to get 15% off an Annual membership to Overstreet Access™?
Use this code to get 15% off Bronze, Silver, or Gold Annual Membership for Overstreet Access!
LOST24
Coupon expires December 31, 2024
Visit OverstreetAccess.com for more info

TABLE OF CONTENTS

GEMSTONE PUBLISHING

EVERY WEEK, *NEW COMICS* ARE RELEASED, OFFERING NEW TALES AND OPENING *NEW WORLDS* TO THEIR READERS.

BUT THEY *CAN'T* BEGIN TO APPROACH THE *NUMBER* OF COMICS THAT HAVE BEEN PRODUCED SINCE COMIC BOOKS *FIRST APPEARED* ON THE SCENE.

WITH ALL OF THE *RECORD PRICES* THAT HAVE BEEN *PAID* IN THE PAST FEW YEARS, CLEARLY *MANY PEOPLE* HAVE RECOGNIZED THE *VALUE.*

BUT THERE ARE STILL *MANY BARGAINS* TO BE HAD!

AMONG THE REALITIES YOU CAN VISIT ARE *"LOST UNIVERSES,"* PUBLISHERS OR IMPRINTS THAT HAVE *COME* AND *GONE...*

AND *SOMETIMES* COME *AGAIN...*

SO LET'S TAKE A FEW MINUTES AND TALK ABOUT THESE LOST UNIVERSES!

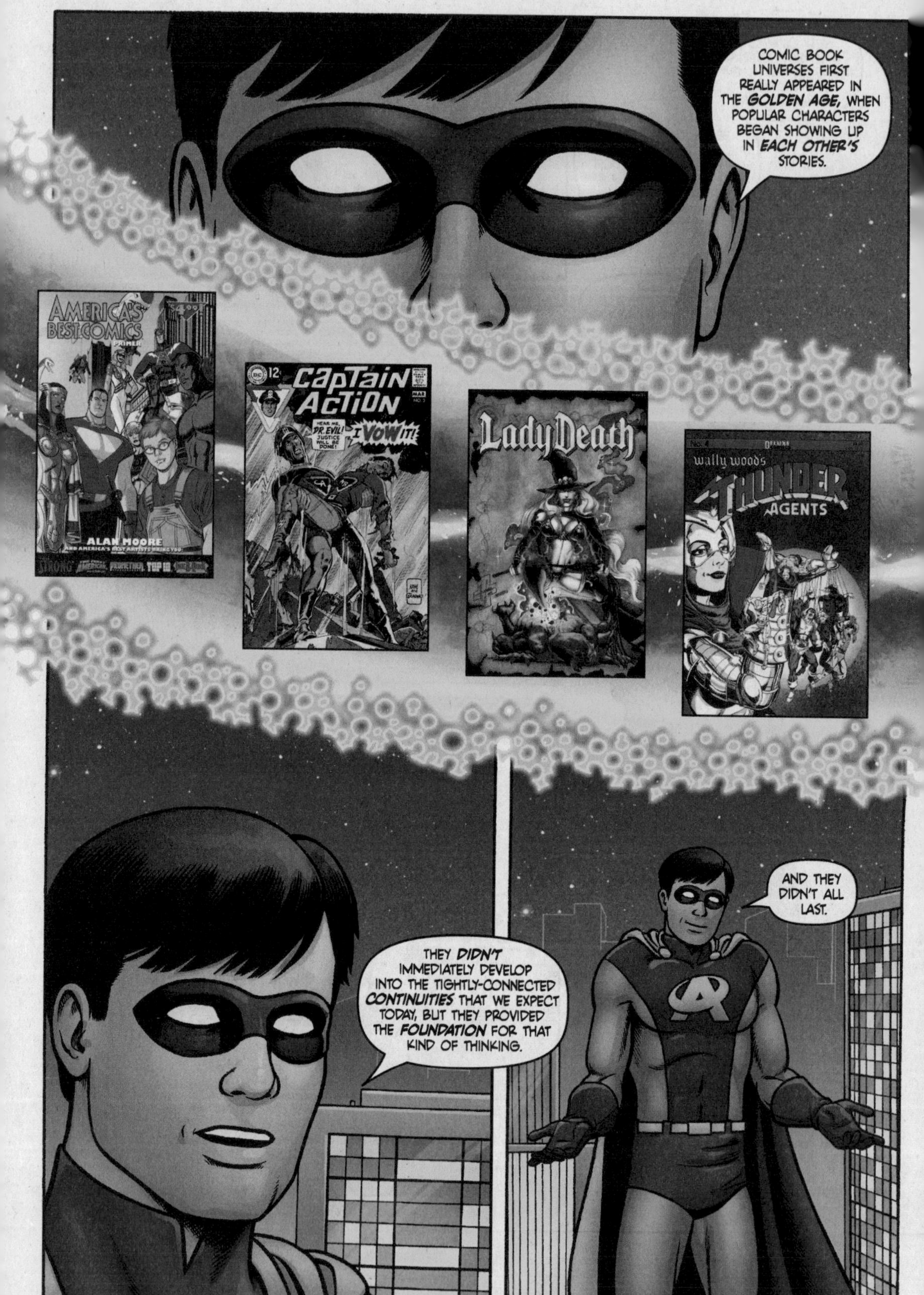
COMIC BOOK UNIVERSES FIRST REALLY APPEARED IN THE *GOLDEN AGE,* WHEN POPULAR CHARACTERS BEGAN SHOWING UP IN *EACH OTHER'S* STORIES.
AMERICA'S BEST COMICS
PRIMER
ALAN MOORE
CAPTAIN ACTION
I VOW IT!
Lady Death
wally wood's
THUNDER AGENTS
THEY *DIDN'T* IMMEDIATELY DEVELOP INTO THE TIGHTLY-CONNECTED *CONTINUITIES* THAT WE EXPECT TODAY, BUT THEY PROVIDED THE *FOUNDATION* FOR THAT KIND OF THINKING.
AND THEY DIDN'T ALL LAST.

SOMETIMES THE PUBLISHERS OR EDITORS HAD A *PLAN*. OFTEN IT WAS JUST A WAY TO *SELL MORE COMICS*...

BUT WHETHER ON PURPOSE OR NOT, *SOMETIMES* THESE CROSSOVERS *CAUGHT ON*.

MLJ, AS ARCHIE COMICS WAS ORIGINALLY KNOWN, HAD SUPERHEROES *BEFORE* THEY HAD ARCHIE...

AND THEIR *HEROES* HAVE COME BACK *MANY TIMES* OVER THE YEARS.

THEY'RE JUST ONE EXAMPLE OF *LOST UNIVERSES*, BUT THEY'VE SPANNED THE *GOLDEN AGE* TO THE PRESENT!

BUT *ALL* OF THE LOST UNIVERSES *HAVEN'T* BEEN AROUND *THAT LONG*, HAVE THEY?

NO. COMIC COMPANIES HAVE *STARTED UP* AND *DISAPPEARED* ACROSS THE WHOLE HISTORY OF THE MEDIUM, BUT MANY HAVE HAPPENED IN RECENT YEARS.

OH, LIKE THE ORIGINAL *VALIANT* AND *MILESTONE?*

EXACTLY! AND JUST LIKE THOSE TWO AND LIKE ARCHIE'S HEROES, *SOME* OF THEM RETURN FROM THE LAND OF *CANCELATION!*

BUT *NOT ALL* OF THEM COME BACK, RIGHT?

SOMETIMES "*DEAD*" IS A BIT MORE *FINAL* THAN IT OFTEN IS IN COMIC BOOKS, BUT EVEN THEN...

BUT WHAT IF *I* LIKE A LOST UNIVERSE OR EVEN JUST ONE COMIC FROM ONE AND MY FRIENDS *DON'T?* I LOVED *RUSE* FROM CROSSGEN!

YOU MIGHT GET TIRED OF US SAYING "*COLLECT WHAT YOU LOVE!*" BUT IT'S ABOUT WHAT *YOU* LIKE, *NOT* WHAT *OTHER* PEOPLE LIKE.

THAT MAKES *SENSE!* THERE'S SO MUCH OUT THERE TO *DISCOVER!* WHY *LIMIT* YOURSELF?

ONE OF THE *GREAT THINGS* ABOUT LOST UNIVERSES IS THAT THEY'RE *FINITE SETS.* YOU KNOW RIGHT AWAY *WHAT IT TAKES* TO COLLECT A *FULL RUN!*

ISN'T IT *WEIRD* FOR A PRICE GUIDE TO SAY "COLLECT WHAT YOU LOVE" WHEN YOU LIST ALL THOSE *PRICES?*

TO US, IT WOULD BE WEIRD *NOT* TO THINK THAT WAY!

THINK ABOUT *HOW MANY* BACK ISSUE COMICS THERE ARE. YOU KNOW THERE'S A SERIES OUT THERE *FOR YOU,* RIGHT?

IT *DOESN'T* HAVE TO BE ONE OF THE *LOST UNIVERSES.* IN FACT, IT COULD BE ONE *JUST STARTING* OUT NOW...

BUT AS THE PRICES ON *HIGH PROFILE* COMICS HAVE GONE *CRAZY,* THE LOST UNIVERSES REPRESENT COMICS THAT ARE OFTEN *VERY ACCESSIBLE,* PRICE-WISE!

WHATEVER *YOU* DECIDE, I'LL SEE YOU AT YOUR COMIC SHOP!

Written by J.C. VAUGHN
Illustrated by BRENDON & BRIAN FRAIM
Colored by Hi-Fi's BRIAN MILLER
Lettered by MINDY LOPKIN
Edited by AMANDA SHERIFF & MARK HUESMAN

Welcome to the second edition of Overstreet's *Lost Universes* series. When we were just part of the way through the first volume, we knew that it was coming together to make a very special book. Thankfully, enough of you agreed – and there are still plenty of lost universes left to cover.

During the Covid-19 lock-downs, we saw certain comic book prices go every bit as crazy as those of other collect-ibles. The truth is, though, that you'd pretty much have to hit Powerball or Mega Millions to put together a full run of comics from legacy publishers such as Marvel or DC.

But that's not true of many lost universes. We're talking about finite sets, often with short pub-lishing histories and a limited number of comics. For every high-end collector's dream of a com-plete run of the MLJ/Archie superheroes (seen in Volume 1) or Fawcett's Marvel Family titles (in this edition), you have many others that are extremely affordable.

The trick, as with every other comic, is one's ability to find it in grade. Some issues are super easy, but sometimes when a comic has been reg-ularly classified as dollar box material, it's next to impossible to find that same issue in high grade. In the end, that's part of the thrill of the hunt.

But another part of the excite-ment is collecting a set, finite group of comics. The ability to collect them all. That's a rare thing in this era of record prices.

In assembling these Lost Universes books, we've done our best to create a visual checklist, a book that will have lasting value long after the pric-es listed have become outdated. In this one, the range is incred-ibly wide. We get to look at all those wonderful *Captain Marvel, Jr.* and *Master Comics* covers and I get a chance to talk about *Dinosaurs For Hire*. All in the same book! Talk about diversity!

As always, our projects rise and fall based on your feedback. Please let us know what you think of this volume. We look forward to hear-ing from you!

Sincerely,

J.C. Vaughn
President

Values for items listed and pictured in this book are based on author's experience, consultations with a network of advisors including collectors specializing in various categories, and actual prices realized for specific items sold through private sales and auctions. The values offered in this book are approximations influenced by many factors including condition, rarity and demand, and they should serve only as guidelines, presenting an average range of what one might expect to pay for the items.

In the marketplace, knowledge and opinions held by both sellers and buyers determine prices asked and prices paid. This is not a price list of items for sale or items wanted by the author or publisher. The author and the publisher shall not be held responsible for losses that may occur in the purchase, sale or other transaction of property because of information contained herein. Efforts have been made to present accurate information, but the possibility of error exists.

Unlike the main edition of *The Overstreet Comic Book Price Guide*, this book only includes three pricing columns, representing the grades 2.0 (Good or GD), 6.0 (Fine or FN), and 9.2 (Near Mint-minus or NM-). You will see the three prices listed under the images of the comics, as in the top example.

However, some of the comics listed in this volume have yet to accrue significant value below grade 9.2 (Near Mint-minus or NM-). For such issues, we have only listed the single 9.2 price, as in the lower example.

It may seem odd advice to get from a price guide, but whatever price the market assesses to your comics, remember that in the end you determine what they are worth *to you*. Collect what you love and it's difficult to overpay!

The Overstreet Comic Book Price Guide is now online at **OverstreetAccess.com**. It's a price guide, a collection management system, and more. See our ads elsewhere in this book

Readers who believe that they have discovered an error are invited to mail corrective information to the author, Robert M. Overstreet, at Gemstone Publishing, 10150 York Rd., Suite 300, Hunt Valley, MD 21030. Verified corrections will be incorporated into future editions.

CAPTAIN MARVEL ADVENTURES #18
DECEMBER 1942
$1000 $3000 $20,000

SPIDER-MAN 2099 #38
DECEMBER 1995
$5

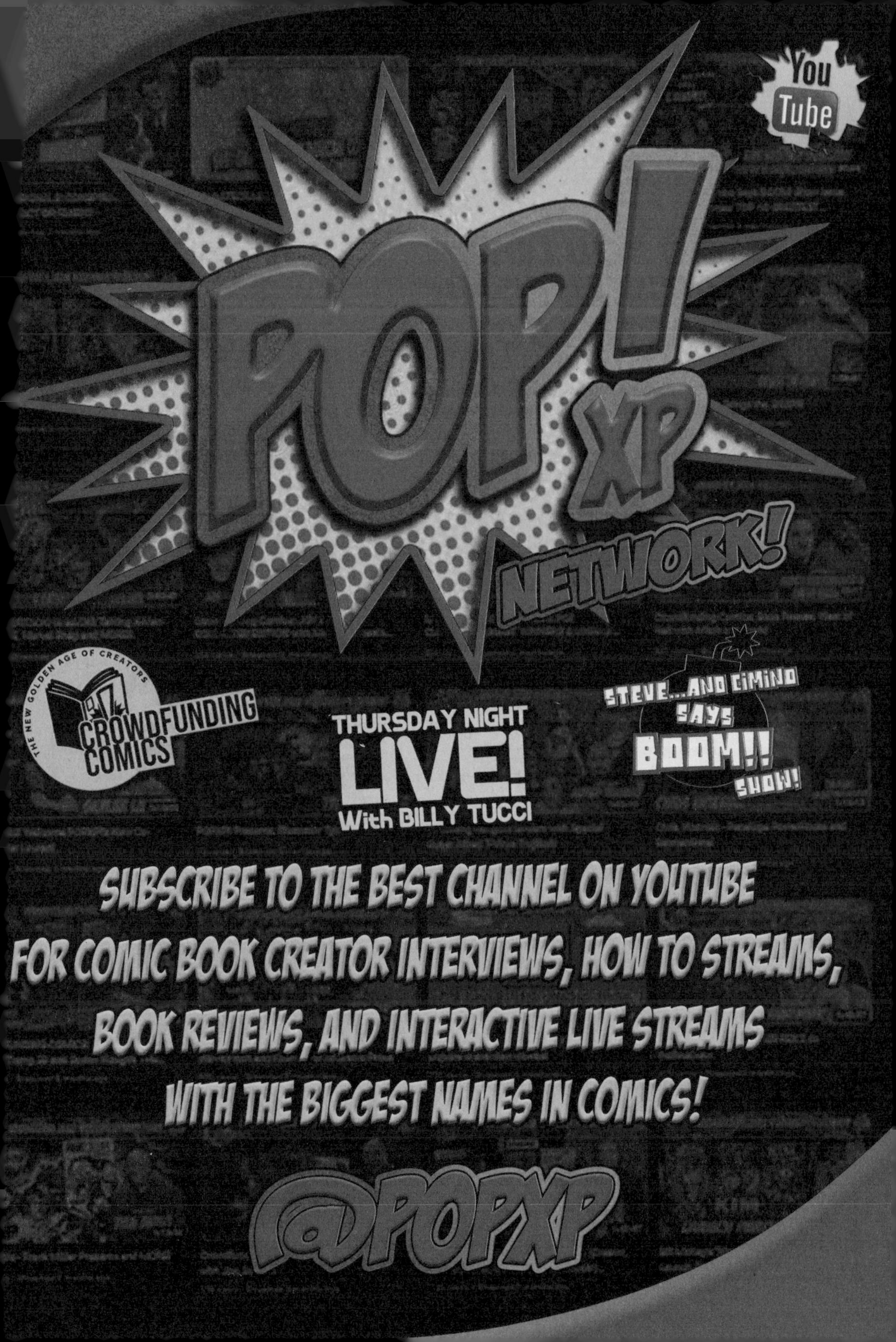

You Tube
POP! XP
NETWORK!
THE NEW GOLDEN AGE OF CREATORS
CROWDFUNDING COMICS
THURSDAY NIGHT LIVE! With BILLY TUCCI
STEVE...AND CIMINO SAYS BOOM!! SHOW!
SUBSCRIBE TO THE BEST CHANNEL ON YOUTUBE
FOR COMIC BOOK CREATOR INTERVIEWS, HOW TO STREAMS,
BOOK REVIEWS, AND INTERACTIVE LIVE STREAMS
WITH THE BIGGEST NAMES IN COMICS!
@POPXP

WWW.NICKKATRADIS.COM

WANTED

THE GREATEST COMICS OF ALL TIME!

I WANT THESE BACK!

I'm looking for all those great comics you saw on the previous page, and for many others as well! Some people thought when I donated a major collection to the Library of Congress that I stopped collecting. Nothing could be further from the truth!

I'm buying all the time! Are you in the market to sell your Pre-1965 comics? Send me your list!

Steve Geppi
gsteve@diamondcomics.com

The Inside
COLLECTOR

July/
August 1991
Volume 2
Number 2

$3.95
Canada
$4.95

**Scandal Rocks
Toy World**

Jewels by Jumeau

Fireworks!!

Claymation Art

**Comics King
Steve Geppi**

**10150 York Road, Suite 300
Hunt Valley, MD 21030**

410.598.1773

Named after the popular Golden Age title from Nedor Publications, America's Best Comics was an imprint initiated at Jim Lee's Wildstorm Productions studio at Image Comics prior to Lee selling his company to DC. Beginning in the late 1990s, Alan Moore developed all of the imprint's titles, and he wrote or co-plotted the bulk of the line. Moore had famously vowed to not work with DC Comics again, but when Wildstorm merged into DC, he honored his agreement to lead the line.

Moore and artist Kevin O'Neill co-created *The League of Extraordinary Gentlemen*, a story set in the late 1800s that starred Victorian Age public domain characters created by Bram Stoker, H. Rider Haggard, Jules Verne, Robert Louis Stevenson, H.G. Wells, Sir Arthur Conan Doyle, and Sax Rohmer.

In the first volume, Mina Murray puts together the team of Allan Quartermain, Captain Nemo, Dr. Jekyll, and the Invisible Man, to try to stop a war between Professor Moriarty (Sherlock Holmes' nemesis) and Fu Manchu. The second volume put the heroes into H.G. Wells' *The War of the Worlds*, while utilizing characters and story elements from writers like Doyle, Ian Fleming, and Edgar Rice Burroughs. Moore and O'Neill's final entry under ABC was *Black Dossier*, a "sourcebook" with prose stories, letters, guidebooks, maps, and more.

FIRST PUBLICATION:
The League of Extraordinary Gentlemen Vol. 1 #1
(March 1999)

LAST PUBLICATION:
The League of Extraordinary Gentlemen: Black Dossier
(November 2007)

REVIVAL(S): *L.O.E.G. Vol. 3: Century* (Top Shelf Prods. and Knockabout Comics, 2009), *L.O.E.G.: Nemo Trilogy* (Top Shelf Prods. and Knockabout Comics, 2013), *L.O.E.G. Vol. 4: The Tempest* (Top Shelf Prods and Knockabout Comics, 2018)

Tom Strong, created by Moore and artist Chris Sprouse, paid homage to pulp magazines and heroes such as Doc Savage and Tarzan. The title character was a science-based hero, joined by his wife and daughter (who had special mental and physical abilities), Pneuman (a steam powered robot) and King Solomon (a human-like gorilla). The series ventured into different universes and timelines, exploring multiple pulp themes along the way.

Moore and artists Gene Ha and Zander Cannon collaborated on *Top 10*, a police procedural and superhero mashup. Similar in tone to police shows like *Hill Street Blues*, the book follows the work and personal lives of police officers in the city of Neopolis where nearly everyone has superpowers. It was followed by multiple spinoffs, including *Smax* (set after the original series' conclusion), *Top 10: The Forty-Niners* (set in 1949), and *Top Ten: Beyond the Farthest Precinct* (taking place five years after the first series).

Moore presented his views on magic in *Promethea*, co-created by J.H. Williams III and Mick Gray. Set in an alternate version of New York City in 1999, the title stars college student Sophie Bangs, who becomes the embodiment of the magical entity Promethea. Sophie studies magic, learns about Promethea's powers and her past, and ultimately gives in to Promethea's final mission of bringing about the apocalypse.

Spinoffs within the ABC line included *Terra Obscura*, a *Tom Strong* extension on an alternate Earth where the Society of Major American Science Heroes protect the planet. It was written by Peter Hogan, co-plotted by Moore, with art by Yanick Paquette, Karl Story, and others. *Tomorrow Stories* was a short story collection featuring pulp-inspired characters and others that played on superhero archetypes, from a slate of creatives that included Moore, Rick Veitch, Melinda Gebbie, Kevin Nowlan, Jim Baikie, and Hilary Barta.

America's Best Comics: A to Z was planned as a six-part series by Peter Hogan and Steve Moore that would present facts and reveal secrets about characters from across the ABC line. Signaling the end of America's Best Comics, the title ended early after four issues.

Moore effectively ended the ABC imprint deliberately through an apocalypse, which was achieved with the conclusion of *Promethea*. He then wrote the final *Tom Strong* issue and a pair of *Tomorrow Stories* 64-page specials that closed the chapter on ABC characters.

– Amanda Sheriff

Gene Ha's original art for the back cover of *America's Best Comics Special #1* (2001).
Image courtesy of Heritage Auctions.

ABC: A-Z Greyshirt and Cobweb #1
JANUARY 2006
$6

ABC: A-Z Terra Obscura and Splash Brannigan #1
MARCH 2006
$6

ABC: A-Z Tom Strong and Jack B. Quick #1
NOVEMBER 2005
$4

ABC: A-Z Top 10 and Teams #1
JULY 2006
$4

America's Best Comics Preview
1999
$4

America's Best Comics Primer
2008
$5

America's Best Comics Sketchbook #1
2002
$6

America's Best Comics Special #1
FEBRUARY 2001
$7

Greyshirt: Indigo Sunset #1
DECEMBER 2001
$3.50

**GREYSHIRT:
INDIGO SUNSET #2**
JANUARY 2002
$3.50

**GREYSHIRT:
INDIGO SUNSET #3**
FEBRUARY 2002
$3.50

**GREYSHIRT:
INDIGO SUNSET #4**
APRIL 2002
$3.50

**GREYSHIRT:
INDIGO SUNSET #5**
JUNE 2002
$3.50

**GREYSHIRT:
INDIGO SUNSET #6**
AUGUST 2002
$3.50

**THE LEAGUE OF EXTRAORDINARY
GENTLEMEN #1**
MARCH 1999
$3 $9 $26

**THE LEAGUE OF EXTRAORDINARY
GENTLEMEN #1**
DYNAMIC FORCES EDITION • MARCH 1999
$3 $9 $32

**THE LEAGUE OF EXTRAORDINARY
GENTLEMEN #2**
APRIL 1999
$6

**THE LEAGUE OF EXTRAORDINARY
GENTLEMEN #3**
MAY 1999
$6

**THE LEAGUE OF EXTRAORDINARY
GENTLEMEN #4**
NOVEMBER 1999
$4

**THE LEAGUE OF EXTRAORDINARY
GENTLEMEN #5** • JUNE 2000
RECALLED EDITION $14 $42 $315
REVISED SECOND PRINTING $4

**THE LEAGUE OF EXTRAORDINARY
GENTLEMEN #6**
SEPTEMBER 2000
$4

**THE LEAGUE OF EXTRAORDINARY
GENTLEMEN BUMPER COMPENDIUM #1**
JUNE 1999
$6

**THE LEAGUE OF EXTRAORDINARY
GENTLEMEN BUMPER COMPENDIUM #2**
1999
$6

**THE LEAGUE OF EXTRAORDINARY
GENTLEMEN VOL. 2 #1**
SEPTEMBER 2002
$5

**THE LEAGUE OF EXTRAORDINARY
GENTLEMEN VOL. 2 #2**
OCTOBER 2002
$5

**THE LEAGUE OF EXTRAORDINARY
GENTLEMEN VOL. 2 #3**
NOVEMBER 2002
$5

**THE LEAGUE OF EXTRAORDINARY
GENTLEMEN VOL. 2 #4**
APRIL 2003
$5

THE LEAGUE OF EXTRAORDINARY
GENTLEMEN VOL. 2 #5
JULY 2003
$5

THE LEAGUE OF EXTRAORDINARY
GENTLEMEN VOL. 2 #6
NOVEMBER 2003
$5

THE LEAGUE OF EXTRAORDINARY
GENTLEMEN BUMPER COMPENDIUM #1
VOLUME 2 • DECEMBER 2002
$6

THE LEAGUE OF EXTRAORDINARY
GENTLEMEN BUMPER COMPENDIUM #2
VOLUME 2 • APRIL 2003
$6

THE LEAGUE OF EXTRAORDINARY
GENTLEMEN BLACK DOSSIER
HARDCOVER • 2007
$30

MANY WORLDS OF
TESLA STRONG #1
JULY 2003
$6

MANY WORLDS OF
TESLA STRONG #1
VARIANT COVER • JULY 2003
$6

PROMETHEA #1
AUGUST 1999
$1 $4 $10

PROMETHEA #1
VARIANT COVER • AUGUST 1999
$2 $6 $12

PROMETHEA #2
SEPTEMBER 1999
$4

PROMETHEA #3
OCTOBER 1999
$4

PROMETHEA #4
NOVEMBER 1999
$4

PROMETHEA #5
FEBRUARY 2000
$4

PROMETHEA #6
MARCH 2000
$4

PROMETHEA #7
APRIL 2000
$4

PROMETHEA #8
JULY 2000
$4

PROMETHEA #9
SEPTEMBER 2000
$4

PROMETHEA #10
OCTOBER 2000
$4

PROMETHEA #11
DECEMBER 2000
$4

PROMETHEA #12
FEBRUARY 2001
$4

PROMETHEA #13
APRIL 2001
$4

PROMETHEA #14
JUNE 2001
$4

PROMETHEA #15
AUGUST 2001
$4

PROMETHEA #16
OCTOBER 2001
$4

PROMETHEA #17
DECEMBER 2001
$4

PROMETHEA #18
FEBRUARY 2002
$4

PROMETHEA #19
APRIL 2002
$4

PROMETHEA #20
JUNE 2002
$4

PROMETHEA #21
AUGUST 2002
$4

PROMETHEA #22
NOVEMBER 2002
$4

PROMETHEA #23
DECEMBER 2002
$4

PROMETHEA #24
FEBRUARY 2003
$4

PROMETHEA #25
MAY 2003
$4

PROMETHEA #26
AUGUST 2003
$4

PROMETHEA #27
NOVEMBER 2003
$4

PROMETHEA #28
JANUARY 2004
$4

PROMETHEA #29
MAY 2004
$4

PROMETHEA #30
JULY 2004
$4

PROMETHEA #31
OCTOBER 2004
$4

PROMETHEA #32
APRIL 2005
$3 $9 $28

PROMETHEA #32
COVERS COLLECTION • MAY 2005
LIMITED EDITION WITH POSTERS $120

SMAX #1
OCTOBER 2003
$3

SMAX #2
NOVEMBER 2003
$3

SMAX #3
DECEMBER 2003
$3

SMAX #4
FEBRUARY 2004
$3

SMAX #5
MAY 2004
$3

TERRA OBSCURA #1
AUGUST 2003
$3

TERRA OBSCURA #2
SEPTEMBER 2003
$3

TERRA OBSCURA #3
OCTOBER 2003
$3

TERRA OBSCURA #4
NOVEMBER 2003
$3

TERRA OBSCURA #5
DECEMBER 2003
$3

TERRA OBSCURA #6
FEBRUARY 2004
$3

**TERRA OBSCURA
VOLUME 2 #1**
OCTOBER 2004
$3

**TERRA OBSCURA
VOLUME 2 #2**
NOVEMBER 2004
$3

**TERRA OBSCURA
VOLUME 2 #3**
DECEMBER 2004
$3

**TERRA OBSCURA
VOLUME 2 #4**
JANUARY 2005
$3

**TERRA OBSCURA
VOLUME 2 #5**
MARCH 2005
$3

**TERRA OBSCURA
VOLUME 2 #6**
MAY 2005
$3

TOMORROW STORIES #1
OCTOBER 1999
$4

TOMORROW STORIES #1
VARIANT COVER • OCTOBER 1999
$4

TOMORROW STORIES #2
NOVEMBER 1999
$3

TOMORROW STORIES #3
DECEMBER 1999
$3

TOMORROW STORIES #4
JANUARY 2000
$3

TOMORROW STORIES #5
FEBRUARY 2000
$3

TOMORROW STORIES #6
MARCH 2000
$3

TOMORROW STORIES #7
JUNE 2000
$3

TOMORROW STORIES #8
JANUARY 2001
$3

TOMORROW STORIES #9
FEBRUARY 2001
$3

TOMORROW STORIES #10
JUNE 2001
$3

TOMORROW STORIES #11
OCTOBER 2001
$3

TOMORROW STORIES #12
APRIL 2002
$3

**TOMORROW STORIES
SPECIAL #1**
JANUARY 2006
$7

TOMORROW STORIES
SPECIAL #2
MAY 2006
$7

TOM STRONG #1
JUNE 1999
$4

TOM STRONG #1
VARIANT COVER • JUNE 1999
$4

TOM STRONG #2
JULY 1999
$3

TOM STRONG #3
AUGUST 1999
$3

TOM STRONG #4
OCTOBER 1999
$3

TOM STRONG #5
DECEMBER 1999
$3

TOM STRONG #6
FEBRUARY 2000
$3

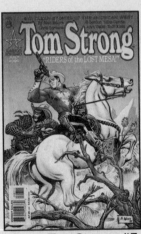

TOM STRONG #7
MARCH 2000
$3

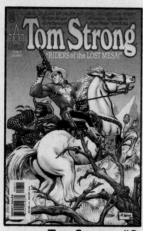

TOM STRONG #8
JULY 2000
$3

TOM STRONG #9
SEPTEMBER 2000
$3

TOM STRONG #10
NOVEMBER 2000
$3

TOM STRONG #11
JANUARY 2001
$3

TOM STRONG #12
JUNE 2001
$3

TOM STRONG #13
JULY 2001
$3

TOM STRONG #14
OCTOBER 2001
$3

TOM STRONG #15
MARCH 2002
$3

TOM STRONG #16
APRIL 2002
$3

TOM STRONG #17
AUGUST 2002
$3

TOM STRONG #18
DECEMBER 2002
$3

TOM STRONG #19
APRIL 2003
$3

TOM STRONG #20
JUNE 2003
$3

TOM STRONG #21
OCTOBER 2003
$3

TOM STRONG #22
DECEMBER 2003
$3

TOM STRONG #23
JANUARY 2004
$3

TOM STRONG #24
MARCH 2004
$3

TOM STRONG #25
MAY 2004
$3

TOM STRONG #26
JULY 2004
$3

TOM STRONG #27
SEPTEMBER 2004
$3

TOM STRONG #28
NOVEMBER 2004
$3

TOM STRONG #29
DECEMBER 2004
$3

TOM STRONG #30
FEBRUARY 2005
$3

TOM STRONG #31
APRIL 2005
$3

TOM STRONG #32
JUNE 2005
$3

TOM STRONG #33
AUGUST 2005
$3

TOM STRONG #34
OCTOBER 2005
$3

TOM STRONG #35
JANUARY 2006
$3

TOM STRONG #36
MAY 2006
$3

**TOM STRONG AND THE
PLANET OF PERIL #1**
SEPTEMBER 2013
$3

**TOM STRONG AND THE
PLANET OF PERIL #1**
VARIANT COVER • SEPTEMBER 2013
$3

**TOM STRONG AND THE
PLANET OF PERIL #2**
OCTOBER 2013
$3

**TOM STRONG AND THE
PLANET OF PERIL #3**
NOVEMBER 2013
$3

**TOM STRONG AND THE
PLANET OF PERIL #4**
DECEMBER 2013
$3

**TOM STRONG AND THE
PLANET OF PERIL #5**
JANUARY 2014
$3

**TOM STRONG AND THE
PLANET OF PERIL #6**
FEBRUARY 2014
$3

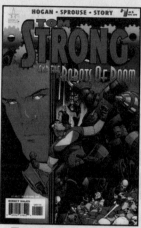

**TOM STRONG AND THE
ROBOTS OF DOOM #1**
AUGUST 2010
$4

**TOM STRONG AND THE
ROBOTS OF DOOM #1**
VARIANT COVER • AUGUST 2010
$4

**TOM STRONG AND THE
ROBOTS OF DOOM #2**
SEPTEMBER 2010
$4

**TOM STRONG AND THE
ROBOTS OF DOOM #3**
OCTOBER 2010
$4

**TOM STRONG AND THE
ROBOTS OF DOOM #4**
NOVEMBER 2010
$4

**TOM STRONG AND THE
ROBOTS OF DOOM #5**
DECEMBER 2010
$4

**TOM STRONG AND THE
ROBOTS OF DOOM #6**
JANUARY 2011
$4

**TOM STRONG'S
TERRIFIC TALES #1**
JANUARY 2002
$3.50

**TOM STRONG'S
TERRIFIC TALES #2**
MARCH 2002
$3

TOM STRONG'S
TERRIFIC TALES #3
JUNE 2002
$3

TOM STRONG'S
TERRIFIC TALES #4
NOVEMBER 2002
$3

TOM STRONG'S
TERRIFIC TALES #5
JANUARY 2003
$3

TOM STRONG'S
TERRIFIC TALES #6
APRIL 2003
$3

TOM STRONG'S
TERRIFIC TALES #7
JULY 2003
$3

TOM STRONG'S
TERRIFIC TALES #8
DECEMBER 2003
$3

TOM STRONG'S
TERRIFIC TALES #9
APRIL 2004
$3

TOM STRONG'S
TERRIFIC TALES #10
JUNE 2004
$3

TOM STRONG'S
TERRIFIC TALES #11
SEPTEMBER 2004
$3

**TOM STRONG'S
TERRIFIC TALES #12**
JANUARY 2005
$3

TOP 10 #1
SEPTEMBER 1999
$3.50

TOP 10 #1
VARIANT COVER • SEPTEMBER 1999
$3.50

TOP 10 #2
OCTOBER 1999
$3

TOP 10 #3
NOVEMBER 1999
$3

TOP 10 #4
DECEMBER 1999
$3

TOP 10 #5
JANUARY 2000
$3

TOP 10 #6
FEBRUARY 2000
$3

TOP 10 #7
APRIL 2000
$3

Top 10 #8
JUNE 2000
$3

Top 10 #9
OCTOBER 2000
$3

Top 10 #10
JANUARY 2001
$3

Top 10 #11
MAY 2001
$3

Top 10 #12
OCTOBER 2001
$3

**Top 10: Beyond the
Farthest Precinct #1**
OCTOBER 2005
$3

**Top 10: Beyond the
Farthest Precinct #2**
NOVEMBER 2005
$3

**Top 10: Beyond the
Farthest Precinct #3**
DECEMBER 2005
$3

**Top 10: Beyond the
Farthest Precinct #4**
JANUARY 2006
$3

TOP 10: BEYOND THE FARTHEST PRECINCT #5
FEBRUARY 2006
$3

TOP 10 SEASON TWO #1
DECEMBER 2008
$3

TOP 10 SEASON TWO #2
JANUARY 2009
$3

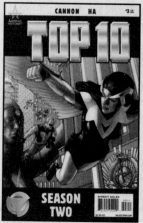

TOP 10 SEASON TWO #3
FEBRUARY 2009
$3

TOP 10 SEASON TWO #4
MARCH 2009
$3

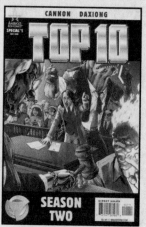

TOP 10 SEASON TWO SPECIAL #1
MAY 2009
$3

Promethea #19 pages 6,7 original art by J.H. Williams III and Mick Gray (2002). Image courtesy of Heritage Auctions.

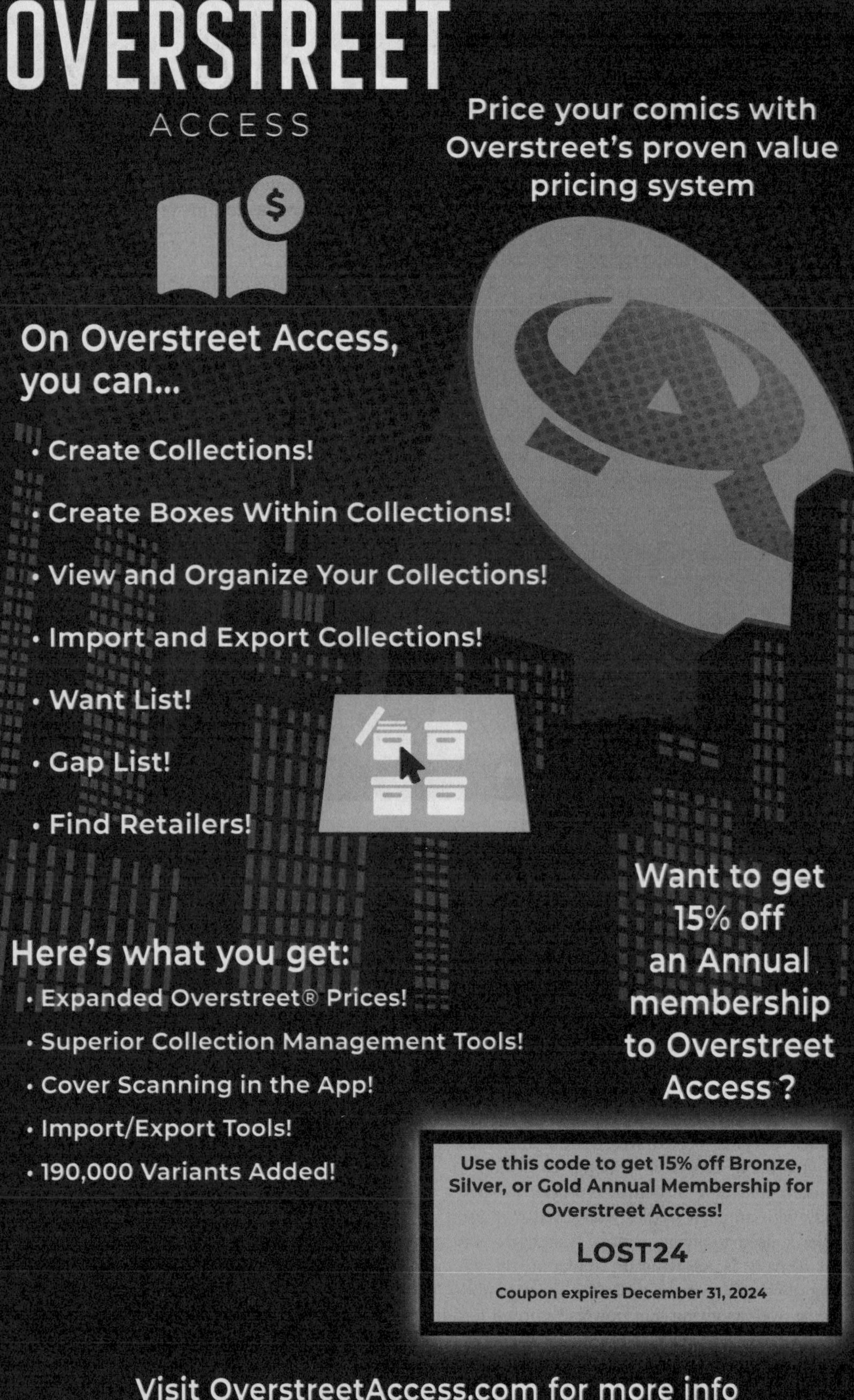
OVERSTREET
ACCESS
Price your comics with Overstreet's proven value pricing system
On Overstreet Access, you can...
• Create Collections!
• Create Boxes Within Collections!
• View and Organize Your Collections!
• Import and Export Collections!
• Want List!
• Gap List!
• Find Retailers!
Here's what you get:
• Expanded Overstreet® Prices!
• Superior Collection Management Tools!
• Cover Scanning in the App!
• Import/Export Tools!
• 190,000 Variants Added!
Want to get 15% off an Annual membership to Overstreet Access?
Use this code to get 15% off Bronze, Silver, or Gold Annual Membership for Overstreet Access!
LOST24
Coupon expires December 31, 2024
Visit OverstreetAccess.com for more info

BOOM! Studios' Stan Lee Comics

In addition to making regular cameos in the Marvel Cinematic Universe and becoming an icon to movie fans who had never read a comic book, Stan Lee kept on creating new works long past the time many expected him to just coast.

Ross Richie founded BOOM! Studios, in 2005 out of his spare bedroom, and by 2010 the company had already twice been named "Best Publisher (under 5% market share)" by Diamond Comic Distributors. With a number of high-profile creator-driven projects, licensed titles, and numerous newcomers, it still didn't necessarily seem like an automatic fit for Stan Lee.

Unless you considered that Richie wasn't just a creative executive, he was a lifelong comic book collector. If Stan Lee had been writing it, it wouldn't just have made sense, their collaboration would have been destined to happen.

In 2010, BOOM! kicked off a marketing campaign built around the phrase "Stan's Back!" – and kept everyone guessing for a week what was going on. At Comic-Con International: San Diego that year, they released the details: Lee and his company, POW! Entertainment (Purveyors of Wonder), would collaborate with BOOM! and a stable of creators to launch three new titles.

Soldier Zero was the first of three Lee created for BOOM!, initially written by Paul Cornell (*Doctor Who*) and illustrated by Javier Pina (*Superman*). At its release in October, it quickly became the company's best-selling comic book up that point.

"A former U.S. Marine, paralyzed from the waist down after being caught in a bomb explosion in Afghanistan, and now a pacifist, is forced to share his body with an alien soldier who's fled to Earth. The alien's used to living with a host body, and Stewart Travers is its reluctant replacement. The bonding allows Stewart to walk, for short periods of time, as well as giving him powers," Cornell told our *Scoop* email newsletter at the time. "The series

FIRST PUBLICATION:
Soldier Zero #1
(October 2010)

LAST PUBLICATION:
Starborn #12
(November 2011)

REVIVAL(S):
None.

is an action adventure with a large chunk of family drama about how he and his brother deal with the situation."

Cornell left after the fourth issue and was replaced by the then-prolific team of Dan Abnett and Andy Lanning, known for their work on *Annihilation*, *Nova*, *Guardians of the Galaxy*, *War of Kings*, *Thanos Imperative*, and *Legion of Super-Heroes*

"We were invited by BOOM! as soon as they realized Paul wasn't able to continue past the launch arc. We think they thought our 'cosmic' mindset might come in handy," Abnett and Lanning told *Scoop*.

The Traveler was written by Overstreet Hall of Fame inductee Mark Waid, who at the time was also serving as the company's Chief Creative Officer, and illustrated by Chad Hardin (*Amazing Spider-Man*). *The Traveler* #1 debuted in November 2010, and it featured, in their words, "…a mysterious new superhero with time-traveling powers battling the Split-Second Men, super-powered assassins from the future."

Chris Roberson (*iZombie*) and Khary Randolph (*X-Men*) followed in December of that year with *Starborn*, the story of a regular guy who discovers he's the heir to an intergalactic empire, which puts him the center of a war between five alien races.

While it wasn't celebrated as much as the involvement of Lee himself was, in tone and story it was clear to readers from the beginning that the titles were related. Then, for the 2011 edition of the Emerald City Comicon, artist Scott Clark created a triptych Stan Lee's *Starborn* #3, *The Traveler* #4, and *Soldier Zero* #5, and the three covers formed one larger image.

Soldier Zero ran 12 issues, as did *The Traveler* and *Starborn*. In the end, the central characters of each of the series came together to fight a huge threat and defend civilization. Each of the series was also collected into three paperbacks per title.

Monoprints (unique one-of-one artist proofs) of *Soldier Zero* #1 Pages 1-4
by Javier Pina. Printed in German Etching 310 of Hahnemühle paper.
Images courtesy of the artist.

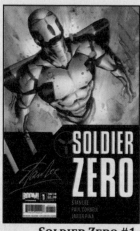

SOLDIER ZERO #1
OCTOBER 2010
$4

SOLDIER ZERO #1
VARIANT COVER
OCTOBER 2010
$4

SOLDIER ZERO #1
VARIANT COVER
OCTOBER 2010
$4

SOLDIER ZERO #1
VARIANT COVER
OCTOBER 2010
$4

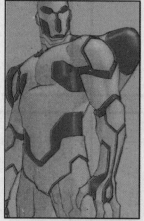

SOLDIER ZERO #1
VARIANT COVER
OCTOBER 2010
$4

SOLDIER ZERO #1
VARIANT COVER
OCTOBER 2010
$4

SOLDIER ZERO #1
VARIANT COVER
OCTOBER 2010
$4

SOLDIER ZERO #1
VARIANT COVER
OCTOBER 2010
$4

SOLDIER ZERO #1
HASTINGS VARIANT COVER
OCTOBER 2010
$4

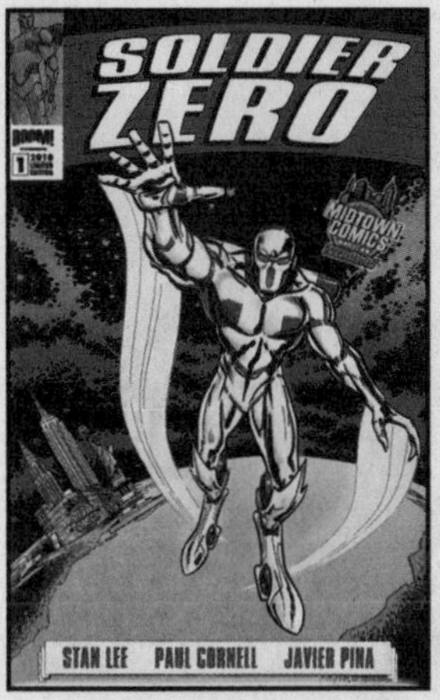
SOLDIER ZERO
MIDTOWN COMICS
STAN LEE PAUL CORNELL JAVIER PINA

Soldier Zero #1
Midtown Comics variant cover
October 2010
$4

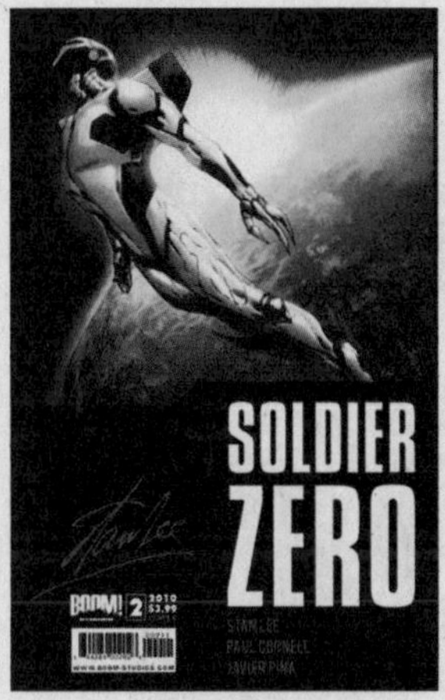
SOLDIER ZERO
BOOM!

Soldier Zero #2
November 2010
$4

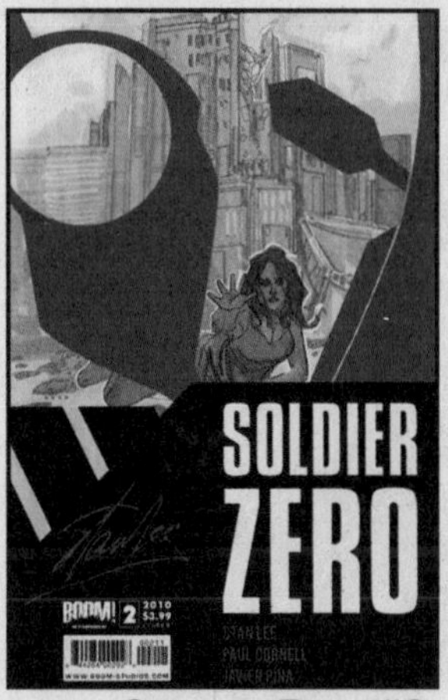
SOLDIER ZERO
BOOM!

Soldier Zero #2
Variant cover
November 2010
$4

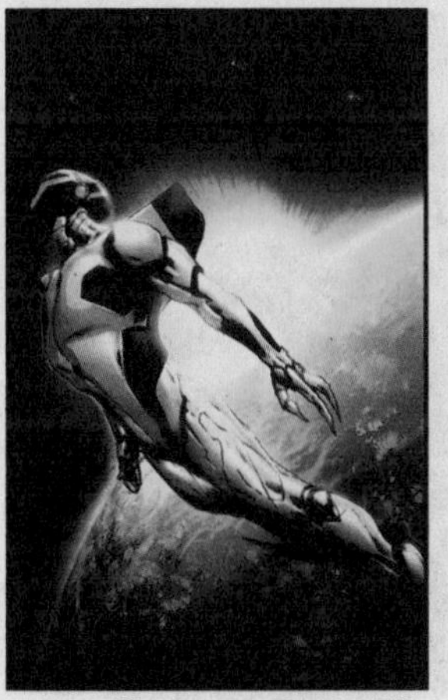

Soldier Zero #2
Variant cover
November 2010
$4

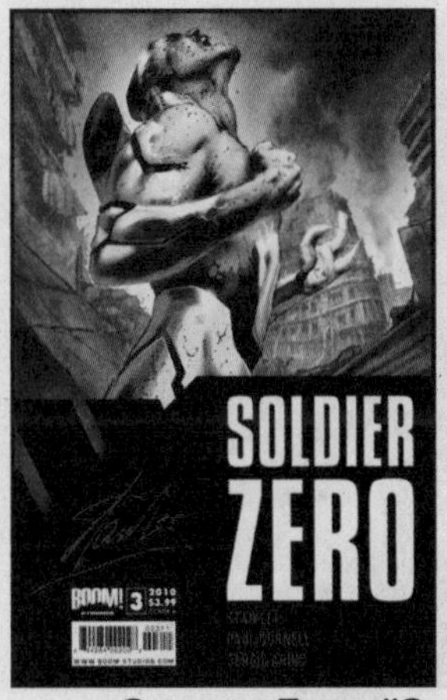
SOLDIER ZERO
BOOM!

Soldier Zero #3
December 2010
$4

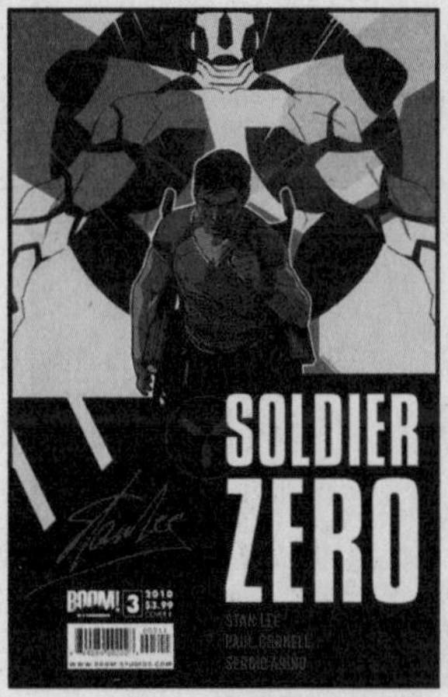
SOLDIER ZERO
BOOM!

Soldier Zero #3
Variant cover
December 2010
$4

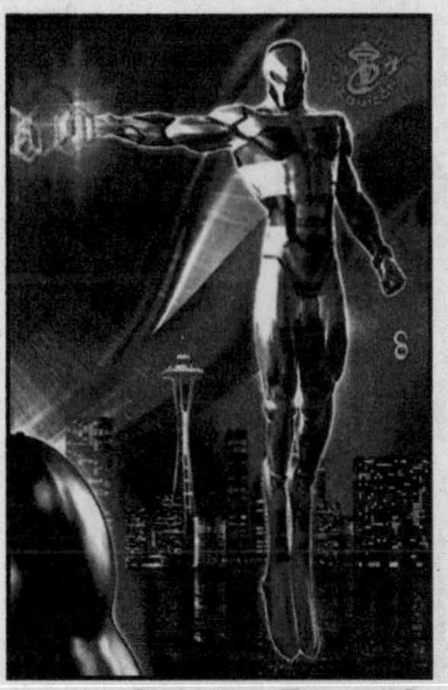

Soldier Zero #3
Emerald City Comicon cover
December 2010
$4

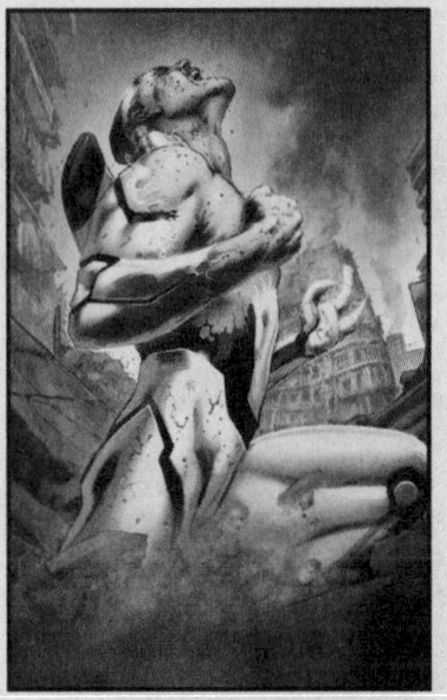

Soldier Zero #3
Variant cover
December 2010
$4

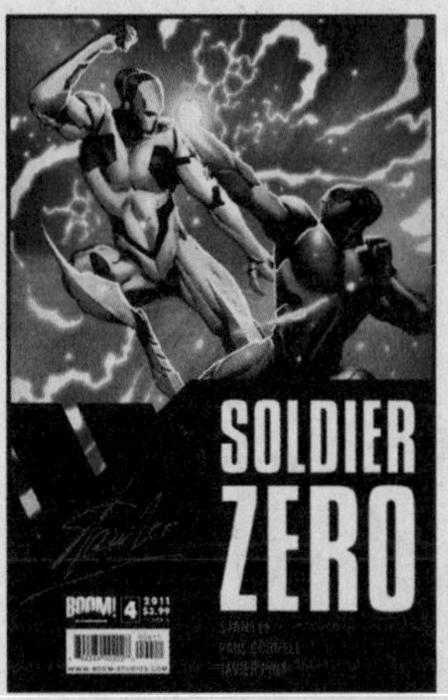
SOLDIER ZERO
BOOM!

Soldier Zero #4
January 2011
$4

SOLDIER ZERO #4
VARIANT COVER
JANUARY 2011
$4

SOLDIER ZERO #4
VARIANT COVER
JANUARY 2011
$4

SOLDIER ZERO #5
FEBRUARY 2011
$4

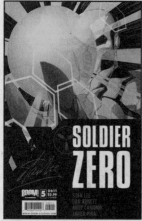

SOLDIER ZERO #5
VARIANT COVER
FEBRUARY 2011
$4

SOLDIER ZERO #5
VARIANT COVER
FEBRUARY 2011
$4

SOLDIER ZERO #6
MARCH 2011
$4

SOLDIER ZERO #6
VARIANT COVER
MARCH 2011
$4

SOLDIER ZERO #6
VARIANT COVER
MARCH 2011
$4

SOLDIER ZERO #7
APRIL 2011
$4

SOLDIER ZERO #7
VARIANT COVER
APRIL 2011
$4

SOLDIER ZERO #7
VARIANT COVER
APRIL 2011
$4

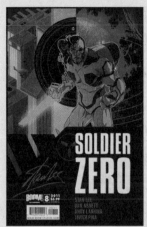

SOLDIER ZERO #8
MAY 2011
$4

SOLDIER ZERO #8
VARIANT COVER
MAY 2011
$4

SOLDIER ZERO #8
VARIANT COVER
MAY 2011
$4

SOLDIER ZERO #9
JUNE 2011
$4

SOLDIER ZERO #9
VARIANT COVER
JUNE 2011
$4

SOLDIER ZERO #9
VARIANT COVER
JUNE 2011
$4

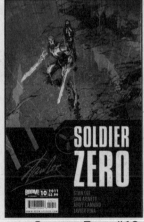

SOLDIER ZERO #10
JULY 2011
$4

SOLDIER ZERO #10
VARIANT COVER
JULY 2011
$4

SOLDIER ZERO #11
AUGUST 2011
$4

SOLDIER ZERO #11
VARIANT COVER
AUGUST 2011
$4

SOLDIER ZERO #12
SEPTEMBER 2011
$4

SOLDIER ZERO #12
VARIANT COVER
SEPTEMBER 2011
$4

STARBORN #1
DECEMBER 2010
$4

STARBORN #1
VARIANT COVER
DECEMBER 2010
$4

STARBORN #1
VARIANT COVER
DECEMBER 2010
$4

STARBORN #1
VARIANT COVER
DECEMBER 2010
$4

STARBORN #1
VARIANT COVER
DECEMBER 2010
$4

STARBORN #1
VARIANT COVER
DECEMBER 2010
$4

STARBORN #1
VARIANT COVER
DECEMBER 2010
$4

STARBORN #1
MIDTOWN COMICS VARIANT COVER
DECEMBER 2010
$4

STARBORN #2
JANUARY 2011
$4

STARBORN #2
VARIANT COVER
JANUARY 2011
$4

STARBORN #2
VARIANT COVER
JANUARY 2011
$4

STARBORN #3
FEBRUARY 2011
$4

STARBORN #3
VARIANT COVER
FEBRUARY 2011
$4

STARBORN #3
Variant cover
February 2011
$4

STARBORN #3
Emerald City Comicon cove
February 2011
$4

STARBORN #4
March 2011
$4

STARBORN #4
Variant cover
March 2011
$4

STARBORN #4
Variant cover
March 2011
$4

STARBORN #5
April 2011
$4

STARBORN #5
Variant cover
April 2011
$4

STARBORN #5
Variant cover
April 2011
$4

STARBORN #6
May 2011
$4

STARBORN #6
Variant cover
May 2011
$4

STARBORN #6
Variant cover
May 2011
$4

STARBORN #7
June 2011
$4

STARBORN #7
Variant cover
June 2011
$4

STARBORN #7
Variant cover
June 2011
$4

STARBORN #8
July 2011
$4

STARBORN #8
Variant cover
July 2011
$4

STARBORN #9
August 2011
$4

STARBORN #9
Variant cover
August 2011
$4

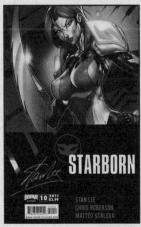

STARBORN #10
SEPTEMBER 2011
$4

STARBORN #10
VARIANT COVER
SEPTEMBER 2011
$4

STARBORN #11
OCTOBER 2011
$4

STARBORN #11
VARIANT COVER
OCTOBER 2011
$4

STARBORN #12
NOVEMBER 2011
$4

STARBORN #12
VARIANT COVER
NOVEMBER 2011
$4

THE TRAVELER #1
NOVEMBER 2010
$4

THE TRAVELER #1
VARIANT COVER
NOVEMBER 2010
$4

THE TRAVELER #1
VARIANT COVER
NOVEMBER 2010
$4

THE TRAVELER #1
VARIANT COVER
NOVEMBER 2010
$4

THE TRAVELER #1
VARIANT COVER
NOVEMBER 2010
$4

THE TRAVELER #1
VARIANT COVER
NOVEMBER 2010
$4

THE TRAVELER #1
VARIANT COVER
NOVEMBER 2010
$4

THE TRAVELER #1
VARIANT COVER
NOVEMBER 2010
$4

THE TRAVELER #1
MIDTOWN COMICS VARIANT COVER
NOVEMBER 2010
$4

THE TRAVELER #2
DECEMBER 2010
$4

THE TRAVELER #2
VARIANT COVER
DECEMBER 2010
$4

THE TRAVELER #2
VARIANT COVER
DECEMBER 2010
$4

THE TRAVELER #3
JANUARY 2011
$4

THE TRAVELER #3
VARIANT COVER
JANUARY 2011
$4

THE TRAVELER #3
VARIANT COVER
JANUARY 2011
$4

THE TRAVELER #4
FEBRUARY 2011
$4

THE TRAVELER #4
VARIANT COVER
FEBRUARY 2011
$4

THE TRAVELER #4
VARIANT COVER
FEBRUARY 2011
$4

THE TRAVELER #4
EMERALD CITY COMICON COVER
FEBRUARY 2011
$4

THE TRAVELER #5
MARCH 2011
$4

THE TRAVELER #5
VARIANT COVER
MARCH 2011
$4

THE TRAVELER #5
Variant cover
March 2011
$4

THE TRAVELER #6
April 2011
$4

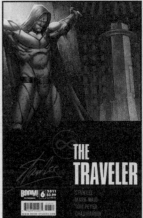

THE TRAVELER #6
Variant cover
April 2011
$4

THE TRAVELER #6
Variant cover
April 2011
$4

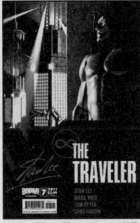

THE TRAVELER #7
May 2011
$4

THE TRAVELER #7
Variant cover
May 2011
$4

THE TRAVELER #7
Variant cover
May 2011
$4

THE TRAVELER #8
June 2011
$4

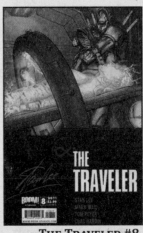

THE TRAVELER #8
Variant cover
June 2011
$4

THE TRAVELER #8
VARIANT COVER
JUNE 2011
$4

THE TRAVELER #9
JULY 2011
$4

THE TRAVELER #9
VARIANT COVER
JULY 2011
$4

THE TRAVELER #10
VARIANT COVER
AUGUST 2011
$4

THE TRAVELER #10
AUGUST 2011
$4

THE TRAVELER #11
SEPTEMBER 2011
$4

THE TRAVELER #11
VARIANT COVER
SEPTEMBER 2011
$4

THE TRAVELER #12
OCTOBER 2011
$4

THE TRAVELER #12
VARIANT COVER
OCTOBER 2011
$4

BROADWAY COMICS

"I formed Broadway Comics in partnership with Broadway Video Entertainment, a division of Broadway Video, *Saturday Night Live* producer Lorne Michaels' company. Our purpose was to make great and successful comics, of course, but with an eye towards properties that had potential for TV and film," Jim Shooter wrote in 2011.

"Among the experiments tried at Broadway Comics was writing comics sort of in the same manner that many TV shows are written—a group of writers working together," he said.

Janet "JayJay" Jackson, Joe James and Pauline Weiss, the company's three Executive Editors, joined Shooter in the writer's room. They were occasionally joined by others in what was dubbed "The Fifth Chair."

"Each member of the group had special strengths. JayJay, besides being generally brilliant and having a gift for dialogue, is a great designer. She was wonderful with clothing and costumes. She also created floor plans of locations. She was always sketching. JayJay, an excellent photographer, also took photos of me and whomever acting out some bits, as well as shots of settings. We often went out to film 'on location,'" he wrote.

"Joe is a terrific designer and a superb artist. He thumbnailed panels and choreographed action as we went along. He also was good with current slang, real-people talk and such. Pauline can type faster than you can talk. She was the scribe. She took down every word uttered in our sessions," he said, adding that taking down everyone else's thoughts didn't stop Weiss from contributing her own.

They launched with black and white preview editions delivered to the retailers in time to impact their distributor orders. *Powers That Be* #1 featured Fatale (with J.G. Jones artwork) and Star Seed, a super-powered half-alien boy finding his way in the world.

FIRST PUBLICATION:
Powers That Be #1
Preview Edition
(August 1995)

LAST PUBLICATION:
Inherit The Earth SC/HC
(November 1996)

REVIVAL(S):
None

"*Fatale* was an experiment in many ways. Fatale was created to be Broadway Comics' answer to the 'Bad Girl' trend, popular in the 1990s. Being me, I wanted to do a Bad Girl who was every bit as extreme as those pneumatic vixens who led the charge but less puerile and more real," he said.

We had so much faith in Fatale that we debuted her in the first Broadway Comics offering, *Powers That Be* #1 (starring Star Seed) and in the first two issues of *Shadow State*, our second series launch," he said.

Shadow State featured a sort of comic-within-a-comic story "Till Death Do Us Part" and "Blood S.C.R.E.A.M." The title also served as a vehicle for Fatale, until she got her own series.

The company would also launch *Knights on Broadway* (a science fiction tale inspired by a dystopic take on the turn of the millennium), *Fatale* in her own series, and retitle *Powers That Be* to *Star Seed*. Despite launching at a time when the market was nearing a freefall drop *Fatale* and *Star Seed* found themselves in profitable territory, but then their parent firm was sold to Golden Books.

With numerous other properties developed, including ones that would have more clearly made Broadway Comics a universe (there were clues in several of the books) – as well as a line of creator-owned material – it was not to be.

At the meet-and-greet with the Shooter and the leaders of the various divisions, the head of Golden Books, with a glance over his shoulder, told Shooter, "Oh, I'm shutting you down," Shooter said.

Inherit The Earth, the trade paperback collecting Fatale's *Powers That Be* and *Shadow State* adventures in addition to *Fatale* #1-6, would be the company's last publication. A limited edition hardcover, signed by Shooter, J.G. Jones, and Frank McLaughlin still commands a premium, as does their promotional comic, *Miracle on Broadway*.

J.G. Jones and Frank McLaughlin's original cover art for Broadway's
Powers That Be #1 (1995) featuring Fatale. From collection of J.C. Vaughn.

BABES OF BROADWAY #1
MAY 1996
$5

FATALE PREVIEW EDITION #1
SEPTEMBER 1995
$4

FATALE #1
JANUARY 1996
$4

FATALE #2
FEBRUARY 1996
$4

FATALE #3
MARCH 1996
$4

FATALE #4
MAY 1996
$4

FATALE #5
JULY 1996
$4

FATALE #6
OCTOBER 1996
$4

INHERIT THE EARTH
HARDCOVER • 1996
$75

INHERIT THE EARTH
SOFT COVER • 1996
$75

KNIGHTS ON BROADWAY #1
JULY 1996
$4

KNIGHTS ON BROADWAY #2
AUGUST 1996
$4

KNIGHTS ON BROADWAY #3
OCTOBER 1996
$4

MIRACLE ON BROADWAY #1
1995
$6 **$18** **$100**

**POWERS THAT BE
#1 PREVIEW EDITION**
AUGUST 1995
$4

**POWERS THAT BE
#2 PREVIEW EDITION**
SEPTEMBER 1995
$4

**POWERS THAT BE
#3 PREVIEW EDITION**
OCTOBER 1995
$4

POWERS THAT BE #1
NOVEMBER 1995
$4

POWERS THAT BE #2
DECEMBER 1995
$4

POWERS THAT BE #3
JANUARY 1996
$4

POWERS THAT BE #4
FEBRUARY 1996
$4

POWERS THAT BE #5
APRIL 1996
$4

POWERS THAT BE #6
MAY 1996
$4

**SHADOW STATE
#1 PREVIEW EDITION**
OCTOBER 1995
$4

**SHADOW STATE
#2 PREVIEW EDITION**
NOVEMBER 1995
$4

SHADOW STATE #1
DECEMBER 1995
$4

SHADOW STATE #2
JANUARY 1996
$4

SHADOW STATE #3
MARCH 1996
$4

SHADOW STATE #4
APRIL 1996
$4

SHADOW STATE #5
MAY 1996
$4

STAR SEED #7
JULY 1996
$4

STAR SEED #8
AUGUST 1996
$4

STAR SEED #9
SEPTEMBER 1996
$4

J.G. Jones and Frank McLaughlin's original art for *Fatale* #5 Page 2 (1996).
Image courtesy of Heritage Auctions.

"I WAS RAISED BY A *WIZARD* IN A *SMALL COMIC BOOK SHOP*...BUT I'M GETTING AHEAD OF MYSELF."

"MY EARLIEST MEMORY IS DRAWING ON LARGE PIECES OF PAPER ON THE LIVING ROOM FLOOR..."

WRITTEN & ILLUSTRATED BY JOE JAMES
COLORED BY JAYJAY JACKSON
LETTERED BY MINDY LOPKIN
EDITED BY J.C. VAUGHN & AMANDA SHERIFF

"...BY THE LIGHT OF A *BLACK AND WHITE TV* IN OUR TENEMENT APARTMENT IN DOWNTOWN *NEW YORK CITY.*"

"I WAS EXPOSED TO MY FIRST *SPINNING COMIC BOOK RACK* AT A LOCAL STATIONARY STORE;"

"THAT DAY, I GOT A FEW ISSUES OF *THE DEFENDERS, FLASH, GHOST RIDER, CHAMPIONS,* AND THE *TREASURY-SIZED EDITION* OF *STAR WARS!*"

"THE PICTURES, THE WORDS, THE SOUND OF THE *ONOMATOPOEIAS* CRACKLED IN MY MIND'S EAR. SUDDENLY I *KNEW* WHAT I WANTED TO DO."

"I WAS DETERMINED TO BECOME AN *ARTIST.*"

"BUT I ALSO LOVED MOVIES AND FOUND MYSELF FASCINATED BY THE *CONCEPTUAL DESIGNS* I WOULD SEE ON SCREEN."

"THAT'S RIGHT, I WAS THAT KID WHO OBSESSED OVER THE SET DESIGN OF *SWEETHAVEN* ON THE MOVIE *POPEYE.*"

"I'D SPENT HOURS DRAWING THE SHIPS FROM *CLOSE ENCOUNTERS OF THE THIRD KIND,* THE *SIX MILLION DOLLAR MAN,* OR JUST ABOUT ANYTHING FROM *STAR WARS.*"

"AT THE TENDER AGE OF 12, I GOT A JOB AT A SMALL COMIC BOOK SHOP, AND I WAS WELCOMED INTO A WORLD OF *COMIC BOOK STORYTELLING.*"

"THE SHOP WAS CALLED *WONDERWORLD* AND WAS OWNED BY A *WIZARD.*"

"EVERY DAY AFTER SCHOOL, I READ EVERYTHING FROM *WILL EISNER'S THE DREAMER* TO *SECRET WARS,* THE *NEW MUTANTS* TO *LONE WOLF AND CUB* AND *CEREBUS.*"

"AN *ADDED BENEFIT* OF BEING RAISED IN THE SHOP WAS THE WIZARD WHO *OWNED* IT. YOU SEE, HE HAD BEEN AN ACTUAL *MAGICIAN'S ASSISTANT* FOR MANY YEARS..."

"...AND, AS A RESULT, WAS A *COLLECTOR* OF COMICS AND *CURATOR* OF ALL THINGS STRANGE. THE WIZARD WOULD LECTURE ME ON THE HISTORY AND CHARACTERS OF EACH COMIC I READ.

"COMICS WERE ABLE TO GO FROM *AUTOBIOGRAPHICAL* TO *UNIVERSE EXPANDING* ADVENTURE.

"THEY WERE BOTH *INTIMATE* AND *MIND-BLOWING,* AND AS WITH A GREAT NOVEL, IT ALL HAPPENED IN THE *INTIMACY* OF YOUR *MIND.*"

"I LOVED THE POWER OF *PICTURES* AND *WORDS,* AND I KNEW THIS WAS WHAT I WANTED TO *DO.*"

"SOON, THE WIZARD HELPED ME PUT TOGETHER THE FOUR-PAGE SAMPLE PORTFOLIO THAT GOT ME INTO AN ART SCHOOL; I THOUGHT THAT I COULD PROBABLY BUILD A LIFE DOING THIS.

"AFTER SOME YEARS, I KEPT SHOWING UP TO THE OFFICES OF DC COMICS ON 5TH AVENUE WITH MY SAMPLE PAGES, AND *DICK GIORDANO* WAS KIND ENOUGH TO GIVE ME A FEW MINUTES AND SOME POINTERS.

"HE TOOK ME UNDER HIS WING, SCRUTINIZED MY COMPOSITION, AND TOLD ME STORIES ABOUT THE GREAT *OLD DAYS OF COMICS.*"

"SOON I GOT A JOB WORKING FOR DENYS COWAN ON BOOKS LIKE *THE QUESTION*, *GREEN ARROW*, *FOOLKILLER*."

"DENYS SPOTTED ME AT A CONVENTION AND OFFERED ME A POSITION TO BE HIS ASSISTANT."

"BY THE FOLLOWING MONDAY, I WAS WORKING FULL-TIME IN HIS STUDIO. I LEARNED THE CRAFT AND DISCIPLINE OF DRAWING BY WORKING WITH HIM."

"THE FORMATIVE MEETINGS FOR *MILESTONE MEDIA*, THE HOME OF *HARDWARE*, *ICON*, AND *STATIC SHOCK*, TOOK PLACE AT DENYS' STUDIO. I BEGAN WORKING WITH DENYS ON MUCH OF THE CONCEPTUAL ART FOR THE WORLD OF DAKOTA CITY."

"THAT RESULTED IN *DWAYNE MCDUFFIE*, *EDITOR IN CHIEF OF MILESTONE*, OFFERING ME A JOB AS A CREATIVE ASSOCIATE BEFORE PUBLISHING THEIR BOOKS UNDER THE *DC COMICS* BANNER."

"DWAYNE UNDERSTOOD THAT I WAS COMPLETELY COMFORTABLE TALKING *"ONOMATOPOEIA."* AT FIRST, HE WAS AMUSED AT MY TENDENCY TO SPEAK IN SWISHES AND CRACKLES IN DESCRIBING ART OR SEQUENCES, BUT EVENTUALLY, HE WOULD TALK BACK IN THE SAME WAY."

"IN FACT, HE WOULD SUBSEQUENTLY LIMIT HIS DIRECTION TO SOUNDS."

YEAH, JUST MAKE IT MORE... *KRRRRAUUUAGH.* COOL?

"DWAYNE TOOK ME UNDER HIS WING AND TAUGHT ME THE STEPS OF DRAWING AND PRODUCING A COMIC BOOK FROM THE GROUND UP."

"*JAYJAY JACKSON* WAS DESIGNING LOGOS FOR *DEFIANT* AND ASKED ME TO COME IN AND HELP."

"OVER COFFEE, WE CAME UP WITH SOME EXCELLENT IDEAS SKETCHED OUT ON NAPKINS."

"EVENTUALLY, THOSE BECAME THE LOGOS FOR *PLASM*, *DARK DOMINION* AND *DOGS OF WAR*."

"SOON I CREATED SOME ART FOR THE *DARK DOMINION* TRADING CARD SET, WHICH FEATURED WORK BY *STEVE DITKO*. EDITOR DEBORAH PURCELL OFFERED ME A STAFF JOB, AND I TOOK IT."

"IT WAS A CHANCE TO LEARN FROM ONE OF MY HEROES, *JIM SHOOTER*."

"JIM REMINDED ME OF THE *WIZARD.*

"HERE WAS SOMEONE WHO MAINTAINED A *CHILD-LIKE* WONDER FOR THE STORY, CARED FOR THE *EMOTIONAL FOUNDATIONS* OF THE CHARACTER'S JOURNEY, AND KEPT A *CLEAR EYE* ON THE BUILDING BLOCKS OF THE OVERARCHING STORY.

"HIS LESSONS INCLUDED SCRIPTWRITING, CHARACTER DEVELOPMENT, STORYTELLING, SHOT-MAKING, CONCEPTUALIZATION, EDITING.

"AND A FIERCE COMMITMENT TO THE *FANTASTIC!*

"I ALSO WORKED WITH JIM AT *BROADWAY COMICS...*

"...CREATING AND WRITING *KNIGHTS ON BROADWAY.*

"JIM MADE ME INTO A STUDENT OF STORYTELLING, AND TO THIS DAY, HIS *LESSONS* RING IN MY *EARS...*

"...AS I WORK ON STORYBOARDS FOR MOTION PICTURES AND COMMERCIALS WITH MY COMPANY *ST. JAMES STUDIOS.*

"YOU'VE SEEN SOME OF THE PROJECTS I'VE WORKED ON, WHICH INCLUDES A *BAYER* COMMERCIAL THAT FEATURED ME.

"THERE'S NOTHING QUITE LIKE THE FEELING OF OPENING A GRAPHIC NOVEL AND ALLOWING A UNIVERSE TO FLOWER IN MY MIND.

"THAT'S THE POWER OF COMIC BOOKS, THE MOST ANCIENT ART OF STORYTELLING, AND IT STILL BEATS THE REST.

"I HOPE YOU FIND A *WIZARD* WHO CAN HELP PUT YOU ON THE PATH TO SOMETHING YOU *LOVE.* AND A *PARTNER* WHO WILL SHARE THE *JOURNEY* WITH *YOU.*"

There was a seismic shift in toy manufacturing that followed Mattel's introduction of Barbie in 1959 and Hasbro's introduction of G.I. Joe in 1964. Adopting the razor-and-razor-blades model, their respective manufacturers sold kids (and got the kids to sell their parents) first on the figures and then on the specialty clothing, vehicles, and playsets to go with them.

Ideal Toys responded to their competitors' success with their own take on the concept. First imagined by Stan Wesson as Captain Magic, the character was a superhero who would be able to take on the identities of other superheroes with an easy costume change. The name was quickly changed to Captain Action and Wesson's concept was soon put to the test.

The first issue of the Captain Action figure was 12" tall, and he came decked out in a blue and black costume with the initials "CA" emblazoned on his chest. The figure arrived with accessories such as a dark blue captain's hat, a pair of black boots, a belt, a lightning sword, a ray gun, and a fold-out mini poster. Subsequent reissues included more accessories, running the gamut from parachutes to mini-comics to video-matic flasher rings. The costumes that transformed Captain Action into the world's greatest superheroes were sold separately: Superman, Batman, Aquaman, Captain America, the Phantom, Steve Canyon, Flash Gordon, Sgt. Fury, and the Lone Ranger (each with additional accessories).

In 1967, Action Boy was added, along with costumes for Robin, Superboy, or Aqualad. That same year, four more Captain Action costumes were released: Green Hornet, Buck Rogers, Tonto, and Spider-Man.

In 1968, a new version of Action Boy was released, and the villain Dr. Evil also debuted. That same year, DC Comics launched the first issue of the *Captain Action* comic book series. While it only lasted five issues, it contained a number of highlights, including the work of Jim Shooter, Wally Wood, and Gil Kane, covers by Irv Novick, Kane, and Kane teamed with

FIRST PUBLICATION:
Captain Action #1
(October 1968)

LAST PUBLICATION:
Captain Action #5
(July 1969)

REVIVAL(S):
Moonstone: *Captain Action* #1 (October 2008),
Dynamite: *Codename: Action* (September 2013)

Dick Giordano. In addition to strong story and art, *Captain Action* #1 is always great for at least one trivia answer: it was then 16-year-old Jim Shooter's first published credit, though at that point he'd been writing for DC for about three years.

Somewhat paralleling the 1960s rise and fall of Batmania, the toy line ended that same year. Thirty years later, though, in 1998, Captain Action was revived by retro-themed toy company Playing Mantis. While that line did not last, it eventually led to more comics.

In 2005, Captain Action Enterprises was formed and they began developing new products based on the character. In 2008 Moonstone Books launched a new comic book series, including a new back story and the creation of his employer, the A.C.T.I.O.N. Directorate, a secret non-governmental agency. It also included the introduction of Nicola Sinclair, Lady Action.

Moonstone has featured a similarly revised Action Boy. In this version he is Sean Barrett, the son of a famous naturalist whose identity is assumed by Dr. Eville. His stories also take place in the 1960s. Moonstone has also created an original character, Lady Action, who works for the British branch of the A.C.T.I.O.N. Directorate.

In 2013 Dynamite Entertainment released *Codename: Action*, a mini-series that paired Captain Action with a number of pulp and comic book characters to create a rich origin story for the character. They released *Captain Action Cat: The Timestream CATastrophe!*, a four-issue mini-series, in 2014.

IDW published a hardcover collected edition of the original DC series in 2023.

Editor's Note: *We highly recommend Michael Eury's book,* Captain Action: The Original Super-Hero Action Figure, *a truly insightful study of the character. While there have been developments in the years since its publication, it remains nearly definitive.*

Gil Kane and Wally Wood's original art for *Captain Action #2* Page 2 (1969).
Image courtesy of Heritage Auctions.

CAPTAIN ACTION & ACTION BOY
IDEAL TOY CO. GIVEAWAY • 1967
$12 $36 $260

CAPTAIN ACTION #1
NOVEMBER 1968
$7 $21 $135

CAPTAIN ACTION #2
JANUARY 1969
$5 $15 $80

CAPTAIN ACTION #3
MARCH 1969
$5 $15 $80

CAPTAIN ACTION #4
MAY 1969
$4 $12 $65

CAPTAIN ACTION #5
JULY 1969
$5 $15 $80

CAPTAIN ACTION COMICS #0
2008
$3

CAPTAIN ACTION COMICS #0
VARIANT COVER • 2008
$3

CAPTAIN ACTION COMICS #0
VARIANT COVER • 2008
$3

CAPTAIN ACTION COMICS #1
OCTOBER 2008
$4

CAPTAIN ACTION COMICS #1
VARIANT COVER • OCTOBER 2008
$4

CAPTAIN ACTION COMICS #1
VARIANT COVER • OCTOBER 2008
$4

CAPTAIN ACTION COMICS #1
VARIANT COVER • OCTOBER 2008
$4

CAPTAIN ACTION COMICS #2
JANUARY 2009
$4

CAPTAIN ACTION COMICS #2
VARIANT COVER • JANUARY 2009
$4

CAPTAIN ACTION COMICS #2
VARIANT COVER • JANUARY 2009
$4

CAPTAIN ACTION COMICS #2
VARIANT COVER • JANUARY 2009
$4

CAPTAIN ACTION COMICS #3
2009
$4

CAPTAIN ACTION COMICS #3
VARIANT COVER • 2009
$4

CAPTAIN ACTION COMICS #3
VARIANT COVER • 2009
$4

CAPTAIN ACTION COMICS #3.5
2009
$4

CAPTAIN ACTION COMICS #3.5
VARIANT COVER • 2009
$4

CAPTAIN ACTION COMICS #4
VARIANT COVER • 2009
$4

CAPTAIN ACTION COMICS #4
VARIANT COVER • 2009
$4

CAPTAIN ACTION COMICS #5
VARIANT COVER • 2009
$4

CAPTAIN ACTION COMICS #5
VARIANT COVER • 2009
$4

CAPTAIN ACTION COMICS
SPECIAL #1
APRIL 2010
$6

CAPTAIN ACTION COMICS
SPECIAL #1
VARIANT COVER • APRIL 2010
$6

CAPTAIN ACTION COMICS
SPECIAL #1
VARIANT COVER • APRIL 2010
$6

CAPTAIN ACTION
FIRST MISSION, LAST DAY
JULY 2008
$4

CAPTAIN ACTION
FIRST MISSION, LAST DAY
VARIANT COVER • JULY 2008
$4

CAPTAIN ACTION COMICS
KING SIZE SPECIAL #1
JANUARY 2011
$7

CAPTAIN ACTION COMICS
KING SIZE SPECIAL #1
VARIANT COVER • JANUARY 2011
$7

CAPTAIN ACTION
SEASON 2 #1
AUGUST 2010
$4

CAPTAIN ACTION
SEASON 2 #1
VARIANT COVER • AUGUST 2010
$4

CAPTAIN ACTION SEASON 2 #2
SEPTEMBER 2010
$4

CAPTAIN ACTION SEASON 2 #2
VARIANT COVER • SEPTEMBER 2010
$4

CAPTAIN ACTION SEASON 2 #3
NOVEMBER 2010
$4

CAPTAIN ACTION SEASON 2 #3
VARIANT COVER • NOVEMBER 2010
$4

CAPTAIN ACTION COMICS WINTER SPECIAL #1
MARCH 2011
$5

CAPTAIN ACTION COMICS WINTER SPECIAL #1
VARIANT COVER • MARCH 2011
$5

THE PHANTOM - CAPTAIN ACTION #1
APRIL 2010
$4

THE PHANTOM - CAPTAIN ACTION #1
VARIANT COVER • APRIL 2010
$4

THE PHANTOM - CAPTAIN ACTION #1
VARIANT COVER • APRIL 2010
$4

**THE PHANTOM -
CAPTAIN ACTION #2**
VARIANT COVER • JUNE 2010
$4

**THE PHANTOM -
CAPTAIN ACTION #2**
VARIANT COVER • JUNE 2010
$4

**THE PHANTOM -
CAPTAIN ACTION #2**
VARIANT COVER • JUNE 2010
$4

CODENAME: ACTION #1
SEPTEMBER 2013
$4

CODENAME: ACTION #1
VARIANT COVER • SEPTEMBER 2013
$4

CODENAME: ACTION #1
VARIANT COVER • SEPTEMBER 2013
$4

CODENAME: ACTION #1
VARIANT COVER • SEPTEMBER 2013
$4

CODENAME: ACTION #1
VARIANT COVER • SEPTEMBER 2013
$4

CODENAME: ACTION #1
VARIANT COVER • SEPTEMBER 2013
$4

CODENAME: ACTION #1
VARIANT COVER • SEPTEMBER 2013
$4

CODENAME: ACTION #1
VARIANT COVER • SEPTEMBER 2013
$4

CODENAME: ACTION #1
VARIANT COVER • SEPTEMBER 2013
$4

CODENAME: ACTION #2
OCTOBER 2013
$4

CODENAME: ACTION #2
VARIANT COVER • OCTOBER 2013
$4

CODENAME: ACTION #2
VARIANT COVER • OCTOBER 2013
$4

CODENAME: ACTION #2
VARIANT COVER • OCTOBER 2013
$4

CODENAME: ACTION #2
VARIANT COVER • OCTOBER 2013
$4

CODENAME: ACTION #2
NYCC VARIANT • OCTOBER 2013
$4

CODENAME: ACTION #2
NYCC BLANK COVER • OCTOBER 2013
$4

CODENAME: ACTION #3
NOVEMBER 2013
$4

CODENAME: ACTION #3
VARIANT COVER • NOVEMBER 2013
$4

CODENAME: ACTION #3
VARIANT COVER • NOVEMBER 2013
$4

CODENAME: ACTION #3
VARIANT COVER • NOVEMBER 2013
$4

CODENAME: ACTION #4
DECEMBER 2013
$4

CODENAME: ACTION #4
VARIANT COVER • DECEMBER 2013
$4

CODENAME: ACTION #4
VARIANT COVER • DECEMBER 2013
$4

CODENAME: ACTION #5
FEBRUARY 2014
$4

CODENAME: ACTION #5
VARIANT COVER • FEBRUARY 2014
$4

CODENAME: ACTION #5
VARIANT COVER • FEBRUARY 2014
$4

CODENAME: ACTION #5
VARIANT COVER • FEBRUARY 2014
$4

CAPTAIN ACTION CAT:
THE TIMESTREAM CATASTROPHE #1
APRIL 2014
$4

CAPTAIN ACTION CAT:
THE TIMESTREAM CATASTROPHE #2
JUNE 2014
$4

CAPTAIN ACTION CAT:
THE TIMESTREAM CATASTROPHE #3
JULY 2014
$4

CAPTAIN ACTION CAT:
THE TIMESTREAM CATASTROPHE #4
SEPTEMBER 2014
$4

CAPTAIN ACTION: THE
CLASSIC COLLECTION HC
IDW PUBLISHING • MAY 2022
$29.95

CAPTAIN ACTION: THE
CLASSIC COLLECTION HC
DOCTOR EVIL EDITION • IDW PUBL.
MAY 2022 • $39.95

Dick Giordano's original cover art for the variant cover on Moonstone's *Captain Action Comics* #4 (2008), a recreation of Gil Kane's cover DC's *Captain Action* #3, which was inked by Giordano. Image courtesy of Heritage Auctions.

CAPTAIN ACTION

by *Michael Eury*

As Captain Action approaches his 60th anniversary, we are happy to re-present Michael Eury's concise overview of the action figure/comic book character from *The Overstreet Comic Book Price Guide #45*.

Captain Action's history is as jagged as the blade on his lightning sword. Yet over the course of half a century, Captain Action has withstood almost as many reboots as there are plastic boots in his Ideal Toys wardrobe and has become an enduring pop-culture legend.

A MAGICAL BEGINNING

Captain Action started as a 12-inch poseable action figure for boys, introduced by the Ideal Toy Company at the 1966 Toy Fair. Two years earlier, Hasbro rolled out G.I. Joe, an articulated action figure billed as "America's movable fighting man." G.I. Joe's creators, licensing impresario Stan Weston and toy exec Don Levine, appropriated from Mattel's popular Barbie line the "razor/razor blade" marketing approach: sell a kid the "razor" (the primary figure) and she/he will be obliged to buy the "razor blades" (clothing and accessories). Through an expanding array of uniforms, G.I. Joe could become a sailor, a Marine, a frogman—even an astronaut!—and Hasbro dropped a decisive salvo onto war-toy competitors.

Weston, a fan of comics and pulps, was convinced that lightning could strike twice with this "razor/razor blade" concept for boys. He conceived a generic super-hero that could "become" different commercially popular champions with the mere change of a costume—or, from Weston's thinking, via an imagined magical transformation, hence the character's name: Captain Magic. In 1965 Weston proposed the idea to Ideal Toys' Larry Reiner. Reiner was reluctant, fearing that Captain Magic's own identity would be lost behind the rubber masks of the better-known characters' faces, but conceded to Weston's enthusiasm. Ideal designed the hero with military implications including the rank of "Captain" so as not to stray too far from G.I. Joe, but rebranded him with a name more reflective of a super-hero: Captain Action. Meanwhile, Weston recruited multiple licensors' properties to the initial line.

LIKE A QUICKSILVER OF LIGHTNING

And thus, in early 1966, the American public met Captain Action, "the Amazing 9-in-1 Super Hero" who could become Superman, Batman, Aquaman, Captain America, Sgt. Fury, the Phantom, Flash Gordon, Lone Ranger, and Steve Canyon. The Captain Action figure was sold separately in a decorative box sporting a painted image (by an unknown artist) of the hero brandishing his lightning sword and ray gun. *Hawkman* illustrator Murphy Anderson, whose slick artwork epitomized DC Comics' house style at the time, was contracted by Ideal to produce the package art for most of Captain Action's super-hero uniforms. The first Captain Action artist in the minds of most DC readers, however, was *Lois Lane*'s Kurt Schaffenberger, who drew one-page Captain Action house ads appearing in DC titles.

The debut of Captain Action could not have been more fortuitously timed: the overnight success of TV's *Batman* series starring Adam West torch-lit an international super-hero craze. Ideal's Captain Action enjoyed a modestly successful first year, and product expansion briskly followed: several major department stores offered exclusive playsets, and in 1967 Ideal unleashed more costumes (Spider-Man, Green Hornet, and Tonto), a kid sidekick (Action Boy, with his boomerang and pet panther, Khem), Action Boy uniforms (Robin, Superboy, and Aqualad), and a Barbie-like line of "Super Queens" (Supergirl, Batgirl, Wonder Woman, and Mera) marketed at girls. The first Captain Action comic book, a 32-page illustrated catalog drawn by Chic Stone, was also released in 1967 and was inserted into Captain Action products.

While Ideal aggressively pushed Captain Action's and Action Boy's famous alter egos, they also exploited Captain Action as a hero in his own right, releasing a vehicle (the Silver Streak) and accessory packs (including the Directional Communicator). Ideal licensed Captain Action to other vendors for products including an Aurora model kit, a Ben Cooper Halloween costume, and a card game promotion with General Mills' Kool-Pops.

During the product's third year, 1968, no new licensed super-hero costumes were produced. Instead Ideal continued to push Captain Action as *their* super-hero by introducing his nemesis, Dr. Evil, a blue-skinned "sinister invader of Earth" with an exposed brain—and groovy threads (Nehru jacket, sandals, and a medallion). Also released that year was a second-issue Action Boy, clad in a spacesuit. By this time, the *Batman*-inspired super-hero fad was stalling, and so were Captain Action's sales. Revitalization attempts had fizzled, including a giveaway parachute with Captain Action figures and the addition of "Video-Matic" flasher rings to costumes. Ideal discontinued the line at the end of 1968. It's unlikely that a single factor can be blamed for the toy's demise, but former Ideal salesman Larry O'Daly believed that the figure's dual function as a super-hero *and* a super-hero masquerader tended to "fragment the imagery of the basic character."

CAPTAIN ACTION AT DC COMICS

While American boys were playing with Cap-

tain Action, Jim Shooter, a teenager just a few years older than Ideal's target audience, was writing Superman and Legion of Super-Heroes stories for DC Comics' infamously tyrannical editor, Mort Weisinger. In 1968 Shooter was thrilled when he landed the assignment to produce a "new" superhero book for Weisinger ... until Mort rattled off the feature's prerequisites: "His name is Captain Action. He has a sidekick named Action Boy, a threewheeled car, a secret cave..." Nonetheless, Shooter dove into the assignment, a DC comic book starring Captain Action, the result of a licensing agreement with Ideal.

The colorful but vague concept of Ideal's Captain Action presented a super-hero that could take on the guises—and powers—of other super-heroes. That's great for playtime, but improbable for comic-book storytelling. Shooter concocted a backstory: DC's Captain Action was actually archaeologist Clive Arno, who, along with his duplicitous colleague Krellik, unearthed ancient coins imbued with the abilities of the gods of myth. The altruistic Arno wields the tokens as the superhero Captain Action, while Krellik, empowered by the coin of the

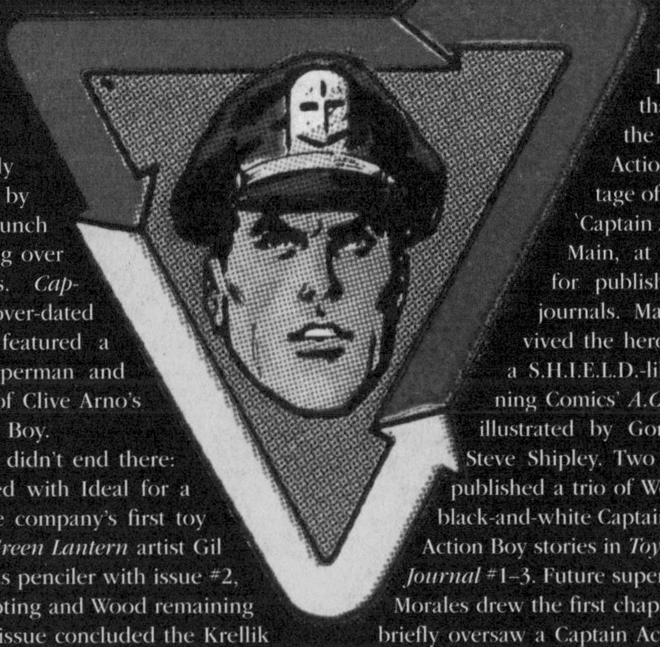

god of evil, Chernobog (Loki), unleashes a crime spree. The amazing Wally Wood was tapped by Weisinger to launch the series, working over Shooter's layouts. *Captain Action* #1, cover-dated Oct.–Nov. 1968, featured a guest-shot by Superman and the introduction of Clive Arno's son Carl as Action Boy.

Yet the series didn't end there: DC had contracted with Ideal for a five-issue run, the company's first toy tie-in. Longtime *Green Lantern* artist Gil Kane stepped in as penciler with issue #2, with Shooter scripting and Wood remaining on as inker. This issue concluded the Krellik storyline.

By the time the third issue of the bimonthly series went into production in late 1968, Weisinger passed off *Captain Action* to editor Julius Schwartz. Schwartz offered Gil Kane the opportunity to write as well as draw *Captain Action*, which Gil relished. Kane brought Ideal Toys' Dr. Evil into comics with issues #3 and 4. Issue #5 pitted Captain Action and Action Boy against a persuasive demagogue. Despite dynamic storytelling and gorgeous artwork, DC's *Captain Action* premiered too late to capitalize upon the toy line's momentum and was not renewed. Kane confessed to me in 1998, "It broke my heart when it ended cold."

FALSE STARTS

Yet Captain Action did not fade from fans' memories. He was included in E. Nelson Bridwell's "Checklist of DC Super-Heroes" in 1971's *DC 100-Page Super Spectacular* #6, and occasionally a *Brave and the Bold* reader would appeal for a Batman/Captain Action team-up. In the early 1980s, writer Mike Tiefenbacher unsuccessfully pitched a Clive Arno revival for the "Whatever Happened To...?" backup series in *DC Comics Presents*, proposing that since DC no longer had the rights to the Captain Action name, Arno and son would be rechristened Captain Triumph and Javelin. However, outside of a wistful review of DC's Silver Age series in Fantagraphics' *Amazing Heroes* #9 in early 1982, *Captain Action* remained banished to back-issue bins.

Until January 1987. With the demise of Ideal Toys in the early 1980s, it appeared that no one owned the rights to Captain Action. Taking advantage of this was longtime Captain Action booster Jim Main, at the time known for publishing toycollecting journals. Main, as writer, revived the hero as the leader of a S.H.I.E.L.D.-like team in Lightning Comics' *A.C.T.I.O.N. Force* #1, illustrated by Gordon Purcell and Steve Shipley. Two years later, Main published a trio of World War II set, black-and-white Captain Action and Action Boy stories in *Toy Collectors' Journal* #1–3. Future superstar Rags Morales drew the first chapter. Main briefly oversaw a Captain Action Fan Club and intended to produce an ongoing comic book, to no avail.

Artist Barry Kraus and writer Michael Luck of Karl Art Publishing had, like Main, grown up with Captain Action, and in 1995 obtained the copyright to the character with the publication of the ashcan comic *Captain Action* #0. Their modernized version included an updated costume, mega-sized firearms, a razor-sharp boomerang, and a retooled Dr. Evil. Kraus and Luck hoped to broker toy and animation deals with their new Captain Action, but no agreements ever materialized.

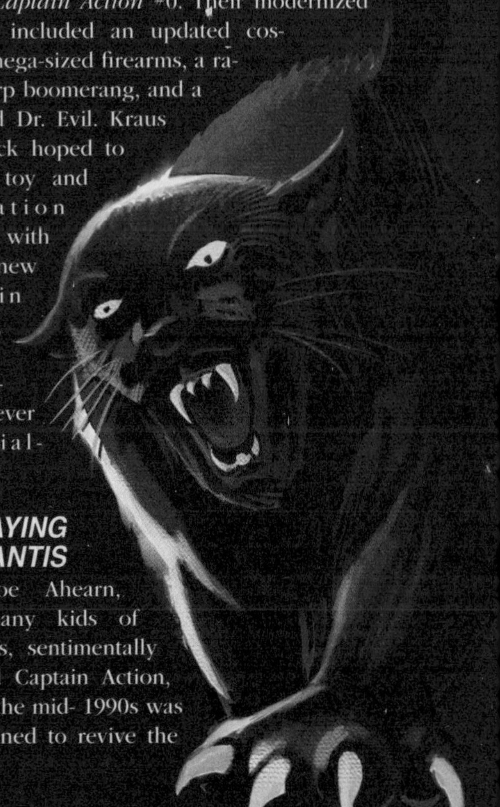

PLAYING MANTIS

Joe Ahearn, like many kids of the '60s, sentimentally recalled Captain Action, and in the mid- 1990s was determined to revive the toy in a marketplace growing accustomed to reissues promoted toward collectors. Ahearn petitioned Tom Lowe, president of Playing Mantis, a manufacturer of collectors' toys, to revive Captain Action, and after an initial rejection Lowe agreed. Playing Mantis signed a licensing agreement with Karl Art Publishing and in 1998 re-released Captain Action and Dr. Evil, plus Captain Action as both the Green Hornet and the never-before-produced Kato. The figures were released in a book-like box, with the Hornet and Kato figures sold on Captain Action figures instead of being released simply as costumes. Package art came from Carmine Infantino, with an uncredited Joe Orlando providing finishes. Three additional Captain Action reissues followed—Lone Ranger, Tonto, and Flash Gordon—plus the first-ever Dr. Evil villain costume, Ming the Merciless, on a now-rare Dr. Evil figure molded in tan instead of blue. Due to the public's unfamiliarity with the characters and a high price point, this Captain Action revival flopped.

At the urging of a persistent Ahearn, Playing Mantis, in conjunction with Diamond Distributors, gave Captain Action another shot, and from 1999 to 2000 rebooted the line, this time in packaging that mimicked Ideal's original boxes. Captain Action and Dr. Evil were back, Action Boy was released but renamed Kid Action due to

a trademark concern, and window-boxed outfits followed: the Phantom, the Phantom's foe Kabai Singh (for Dr. Evil), Lone Ranger (in a blue-suit variation), and Green Hornet and Kato. Speed Racer and Jonny Quest costumes were also in the works. But the line failed to catch on, partially because of the pessimism of some retailers burned by the earlier reissues. Captain Action was once again relegated to the dustbins of nostalgia.

NEW ENTERPRISES

But not for long. In 2002, TwoMorrows Publishing released my history/sourcebook, *Captain Action: The Original Super-Hero Action Figure*. In 1998 and 1999 I interviewed several toy professionals and comics creators involved with Captain Action, and wrote the book the following year for a different publisher, one that was unable to complete the project. Luckily, TwoMorrows publisher John Morrow offered *Captain Action* a home (and a revised second edition in 2009).

During my research I became friends with Joe Ahearn, indisputably Captain Action's most tenacious supporter. We pitched to Marvel Comics a Captain Action-like 12-inch action figure called Marvel Man, who could assume the guises of other Marvel super-heroes, but this went no further than a few conversations.

If Captain Action has a "real" super-power, it is the bottomless resolve of Joe Ahearn. Joe partnered with Ed Catto in 2006 to form Captain Action Enterprises, and they eventually acquired the property. This dynamic duo unleashed a campaign to place Captain Action in the public eye, starting with the announcement of a new comic series to be produced by Moonstone in 2008. A call went out to writers to pitch ideas for a Captain Action revival.

HOLD KHEM FOR ME, ACTION BOY... WHILE I TACKLE THAT PHONEY!
THIS IS A JOB FOR CAPTAIN ACTION AND COMPANY... THE REAL McCOY!
WHAT THE...?
ANOTHER ONE!!
CAPTAIN ACTION
SILVER STREAK
AMPHIBIAN
IDEAL
CAPTAIN ACTION CAT
DYNAMITE
THE TIMESTREAM CATASTROPHE!
FEATURING
ACTION CAT
BY ART BALTAZAR & FRANCO & SMITS
ARCH ENEMY OF ACTION BOY AND CAPTAIN ACTION
DR. EVIL
DISGUISES AND WEAPONS
dr. evil... the sinister invader of earth
POSE HIM IN 1001 POSITIONS

The winner was Fabian Nicieza, who contemporized the concept while paying homage to its roots.

Tackling the identity crisis which helped defeat Ideal's hero, Nicieza made Captain Action a super-spy, an operative for the A.C.T.I.O.N. Directorate, a covert agency that used super-heroes (the Protectors) in a war against a secret otherworldly threat known as the Red Crawl. Miles Drake was the original Captain Action, while his son Cole stepped into his father's role as the new Captain. Nicieza and artist Mark Sparacio introduced original super-heroes into the mix, analogs to the characters licensed by Ideal (Savior for Superman, for example), and the new Captain used a substance called "plasmaderm" to replicate their identities and powers.

At Moonstone, *Captain Action Comics* and its follow-ups also featured the talents of writers Marv Wolfman and Steven Grant, with covers by John Byrne, Mike Allred, Paul Gulacy, Dick Giordano, and other fan-favorites. Action Boy and Dr. Evil were reintroduced, but the breakout character was Lady Action, a British super-spy inspired by model/actress Niki Rubin, whose live promotional appearances as Lady Action at comic conventions earned her—and the character—a fan following. Moonstone also published Captain Action miniseries and specials featuring team-ups with retro heroes the Phantom, Green Hornet and Kato, Honey West, and That (Our) Man Flint.

Meanwhile, Captain Action Enterprises expanded their brand with a torrent of products, including T-shirts, Mego-sized figures, and a comic novella and pulp novel. An agreement with toy manufacturer Round 2 produced a revitalized line of 12-inch figures and costumes, which began in early 2012 with Captain Action and Dr. Evil, plus Spider-Man and Captain America uniforms. The line continued with an arctic Captain Action variation, plus costumes for Thor, Loki, Iron Man, and Wolverine,

along with Hawkeye, whose "Assemble an Avenger" costume was released in stages as bonuses inside the other Marvel ensembles. A line of DC super-hero costumes for Captain Action is planned but at this writing has yet to materialize. Other releases include a 16-inch Lady Action doll from Tonner (with Wonder Woman and Supergirl costumes) and a Captain Action "Amazing Heroes" action figure. A Captain Action animation series is in development, with Marv Wolfman as lead writer.

Dynamite Entertainment became Captain Action's new comic-book home in 2013 with the release of its five-issue miniseries *Codename: Action*, by Chris Roberson and Jonathan Lau. This critically acclaimed Cold War-era epic followed tough-guy spy Operative 1001's evolution into Captain Action, and guest-starred other retro heroes including the Spider and Green Lama. In 2014 Dynamite also published the four-issue miniseries *Captain Action Cat: The Timestream CATastrophe*, by cartoonist Art Baltazar, with Franco and Chris Smits. This all-ages crossover combined feline versions of Captain Action and company with Aw Yeah Comics!'s Action Cat, plus cartoon versions of Dark Horse Comics' X and Ghost.

So, who is this Captain Action? Is he a quick-change super-hero, a spy, a woman, or a cat? He's all of the above, and more. Imagination has driven his various incarnations, from plastic to print, and with that in his weapons arsenal, Captain Action should be fighting injustice for at least *another* fifty years!

Overstreet adviser Michael Eury coined the phrase "The Original Super-Hero Action Figure" as the subtitle of his Captain Action book from TwoMorrows. For that publisher he is the editor-in-chief of BACK ISSUE *magazine and the author of several comics-history books. He has also produced material for a host of clients including Arcadia Publishing, DC, Marvel, Dark Horse, Nike, and Toys R Us.*

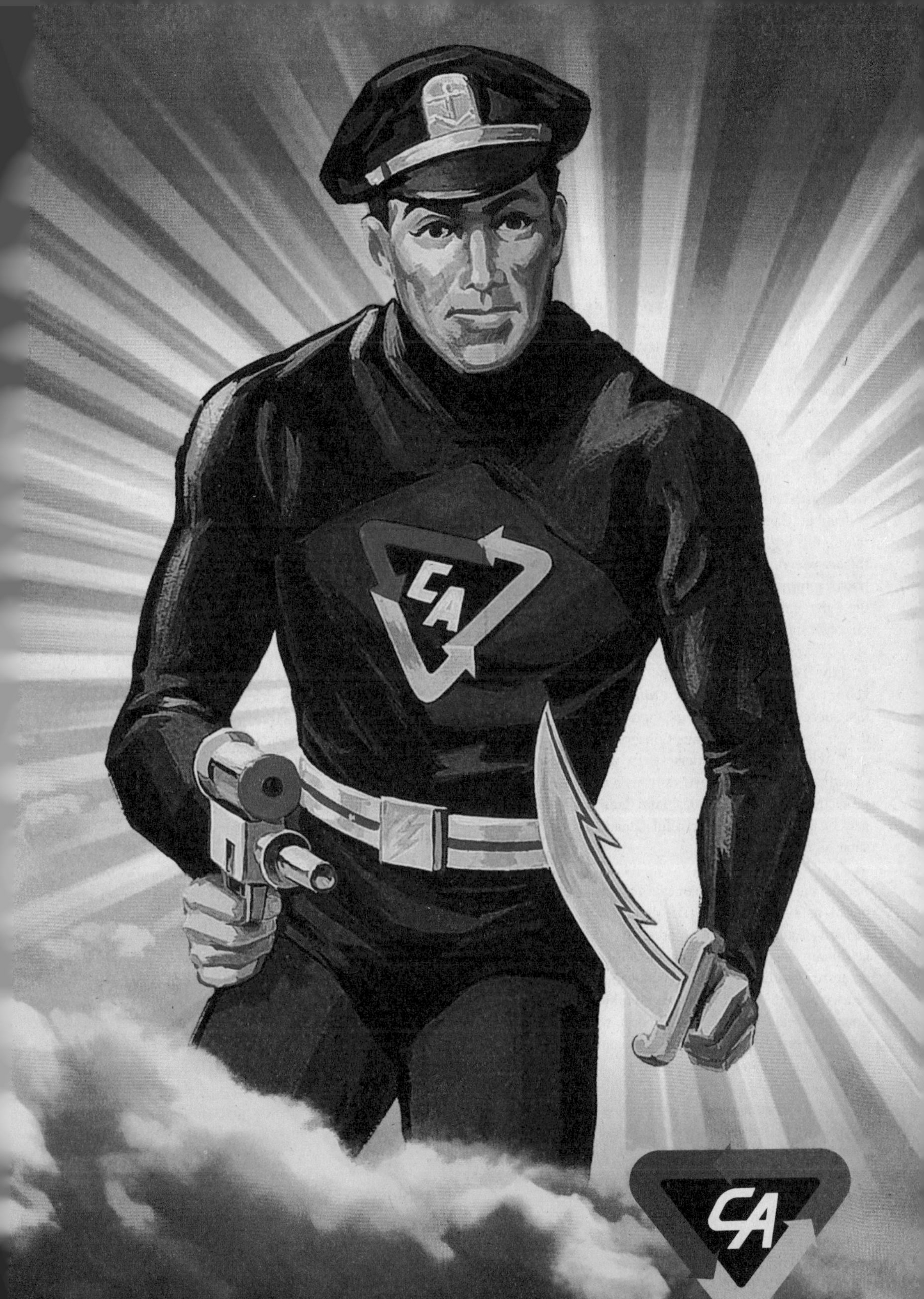
CA
CA

CAPTAIN CANUCK

The Canadian news media gave *Captain Canuck* an unprecedented amount of coverage when the first issue appeared in late May 1975. Even the US media noticed. *Time* magazine covered *Captain Canuck* and several newspapers picked up the wire service articles. Although the comic book has not been published continuously since its debut, he does survive to this day.

In December 1940, the War Exchange Conservation Act was passed. It restricted the importation of goods from the US that were deemed non-essential to combat the trade deficit Canada had with the United States. American comic books were casualties of the Act. The highly collectible "Canadian Whites" were created during this era. At the end of World War II, the act was repealed, and American comic books returned to Canada. By 1956 all of the Canadian comic book publishers were out of business.

In July 1975 Richard Comely and Ron Leishman published *Captain Canuck*, the first successful Canadian comic book since the end of the War Exchange Conservation Act. When one considers that prior Canadian heroes flourished only with the protection of the WECA, Captain Canuck may be the first truly successful Canadian superhero.

Behind the scenes, the character's genesis began in 1971 when Ron Leishman and Richard Comely met at church. It was Leishman who came up with the idea of doing a Canadian superhero comic book series at a time when there were no others. Comely agreed. At that point, though, neither of them had any background in comic book art, publishing, or distribution.

Comely had worked as a sign painter, crest designer, embroidery designer, and illustrator/paste-up artist for a printer. At the time they met in 1971, he was a part-time janitor in his apartment building in Winnipeg.

Leishman wanted to call their hero "Captain Canada." However, Comely had seen a sweatshirt on sale in the Hudson's Bay Company featuring a superhero with a Captain Canada logo. He, in turn, suggested Captain

Canuck. Leishman designed the character's original costume.

Armed with Leishman's character design and four comic pages, Comely spent three years putting together a business plan. Leishman became less involved as the years dragged on, but in 1975 Comely was able to secure an $8,000 loan, a newsstand distributor, and a printer willing to extend credit. This was the launch of Comely Comix and *Captain Canuck*.

FIRST PUBLICATION:
Captain Canuck #1
(July 1975)

LAST PUBLICATION:
Captain Canuck #14
(March 1981)

REVIVAL(S):
Captain Canuck: Reborn #0-3 (1993-1994), Captain Canuck #15 (June 2004), Captain Canuck: Unholy War #1-4 (October 2004 – January 2005), Captain Canuck Legacy (September 2006), Captain Canuck: The Complete Edition (November 2011), Captain Canuck Summer Special Canada Day Edition (2014), Captain Canuck #1-11 (May 2015 – December 2016), All New Classic Captain Canuck #0-4 (February 2016 – April 2017), Captain Canuck: Year One #1 (December 2017), Captain Canuck: Season Five #1 (November 2020), multiple collected editions (2015, 2016, 2019-2021)

The story was sent in the then-near future, 1993, just 18 years away from 1975. Tom Evans lives in that future world in which Canada is an "Essential World Power." Terrorists, communist renegades, space pirates and multi-national drug cartels threaten Canada and the world. The Canadian International Security Organization (C.I.S.O.) was created to deal with these threats. Tom Evans, a C.I.S.O. recruit and dedicated Boy Scout leader, takes his troop camping. After a long hike to a remote location, the troop sets up camp. While the boys are sleeping, Evans has an encounter with the aliens. The next morning he and the boys only have veiled memories of these events. Evans returns to C.I.S.O. training where a strange but mighty change is noticed by all.

"Suddenly I was twice as strong! I could lift twice as much and move twice as fast as I could before! It wasn't long before the heads of C.I.S.O. were also aware of my new power and they had a plan on how to capitalize on it."

"C.I.S.O. directors and specialists created a costume and a code name. They wanted to create an image – a symbol of C.I.S.O. authority and power – a show piece for Canada! Especially now with C.I.S.O.'s elite anti-terrorist squad being used by other countries!"

This was the birth of Captain Canuck. The character continued his adventures in 14 comics from 1975 to 1981. In 2004 a final, 15th issue was published.

– Rik Offenberger

DAPPER DAVE   R.C.

Dear Readers,
Canadian Comix!! brought to you by R.C (the man with the plan). He wanted to see Canadian Comix on Canadian News-stands, with good ol' high quality Canadian content, and here it is ....No.1!! But as they say "We've only just begun". Comely Comix will be bring-ing you the best in read-ing entertainment in titles covering the en-tire Comic. spectrum... and more!
where did Captain Canuck come from?...read on..... A question in everyone's mind in these unpredictable times is what lies ahead in the future of this planet.

well, for Canada its C.I.S.O. and its top Super-agent "Captain Canuck".

1980's to guard against the growing threat of Canada's invasion by outside forces. With our supply of food and natural resources, Canada will hold an im-portant position in Wor-ld affairs of the late 20th Century, and with it the responsibilities of main-taining world peace. Captain Canuck is .... well maybe I shouldn't reveal it all now. I'm sure you'll be following C.C. in his adventures to come and the story will tell itself.

D. Abbott

Original editorial page from *Captain Canuck* #1 (1975).
Image courtesy of Doug Sulipa.

CAPTAIN CANUCK #1
JULY 1975
$3 $9 $40

CAPTAIN CANUCK #2
AUGUST 1975
$1 $4 $10

CAPTAIN CANUCK #3
MAY - JULY 1976
$1 $4 $10

CAPTAIN CANUCK #4
OVERSIZED 1ST PRINTING • FEBRUARY 1979
$10 $30 $215

CAPTAIN CANUCK #4
REGULAR ED. • JULY - AUGUST 1979
$1 $3 $8

CAPTAIN CANUCK #5
AUGUST 1979
$1 $3 $8

CAPTAIN CANUCK #6
OCTOBER - NOVEMBER 1979
$1 $3 $8

CAPTAIN CANUCK #7
DECEMBER 1979 - JANUARY 1980
$1 $3 $8

CAPTAIN CANUCK #8
FEBRUARY - MARCH 1980
$1 $3 $8

CAPTAIN CANUCK #9
APRIL - MAY 1980
$1 $3 $8

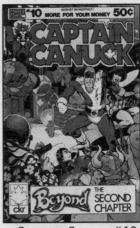

CAPTAIN CANUCK #10
JULY - AUGUST 1980
$1 $3 $8

CAPTAIN CANUCK #11
SEPTEMBER - OCTOBER 1980
$1 $3 $8

CAPTAIN CANUCK #12
NOVEMBER - DECEMBER 1980
$1 $3 $8

CAPTAIN CANUCK #13
JANUARY - FEBRUARY 1981
$1 $3 $8

CAPTAIN CANUCK #14
MARCH - APRIL 1981
$1 $3 $8

CAPTAIN CANUCK #15
AUGUST 2004
$8 $24 $140

**CAPTAIN CANUCK
SUMMER SPECIAL #1**
SEPTEMBER 1980
$6

Comics historian and journalist Rik Offenberger first discovered Captain Canuck *on the rack at his local comic shop. He said it was an interesting comic, and fit in well with his expanding tastes in indie comics, but that he had no idea he was looking at a Canadian national treasure. Despite a long career in the industry, he had never previously had the opportunity to talk with* Captain Canuck *creator Richard Comely prior to this interview.*

Overstreet: Are you a native-born Canadian?

Richard Comely (RC): I was born in Oxford, England in 1950, and came to Canada in 1953, when my parents immigrated. I became a Canadian citizen in 1983.

Overstreet: Where did you grow up?

RC: From the age of almost 5 years old until I was 17, we lived near Portage la Prairie, Manitoba.

Overstreet: When did you discover comics?

RC: The first comic books I was exposed to was at a neighbor's home when I was a small child. *Dennis the Menace, Tarzan,* and war comics were the comics I remember seeing.

Overstreet: What attracted you to them?

RC: I, like most children, liked to draw and I was encouraged. I loved reading the weekend comic pages in the local newspapers, but I didn't buy comic books at that

time. I started buying comic books and seriously looking at them after I decided I wanted to write and illustrate *Captain Canuck*.

Overstreet: Which comics were your favorites?

RC: I don't remember having any particular favorites. I liked Superman, Batman, and Deathlok. I looked at them all. Tin Tin was one of my favorites.

Overstreet: When did you start drawing superheroes?

RC: I started drawing superheroes after I decided to publish *Captain Canuck*. I'm sure I dabbled in drawing superheroes earlier on. I seriously started studying human anatomy and drawing superheroes after I decided to produce a *Captain Canuck* comic book series.

Overstreet: Where did you study art?

RC: In 1970, I won a bursary to take a two-year advertising art course at Red River College in Winnipeg Manitoba. At the time I was working as a crest and embroidery designer. I dropped out after the first five months, which was the first term to work in fashion design for a while. Life Drawing and Photography were the subjects that I felt I gained the most benefit from.

Overstreet: How did you meet Ron Leishman?

RC: I met Ron Leishman at church in late 1971 or early 1972. We are both members of The Church of Jesus Christ of Latter-Day Saints

Overstreet: What made you and Ron think it was the right time for a Canadian patriotic hero?

RC: I can only suggest that we were probably influenced by events taking place at that time and that it was more of a subconscious awareness on our part. Canada got a new flag in 1965. I had submitted a flag design along with many others. Canada had close British ties and was also strongly influenced by and connected to the U.S.. I think there was a growing change in attitude in Canada. Americans were proud of their country. Why shouldn't Canadians have the same pride for Canada?

Overstreet: Why is he named Captain Canuck instead of Captain Canada?

RC: Ron and I considered both names. In 1973 I came across three other Captain Canada characters in use. One had moose horns. That convinced me that we had to go with Captain Canuck. Shortly after this Ron moved to Alberta to work in the oil industry to raise money to support himself while he served a church mission. Initially, it was his idea to produce Captain Canuck and I had assumed that we would produce

it together. I ended up doing it myself and started working on it in the summer of 1974.

Overstreet: This was the first color Canadian comic, how did you fund the project?

RC: I got a $7,000 line of credit with my parents co-signing for it and I found a printer in Winnipeg who would extend credit. The print runs were 200,000 copies per issue for the first three editions.

Overstreet: How did you get distribution?

RC: I found a mass market newsstand distributor based in Oakville, Ontario who agreed to take on distribution. I first made contact with them in 1973. At that time there were only a few comic book stores in the world.

Overstreet: Why did Comely Comix stop production?

RC: I ran out of money.

Overstreet: Was there always a plan to resume production?

RC: Yes. I was out of money in 1976, and I accepted an offer to run a weekly newspaper in Cardston, Alberta. My wife and I and our three children as well as George Freeman and Claude St. Aubin moved to Cardston in August 1976. We were hoping that the newspaper would support us financially while I looked for an investor.

Overstreet: When you resumed production why did you change the name of the company from Comely Comics to CKR?

RC: I found an investor in 1978 after we had moved to Calgary. He brought on another minor investor who became the office manager and we formed CKR Productions. We continued to use the Comely Comix brand until issue #12.

Overstreet: How were the CKR Captain Canuck comics different from the Comely Comics version?
RC: There was no real difference other than we moved printing to World Color Press in Sparta, Illinois where most comic books were printed. This saved us over half the cost of printing but the printing quality was not as good as the first three issues printed in Winnipeg.

Overstreet: Why did CKR stop publication?
RC: Funding dried up. A new mass market distributor signed on by the two investors proved to be a big disappointment, and I had some differences with the investors shortly after. I was gone about six months before they shut it down.

Overstreet: Why did you reboot with *Captain Canuck Reborn* instead of continuing with Tom Evans as Captain Canuck?
RC: At the time I wanted to introduce a new cast of characters and get away from time travel stories. Stopping a world dictatorship conspiracy was the all-encompassing challenge for the hero who would take on the mantle of Captain Canuck. It seemed less convoluted and cleaner to start anew with Darren Oak.

Overstreet: How did Captain Canuck end up in a newspaper strip?
RC: Back in 1980 we had put together a presentation for newspaper syndicates to pitch the strip. George and Claude did the art. I wrote and did the lettering. There was avid interest in syndication to Canadian newspapers but because of other problems, the project was sidetracked at the time.

Overstreet: Did the newspaper strip feature Tom Evens or Darren Oak?
RC: The 1980 strip starred Tom Evans.

Overstreet: With *Captain Canuck: Unholy War* you switched Captain Canuck from Darren Oak to David Semple. Why not bring back Tom Evans?
RC: Tom Evans does appear towards the end of that series. David Semple is a Mountie who decides he will be the West Coast Captain Canuck and makes his costume. Riel did a very nice job with the script.

Overstreet: You became an instructor at Mohawk College. How did that come about?
RC: I had been teaching continuing education courses in the evening for illustration, cartooning, and sequential art at Mohawk College and Conestoga College. Mohawk asked me to help them develop a one-year post-graduate course on sequential art. In 2007 I taught two of the subjects for the first year.

Overstreet: How did you end up working with Fadi Hakim and Chapterhouse Comics?
RC: Fadi contacted me sometime in 2009. He had lots of ideas which we discussed for a few years and it went from there.

Overstreet: How did the animated show come about?
RC: This was Fadi's idea. He produced it after raising the funding through a Kickstarter campaign.

Overstreet: Did you change the uniform before the animated show, or did the show change the uniform?
RC: Fadi brought on Kalman Andrasofszky to design the costume and a new look as well as

to write and illustrate the new 2015 series. Like many characters, Captain Canuck has more than one outfit.

Overstreet: What is going on with the Captain Canuck feature film from Minds Eye Entertainment?
RC: That option agreement expired a while ago. We are currently talking to a few other production companies. There is lots of interest and Fadi has gone through many meetings. He is still looking for the arrangement that will make the most sense.

Overstreet:. When did you discover the LDS church?
RC: I was not raised in any particular faith. I was christened in an Anglican Church Abby before we came to Canada and attended different Protestant churches in my youth. I was baptized a member of The Church of Jesus Christ of Latter-day Saints in May 1971. I was 20. My conversion and acceptance was a powerful life-changing experience.

Overstreet: How has your faith interacted with Captain Canuck?
RC: My approach to storytelling, my attitude towards morality, and every aspect of my life are affected by my faith.

Overstreet: What was it like to have Captain Canuck recognized at Brigham Young University's Comics and Mormons exhibit?
RC: I wasn't aware of that exhibit at BYU. I think I got an email about it but wasn't sure it was an event. I was informed there will be an exhibit of my work at BYU in 2024.

Overstreet: How did Captain Canuck get to be on Canadian postage stamps?
RC: I got a phone call one day in 1993 from someone at Canada Post asking for permission.

Overstreet: In 2010, the Captain Canuck creators were inducted into the Joe Shuster Awards Hall of Fame. What other awards has Captain Canuck won?
RC: The animated series won an award; the Geeky Award I believe. There was an award years ago out of Montreal, but I can't remember what and from whom.

Overstreet: Captain Canuck has had letters published from Governor General David Johnston and Prime Minister Justin Trudeau. What other influential or famous fans have written into Captain Canuck?
RC: Other than the creator of *Corner Gas* and Rick Mercer making nice comments, I can't think of any other people of note sending us anything.

Overstreet: Captain Canuck is arguably the most famous Canadian superhero in history. What are you most proud of about Captain Canuck and his place in comics?
RC: I often have people tell me how much they enjoyed reading Captain Canuck and how many times they had read a particular issue. The 1980 *Summer Special* was very much liked by many. Many Canadians tell me they are happy and proud to call Captain Canuck our own.

– Rik Offenberger

Rik Offenberger is a 30-year comic book industry veteran who has been a retailer, journalist, writer, publicist, publisher, and even a judge for the Eisner Awards. You can find his work at firstcomics-news.com and G-Man Comics.

CHAOS! COMICS

Ernest Fairchild, better known as Evil Ernie, first appeared in the pages of *Evil Ernie* #1 (December 1991) from Eternity Comics (later better known as part of Malibu). Writer Brian Pulido and artist Steven Hughes unleashed the story of the character, a formerly happy youngster who now is on a decidedly dark mission. Accompanied by Smiley, the psychotic smiley face button, he wants to unleash "Megadeath," which is basically the nuclear destruction of everyone.

The issue and the four that followed carved out a niche, established a tone, and served as a proving ground of sorts for what would follow. Also lurking in its pages was an early incarnation of what would soon become Pulido's signature character, Lady Death. From 1993 until 2002, his company, Chaos! Comics, offered a unique, distinctive voice in comics and the horror genre.

"I've read and collected comic books ever since I was a little kid. The interplay between words and pictures always ignited my imagination and still does to this day. In the '90s, I launched Chaos! Comics. With a unique recipe of heavy metal, horror, and the supernatural, Chaos! Comics established its own genre of comics and changed the face of independent comic book publishing forever," Pulido has written.

Lady Death was born as a normal mortal named Hope in medieval Sweden. Her father, an outwardly pious nobleman, was truly evil. When the people rose up against him, he escaped, but Hope did not. Faced with being burned at the stake, she used an incantation of his. It started her down the road of destruction. *Lady Death* was a hit.

Branded as "Where Darkness Dwells," Chaos! Comics also launched such character-driven titles as *Chastity, Purgatori,* and *Smiley: The Psychotic Button,* which joined *Lady Death* and *Evil Ernie.* There were action figures, a thrash metal album, and more. But it wouldn't last.

"Chaos! roared through the '90s, building a loyal following of ravenous fans known as 'Fiends,' with a stable of characters like Purgatori and Chastity and licensed titles like *WWE, Megadeath, Halloween,* and *Insane Clown Posse.* At one point, Chaos! grew to be the fourth largest comic book publisher in North America. However, my inexperience and strategic miscalculations led to Chaos! Comics going out of business in 2002. I lost all my creations with the exception of Lady Death. I had failed, and failed big," Pulido wrote.

Chaos! Comics filed for bankruptcy in late 2002. Prior to the bankruptcy, they sold Lady Death to CrossGen Entertainment. The other characters in the Chaos! stable were sold to retailer Tales of Wonder, who in turn sold the rights to Devil's Due Publishing. When Devil's Due ran into its own troubles, Dynamite Entertainment acquired the characters and the Chaos! brand.

Lady Death, as it turns out, was much pretty hard to kill off. After Pulido produced new work at CrossGen, that company failed, too. Pulido then partnered with Avatar Press to launch Boundless Comics, to produce the character. There, too, problems abound.

"I lost all confidence and limped along in a daze for almost ten years. Lady Death was being published, but unresolvable differences forced me to litigate against the publisher. In the settlement, I regained complete control of Lady Death, and frankly, the lawsuit fired me up and gave me my *drive* back," he wrote.

"By 2015, it had been 13 years since I had been a publisher. The comic book world had become devoid of the rebel sprit that drives everything I do. I saw an opportunity, Pulido wrote.

This sparked the creation of Coffin Comics and a whole new host of characters, which seems to have taken the world of crowdfunded comics by storm (even as they continue to be available in comic shops).

The other original Chaos! characters continue at Dynamite.

FIRST PUBLICATION:
Evil Ernie: Ressurection #1
(July 1993)

LAST PUBLICATIONS:
Lady Death: Dark Alliance #3 and *Lady Death: Goddess Returns #2* (both August 2002)

REVIVAL(S):
Lady Death - Medieval Lady Death (CrossGen), numerous titles at Boundless Comics, numerous titles at Coffin Comics. Other Chaos! characters — numerous titles at Dynamite.

Ivan Reis and Joe Pimentel's original cover art for *Armageddon #2* (1999).
Image courtesy of Heritage Auctions.

AFTERMATH #1
FEBRUARY 2000
$4

AFTERMATH #1
PREMIUM COVER • FEBRUARY 2000
$4

AFTERMATH #1
DYNAMIC FORCES • FEBRUARY 2000
$4

ARMAGEDDON #0
SEPTEMBER 1999
$2 $6 $20

ARMAGEDDON #1
OCTOBER 1999
$4

ARMAGEDDON #2
NOVEMBER 1999
$4

ARMAGEDDON #3
DECEMBER 1999
$4

ARMAGEDDON #4
JANUARY 2000
$4

CHAOS! BIBLE #1
NOVEMBER 1995
$4

CHAOS! CHRONICLES #1
FEBRUARY 2000
$3.50

CHAOS! CHRONICLES #1
VARIANT COVER • FEBRUARY 2000
$3.50

CHAOS! GALLERY #1
AUGUST 1997
$5

CHAOS! QUARTERLY #1
OCTOBER 1995
$5

CHAOS! QUARTERLY #1
PREMIUM EDITION • OCTOBER 1995
$25

CHAOS! QUARTERLY #2
JANUARY 1996
$5

CHAOS! QUARTERLY #3
MAY 1996
$5

EVIL ERNIE #1
DECEMBER 1991
$17 **$51** **$400**

EVIL ERNIE #2
JANUARY 1992
$9 **$27** **$195**

EVIL ERNIE #3
FEBRUARY 1992
$5 $15 $80

EVIL ERNIE #4
MARCH 1992
$5 $15 $70

EVIL ERNIE #5
APRIL 1992
$4 $12 $55

EVIL ERNIE #0
DECEMBER 1993
$5

EVIL ERNIE #1
JULY 1998
$1 $4 $10

EVIL ERNIE #1
PREMIUM EDITION • JULY 1998
$2 $6 $12

EVIL ERNIE #2
AUGUST 1998
$4

EVIL ERNIE #3
SEPTEMBER 1998
$4

EVIL ERNIE #4
OCTOBER 1998
$4

EVIL ERNIE #5
NOVEMBER 1998
$4

EVIL ERNIE #6
DECEMBER 1998
$4

EVIL ERNIE #7
JANUARY 1999
$4

EVIL ERNIE #8
FEBRUARY 1999
$4

EVIL ERNIE #9
MARCH 1999
$4

EVIL ERNIE #10
APRIL 1999
$4

**EVIL ERNIE
BADDEST BATTLES #1**
JANUARY 1997
$5

**EVIL ERNIE:
DEPRAVED PREVIEW**
MAY 1999
$4

**EVIL ERNIE:
DEPRAVED #1**
JULY 1999
$4

EVIL ERNIE:
DEPRAVED #2
AUGUST 1999
$4

EVIL ERNIE:
DEPRAVED #3
SEPTEMBER 1999
$4

EVIL ERNIE:
DESTROYER PREVIEW
SEPTEMBER 1997
$4

EVIL ERNIE:
DESTROYER #1
OCTOBER 1997
$4

EVIL ERNIE:
DESTROYER #2
NOVEMBER 1997
$4

EVIL ERNIE:
DESTROYER #3
DECEMBER 1997
$4

EVIL ERNIE:
DESTROYER #4
JANUARY 1998
$4

EVIL ERNIE:
DESTROYER #5
FEBRUARY 1998
$4

EVIL ERNIE:
DESTROYER #6
MARCH 1998
$4

**EVIL ERNIE:
DESTROYER #7**
APRIL 1998
$4

**EVIL ERNIE:
DESTROYER #8**
MAY 1998
$4

**EVIL ERNIE:
DESTROYER #9**
JUNE 1998
$4

**EVIL ERNIE
PIECES OF ME #1**
OCTOBER 2000
$4

**EVIL ERNIE
PIECES OF ME #1**
VARIANT COVER • OCTOBER 2000
$4

**EVIL ERNIE
RELENTLESS #1**
MAY 2002
$5

**EVIL ERNIE
RELENTLESS #1**
PREMIUM EDITION • MAY 2002
$5

**EVIL ERNIE
RETURNS #1**
NOVEMBER 2001
$4

**EVIL ERNIE
RETURNS #1**
VARIANT COVER • NOVEMBER 2001
$4

EVIL ERNIE: REVENGE #1
OCTOBER 1994
$2 **$6** **$12**

EVIL ERNIE: REVENGE #1
VARIANT COVER • OCTOBER 1994
$2 **$6** **$16**

EVIL ERNIE: REVENGE #2
DECEMBER 1994
$4

EVIL ERNIE: REVENGE #3
JANUARY 1995
$4

EVIL ERNIE: REVENGE #4
FEBRUARY 1995
$4

EVIL ERNIE:
STRAIGHT TO HELL #1
OCTOBER 1995
$2 **$6** **$12**

EVIL ERNIE:
STRAIGHT TO HELL #2
DECEMBER 1995
$4

EVIL ERNIE:
STRAIGHT TO HELL #3
JANUARY 1996
$4

EVIL ERNIE:
STRAIGHT TO HELL #3
CHASTITY COVER • JANUARY 1996
$20

EVIL ERNIE:
STRAIGHT TO HELL #4
MARCH 1996
$4

EVIL ERNIE:
STRAIGHT TO HELL #5
MAY 1996
$4

EVIL ERNIE:
THE RESURRECTION #1
JULY 1993
$2 $6 $12

EVIL ERNIE:
THE RESURRECTION #2
AUGUST 1993
$1 $3 $8

EVIL ERNIE:
THE RESURRECTION #3
SEPTEMBER 1993
$1 $3 $8

EVIL ERNIE:
THE RESURRECTION #4
OCTOBER 1993
$1 $3 $8

EVIL ERNIE VS.
THE MOVIE MONSTERS #1
MARCH 1997
$4

EVIL ERNIE VS.
THE MOVIE MONSTERS #1
VARIANT COVER • MARCH 1997
$1 $4 $10

EVIL ERNIE VS.
THE SUPER HEROES #1
AUGUST 1995
$4

EVIL ERNIE VS. THE SUPER HEROES #1
VARIANT COVER • AUGUST 1995
$2 $6 $20

EVIL ERNIE VS. THE SUPER HEROES #1
VARIANT COVER • AUGUST 1995
$2 $6 $20

EVIL ERNIE VS. THE SUPER HEROES #2
SEPTEMBER 1998
$4

EVIL ERNIE: WAR OF THE DEAD #1
NOVEMBER 1999
$4

EVIL ERNIE: WAR OF THE DEAD #1
VARIANT COVER • NOVEMBER 1999
$4

EVIL ERNIE: WAR OF THE DEAD #1
VARIANT COVER • NOVEMBER 1999
$4

EVIL ERNIE: WAR OF THE DEAD #2
DECEMBER 1999
$4

EVIL ERNIE: WAR OF THE DEAD #3
JANUARY 2000
$4

EVIL ERNIE: WAR OF THE DEAD #1
VARIANT COVER • JANUARY 2000
$4

LADY DEATH #1
JANUARY 1994
$2 $6 $18

LADY DEATH #1
CHROMIUM COVER • JANUARY 1994
$2 $6 $20

LADY DEATH #2
FEBRUARY 1994
$1 $4 $10

LADY DEATH #3
MARCH 1994
$5

LADY DEATH #1/2
JANUARY 1994
$1 $4 $10

LADY DEATH #0
NOVEMBER 1997
$4

LADY DEATH #1
FEBRUARY 1998
$2 $6 $15

LADY DEATH #1
SDCC VARIANT • FEBRUARY 1998
$2 $6 $15

LADY DEATH #2
MARCH 1998
$4

LADY DEATH #3
APRIL 1998
$4

LADY DEATH #4
MAY 1998
$4

LADY DEATH #5
JUNE 1998
$4

LADY DEATH #5
JUNE 1998
$4

LADY DEATH #6
JULY 1998
$4

LADY DEATH #7
AUGUST 1998
$4

LADY DEATH #8
SEPTEMBER 1998
$4

LADY DEATH #9
OCTOBER 1998
$4

LADY DEATH #10
OCTOBER 1998
$4

LADY DEATH #11
DECEMBER 1998
$4

LADY DEATH #12
JANUARY 1999
$4

LADY DEATH #13
FEBRUARY 1999
$4

LADY DEATH #14
MARCH 1999
$4

LADY DEATH #15
APRIL 1999
$4

LADY DEATH #16
MAY 1999
$4

**LADY DEATH II: BETWEEN
HEAVEN AND HELL #1**
JANUARY 1995
$1 **$3** **$8**

**LADY DEATH II: BETWEEN
HEAVEN AND HELL #2**
APRIL 1995
$3.50

**LADY DEATH II: BETWEEN
HEAVEN AND HELL #3**
MAY 1995
$3.50

LADY DEATH II: BETWEEN HEAVEN AND HELL #4
JUNE 1995
$3.50

LADY DEATH II: BETWEEN HEAVEN AND HELL #4
LADY DEMON VARIANT • MAY 1995
$1 $3 $9

LADY DEATH: ALIVE #1
MAY 2001
$3

LADY DEATH: ALIVE #1
VARIANT COVER • MAY 2001
$3

LADY DEATH: ALIVE #2
JUNE 2001
$3

LADY DEATH: ALIVE #3
JULY 2001
$3

LADY DEATH: ALIVE #4
AUGUST 2001
$3

LADY DEATH: ALIVE #4
VARIANT COVER • AUGUST 2001
$3

LADY DEATH AND JADE #1
APRIL 2002
$3

LADY DEATH AND JADE #1
VARIANT COVER • APRIL 2002
$3

LADY DEATH AND THE WOMEN OF CHAOS! GALLERY #1
NOVEMBER 1996
$3

LADY DEATH AND THE WOMEN OF CHAOS! GALLERY #1
VARIANT COVER • NOVEMBER 1996
$3

LADY DEATH / BAD KITTY #1
SEPTEMBER 2001
$3

LADY DEATH / BAD KITTY #1
VARIANT COVER • SEPTEMBER 2001
$3

LADY DEATH / BEDLAM #1
JUNE 2002
$3

LADY DEATH / BEDLAM #1
VARIANT COVER • JUNE 2002
$3

LADY DEATH BY STEVEN HUGHES
2000
$3

LADY DEATH / CHASTITY #1
JANUARY 2002
$3

**LADY DEATH / CHASTITY /
BAD KITTY: UNITED #1**
MAY 2002
$3

**LADY DEATH / CHASTITY /
BAD KITTY: UNITED #1**
VARIANT COVER • MAY 2002
$3

**LADY DEATH:
DARK ALLIANCE #1**
JULY 2002
$3

**LADY DEATH:
DARK ALLIANCE #1**
VARIANT COVER • JULY 2002
$3

**LADY DEATH:
DARK ALLIANCE #2**
AUGUST 2002
$3

**LADY DEATH:
DARK ALLIANCE #2**
VARIANT COVER • AUGUST 2002
$3

**LADY DEATH:
DARK ALLIANCE #3**
AUGUST 2002
$3

**LADY DEATH:
DARK ALLIANCE #3**
VARIANT COVER • AUGUST 2002
$3

**LADY DEATH:
DARK MILLENNIUM #1**
FEBRUARY 2000
$3

**LADY DEATH:
DARK MILLENNIUM #1**
VARIANT COVER • FEBRUARY 2000
$3

**LADY DEATH:
DARK MILLENNIUM #1**
VARIANT COVER • FEBRUARY 2000
$3

**LADY DEATH:
DARK MILLENNIUM #1**
VARIANT COVER • FEBRUARY 2000
$3

**LADY DEATH:
DARK MILLENNIUM #2**
MARCH 2000
$3

**LADY DEATH:
DARK MILLENNIUM #3**
APRIL 2000
$3

**LADY DEATH:
DRAGON WARS #1**
APRIL 1998
$3

**LADY DEATH FAN EDITION:
ALL HALLOW'S EVE #1**
JANUARY 1997
$5

**LADY DEATH:
GODDESS RETURNS #1**
JUNE 2002
$3

**LADY DEATH:
GODDESS RETURNS #1**
VARIANT COVER • JUNE 2002
$3

LADY DEATH:
GODDESS RETURNS #2
AUGUST 2002
$3

LADY DEATH:
GODDESS RETURNS #2
VARIANT COVER • AUGUST 2002
$3

LADY DEATH:
HEARTBREAKER #1
MARCH 2002
$3

LADY DEATH:
HEARTBREAKER #1
VARIANT COVER • MARCH 2002
$3

LADY DEATH:
HEARTBREAKER #1
VARIANT COVER • MARCH 2002
$3

LADY DEATH
IN LINGERIE #1
SIDEWAYS COVER • AUGUST 1995
$3

LADY DEATH
IN LINGERIE #1
LEATHER COVER • AUGUST 1995
$12

LADY DEATH:
JUDGEMENT WAR PRELUDE
1999
$4

LADY DEATH:
JUDGEMENT WAR #1
NOVEMBER 1999
$4

LADY DEATH:
JUDGEMENT WAR #1
VARIANT COVER • NOVEMBER 1999
$4

LADY DEATH:
JUDGEMENT WAR #1
VARIANT COVER • NOVEMBER 1999
$4

LADY DEATH:
JUDGEMENT WAR #2
DECEMBER 1999
$4

LADY DEATH:
JUDGEMENT WAR #3
JANUARY 2000
$4

LADY DEATH:
JUDGEMENT WAR #3
VARIANT COVER • JANUARY 2000
$4

LADY DEATH:
LAST RITES #1
OCTOBER 2001
$3

LADY DEATH:
LAST RITES #1
VARIANT COVER • OCTOBER 2001
$3

LADY DEATH:
LAST RITES #2
DECEMBER 2001
$3

LADY DEATH:
LAST RITES #2
VARIANT COVER • DECEMBER 2001
$3

**LADY DEATH:
LAST RITES #3**
JANUARY 2002
$3

**LADY DEATH:
LAST RITES #3**
VARIANT COVER • JANUARY 2002
$3

**LADY DEATH:
LAST RITES #4**
FEBRUARY 2002
$3

**LADY DEATH:
LOVE BITES #3**
MARCH 2001
$3

**LADY DEATH:
LOVE BITES #3**
VARIANT COVER • MARCH 2001
$3

**LADY DEATH/MEDIEVAL
WITCHBLADE PREVIEW**
AUGUST 2001
$3

**LADY DEATH/
MEDIEVAL WITCHBLADE #1**
AUGUST 2001
$3.50

**LADY DEATH/
MEDIEVAL WITCHBLADE #1**
VARIANT COVER • AUGUST 2001
$3.50

**LADY DEATH/
MEDIEVAL WITCHBLADE #1**
VARIANT COVER • AUGUST 2001
$3.50

**LADY DEATH/
MEDIEVAL WITCHBLADE #1**
VARIANT COVER • AUGUST 2001
$3.50

**LADY DEATH:
MISCHIEF NIGHT #1**
NOVEMBER 2001
$3

**LADY DEATH:
MISCHIEF NIGHT #1**
VARIANT COVER • NOVEMBER 2001
$3

**LADY DEATH:
MISCHIEF NIGHT #1**
VARIANT COVER • NOVEMBER 2001
$3

**LADY DEATH:
RE-IMAGINED #1**
JULY 2002
$3

**LADY DEATH:
RE-IMAGINED #1**
VARIANT COVER • JULY 2002
$3

**LADY DEATH:
RE-IMAGINED #1**
VARIANT COVER • JULY 2002
$3

**LADY DEATH:
RETRIBUTION #1**
AUGUST 1998
$4

**LADY DEATH:
RETRIBUTION #1**
VARIANT COVER • AUGUST 1998
$6

**LADY DEATH:
RIVER OF FEAR #1**
APRIL 2001
$3

**LADY DEATH:
RIVER OF FEAR #1**
VARIANT COVER • APRIL 2001
$3

**LADY DEATH
SWIMSUIT SPECIAL #1**
MAY 1994
$3

**LADY DEATH
SWIMSUIT 2001 #1**
JUNE 2001
$3

**LADY DEATH:
THE CRUCIBLE #1/2**
WIZARD EDITION • JULY 1996
$4

**LADY DEATH:
THE CRUCIBLE #1**
NOVEMBER 1996
$5

**LADY DEATH:
THE CRUCIBLE #2**
JANUARY 1997
$4

**LADY DEATH:
THE CRUCIBLE #3**
MARCH 1997
$4

**LADY DEATH:
THE CRUCIBLE #5**
JULY 1997
$4

**LADY DEATH:
THE CRUCIBLE #6**
OCTOBER 1997
$4

**LADY DEATH:
THE GAUNTLET #1**
APRIL 2002
$4

**LADY DEATH:
THE GAUNTLET #2**
MAY 2002
$4

**LADY DEATH:
THE ODYSSEY PREVIEW #1**
APRIL 1996
$4

**LADY DEATH:
THE ODYSSEY #1**
APRIL 1996
$5

**LADY DEATH:
THE ODYSSEY #1**
VARIANT COVER • APRIL 1996
$20

**LADY DEATH:
THE ODYSSEY #1**
VARIANT COVER • APRIL 1996
$5

**LADY DEATH:
THE ODYSSEY #1**
VARIANT COVER • APRIL 1996
$5

**LADY DEATH:
THE ODYSSEY #2**
MAY 1996
$5

**LADY DEATH:
THE ODYSSEY #3**
JUNE 1996
$5

**LADY DEATH:
THE ODYSSEY #4**
AUGUST 1996
$3

**LADY DEATH:
THE ODYSSEY #4**
VARIANT COVER • AUGUST 1996
$3

**LADY DEATH:
THE RAPTURE PREVIEW**
APRIL 1999
$4

**LADY DEATH:
THE RAPTURE #1**
JUNE 1999
$4

**LADY DEATH:
THE RAPTURE #2**
JULY 1999
$4

**LADY DEATH:
THE RAPTURE #3**
AUGUST 1999
$4

**LADY DEATH:
THE RAPTURE #4**
SEPTEMBER 1999
$4

LADY DEATH: TRIBULATION #1
DECEMBER 2000
$3

LADY DEATH: TRIBULATION #1
VARIANT COVER • DECEMBER 2000
$3

LADY DEATH: TRIBULATION #1
VARIANT COVER • DECEMBER 2000
$3

LADY DEATH: TRIBULATION #2
JANUARY 2001
$3

LADY DEATH: TRIBULATION #3
FEBRUARY 2001
$3

LADY DEATH: TRIBULATION #4
MARCH 2001
$3

LADY DEATH/ VAMPIRELLA
MARCH 1999
$3.50

LADY DEATH/ VAMPIRELLA II PREVIEW
FEBRUARY 2000
$3.50

LADY DEATH/ VAMPIRELLA II
MARCH 2000
$3.50

LADY DEATH VS. PURGATORI
DECEMBER 1999
$3.50

LADY DEATH VS. PURGATORI
DYNAMIC FORCES • DECEMBER 1999
$3.50

LADY DEMON #0
JANUARY 2000
$3

LADY DEMON #1
MARCH 2000
$3

LADY DEMON #2
APRIL 2000
$3

LADY DEMON #3
MAY 2000
$3

PURGATORI VS. LADY DEATH
#1
JANUARY 2001
$3

PURGATORI VS. LADY DEATH
#1
JANUARY 2001
$3

SMILEY #1
JULY 1998
$4

**SMILEY ANTI-HOLIDAY
SPECIAL #1**
JANUARY 1999
$4

**SMILEY'S SPRING BREAK
#1**
APRIL 1999
$4

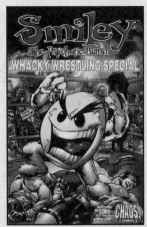

**SMILEY WHACKY
WRESTLING SPECIAL #1**
JANUARY 1998
$4

**A TRIBUTE TO
STEVEN HUGHES #1**
SEPTEMBER 2000
$7

**UNTOLD TALES
OF LADY DEATH #1**
NOVEMBER 2000
$3

**UNTOLD TALES
OF LADY DEATH #1**
PREMIUM EDITION • NOVEMBER 2000
$3

**VAMPIRELLA/
LADY DEATH #1**
NOVEMBER 2000
$4

**VAMPIRELLA/
LADY DEATH #1**
FOIL COVER • NOVEMBER 2000
$4

**WITCHBLADE/
LADY DEATH #1**
NOVEMBER 2001
$5

Capitalizing on both the James Bond-inspired spy craze and the revival of superhero comics that was in full swing at the time, writer Len Brown and artist Wally Wood developed the T.H.U.N.D.E.R. Agents for Tower Comics in 1965. "T.H.U.N.D.E.R." stood for The Higher United Nations Defense Enforcement Reserves, which served as the springboard for the adventures of agents such as Dynamo, NoMan, Menthor, Raven, Lightning, and Undersea Agent.

The project had no problem attracting talent. Larry Ivie, Reed Crandall, Gil Kane, George Tuska, Mike Esposito, Mike Sekowsky, Frank Giacoia, Dan Adkins, Dick Ayers, Joe Orlando, Steve Skeates, Steve Ditko, Ralph Reese, Chic Stone, and Joe Giella all signed up. Artists and writers such as Paul Reinman, Ray Bailey, Sheldon Moldoff, John Giunta, Manny Stallman, Ogden Whitney, and Jack Abel also worked on the series.

Despite the creative firepower, Tower Comics folded in 1969.

The team, though, was still attractive to collectors and would-be publishers. Eventually, John Carbonaro was recognized as the rights holder. In May 1983 he launched JC Comics, which produced three issues under its own banner. January 1983 also saw the team front and center on the cover of Texas Comics' *Justice Machine Annual* #1 (which also featured the debut of Bill Willingham's Elementals).

Then came publisher David M. Singer's Deluxe Comics.

In 1984, Singer launched *Wally Wood's T.H.U.N.D.E.R. Agents*. Printed on nice paper and aimed clearly at the burgeoning comic book specialty market, Singer and company attempted to replicate the caliber of Tower Comics' all-star line-up with one of their own. Roy & Dann Thomas, George Pérez, Dave Cockrum, Steve Ditko, Keith Giffen, Jerry Ordway, Stan Drake, Steve Englehart, Murphy Anderson, Tom & Mary Bierbaum, Ron Lim, and Roger McKenzie were among those who plied their crafts for the upstart publisher.

The content was on par with what the major publishers were producing. As with the original series, which included the death of an agent, there were consequences of the heroes using their powers. Whether it was Pérez on Raven, Ditko on No-Man, Giffen on Lightning or any other on the others, all of the main characters got time in the spotlight and the creators made it pay off for the readers.

There was just one problem. Singer claimed T.H.U.N.D.E.R. Agents were in the public domain. Carbonaro claimed otherwise and filed suit. The U.S. District Court found in favor of Carbonaro, and he received all rights to *Wally Wood's T.H.U.N.D.E.R. Agents*. Despite the obvious failing associated with the series, Deluxe Comics' tenure with the characters is widely considered the best since Tower Comics' original series.

They were followed by a T.H.U.N.D.E.R. Agents project from Solson (1987, one issue of a projected four). Rob Liefeld's Extreme Studios announced a T.H.U.N.D.E.R. Agents project with artist Dave Cockrum, but it never came to fruition. Penthouse Comics intended the team for their *Omni Comics* #3 with art by Paul Gulacy and Terry Austin. DC Comics collected the original Tower material in *The T.H.U.N.D.E.R. Agents Archives* (followed by an inferior quality volume of the Deluxe issues), and then released new material in two series (2011, 2012). They were followed by IDW Publishing, which produced archival trade paperbacks and an eight-issue new series (2013).

FIRST PUBLICATION:
Wally Wood's T.H.U.N.D.E.R. Agents #1 (November 1984)

LAST PUBLICATION:
Wally Wood's T.H.U.N.D.E.R. Agents #5 (February 1986)

REVIVAL(S):
T.H.U.N.D.E.R. Agents #1 (Solson (1987), *The T.H.U.N.D.E.R. Agents Archives* (DC Comics), *T.H.U.N.D.E.R. Agents* #1-10 (DC Comics, 2011), *T.H.U.N.D.E.R. Agents* #1-6 (DC Comics, 2012), *T.H.U.N.D.E.R. Agents* #1-8 (IDW Publishing, 2013)

The original cover art for Wally Wood's T.H.U.N.D.E.R. Agents #4
by George Pérez (1986). Image courtesy of Heritage Auctions.

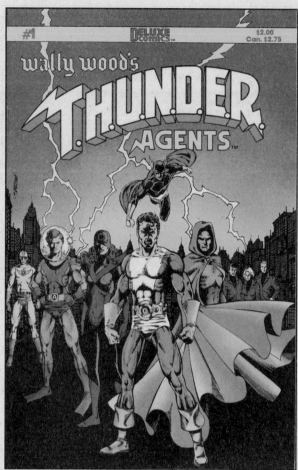

**WALLY WOOD'S
T.H.U.N.D.E.R. AGENTS #2**
JANUARY 1985
$6

WALLY WOOD'S
T.H.U.N.D.E.R. AGENTS #1
NOVEMBER 1984
$6

**WALLY WOOD'S
T.H.U.N.D.E.R. AGENTS #3**
NOVEMBER 1985
$6

**WALLY WOOD'S
T.H.U.N.D.E.R. AGENTS #4**
FEBRUARY 1986
$6

**WALLY WOOD'S
T.H.U.N.D.E.R. AGENTS #5**
OCTOBER 1985
$6

**T.H.U.N.D.E.R. AGENTS
ARCHIVE #7**
HC REPRINTS • DC COMICS • 2011
$60

After Tower but before Deluxe, J.C. Comics published Steve Ditko and Willie Blyberg's cover for *Hall of Fame Featuring the T.H.U.N.D.E.R. Agents* #2 (1983).

Published by Eclipse, the DNAgents family of titles includes *DNAgents*, *Crossfire*, the limited series *Crossfire and Rainbow* and *Surge*, *Whodunnit?*, and *Three Dimensional DNAgents*. Both *DNAgents* and *Crossfire* enjoyed good runs, carving out their own universe in the non-universe that was Eclipse.

Writer Mark Evanier made his first sale in 1969, and almost immediately was taken on as an assistant to Jack Kirby. While apprenticing under Kirby, he wrote foreign comic books for Disney. This led to work for Gold Key, and then the Edgar Rice Burroughs estate. He subsequently wrote for such TV shows as *The Nancy Walker Show*, *The McLean Stevenson Show*, and *Welcome Back, Kotter*. After *Kotter* ended, he wrote for such cartoons as *Scooby Doo*, *Plastic Man*, *Thundarr the Barbarian*, *The ABC Weekend Special*, *Richie Rich*, *The Wuzzles*, *Dungeons & Dragons*, and *Garfield and Friends*. He also migrated back into comic books, with projects such as Sergio Aragones' *Groo*, *Blackhawk*, *Mister Miracle*, and *New Gods* series, among others.

He teamed with artist-producer Will Meugniot to create *DNAgents* #1 (March 1983), and a story so far ahead of its time that it's just now contemporary. Developed by a major conglomerate known as Matrix Technologies, the characters were genetically modified, test-tube creations intended to be slave special agents for their corporate masters. The team consisted of the mistress of mirage Rainbow, juggernaut Tank, hothead Surge, aerial angel Amber, and oh-so-shy Sham. The agents had minds and personalities of their own, so drama, conflict, and action followed.

Evanier said that creating a new universe had its challenges, but it wasn't overly burdensome.

"I think once you get off the notion that you have

to construct an entire universe from scratch all at once... once you realize you can figure it out as you go along... it's pretty simple. Especially when you're only doing one comic at the time," he said. "I think the main thing our comic provided was that it wasn't the work of a whole mess of different creators with different views all switching-off and trying to change things their way or emulate what others had done. And I think a lot of folks liked the idea of collecting a new 'universe' of superheroes and being able to have complete collections. Even if you came in late, it wasn't difficult or expensive to get a complete set."

Meugniot illustrated the first 14 issues, and was followed by Richard Howell, Dan Spiegle (who also illustrated *Crossfire*), Jerry Ordway, and Mitch Schauer. After *DNAgents* #24, the series was restarted as *The New DNAgents* with Schauer as the regular artist, along with work by Chuck Patton, Mike Sekowsky, and Rick Hoberg. Image co-founder and Savage Dragon creator Erik Larsen illustrated the last five issues.

Jeff Baker, the original Crossfire, first appeared in *DNAgents* #4. His successor, bail bondsman Jay Endicott, first appeared in *DNAgents* #9. His solo adventures, steeped in Hollywood history and more grounded in the real world, were illustrated by Dan Spiegle. *Crossfire* ran 26 issues, initially in color and then from #18 until the end of the series in black and white.

Endicott, doubled as the romantic interest of DNAgent Rainbow (they even had their four-issue mini-series), was also the lead character in *Whodunnit?*, a three-issue mystery series in which he tried to solve crimes in his civilian identity. Readers were invited to submit their suspects in the crimes for a potential cash prize.

– *Scott Braden*

FIRST PUBLICATION:
DNAgents #1
(March 1983)

LAST PUBLICATION:
Crossfire #26
(February 1988)

REVIVAL(S):
DNAgents Super Special #1 (Antarctic Press, April 1994), *The DNAgents Industrial Strength Edition* (About Comics, 2008), *The DNAgents Industrial Strength Edition* (Image Comics, 2008)

Will Meugniot and Al Gordon's original art for *DNAgents* #10 Page 20 (1984).
Image courtesy of Heritage Auctions.

DNAGENTS #1
MARCH 1983
$5

DNAGENTS #2
APRIL 1983
$4

DNAGENTS #3
MAY 1983
$4

DNAGENTS #4
JULY 1983
$4

DNAGENTS #5
AUGUST 1983
$4

DNAGENTS #6
OCTOBER 1983
$4

DNAGENTS #7
NOVEMBER 1983
$4

DNAGENTS #8
JANUARY 1984
$4

DNAGENTS #9
FEBRUARY 1984
$4

DNAgents #10
MARCH 1984
$4

DNAgents #11
MAY 1984
$4

DNAgents #12
MAY 1984
$4

DNAgents #13
JUNE 1984
$4

DNAgents #14
JULY 1984
$4

DNAgents #15
AUGUST 1984
$4

DNAgents #16
OCTOBER 1984
$4

DNAgents #17
DECEMBER 1984
$4

DNAgents #18
JANUARY 1985
$4

DNAGENTS #19
FEBRUARY 1985
$4

DNAGENTS #20
MARCH 1985
$4

DNAGENTS #21
APRIL 1985
$4

DNAGENTS #22
MAY 1985
$4

DNAGENTS #23
JUNE 1985
$4

DNAGENTS #24
JULY 1985
$6 **$18** **$100**

NEW DNAGENTS #1
OCTOBER 1985
$4

NEW DNAGENTS #2
NOVEMBER 1985
$4

NEW DNAGENTS #3
NOVEMBER 1985
$4

NEW DNAGENTS #4
DECEMBER 1985
$4

NEW DNAGENTS #5
JANUARY 1986
$4

NEW DNAGENTS #6
FEBRUARY 1986
$4

NEW DNAGENTS #7
APRIL 1986
$4

NEW DNAGENTS #8
APRIL 1986
$4

NEW DNAGENTS #9
JUNE 1986
$4

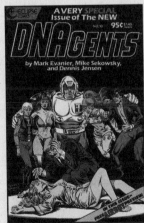

NEW DNAGENTS #10
JUNE 1986
$4

NEW DNAGENTS #11
AUGUST 1986
$4

NEW DNAGENTS #12
AUGUST 1986
$4

NEW DNAGENTS #13
OCTOBER 1986
$4

NEW DNAGENTS #14
NOVEMBER 1986
$4

NEW DNAGENTS #15
DECEMBER 1986
$4

NEW DNAGENTS #16
JANUARY 1987
$4

NEW DNAGENTS #17
MARCH 1987
$4

CROSSFIRE #1
MAY 1984
$4

CROSSFIRE #2
JUNE 1984
$4

CROSSFIRE #3
JULY 1984
$4

CROSSFIRE #4
AUGUST 1984
$4

CROSSFIRE #5
SEPTEMBER 1984
$4

CROSSFIRE #6
NOVEMBER 1984
$4

CROSSFIRE #7
DECEMBER 1984
$4

CROSSFIRE #8
JANUARY 1985
$4

CROSSFIRE #9
MARCH 1985
$4

CROSSFIRE #10
APRIL 1985
$4

CROSSFIRE #11
MAY 1985
$4

CROSSFIRE #12
JUNE 1985
$5   **$15**   **$75**

CROSSFIRE #13
JULY 1985
$1   **$4**   **$10**

CROSSFIRE #14
AUGUST 1985
$4

CROSSFIRE #15
SEPTEMBER 1985
$4

CROSSFIRE #16
JANUARY 1986
$4

CROSSFIRE #17
MARCH 1986
$4

CROSSFIRE #18
JANUARY 1987
$4

CROSSFIRE #19
FEBRUARY 1987
$4

CROSSFIRE #20
MARCH 1987
$4

CROSSFIRE #21
APRIL 1987
$4

CROSSFIRE #22
JUNE 1987
$4

CROSSFIRE #23
JULY 1987
$4

CROSSFIRE #24
AUGUST 1987
$4

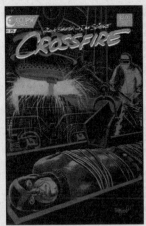

CROSSFIRE #25
OCTOBER 1987
$4

CROSSFIRE #26
FEBRUARY 1988
$4

CROSSFIRE AND RAINBOW #1
JUNE 1986
$4

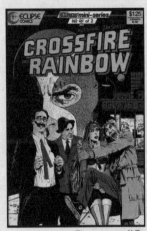

CROSSFIRE AND RAINBOW #2
JULY 1986
$4

CROSSFIRE AND RAINBOW #3
AUGUST 1986
$4

CROSSFIRE AND RAINBOW #4
SEPTEMBER 1986
$3　**$9**　**$25**

SURGE #1
JULY 1984
$4

SURGE #2
AUGUST 1984
$4

SURGE #3
OCTOBER 1984
$4

SURGE #4
JANUARY 1985
$4

**THREE-DIMENSIONAL
DNAGENTS #1**
JANUARY 1986
$4

WHODUNNIT? #1
JUNE 1986
$4

WHODUNNIT? #2
NOVEMBER 1986
$4

WHODUNNIT? #3
APRIL 1987
$4

**DNAGENTS
SUPER SPECIAL #1**
ANTARCTIC PRESS • 1994
$4

DNAGENTS VOLUME 1
ABOUT COMICS • JULY 2004
$10

DNAGENTS VOLUME 2
About Comics • March 2005
$10

**DNAGENTS INDUSTRIAL
STRENGTH EDITION**
Image Comics • 2008
$25

UNOFFICIAL CROSSOVER: THE DNAGENTS AND THE NEW TEEN TITANS

DNAgents co-creator Mark Evanier and *Nexus* co-creator Steve Rude, who also worked together on a *Space Ghost* one-shot for Comico and a *Mister Miracle* one-shot for DC, teamed with *New Teen Titans* writer Marv Wolfman to make their contributions to the long comic book history of unofficial crossovers.

In the pages of *Tales of the Teen Titans* #48, Wolfman and Rude introduced "RECOMBatants," characters that were clearly modeled on the DNAgents. For his part, Meugniot transformed the members of the Titans into the pastiche super-team codenamed "Project Youngblood" in *DNAgents* #14.

"Marv Wolfman, who of course was writing the *Titans*, is one of my best buddies. We got talking one day –I forget if it was his idea or mine – and it sounded like too much fun to pass up. So, we just coordinated and did our issues at the same time," Evanier said.

Rude also contributed a back-up story in *Surge* #4.

EVANGELINE

While Comico's short-lived anthology title *Primer* is best known for the first appearances of Matt Wagner's Grendel (#2) and Sam Kieth's The Maxx (as Max the Hare, #5), it also should be remembered for the debut of Chuck Dixon and Judith Hunt's Evangeline in *Primer* #6.

The title character, a powerful, devout nun, a sometimes assassin in the service of the Roman Catholic Church in an undefined future. It would become grim and gritty punctuated by moments of beauty, comradeship, and even kindness. Strictly speaking, her series and her worlds were not a comic book universe, but they do indeed suggest a universe of possibilities.

Much like John K. Snyder III's *Fashion In Action* and Max Alan Collins and Terry Beatty's *Ms. Tree*, Evangeline was something of an anomaly in the 1980s as it show-cased a non-super-powered, incredibly competent female action hero. Even with the sea change brought about by creator ownership and the arrival of independent publishers such as First Comics, Eclipse, and Comico, among others, such female characters were not that common. In hind-sight, what's most refreshing about this story is that Evangeline doesn't spend a whole lot of time telling people she's a powerful woman; she just goes out and does what she needs to do.

One of the other truly attractive things about the series that followed this one-shot appearance is that the Catholic church was neither portrayed as all good nor all evil. That shouldn't be amazing, really, but in the world of comics it sort of is.

There's a roughness to this first story that quickly disappeared with the next installments, but the com-pelling undercurrents are already present in this one.

After *Primer* #6, there were only two issues of *Evangeline* at Comico. From Comico, Evangeline moved to Lodestone Publishing for the one-shot

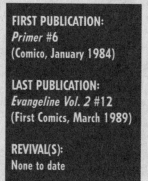

FIRST PUBLICATION:
Primer #6
(Comico, January 1984)

LAST PUBLICATION:
Evangeline Vol. 2 #12
(First Comics, March 1989)

REVIVAL(S):
None to date

Evangeline Special #1, which reprinted the first two Comico issues with some additional material. Reading the editorial matter in that issue, it seems like Lodestone Publisher David Singer expected more issues to follow under that banner (Singer was probably best known for publishing *Wally Wood's T.H.U.N.DE.R. Agents* under his Deluxe Comics imprint, and for the legal fight that followed).

After going through two publish-ers in a relatively short order, the property ended up at First Comics, where its only lengthy run – 12 issues – came to pass, beginning with the "Dinosaur Farm" story that had been teased back in the Comico *Evangeline* #2.

Judith Hunt left the series after *Evangeline* #4 (actually after the cover on #5), and she and Dixon divorced. She was followed on the penciling duties by Cara Sherman-Tereno, John Statema, and Jim Balent. Ricardo Villagran, who had also inked Hunt on the series, was perhaps the saving grace during these artistic changes, stayed with the book, as did Dixon.

"He was strong at rendering the straightforward, and often ignored the flashy. As such his figures, faces, and characters were always spot-on. The landscapes he created were lush in detail, and his backgrounds were smart and solid," frequent *Overstreet* contributor Ed Catto wrote in *Back Issue* #149. "Villagran never was the artist to glamorize the shiny metal of weapons or space-ships. Instead, in an almost workmanlike way, he'd render such objects with a straightforward, working man's level of professionalism. These aspects of his talents were especially helpful in rendering the tired, scuffed world of Evangeline's near-future."

Given that the marketplace is considerably more open to strong female characters of the non-super-hero variety than they were back in the day, it seems a shame that the character hasn't resurfaced, but complicated legal issues apparently surround her and make it less than likely she'll get another chance.

Judith Hunt and Ricardo Villagrán's original art for page 19 of *Evangeline #3*
(First Comics,1987). Image courtesy of Heritage Auctions.

PRIMER #6
JANUARY 1984
$3 **$9** **$24**

EVANGELINE #1
JANUARY 1984
$4

EVANGELINE #2
MARCH 1984
$4

EVANGELINE SPECIAL #1
MAY 1986
$4

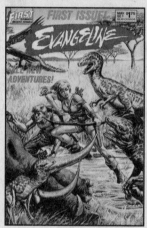

EVANGELINE VOL. 2 #1
MAY 1987
$4

EVANGELINE VOL. 2 #2
JULY 1987
$4

EVANGELINE VOL. 2 #3
SEPTEMBER 1987
$4

EVANGELINE VOL. 2 #4
NOVEMBER 1987
$4

EVANGELINE VOL. 2 #5
JANUARY 1988
$4

EVANGELINE VOL. 2 #6
MARCH 1988
$4

EVANGELINE VOL. 2 #7
MAY 1988
$4

EVANGELINE VOL. 2 #8
JULY 1988
$4

EVANGELINE VOL. 2 #9
SEPTEMBER 1988
$4

EVANGELINE VOL. 2 #10
NOVEMBER 1988
$4

Judith Hunt and
Ricardo Villagrán's
original art panel
from page 24
of *Evangeline* #3
(First Comics,1987).
Image courtesy of
Heritage Auctions.

EVANGELINE VOL. 2 #11
JANUARY 1989
$4

EVANGELINE VOL. 2 #12
MARCH 1989
$4

FAWCETT'S MARVEL FAMILY

It all started with Billy Batson and the magic word turned a young boy into the world's mightiest mortal, Captain Marvel: "Shazam!" First hitting the stands in the February 1940 cover-dated *Whiz Comics* #2 (#1).

Artist C.C. Beck and writer Bill Parker created the character for Fawcett Publications, a successful publishing house in the magazine business that had branched into comic books.

The success of the character quickly spun into a whole family of characters. While Captain Marvel may receive the most acclaim, he was joined in his battles for good by several cohorts, who were eventually dubbed The Marvel Family.

Though they all share the Marvel moniker in their superheroic states, only two of them are actually related. Billy Batson and Mary Batson (also known as Mary Marvel) were long-lost siblings who discovered each other – not to mention their shared Shazam-imparted powers – and teamed up to fight the forces of evil.

Captain Marvel Jr., on the other hand, is a mere friend of the literal family. Known in his everyman-indentity as newspaper boy Freddy Freeman, he was inducted into the pantheon of protagonists after becoming gravely injured in a battle with Captain Nazi. Captain Marvel and Mary Marvel imparted a portion of their powers to help him heal and their effects were permanent.

The extended family included Uncle Marvel (who was Uncle Dudley, Billy's guardian), who had no powers, and three Lieutenants Marvel (Tall Billy Batson, Fat Billy Batson and Hill Billy Batson). The unrelated trio just happened to also be named Billy Batson. When the original would get in trouble, they would shout the magic word. Since there could only be one Captain Marvel, it was presumed they must be Lieutenants. Baby Marvel showed up on the family's doorstep in *Marvel Family* #1. And then there was Hoppy, The Marvel Bunny, who actually turned out to be one of the most prized Captain Marvel-related collectibles.

FIRST PUBLICATION:
Whiz Comics #2 (#1)
(February 1940)

LAST PUBLICATION:
Marvel Family #89
(January 1954)

REVIVAL(S):
Shazam! #1- 35
(DC Comics, February 1973 – June 1978) and many subsequent.

The books were all top sellers in their day. Dozens of toys, novelties and premiums were issued. *The Adventures of Captain Marvel*, a 12-episode chapter play starring Tom Tyler as the Captain and Frank Coghlan Jr. as Billy was released by Republic Pictures in 1941.

Across titles such as *Captain Marvel Adventures*, *Captain Marvel Jr.*, *Mary Marvel*, *Master Comics*, and *Wow Comics*, in addition to *Whiz Comics*, creators such as writer Otto Binder and artists Mac Raboy and Kurt Schaffenberger helped make and keep the characters popular with a generation of fans.

The Marvels subdued criminals and mad scientists for 13 years until it turned into a legal battle with DC, which sued over similarities to Superman. In fact, it was three lawsuits, Roscoe Fawcett told writer P.C Hamerlinck (in an interview published in TwoMorrow's *Fawcett Companion*.

"We won the first, lost the second, won the third...but then there was a problem. One artist, I don't know who, took either a page or a panel from Superman comics and traced it exactly...and simply inserted Marvel where Superman was. That killed us. We settled out of court. We paid them $400,000. The settlement said that we do not admit to copying Superman but promised never to publish Captain Marvel ever again," Fawcett said in the interview.

So, Captain Marvel disappeared from the stands, seemingly forever... but this is comics. Almost two decades later, in 1973, the original returned, when DC leased the characters and began publishing his adventures. Because Marvel Comics had trademarked the name, the new comic was titled *Shazam!*. The series lasted five years. In 1974, a live action television series was produced by Filmation Studios.

Later, DC acquired the characters from Fawcett outright, and further incorporated them into the DC universe, subsequently revamping them with different levels of success. The characters have also appeared in feature films in recent years.

C.C. Beck and Pete Constanza's original cover art for *Whiz Comics* #17 (1941).
Image courtesy of Heritage Auctions.

ALL HERO COMICS #1
MARCH 1943
$206 $618 $3200

AMERICA'S GREATEST COMICS #1
FALL 1941
$371 $1113 $6500

AMERICA'S GREATEST COMICS #2
FEBRUARY - MAY 1942
$161 $483 $2500

AMERICA'S GREATEST COMICS #3
MAY - AUGUST 1942
$123 $369 $1900

AMERICA'S GREATEST COMICS #4
AUGUST - NOVEMBER 1942
$84 $252 $1300

AMERICA'S GREATEST COMICS #5
DECEMBER 1942
$84 $252 $1300

AMERICA'S GREATEST COMICS #6
FEBRUARY 1943
$74 $222 $1150

AMERICA'S GREATEST COMICS #7
MAY 1943
$74 $222 $1150

AMERICA'S GREATEST COMICS #8
SUMMER 1943
$77 $231 $1200

CAPTAIN MARVEL ADVENTURES NN (#1)
MARCH 1941
$7800 $31,200 $140,000

CAPTAIN MARVEL ADVENTURES #2
JUNE 1941
$497 $1491 $9200

CAPTAIN MARVEL ADVENTURES #3
SEPTEMBER 1941
$349 $1047 $6100

CAPTAIN MARVEL ADVENTURES #4
OCTOBER 1941
$252 $756 $3900

CAPTAIN MARVEL ADVENTURES #5
DECEMBER 1941
$213 $639 $3300

CAPTAIN MARVEL ADVENTURES #6
JANUARY 1942
$148 $444 $2300

CAPTAIN MARVEL ADVENTURES #7
FEBRUARY 1942
$148 $444 $2300

CAPTAIN MARVEL ADVENTURES #8
MARCH 1942
$148 $444 $2300

CAPTAIN MARVEL ADVENTURES #9
APRIL 1942
$148 $444 $2300

**CAPTAIN MARVEL
ADVENTURES #10**
MAY 1942
$148 $444 $2300

**CAPTAIN MARVEL
ADVENTURES #11**
MAY 1942
$116 $348 $1800

**CAPTAIN MARVEL
ADVENTURES #12**
JUNE 1942
$116 $348 $1800

**CAPTAIN MARVEL
ADVENTURES #13**
JULY 1942
$116 $348 $1800

**CAPTAIN MARVEL
ADVENTURES #14**
AUGUST 1942
$116 $348 $1800

**CAPTAIN MARVEL
ADVENTURES #15**
SEPTEMBER 1942
$116 $348 $1800

**CAPTAIN MARVEL
ADVENTURES #16**
OCTOBER 1942
$110 $330 $1700

**CAPTAIN MARVEL
ADVENTURES #17**
NOVEMBER 1942
$110 $330 $1700

**CAPTAIN MARVEL
ADVENTURES #18**
DECEMBER 1942
$1000 $3000 $20,000

Captain Marvel Adventures #19
January 1943
$116 $348 $1800

Captain Marvel Adventures #20
January 1943
$481 $1443 $8900

Captain Marvel Adventures #21
February 1943
$481 $1443 $8900

Captain Marvel Adventures #22
March 1943
$123 $369 $1900

Captain Marvel Adventures #23
April 1943
$481 $1443 $8900

Captain Marvel Adventures #24
June 1943
$77 $231 $1200

Captain Marvel Adventures #25
July 1943
$77 $231 $1200

Captain Marvel Adventures #26
August 1943
$61 $183 $950

Captain Marvel Adventures #27
September 1943
$61 $183 $950

**CAPTAIN MARVEL
ADVENTURES #28**
OCTOBER 1943
$61 $183 $950

**CAPTAIN MARVEL
ADVENTURES #29**
NOVEMBER 1943
$81 $243 $1250

**CAPTAIN MARVEL
ADVENTURES #30**
DECEMBER 1943
$61 $183 $950

**CAPTAIN MARVEL
ADVENTURES #31**
JANUARY 1944
$55 $165 $850

**CAPTAIN MARVEL
ADVENTURES #32**
FEBRUARY 1944
$55 $165 $850

**CAPTAIN MARVEL
ADVENTURES #33**
MARCH 1944
$55 $165 $850

**CAPTAIN MARVEL
ADVENTURES #34**
APRIL 1943
$55 $165 $850

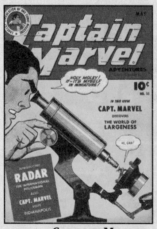

**CAPTAIN MARVEL
ADVENTURES #35**
MAY 1943
$55 $165 $850

**CAPTAIN MARVEL
ADVENTURES #36**
JUNE 1944
$52 $156 $775

CAPTAIN MARVEL
ADVENTURES #37
JULY 1944
$52 $156 $775

CAPTAIN MARVEL
ADVENTURES #38
AUGUST 1944
$52 $156 $775

CAPTAIN MARVEL
ADVENTURES #39
SEPTEMBER 1944
$52 $156 $775

CAPTAIN MARVEL
ADVENTURES #40
OCTOBER 1944
$52 $156 $775

CAPTAIN MARVEL
ADVENTURES #41
NOVEMBER 1944
$42 $126 $625

CAPTAIN MARVEL
ADVENTURES #42
JANUARY 1945
$42 $126 $625

CAPTAIN MARVEL
ADVENTURES #43
FEBRUARY 1945
$42 $126 $625

CAPTAIN MARVEL
ADVENTURES #44
MARCH 1945
$42 $126 $625

CAPTAIN MARVEL
ADVENTURES #45
APRIL 1945
$42 $126 $625

Captain Marvel Adventures #46
MAY 1945

$42 $126 $625

Captain Marvel Adventures #47
JULY 1945

$40 $120 $575

Captain Marvel Adventures #48
SEPTEMBER 1945

$40 $120 $575

Captain Marvel Adventures #49
NOVEMBER 1945

$40 $120 $575

Captain Marvel Adventures #50
DECEMBER 1945

$40 $120 $575

Captain Marvel Adventures #51
JANUARY 1946

$36 $108 $475

Captain Marvel Adventures #52
JANUARY 1946

$36 $108 $475

Captain Marvel Adventures #53
FEBRUARY 1946

$36 $108 $475

Captain Marvel Adventures #54
FEBRUARY 1946

$39 $117 $525

CAPTAIN MARVEL ADVENTURES #55
MARCH 1946
$36 $108 $475

CAPTAIN MARVEL ADVENTURES #56
MARCH 1946
$36 $108 $475

CAPTAIN MARVEL ADVENTURES #57
MARCH 1946
$36 $108 $475

CAPTAIN MARVEL ADVENTURES #58
APRIL 1946
$36 $108 $475

CAPTAIN MARVEL ADVENTURES #59
APRIL 1946
$36 $108 $475

CAPTAIN MARVEL ADVENTURES #60
MAY 1946
$36 $108 $475

CAPTAIN MARVEL ADVENTURES #61
MAY 1946
$39 $117 $500

CAPTAIN MARVEL ADVENTURES #62
JUNE 1946
$34 $102 $460

CAPTAIN MARVEL ADVENTURES #63
JULY 1946
$34 $102 $460

CAPTAIN MARVEL
ADVENTURES #64
AUGUST 1946

$34 **$102** **$460**

CAPTAIN MARVEL
ADVENTURES #65
SEPTEMBER 1946

$34 **$102** **$460**

CAPTAIN MARVEL
ADVENTURES #66
OCTOBER 1946

$43 **$129** **$650**

CAPTAIN MARVEL
ADVENTURES #67
NOVEMBER 1946

$31 **$93** **$420**

CAPTAIN MARVEL
ADVENTURES #68
DECEMBER 1946

$31 **$93** **$420**

CAPTAIN MARVEL
ADVENTURES #69
FEBRUARY 1947

$31 **$93** **$420**

CAPTAIN MARVEL
ADVENTURES #70
MARCH 1947

$31 **$93** **$420**

CAPTAIN MARVEL
ADVENTURES #71
APRIL 1947

$31 **$93** **$420**

CAPTAIN MARVEL
ADVENTURES #72
MAY 1947

$31 **$93** **$420**

**CAPTAIN MARVEL
ADVENTURES #73**
JUNE 1947
$31 $93 $420

**CAPTAIN MARVEL
ADVENTURES #74**
JULY 1947
$31 $93 $420

**CAPTAIN MARVEL
ADVENTURES #75**
AUGUST 1947
$31 $93 $420

**CAPTAIN MARVEL
ADVENTURES #76**
SEPTEMBER 1947
$31 $93 $420

**CAPTAIN MARVEL
ADVENTURES #77**
OCTOBER 1947
$31 $93 $420

**CAPTAIN MARVEL
ADVENTURES #78**
NOVEMBER 1947
$37 $111 $490

**CAPTAIN MARVEL
ADVENTURES #79**
DECEMBER 1947
$31 $93 $420

**CAPTAIN MARVEL
ADVENTURES #80**
JANUARY 1948
$97 $291 $1500

**CAPTAIN MARVEL
ADVENTURES #81**
FEBRUARY 1948
$31 $93 $420

CAPTAIN MARVEL
ADVENTURES #82
MARCH 1948
$31 $93 $420

CAPTAIN MARVEL
ADVENTURES #83
APRIL 1948
$31 $93 $420

CAPTAIN MARVEL
ADVENTURES #84
MAY 1948
$31 $93 $420

CAPTAIN MARVEL
ADVENTURES #85
JUNE 1948
$35 $105 $470

CAPTAIN MARVEL
ADVENTURES #86
JULY 1948
$31 $93 $420

CAPTAIN MARVEL
ADVENTURES #87
AUGUST 1948
$31 $93 $420

CAPTAIN MARVEL
ADVENTURES #88
SEPTEMBER 1948
$31 $93 $420

CAPTAIN MARVEL
ADVENTURES #89
OCTOBER 1948
$31 $93 $420

CAPTAIN MARVEL
ADVENTURES #90
NOVEMBER 1948
$31 $93 $420

**CAPTAIN MARVEL
ADVENTURES #91**
DECEMBER 1948
$30 $90 $400

**CAPTAIN MARVEL
ADVENTURES #92**
JANUARY 1949
$30 $90 $400

**CAPTAIN MARVEL
ADVENTURES #93**
FEBRUARY 1949
$30 $90 $400

**CAPTAIN MARVEL
ADVENTURES #94**
MARCH 1949
$30 $90 $400

**CAPTAIN MARVEL
ADVENTURES #95**
APRIL 1949
$30 $90 $400

**CAPTAIN MARVEL
ADVENTURES #96**
MAY 1949
$30 $90 $400

**CAPTAIN MARVEL
ADVENTURES #97**
JUNE 1948
$30 $90 $400

**CAPTAIN MARVEL
ADVENTURES #98**
JULY 1948
$30 $90 $400

**CAPTAIN MARVEL
ADVENTURES #99**
AUGUST 1949
$30 $90 $400

CAPTAIN MARVEL ADVENTURES #100
SEPTEMBER 1949
$57 $171 $875

CAPTAIN MARVEL ADVENTURES #101
OCTOBER 1949
$30 $90 $400

CAPTAIN MARVEL ADVENTURES #102
NOVEMBER 1949
$30 $90 $400

CAPTAIN MARVEL ADVENTURES #103
DECEMBER 1949
$30 $90 $400

CAPTAIN MARVEL ADVENTURES #104
JANUARY 1950
$30 $90 $400

CAPTAIN MARVEL ADVENTURES #105
FEBRUARY 1950
$30 $90 $400

CAPTAIN MARVEL ADVENTURES #106
MARCH 1950
$30 $90 $400

CAPTAIN MARVEL ADVENTURES #107
APRIL 1950
$30 $90 $400

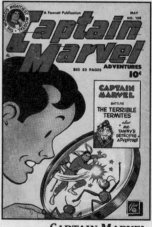

CAPTAIN MARVEL ADVENTURES #108
MAY 1950
$30 $90 $400

**CAPTAIN MARVEL
ADVENTURES #109**
JUNE 1950
$30 $90 $400

**CAPTAIN MARVEL
ADVENTURES #110**
JULY 1950
$30 $90 $400

**CAPTAIN MARVEL
ADVENTURES #111**
AUGUST 1950
$30 $90 $400

**CAPTAIN MARVEL
ADVENTURES #112**
SEPTEMBER 1950
$30 $90 $400

**CAPTAIN MARVEL
ADVENTURES #113**
OCTOBER 1950
$30 $90 $400

**CAPTAIN MARVEL
ADVENTURES #114**
NOVEMBER 1950
$30 $90 $400

**CAPTAIN MARVEL
ADVENTURES #115**
DECEMBER 1950
$30 $90 $400

**CAPTAIN MARVEL
ADVENTURES #116**
JANUARY 1951
$37 $111 $490

**CAPTAIN MARVEL
ADVENTURES #117**
FEBRUARY 1951
$30 $90 $400

**CAPTAIN MARVEL
ADVENTURES #118**
MARCH 1951
$30 $90 $400

**CAPTAIN MARVEL
ADVENTURES #119**
APRIL 1951
$30 $90 $400

**CAPTAIN MARVEL
ADVENTURES #120**
MAY 1951
$30 $90 $400

**CAPTAIN MARVEL
ADVENTURES #121**
JUNE 1951
$39 $117 $550

**CAPTAIN MARVEL
ADVENTURES #122**
JULY 1951
$30 $90 $400

**CAPTAIN MARVEL
ADVENTURES #123**
AUGUST 1951
$30 $90 $400

**CAPTAIN MARVEL
ADVENTURES #124**
SEPTEMBER 1951
$30 $90 $400

**CAPTAIN MARVEL
ADVENTURES #125**
OCTOBER 1951
$30 $90 $400

**CAPTAIN MARVEL
ADVENTURES #126**
NOVEMBER 1951
$30 $90 $400

**Captain Marvel
Adventures #127**
December 1951
$30 $90 $400

**Captain Marvel
Adventures #128**
January 1952
$30 $90 $400

**Captain Marvel
Adventures #129**
February 1952
$30 $90 $400

**Captain Marvel
Adventures #130**
March 1952
$30 $90 $400

**Captain Marvel
Adventures #131**
April 1952
$30 $90 $400

**Captain Marvel
Adventures #132**
May 1952
$30 $90 $400

**Captain Marvel
Adventures #133**
June 1952
$30 $90 $400

**Captain Marvel
Adventures #134**
July 1952
$30 $90 $400

**Captain Marvel
Adventures #135**
August 1952
$30 $90 $400

**CAPTAIN MARVEL
ADVENTURES #136**
SEPTEMBER 1952
$30 $90 $400

**CAPTAIN MARVEL
ADVENTURES #137**
OCTOBER 1952
$30 $90 $400

**CAPTAIN MARVEL
ADVENTURES #138**
NOVEMBER 1952
$39 $117 $525

**CAPTAIN MARVEL
ADVENTURES #139**
DECEMBER 1952
$30 $90 $400

**CAPTAIN MARVEL
ADVENTURES #140**
JANUARY 1953
$30 $90 $400

**CAPTAIN MARVEL
ADVENTURES #141**
FEBRUARY 1953
$39 $117 $550

**CAPTAIN MARVEL
ADVENTURES #142**
MARCH 1953
$34 $102 $460

**CAPTAIN MARVEL
ADVENTURES #143**
APRIL 1953
$34 $102 $460

**CAPTAIN MARVEL
ADVENTURES #144**
MAY 1953
$34 $102 $460

**CAPTAIN MARVEL
ADVENTURES #145**
JUNE 1953
$34 $102 $460

**CAPTAIN MARVEL
ADVENTURES #146**
JULY 1953
$34 $102 $460

**CAPTAIN MARVEL
ADVENTURES #147**
AUGUST 1953
$34 $102 $460

**CAPTAIN MARVEL
ADVENTURES #148**
SEPTEMBER 1953
$34 $102 $460

**CAPTAIN MARVEL
ADVENTURES #149**
OCTOBER 1953
$34 $102 $460

**CAPTAIN MARVEL
ADVENTURES #150**
NOVEMBER 1953
$71 $213 $1100

**CAPTAIN MARVEL AND
THE GOOD HUMOR MAN**
1950
$61 $183 $950

CAPTAIN MARVEL, JR. #1
NOVEMBER 1942
$757 $2271 $14,000

CAPTAIN MARVEL, JR. #2
DECEMBER 1942
$239 $717 $3700

Captain Marvel, Jr. #3
January 1943
$135 $405 $2100

Captain Marvel, Jr. #4
February 1943
$245 $735 $3800

Captain Marvel, Jr. #5
March 1943
$116 $348 $1800

Captain Marvel, Jr. #6
April 1943
$93 $288 $1450

Captain Marvel, Jr. #7
May 1943
$93 $288 $1450

Captain Marvel, Jr. #8
June 1943
$93 $288 $1450

Captain Marvel, Jr. #9
July 1943
$119 $357 $1850

Captain Marvel, Jr. #10
August 1943
$300 $900 $5200

Captain Marvel, Jr. #11
September 1943
$87 $261 $1350

CAPT. MARVEL JR. SCUTTLES THE AXIS ISLE IN THE SKY!

CAPTAIN MARVEL, JR. #12
OCTOBER 1943
$87 $261 $1350

CAPT. MARVEL JR. CARRIES THE BALL FOR DEMOCRACY!

CAPTAIN MARVEL, JR. #13
NOVEMBER 1943
$300 $900 $5200

CAPT. MARVEL JR. wishes his readers a Merry Christmas!

CAPTAIN MARVEL, JR. #14
DECEMBER 1943
$61 $183 $950

FOUR PUNCH-PACKED CAPTAIN MARVEL JR. ADVENTURE STORIES!

CAPTAIN MARVEL, JR. #15
JANUARY 1944
$87 $261 $1350

CAPT. MARVEL JR. CAPTURES POGO JAP MONSTER OF THE DEEP!

CAPTAIN MARVEL, JR. #16
FEBRUARY 1944
$61 $183 $950

CAPT. MARVEL JR. MEETS HIMSELF IN THE FUTURE!!

CAPTAIN MARVEL, JR. #17
MARCH 1944
$61 $183 $950

CAPTAIN MARVEL JR. BATTLES THE BIRDS OF DOOM!

CAPTAIN MARVEL, JR. #18
APRIL 1944
$61 $183 $950

CAPT. MARVEL JR. THE AMERICAN BLOCK-BUSTER

CAPTAIN MARVEL, JR. #19
MAY 1944
$61 $183 $950

CAPT. MARVEL JR. GOES ON THE WARPATH!

CAPTAIN MARVEL, JR. #20
JUNE 1944
$61 $183 $950

CAPTAIN MARVEL, JR. #21
JULY 1944
$48 $144 $725

CAPTAIN MARVEL, JR. #22
AUGUST 1944
$48 $144 $725

CAPTAIN MARVEL, JR. #23
SEPTEMBER 1944
$48 $144 $725

CAPTAIN MARVEL, JR. #24
OCTOBER 1944
$48 $144 $725

CAPTAIN MARVEL, JR. #25
NOVEMBER 1944
$48 $144 $725

CAPTAIN MARVEL, JR. #26
JANUARY 1945
$48 $144 $725

CAPTAIN MARVEL, JR. #27
FEBRUARY 1945
$48 $144 $725

CAPTAIN MARVEL, JR. #28
MARCH 1945
$48 $144 $725

CAPTAIN MARVEL, JR. #29
APRIL 1945
$48 $144 $725

CAPTAIN MARVEL, JR. #30
MAY 1945
$48 $144 $725

CAPTAIN MARVEL, JR. #31
JULY 1945
$35 $105 $470

CAPTAIN MARVEL, JR. #32
SEPTEMBER 1945
$35 $105 $470

CAPTAIN MARVEL, JR. #33
NOVEMBER 1945
$35 $105 $470

CAPTAIN MARVEL, JR. #35
FEBRUARY 1946
$36 $108 $480

CAPTAIN MARVEL, JR. #36
MARCH 1946
$35 $105 $470

ISSUE #34 DOESN'T EXIST

CAPTAIN MARVEL, JR. #37
APRIL 1946
$35 $105 $470

CAPTAIN MARVEL, JR. #38
MAY 1946
$35 $105 $470

CAPTAIN MARVEL, JR. #39
JUNE 1946
$35 $105 $470

CAPTAIN MARVEL, JR. #40
JULY 1946
$35 $105 $470

CAPTAIN MARVEL, JR. #41
AUGUST 1946
$31 $93 $410

CAPTAIN MARVEL, JR. #42
SEPTEMBER 1946
$31 $93 $410

CAPTAIN MARVEL, JR. #43
OCTOBER 1946
$31 $93 $410

CAPTAIN MARVEL, JR. #44
NOVEMBER 1946
$31 $93 $410

CAPTAIN MARVEL, JR. #45
DECEMBER 1946
$31 $93 $410

CAPTAIN MARVEL, JR. #46
FEBRUARY 1947
$31 $93 $410

CAPTAIN MARVEL, JR. #47
MARCH 1947
$31 $93 $410

CAPTAIN MARVEL, JR. #48
APRIL 1947
$31 $93 $410

CAPTAIN MARVEL, JR. #49
MAY 1947
$31 $93 $410

CAPTAIN MARVEL, JR. #50
JUNE 1947
$31 $93 $410

CAPTAIN MARVEL, JR. #51
JULY 1947
$31 $93 $410

CAPTAIN MARVEL, JR. #52
AUGUST 1947
$31 $93 $410

CAPTAIN MARVEL, JR. #53
SEPTEMBER 1947
$41 $123 $600

CAPTAIN MARVEL, JR. #54
OCTOBER 1947
$31 $93 $410

CAPTAIN MARVEL, JR. #55
NOVEMBER 1947
$31 $93 $410

CAPTAIN MARVEL, JR. #56
DECEMBER 1947
$31 $93 $410

CAPTAIN MARVEL, JR. #57
JANUARY 1948
$31 $93 $410

CAPTAIN MARVEL, JR. #58
FEBRUARY 1948
$31 $93 $410

CAPTAIN MARVEL, JR. #59
MARCH 1948
$31 $93 $410

CAPTAIN MARVEL, JR. #60
APRIL 1948
$31 $93 $410

CAPTAIN MARVEL, JR. #61
MAY 1948
$31 $93 $410

CAPTAIN MARVEL, JR. #62
JUNE 1948
$31 $93 $410

CAPTAIN MARVEL, JR. #63
JULY 1948
$31 $93 $410

CAPTAIN MARVEL, JR. #64
AUGUST 1948
$31 $93 $410

CAPTAIN MARVEL, JR. #65
SEPTEMBER 1948
$31 $93 $410

CAPTAIN MARVEL, JR. #66
OCTOBER 1948
$31 $93 $410

CAPTAIN MARVEL, JR. #67
NOVEMBER 1948
$31 $93 $410

CAPTAIN MARVEL, JR. #68
DECEMBER 1948
$31 $93 $410

CAPTAIN MARVEL, JR. #69
JANUARY 1949
$31 $93 $410

CAPTAIN MARVEL, JR. #70
FEBRUARY 1949
$31 $93 $410

CAPTAIN MARVEL, JR. #71
MARCH 1949
$27 $81 $370

CAPTAIN MARVEL, JR. #72
APRIL 1949
$27 $81 $370

CAPTAIN MARVEL, JR. #73
MAY 1949
$27 $81 $370

CAPTAIN MARVEL, JR. #74
JUNE 1949
$27 $81 $370

CAPTAIN MARVEL, JR. #75
JULY 1949
$27 $81 $370

CAPTAIN MARVEL, JR. #76
AUGUST 1949
$27 $81 $370

CAPTAIN MARVEL, JR. #77
SEPTEMBER 1949
$27 $81 $370

CAPTAIN MARVEL, JR. #78
OCTOBER 1949
$27 $81 $370

CAPTAIN MARVEL, JR. #79
NOVEMBER 1949
$27 $81 $370

CAPTAIN MARVEL, JR. #80
DECEMBER 1949
$27 $81 $370

CAPTAIN MARVEL, JR. #81
JANUARY 1950
$27 $81 $370

CAPTAIN MARVEL, JR. #82
FEBRUARY 1950
$27 $81 $370

CAPTAIN MARVEL, JR. #83
MARCH 1950
$27 $81 $370

CAPTAIN MARVEL, JR. #84
APRIL 1950
$27 $81 $370

CAPTAIN MARVEL, JR. #85
MAY 1950
$27 $81 $370

CAPTAIN MARVEL, JR. #86
JUNE 1950
$27 $81 $370

CAPTAIN MARVEL, JR. #87
JULY 1950
$27 $81 $370

CAPTAIN MARVEL, JR. #88
AUGUST 1950
$27 $81 $370

CAPTAIN MARVEL, JR. #89
SEPTEMBER 1950
$27 $81 $370

CAPTAIN MARVEL, JR. #90
OCTOBER 1950
$27 $81 $370

CAPTAIN MARVEL, JR. #91
NOVEMBER 1950
$27 $81 $370

CAPTAIN MARVEL, JR. #92
DECEMBER 1950
$27 $81 $370

CAPTAIN MARVEL, JR. #93
JANUARY 1951
$27 $81 $370

CAPTAIN MARVEL, JR. #94
FEBRUARY 1951
$27 **$81** **$370**

CAPTAIN MARVEL, JR. #95
MARCH 1951
$27 **$81** **$370**

CAPTAIN MARVEL, JR. #96
APRIL 1951
$27 **$81** **$370**

CAPTAIN MARVEL, JR. #97
MAY 1951
$27 **$81** **$370**

CAPTAIN MARVEL, JR. #98
JUNE 1951
$27 **$81** **$370**

CAPTAIN MARVEL, JR. #99
JULY 1951
$27 **$81** **$370**

CAPTAIN MARVEL, JR. #100
AUGUST 1951
$31 **$93** **$420**

CAPTAIN MARVEL, JR. #101
SEPTEMBER 1951
$27 **$81** **$370**

CAPTAIN MARVEL, JR. #102
OCTOBER 1951
$27 **$81** **$370**

CAPTAIN MARVEL, JR. #103
NOVEMBER 1951
$27 $81 $370

CAPTAIN MARVEL, JR. #104
DECEMBER 1951
$27 $81 $370

CAPTAIN MARVEL, JR. #105
JANUARY 1952
$30 $90 $400

CAPTAIN MARVEL, JR. #106
FEBRUARY 1952
$30 $90 $400

CAPTAIN MARVEL, JR. #107
MARCH 1952
$30 $90 $400

CAPTAIN MARVEL, JR. #108
APRIL 1952
$30 $90 $400

CAPTAIN MARVEL, JR. #109
MAY 1952
$30 $90 $400

CAPTAIN MARVEL, JR. #110
JUNE 1952
$30 $90 $400

CAPTAIN MARVEL, JR. #111
JULY 1952
$30 $90 $400

CAPTAIN MARVEL, JR. #112
AUGUST 1952
$30 $90 $400

CAPTAIN MARVEL, JR. #113
SEPTEMBER 1952
$30 $90 $400

CAPTAIN MARVEL, JR. #114
OCTOBER 1952
$30 $90 $400

CAPTAIN MARVEL, JR. #115
NOVEMBER 1952
$200 $600 $3100

CAPTAIN MARVEL, JR. #116
DECEMBER 1952
$30 $90 $400

CAPTAIN MARVEL, JR. #117
JANUARY 1953
$30 $90 $400

CAPTAIN MARVEL, JR. #118
APRIL 1953
$30 $90 $400

CAPTAIN MARVEL, JR. #119
JUNE 1953
$93 $288 $1450

**CAPTAIN MARVEL'S
FUN BOOK nn**
1944
$53 $159 $800

**CAPTAIN MARVEL
STORY BOOK #1**
SUMMER 1946
$68　$204　$1050

**CAPTAIN MARVEL
STORY BOOK #2**
WINTER 1947
$48　$144　$725

**CAPTAIN MARVEL
STORY BOOK #3**
SPRING 1948
$48　$144　$725

**CAPTAIN MARVEL
STORY BOOK #4**
1949
$48　$144　$725

FLASH COMICS #1
JANUARY 1940

**CAPTAIN MARVEL
THRILL BOOK #4**
1941
$480　$1440　—

　　Whiz Comics #2 was not Captain Marvel's actual debut. It was preceded by two books, *Flash Comics* and *Thrill Comics*, both dated Jan, 1940, (12 pgs, B&W, regular size) and were not distributed. These two books are identical except for the title, and were sent out to major distributors as ad copies to promote sales. Since DC Comics was also about to publish a book with the same date and title, Fawcett hurriedly printed up the black and white version of *Flash Comics* to secure copyright before DC. The eight page origin story of Captain Thunder is composed of pages 1-7 and 13 of the Captain Marvel story essentially as they appeared in the first issue of *Whiz Comics*. DC acquired the copyright first and Fawcett dropped *Flash* as well as *Thrill* and came out with *Whiz Comics* a month later. All references to Captain Thunder were relettered to Captain Marvel before appearing in *Whiz*. Cover art is by C.C. Beck.

　　Eight copies of *Flash Comics* exist.The most recent sale was a CGC certified 9.4 copy that sold for $85,000 in 2019.

GIFT COMICS #1
1942
$343 $1029 $6000

GIFT COMICS #2
1942
$226 $678 $3500

GIFT COMICS #3
1949
$168 $504 $2600

GIFT COMICS #4
1949
$110 $330 $1700

HOLIDAY COMICS #1
1942
$325 $975 $6800

MARVEL FAMILY #1
DECEMBER 1945
$2580 $7740 $40,000

MARVEL FAMILY #2
JUNE 1946
$87 $261 $1350

MARVEL FAMILY #3
JULY 1946
$60 $180 $925

MARVEL FAMILY #4
SEPTEMBER 1946
$53 $159 $800

MARVEL FAMILY #5
OCTOBER 1946
$53 $159 $800

MARVEL FAMILY #6
NOVEMBER 1946
$41 $123 $600

MARVEL FAMILY #7
DECEMBER 1946
$41 $123 $600

MARVEL FAMILY #8
FEBRUARY 1947
$41 $123 $600

MARVEL FAMILY #9
MARCH 1947
$41 $123 $600

MARVEL FAMILY #10
APRIL 1947
$41 $123 $600

MARVEL FAMILY #11
MAY 1947
$34 $102 $460

MARVEL FAMILY #12
JUNE 1947
$34 $102 $460

MARVEL FAMILY #13
JULY 1946
$34 $102 $460

MARVEL FAMILY #14
AUGUST 1947
$34　$102　$460

MARVEL FAMILY #15
SEPTEMBER 1947
$34　$102　$460

MARVEL FAMILY #16
OCTOBER 1947
$34　$102　$460

MARVEL FAMILY #17
NOVEMBER 1947
$34　$102　$460

MARVEL FAMILY #18
DECEMBER 1947
$34　$102　$460

MARVEL FAMILY #19
JANUARY 1948
$34　$102　$460

MARVEL FAMILY #20
FEBRUARY 1948
$34　$102　$460

MARVEL FAMILY #21
MARCH 1948
$31　$93　$410

MARVEL FAMILY #22
APRIL 1948
$31　$93　$410

MARVEL FAMILY #23
MAY 1948
$31　$93　$410

MARVEL FAMILY #24
JUNE 1948
$31　$93　$410

MARVEL FAMILY #25
JULY 1948
$31　$93　$410

MARVEL FAMILY #26
AUGUST 1948
$31　$93　$410

MARVEL FAMILY #27
SEPTEMBER 1948
$31　$93　$410

MARVEL FAMILY #28
OCTOBER 1948
$31　$93　$410

MARVEL FAMILY #29
NOVEMBER 1948
$31　$93　$410

MARVEL FAMILY #30
DECEMBER 1948
$31　$93　$410

MARVEL FAMILY #31
JANUARY 1949
$27　$81　$360

MARVEL FAMILY #32
FEBRUARY 1949
$27 $81 $360

MARVEL FAMILY #33
MARCH 1949
$27 $81 $360

MARVEL FAMILY #34
APRIL 1949
$27 $81 $360

MARVEL FAMILY #35
MAY 1949
$27 $81 $360

MARVEL FAMILY #36
JUNE 1949
$27 $81 $360

MARVEL FAMILY #37
JULY 1949
$27 $81 $360

MARVEL FAMILY #38
AUGUST 1949
$27 $81 $360

MARVEL FAMILY #39
SEPTEMBER 1949
$27 $81 $360

MARVEL FAMILY #40
OCTOBER 1949
$27 $81 $360

MARVEL FAMILY #41
NOVEMBER 1949
$25 $75 $340

MARVEL FAMILY #42
DECEMBER 1949
$25 $75 $340

MARVEL FAMILY #43
JANUARY 1950
$25 $75 $340

MARVEL FAMILY #44
FEBRUARY 1950
$25 $75 $340

MARVEL FAMILY #45
MARCH 1950
$25 $75 $340

MARVEL FAMILY #46
APRIL 1950
$25 $75 $340

MARVEL FAMILY #47
MAY 1950
$36 $108 $475

MARVEL FAMILY #48
JUNE 1950
$25 $75 $340

MARVEL FAMILY #49
JULY 1950
$25 $75 $340

MARVEL FAMILY #50
AUGUST 1950
$25 $75 $340

MARVEL FAMILY #51
SEPTEMBER 1950
$24 $72 $320

MARVEL FAMILY #52
OCTOBER 1950
$24 $72 $320

MARVEL FAMILY #53
NOVEMBER 1950
$24 $72 $320

MARVEL FAMILY #54
DECEMBER 1950
$24 $72 $320

MARVEL FAMILY #55
JANUARY 1951
$24 $72 $320

MARVEL FAMILY #56
FEBRUARY 1951
$24 $72 $320

MARVEL FAMILY #57
MARCH 1951
$24 $72 $320

MARVEL FAMILY #58
APRIL 1951
$24 $72 $320

MARVEL FAMILY #59
MAY 1951
$24 $72 $320

MARVEL FAMILY #60
JUNE 1951
$24 $72 $320

MARVEL FAMILY #61
JULY 1951
$24 $72 $320

MARVEL FAMILY #62
AUGUST 1951
$24 $72 $320

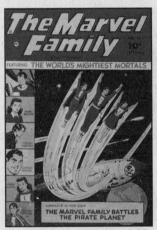

MARVEL FAMILY #63
SEPTEMBER 1951
$24 $72 $320

MARVEL FAMILY #64
OCTOBER 1951
$24 $72 $320

MARVEL FAMILY #65
NOVEMBER 1951
$24 $72 $320

MARVEL FAMILY #66
DECEMBER 1951
$24 $72 $320

MARVEL FAMILY #67
JANUARY 1952
$24 $72 $320

MARVEL FAMILY #68
FEBRUARY 1952
$24 $72 $320

MARVEL FAMILY #69
MARCH 1952
$24 $72 $320

MARVEL FAMILY #70
APRIL 1952
$24 $72 $320

MARVEL FAMILY #71
MAY 1952
$24 $72 $320

MARVEL FAMILY #72
JUNE 1952
$24 $72 $320

MARVEL FAMILY #73
JULY 1952
$24 $72 $320

MARVEL FAMILY #74
AUGUST 1952
$24 $72 $320

MARVEL FAMILY #75
SEPTEMBER 1952
$24 $72 $320

MARVEL FAMILY #76
OCTOBER 1952
$24 $72 $320

MARVEL FAMILY #77
NOVEMBER 1952
$53 $159 $800

MARVEL FAMILY #78
DECEMBER 1952
$27 $81 $370

MARVEL FAMILY #79
JANUARY 1953
$26 $78 $350

MARVEL FAMILY #80
FEBRUARY 1953
$26 $78 $350

MARVEL FAMILY #81
MARCH 1953
$27 $81 $370

MARVEL FAMILY #82
APRIL 1953
$26 $78 $350

MARVEL FAMILY #83
MAY 1953
$26 $78 $350

MARVEL FAMILY #84
JUNE 1953
$26 $78 $350

MARVEL FAMILY #85
JULY 1953
$26 $78 $350

MARVEL FAMILY #86
AUGUST 1953
$26 $78 $350

MARVEL FAMILY #87
SEPTEMBER 1953
$26 $78 $350

MARVEL FAMILY #88
OCTOBER 1953
$26 $78 $350

MARVEL FAMILY #89
JANUARY 1954
$52 $156 $775

MARY MARVEL COMICS #1
DECEMBER 1945
$200 $600 $3100

MARY MARVEL COMICS #2
JUNE 1946
$87 $261 $1350

MARY MARVEL COMICS #3
JULY 1946
$55 $165 $850

MARY MARVEL COMICS #4
AUGUST 1946
$55 $165 $850

MARY MARVEL COMICS #5
SEPTEMBER 1946
$45 $135 $575

MARY MARVEL COMICS #6
OCTOBER 1946
$45 $135 $575

MARY MARVEL COMICS #7
NOVEMBER 1946
$45 $135 $575

MARY MARVEL COMICS #8
DECEMBER 1946
$45 $135 $575

MARY MARVEL COMICS #9
FEBRUARY 1947
$41 $123 $600

MARY MARVEL COMICS #10
MARCH 1947
$41 $123 $600

MARY MARVEL COMICS #11
APRIL 1947
$30 $90 $400

MARY MARVEL COMICS #12
MAY 1947
$30 $90 $400

MARY MARVEL COMICS #13
JUNE 1947
$30 $90 $400

MARY MARVEL COMICS #14
JULY 1947
$30 $90 $400

MARY MARVEL COMICS #15
AUGUST 1947
$30 **$90** **$400**

MARY MARVEL COMICS #16
SEPTEMBER 1947
$30 **$90** **$400**

MARY MARVEL COMICS #17
OCTOBER 1947
$30 **$90** **$400**

MARY MARVEL COMICS #18
NOVEMBER 1947
$30 **$90** **$400**

MARY MARVEL COMICS #19
DECEMBER 1947
$30 **$90** **$400**

MARY MARVEL COMICS #20
JANUARY 1948
$30 **$90** **$400**

MARY MARVEL COMICS #21
FEBRUARY 1948
$27 **$81** **$370**

MARY MARVEL COMICS #22
JULY 1948
$27 **$81** **$370**

MARY MARVEL COMICS #23
JULY 1948
$27 **$81** **$370**

MARY MARVEL COMICS #24
JULY 1948
$27 $81 $370

MARY MARVEL COMICS #25
JUNE 1948
$27 $81 $370

MARY MARVEL COMICS #26
JULY 1948
$27 $81 $370

MARY MARVEL COMICS #27
AUGUST 1948
$27 $81 $370

MARY MARVEL COMICS #28
SEPTEMBER 1948
$27 $81 $370

MASTER COMICS #21
DECEMBER 1941
$1050 $3150 $21,000

MASTER COMICS #22
JANUARY 1942
$865 $2595 $16,000

MASTER COMICS #23
FEBRUARY 1942
$326 $978 $5700

MASTER COMICS #24
MARCH 1942
$152 $456 $2350

MASTER COMICS #25
APRIL 1942
$152 $456 $2350

MASTER COMICS #26
MAY 1942
$148 $444 $2300

MASTER COMICS #27
JUNE 1942
$290 $870 $4500

MASTER COMICS #28
JULY 1942
$148 $444 $2300

MASTER COMICS #29
AUGUST 1942
$400 $1200 $7000

MASTER COMICS #30
SEPTEMBER 1942
$148 $444 $2300

MASTER COMICS #31
OCTOBER 1942
$123 $369 $1900

MASTER COMICS #32
NOVEMBER 1942
$123 $369 $1900

MASTER COMICS #33
DECEMBER 1942
$219 $657 $3400

MASTER COMICS #34
DECEMBER 1942
$206 $618 $3200

MASTER COMICS #35
JANUARY 1943
$123 $369 $1900

MASTER COMICS #36
FEBRUARY 1943
$129 $387 $2000

MASTER COMICS #37
APRIL 1943
$93 $279 $1450

MASTER COMICS #38
MAY 1943
$93 $279 $1450

MASTER COMICS #39
JUNE 1943
$93 $279 $1450

MASTER COMICS #40
JULY 1943
$174 $522 $2700

MASTER COMICS #41
AUGUST 1943
$106 $318 $1650

MASTER COMICS #42
SEPTEMBER 1943
$61 $183 $950

MASTER COMICS #43
OCTOBER 1943
$61 $183 $950

MASTER COMICS #44
NOVEMBER 1943
$61 $183 $950

MASTER COMICS #45
DECEMBER 1943
$61 $183 $950

MASTER COMICS #46
JANUARY 1944
$61 $183 $950

MASTER COMICS #47
FEBRUARY 1944
$71 $213 $1100

MASTER COMICS #48
MARCH 1944
$71 $213 $1100

MASTER COMICS #49
APRIL 1944
$61 $183 $950

MASTER COMICS #50
MAY 1944
$55 $165 $850

MASTER COMICS #51
JUNE 1944
$36 $108 $475

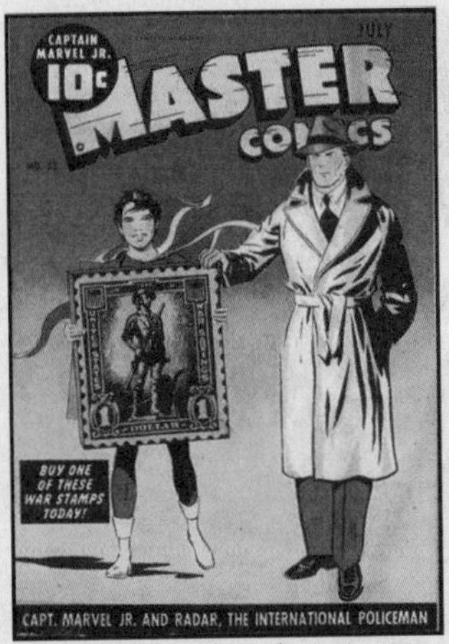
CAPTAIN MARVEL JR.
10¢
MASTER COMICS
JULY
BUY ONE OF THESE WAR STAMPS TODAY!
CAPT. MARVEL JR. AND RADAR, THE INTERNATIONAL POLICEMAN

MASTER COMICS #52
JULY 1944
$36 $108 $475

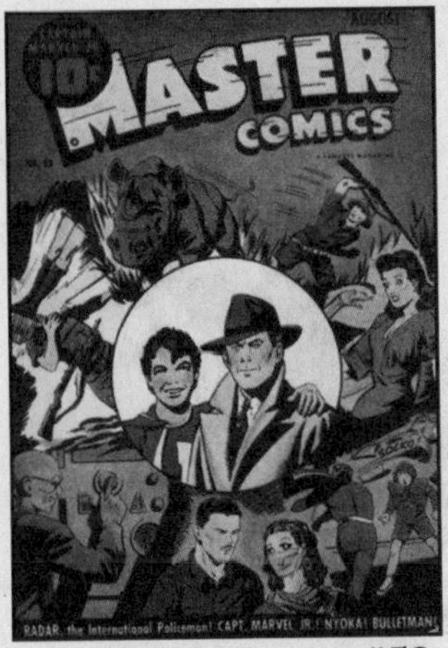
10¢
MASTER COMICS

MASTER COMICS #53
AUGUST 1944
$36 $108 $475

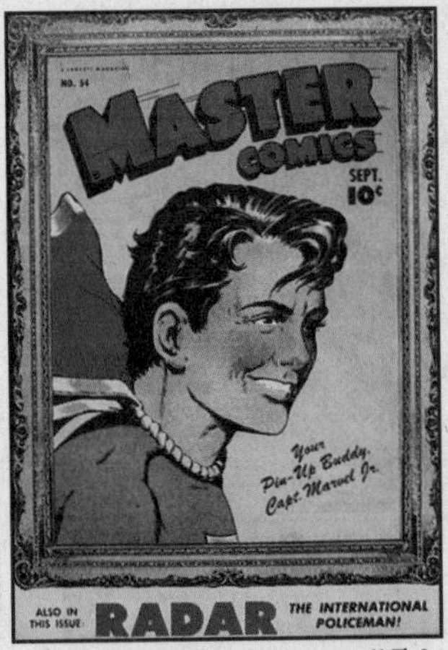
MASTER COMICS
SEPT.
10¢
Your Pin-Up Buddy, Capt. Marvel Jr.
ALSO IN THIS ISSUE
RADAR
THE INTERNATIONAL POLICEMAN!

MASTER COMICS #54
SEPTEMBER 1944
$36 $108 $475

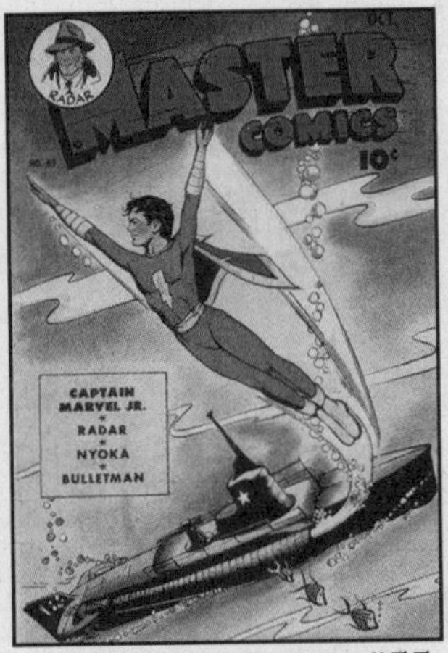
RADAR
MASTER COMICS
10¢
CAPTAIN MARVEL JR.
RADAR
NYOKA
BULLETMAN

MASTER COMICS #55
OCTOBER 1944
$36 $108 $475

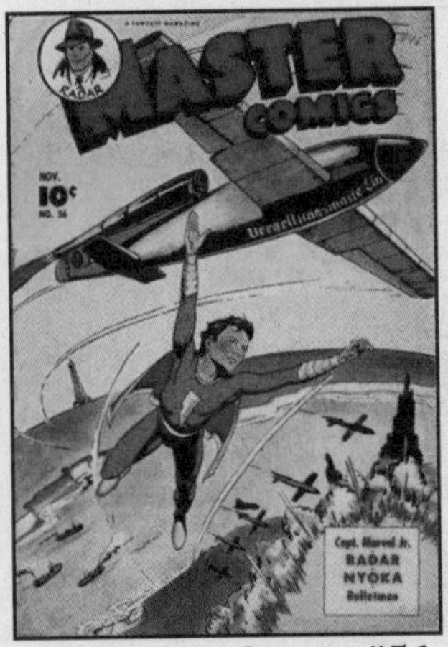
RADAR
MASTER COMICS
NOV.
10¢
Capt. Marvel Jr.
RADAR
NYOKA
Bulletman

MASTER COMICS #56
NOVEMBER 1944
$36 $108 $475

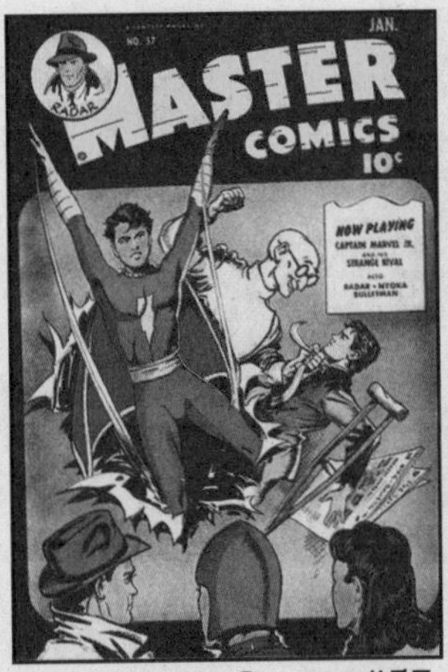
JAN.
RADAR
MASTER COMICS
10¢
NOW PLAYING

MASTER COMICS #57
JANUARY 1945
$36 $108 $475

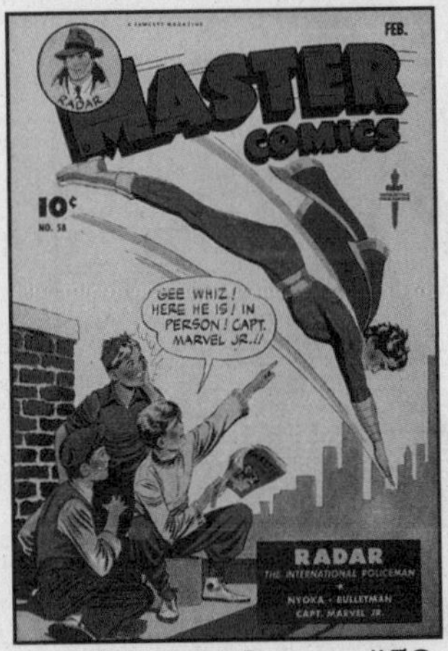
FEB.
RADAR
MASTER COMICS
10¢
GEE WHIZ! HERE HE IS! IN PERSON! CAPT. MARVEL JR.!!
RADAR
THE INTERNATIONAL POLICEMAN
NYOKA · BULLETMAN
CAPT. MARVEL JR.

MASTER COMICS #58
FEBRUARY 1945
$36 $108 $475

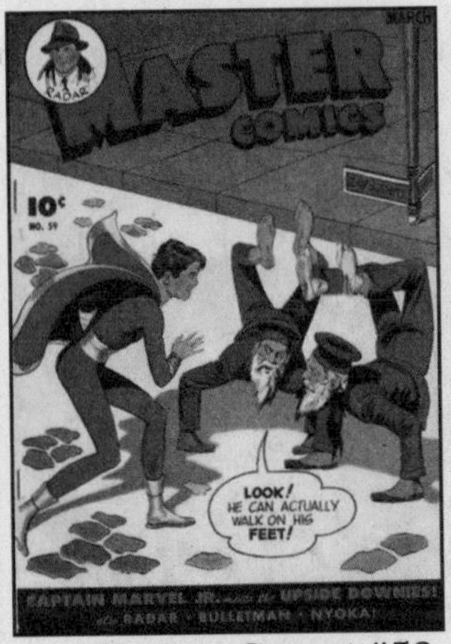
MARCH
RADAR
MASTER COMICS
10¢
LOOK! HE CAN ACTUALLY WALK ON HIS FEET!
CAPTAIN MARVEL JR. meets the UPSIDE DOWNIES!
RADAR · BULLETMAN · NYOKA!

MASTER COMICS #59
MARCH 1945
$37 $111 $500

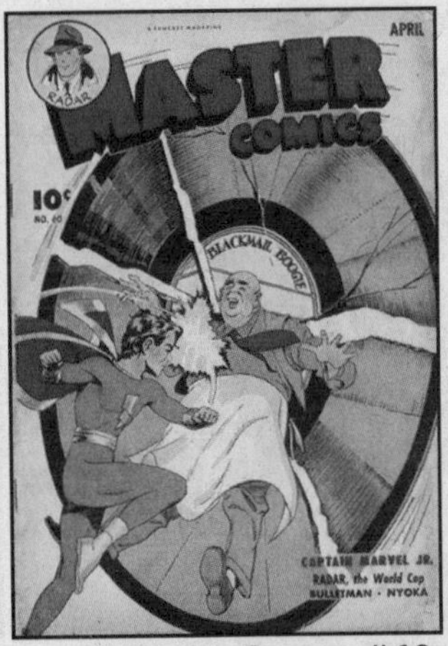
APRIL
RADAR
MASTER COMICS
10¢
CAPTAIN MARVEL JR.
RADAR, the World Cop
BULLETMAN · NYOKA

MASTER COMICS #60
APRIL 1945
$37 $111 $500

MASTER COMICS #61
May 1945
$37 $111 $500

MASTER COMICS #62
July 1945
$37 $111 $500

MASTER COMICS #63
September 1945
$27 $81 $370

MASTER COMICS #64
November 1945
$27 $81 $370

MASTER COMICS #65
January 1946
$27 $81 $370

MASTER COMICS #66
March 1946
$27 $81 $370

MASTER COMICS #67
April 1946
$27 $81 $370

MASTER COMICS #68
May 1946
$$27 $81 $370

MASTER COMICS #69
June 1946
$27 $81 $370

MASTER COMICS #70
JULY 1946
$27 $81 $370

MASTER COMICS #71
AUGUST 1946
$27 $81 $370

MASTER COMICS #72
SEPTEMBER 1946
$27 $81 $370

MASTER COMICS #73
OCTOBER 1946
$27 $81 $370

MASTER COMICS #74
NOVEMBER 1946
$27 $81 $370

MASTER COMICS #75
DECEMBER 1946
$27 $81 $370

MASTER COMICS #76
FEBRUARY 1947
$27 $81 $370

MASTER COMICS #77
MARCH 1947
$27 $81 $370

MASTER COMICS #78
APRIL 1947
$27 $81 $370

MASTER COMICS #79
MAY 1947
$27 **$81** **$370**

MASTER COMICS #80
JUNE 1947
$27 **$81** **$370**

MASTER COMICS #81
JULY 1947
$24 **$72** **$325**

MASTER COMICS #82
AUGUST 1947
$25 **$75** **$340**

MASTER COMICS #83
SEPTEMBER 1947
$24 **$72** **$325**

MASTER COMICS #84
OCTOBER 1947
$24 **$72** **$325**

MASTER COMICS #85
NOVEMBER 1947
$24 **$72** **$325**

MASTER COMICS #86
DECEMBER 1947
$24 **$72** **$325**

MASTER COMICS #87
JANUARY 1948
$24 **$72** **$325**

MASTER COMICS #88
FEBRUARY 1948
$25 $75 $340

MASTER COMICS #89
MARCH 1948
$24 $72 $325

MASTER COMICS #90
APRIL 1948
$24 $72 $325

MASTER COMICS #91
MAY 1948
$24 $72 $325

MASTER COMICS #92
JUNE 1948
$25 $75 $340

MASTER COMICS #93
JULY 1948
$25 $75 $340

MASTER COMICS #94
AUGUST 1948
$25 $75 $340

MASTER COMICS #95
SEPTEMBER 1948
$24 $72 $325

MASTER COMICS #96
OCTOBER 1948
$24 $72 $325

MASTER COMICS #97
NOVEMBER 1948
$24 $72 $325

MASTER COMICS #98
DECEMBER 1948
$24 $72 $325

MASTER COMICS #99
JANUARY 1949
$24 $72 $325

MASTER COMICS #100
FEBRUARY 1949
$28 $84 $380

MASTER COMICS #101
MARCH 1949
$24 $72 $320

MASTER COMICS #102
APRIL 1949
$24 $72 $320

MASTER COMICS #103
MAY 1949
$24 $72 $320

MASTER COMICS #104
JUNE 1949
$24 $72 $320

MASTER COMICS #105
JULY 1949
$24 $72 $320

MASTER COMICS #106
AUGUST 1949
$24 $72 $320

MASTER COMICS #107
SEPTEMBER 1949
$22 $66 $300

MASTER COMICS #108
OCTOBER 1949
$22 $66 $300

MASTER COMICS #109
NOVEMBER 1949
$22 $66 $300

MASTER COMICS #110
DECEMBER 1949
$22 $66 $300

MASTER COMICS #111
JANUARY 1950
$22 $66 $300

MASTER COMICS #112
FEBRUARY 1950
$22 $66 $300

MASTER COMICS #113
MARCH 1950
$22 $66 $300

MASTER COMICS #114
APRIL 1950
$22 $66 $300

MASTER COMICS #115
MAY 1950
$22 **$66** **$300**

MASTER COMICS #116
JUNE 1950
$22 **$66** **$300**

MASTER COMICS #117
JULY 1950
$22 **$66** **$300**

MASTER COMICS #118
OCTOBER 1950
$22 **$66** **$300**

MASTER COMICS #119
DECEMBER 1950
$22 **$66** **$300**

MASTER COMICS #120
FEBRUARY 1951
$22 **$66** **$300**

MASTER COMICS #121
APRIL 1951
$24 **$72** **$330**

MASTER COMICS #122
JUNE 1951
$24 **$72** **$330**

MASTER COMICS #123
AUGUST 1951
$24 **$72** **$330**

MASTER COMICS #124
OCTOBER 1951
$24 $72 $330

MASTER COMICS #125
DECEMBER 1951
$24 $72 $330

MASTER COMICS #126
FEBRUARY 1952
$24 $72 $330

MASTER COMICS #127
APRIL 1952
$24 $72 $330

MASTER COMICS #128
JUNE 1952
$24 $72 $330

MASTER COMICS #129
AUGUST 1952
$24 $72 $330

MASTER COMICS #130
OCTOBER 1952
$24 $72 $330

MASTER COMICS #131
DECEMBER 1952
$24 $72 $330

MASTER COMICS #132
FEBRUARY 1952
$26 $78 $350

MASTER COMICS #133
APRIL 1952
$34 $102 $450

SPECIAL EDITION COMICS #1
AUGUST 1940
$1000 $3000 $20,000

THRILL COMICS ASHCAN
JANUARY 1940
SEE FLASH COMICS

WHIZ COMICS #2 (#1)
FEBRUARY 1940
$39,600 $118,800 $475,000

WHIZ COMICS #3 (#2)
MARCH 1940
$1200 $3600 $24,000

WHIZ COMICS #4 (#3)
APRIL 1940
$530 $1590 $9800

WHIZ COMICS #4
MAY 1940
$423 $1269 $7800

WHIZ COMICS #5
JUNE 1940
$389 $1167 $6800

WHIZ COMICS #6
JULY 1940
$297 $891 $4600

WHIZ COMICS #7
AUGUST 1940
$297 $891 $4600

WHIZ COMICS #8
SEPTEMBER 1940
$297 $891 $4600

WHIZ COMICS #9
OCTOBER 1940
$297 $891 $4600

WHIZ COMICS #10
NOVEMBER 1940
$297 $891 $4600

WHIZ COMICS #11
DECEMBER 1940
$219 $657 $3400

WHIZ COMICS #12
JANUARY 1941
$219 $657 $3400

WHIZ COMICS #13
FEBRUARY 1941
$219 $657 $3400

WHIZ COMICS #14
MARCH 1941
$219 $657 $3400

WHIZ COMICS #15
MARCH 1941
$219 $657 $3400

WHIZ COMICS #16
APRIL 1941
$245 **$735** **$3800**

WHIZ COMICS #17
MAY 1941
$245 **$735** **$3800**

WHIZ COMICS #18
JUNE 1941
$245 **$735** **$3800**

WHIZ COMICS #19
JULY 1941
$239 **$717** **$3700**

WHIZ COMICS #20
AUGUST 1941
$142 **$426** **$2200**

WHIZ COMICS #21
SEPTEMBER 1941
$155 **$465** **$2400**

WHIZ COMICS #22
OCTOBER 1941
$116 **$348** **$1800**

WHIZ COMICS #23
NOVEMBER 1941
$116 **$348** **$1800**

WHIZ COMICS #24
NOVEMBER 1941
$116 **$348** **$1800**

WHIZ COMICS #25
DECEMBER 1941
$1000 $3000 $18,500

WHIZ COMICS #26
JANUARY 1942
$77 $231 $1200

WHIZ COMICS #27
FEBRUARY 1942
$77 $231 $1200

WHIZ COMICS #28
MARCH 1942
$77 $231 $1200

WHIZ COMICS #29
APRIL 1942
$77 $231 $1200

WHIZ COMICS #30
MAY 1942
$77 $231 $1200

WHIZ COMICS #31
JUNE 1942
$66 $198 $1025

WHIZ COMICS #32
JULY 1942
$66 $198 $1025

WHIZ COMICS #33
AUGUST 1942
$87 $261 $1350

WHIZ COMICS #34
SEPTEMBER 1942
$53 $159 $800

WHIZ COMICS #35
OCTOBER 1942
$74 $222 $1150

WHIZ COMICS #36
OCTOBER 1942
$53 $159 $800

WHIZ COMICS #37
NOVEMBER 1942
$53 $159 $800

WHIZ COMICS #38
DECEMBER 1942
$53 $159 $800

WHIZ COMICS #39
JANUARY 1943
$53 $159 $800

WHIZ COMICS #40
FEBRUARY 1943
$53 $159 $800

WHIZ COMICS #41
APRIL 1943
$43 $129 $650

WHIZ COMICS #42
MAY 1943
$43 $129 $650

WHIZ COMICS #43
JUNE 1943
$43 **$129** **$650**

WHIZ COMICS #44
JULY 1943
$43 **$129** **$650**

WHIZ COMICS #45
AUGUST 1943
$43 **$129** **$650**

WHIZ COMICS #46
SEPTEMBER 1943
$43 **$129** **$650**

WHIZ COMICS #47
OCTOBER 1943
$43 **$129** **$650**

WHIZ COMICS #48
NOVEMBER 1943
$43 **$129** **$650**

WHIZ COMICS #49
DECEMBER 1943
$43 **$129** **$650**

WHIZ COMICS #50
JANUARY 1944
$43 **$129** **$650**

WHIZ COMICS #51
FEBRUARY 1944
$37 **$111** **$500**

WHIZ COMICS #52
MARCH 1944
$37 $111 $500

WHIZ COMICS #53
APRIL 1944
$37 $111 $500

WHIZ COMICS #54
MAY 1944
$37 $111 $500

WHIZ COMICS #55
JUNE 1944
$37 $111 $500

WHIZ COMICS #56
JULY 1944
$37 $111 $500

WHIZ COMICS #57
AUGUST 1944
$37 $111 $500

WHIZ COMICS #58
SEPTEMBER 1944
$37 $111 $500

WHIZ COMICS #59
OCTOBER 1944
$37 $111 $500

WHIZ COMICS #60
NOVEMBER 1944
$37 $111 $500

WHIZ COMICS #61
JANUARY 1945
$36 $108 $480

WHIZ COMICS #62
FEBRUARY 1945
$36 $108 $480

WHIZ COMICS #63
MARCH 1945
$36 $108 $480

WHIZ COMICS #64
APRIL 1945
$36 $108 $480

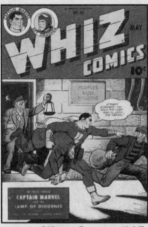

WHIZ COMICS #65
MAY 1945
$36 $108 $480

WHIZ COMICS #66
JULY 1945
$36 $108 $480

WHIZ COMICS #67
SEPTEMBER 1945
$36 $108 $480

WHIZ COMICS #68
NOVEMBER 1945
$36 $108 $480

WHIZ COMICS #69
DECEMBER 1945
$36 $108 $480

WHIZ COMICS #70
JANUARY 1946
$36 $108 $480

WHIZ COMICS #71
FEBRUARY 1946
$33 $99 $440

WHIZ COMICS #72
MARCH 1946
$36 $108 $480

WHIZ COMICS #73
APRIL 1946
$36 $108 $480

WHIZ COMICS #74
MAY 1946
$36 $108 $480

WHIZ COMICS #75
JUNE 1946
$36 $108 $480

WHIZ COMICS #76
JULY 1946
$36 $108 $480

WHIZ COMICS #77
AUGUST 1946
$33 $99 $440

WHIZ COMICS #78
SEPTEMBER 1946
$33 $99 $440

WHIZ COMICS #79
OCTOBER 1946
$33 $99 $440

WHIZ COMICS #80
NOVEMBER 1946
$33 $99 $440

WHIZ COMICS #81
DECEMBER 1946
$33 $99 $440

WHIZ COMICS #82
FEBRUARY 1947
$33 $99 $440

WHIZ COMICS #83
MARCH 1947
$33 $99 $440

WHIZ COMICS #84
APRIL 1947
$33 $99 $440

WHIZ COMICS #85
MAY 1947
$33 $99 $440

WHIZ COMICS #86
JUNE 1947
$41 $123 $600

WHIZ COMICS #87
JULY 1947
$33 $99 $440

WHIZ COMICS #88
AUGUST 1947
$33 **$99** **$440**

WHIZ COMICS #89
SEPTEMBER 1947
$33 **$99** **$440**

WHIZ COMICS #90
OCTOBER 1947
$33 **$99** **$440**

WHIZ COMICS #91
NOVEMBER 1947
$33 **$99** **$440**

WHIZ COMICS #92
DECEMBER 1947
$33 **$99** **$440**

WHIZ COMICS #93
JANUARY 1948
$33 **$99** **$440**

WHIZ COMICS #94
FEBRUARY 1948
$33 **$99** **$440**

WHIZ COMICS #95
MARCH 1948
$33 **$99** **$440**

WHIZ COMICS #96
APRIL 1948
$33 **$99** **$440**

WHIZ COMICS #97
MAY 1948
$33 $99 $440

WHIZ COMICS #98
JUNE 1948
$33 $99 $440

WHIZ COMICS #99
JULY 1948
$33 $99 $440

WHIZ COMICS #100
AUGUST 1948
$43 $129 $650

WHIZ COMICS #101
SEPTEMBER 1948
$34 $102 $460

WHIZ COMICS #102
OCTOBER 1948
$34 $102 $460

WHIZ COMICS #103
NOVEMBER 1948
$34 $102 $460

WHIZ COMICS #104
DECEMBER 1948
$34 $102 $460

WHIZ COMICS #105
JANUARY 1949
$34 $102 $460

WHIZ COMICS #106
FEBRUARY 1949
$34 $102 $460

WHIZ COMICS #107
MARCH 1949
$35 $105 $470

WHIZ COMICS #108
APRIL 1949
$35 $105 $470

WHIZ COMICS #109
MAY 1949
$35 $105 $470

WHIZ COMICS #110
JUNE 1949
$35 $105 $470

WHIZ COMICS #111
JULY 1949
$35 $105 $470

WHIZ COMICS #112
AUGUST 1949
$35 $105 $470

WHIZ COMICS #113
SEPTEMBER 1949
$35 $105 $470

WHIZ COMICS #114
OCTOBER 1949
$35 $105 $470

WHIZ COMICS #115
NOVEMBER 1949
$35 $105 $470

WHIZ COMICS #116
DECEMBER 1949
$35 $105 $470

WHIZ COMICS #117
JANUARY 1950
$35 $105 $470

WHIZ COMICS #118
FEBRUARY 1950
$35 $105 $470

WHIZ COMICS #119
MARCH 1950
$35 $105 $470

WHIZ COMICS #120
APRIL 1950
$35 $105 $470

WHIZ COMICS #121
MAY 1950
$35 $105 $470

WHIZ COMICS #122
JUNE 1950
$35 $105 $470

WHIZ COMICS #123
JULY 1950
$35 $105 $470

WHIZ COMICS #124
AUGUST 1950
$35 $105 $470

WHIZ COMICS #125
SEPTEMBER 1950
$35 $105 $470

WHIZ COMICS #126
OCTOBER 1950
$35 $105 $470

WHIZ COMICS #127
NOVEMBER 1950
$35 $105 $470

WHIZ COMICS #128
DECEMBER 1950
$35 $105 $470

WHIZ COMICS #129
JANUARY 1951
$35 $105 $470

WHIZ COMICS #130
FEBRUARY 1951
$35 $105 $470

WHIZ COMICS #131
MARCH 1951
$35 $105 $470

WHIZ COMICS #132
APRIL 1951
$35 $105 $470

WHIZ COMICS #133
MAY 1951
$35 $105 $470

WHIZ COMICS #134
JUNE 1951
$35 $105 $470

WHIZ COMICS #135
JULY 1951
$35 $105 $470

WHIZ COMICS #136
AUGUST 1951
$35 $105 $470

WHIZ COMICS #137
SEPTEMBER 1951
$35 $105 $470

WHIZ COMICS #138
OCTOBER 1951
$35 $105 $470

WHIZ COMICS #139
NOVEMBER 1951
$35 $105 $470

WHIZ COMICS #140
DECEMBER 1951
$35 $105 $470

WHIZ COMICS #141
JANUARY 1952
$35 $105 $470

Whiz Comics #142
February 1952
$35 $105 $470

Whiz Comics #143
March 1952
$35 $105 $470

Whiz Comics #144
April 1952
$35 $105 $470

Whiz Comics #145
May 1952
$35 $105 $470

Whiz Comics #146
June 1952
$35 $105 $470

Whiz Comics #147
July 1952
$35 $105 $470

Whiz Comics #148
August 1952
$35 $105 $470

Whiz Comics #149
September 1952
$35 $105 $470

Whiz Comics #150
October 1952
$43 $129 $650

WHIZ COMICS #151
NOVEMBER 1952
$43 $129 $650

WHIZ COMICS #152
DECEMBER 1952
$43 $129 $650

WHIZ COMICS #153
JANUARY 1953
$61 $183 $950

WHIZ COMICS #154
APRIL 1953
$61 $183 $950

WHIZ COMICS #155
JUNE 1953
$61 $183 $950

WOW COMICS #9
JANUARY 1943
$326 $978 $5700

WOW COMICS #10
FEBRUARY 1943
$300 $900 $5000

WOW COMICS #11
MARCH 1943
$65 $195 $1000

WOW COMICS #12
APRIL 1943
$65 $195 $1000

WOW COMICS #13
MAY 1943
$65 $195 $1000

WOW COMICS #14
JUNE 1943
$65 $195 $1000

WOW COMICS #15
JULY 1943
$65 $195 $1000

WOW COMICS #16
AUGUST 1943
$65 $195 $1000

WOW COMICS #17
SEPTEMBER 1943
$65 $195 $1000

WOW COMICS #18
OCTOBER 1943
$84 $252 $1300

WOW COMICS #19
NOVEMBER 1943
$65 $195 $1000

WOW COMICS #20
DECEMBER 1943
$65 $195 $1000

WOW COMICS #21
JANUARY 1944
$43 $129 $650

WOW COMICS #22
FEBRUARY 1944
$43 **$129** **$650**

WOW COMICS #23
MARCH 1944
$43 **$129** **$650**

WOW COMICS #24
APRIL 1944
$43 **$129** **$650**

WOW COMICS #25
MAY 1944
$43 **$129** **$650**

WOW COMICS #26
JUNE 1944
$43 **$129** **$650**

WOW COMICS #27
JULY 1944
$43 **$129** **$650**

WOW COMICS #28
AUGUST 1944
$43 **$129** **$650**

WOW COMICS #29
SEPTEMBER 1944
$43 **$129** **$650**

WOW COMICS #30
OCTOBER 1944
$43 **$129** **$650**

WOW COMICS #31
NOVEMBER 1944
$34 $102 $450

WOW COMICS #32
JANUARY 1945
$34 $102 $450

WOW COMICS #33
FEBRUARY 1945
$34 $102 $450

WOW COMICS #34
MARCH 1945
$34 $102 $450

WOW COMICS #35
APRIL 1945
$34 $102 $450

WOW COMICS #36
MAY 1945
$34 $102 $450

WOW COMICS #37
JULY 1945
$34 $102 $450

WOW COMICS #38
SEPTEMBER 1945
$34 $102 $450

WOW COMICS #39
NOVEMBER 1945
$34 $102 $450

WOW COMICS #40
JANAURY 1946
$34 $102 $450

WOW COMICS #41
FEBRUARY 1946
$31 $93 $410

WOW COMICS #42
APRIL 1946
$31 $93 $410

WOW COMICS #43
MAY 1946
$31 $93 $410

WOW COMICS #44
JUNE 1946
$31 $93 $410

WOW COMICS #45
JULY 1946
$31 $93 $410

WOW COMICS #46
AUGUST 1946
$31 $93 $410

WOW COMICS #47
SEPTEMBER 1946
$31 $93 $410

WOW COMICS #48
OCTOBER 1946
$31 $93 $410

WOW COMICS #49
NOVEMBER 1946
$31 $93 $410

WOW COMICS #50
DECEMBER 1946
$31 $93 $410

WOW COMICS #51
FEBRUARY 1947
$28 $84 $380

WOW COMICS #52
MARCH 1947
$28 $84 $380

WOW COMICS #53
APRIL 1947
$28 $84 $380

WOW COMICS #54
MAY 1947
$28 $84 $380

WOW COMICS #55
JUNE 1947
$28 $84 $380

WOW COMICS #56
JULY 1947
$28 $84 $380

WOW COMICS #57
AUGUST 1947
$28 $84 $380

WOW COMICS #58
SEPTEMBER 1947
$28 $84 $380

XMAS COMICS #1
DECEMBER 1941
$514 $1542 $9500

XMAS COMICS #2
DECEMBER 1942
$239 $717 $3700

XMAS COMICS #7
DECEMBER 1947
$103 $309 $1600

XMAS COMICS #4
SECOND SERIES • DECEMBER 1949
$148 $444 $2300

XMAS COMICS #5
SECOND SERIES • DECEMBER 1950
$116 $348 $1800

XMAS COMICS #6
SECOND SERIES • DECEMBER 1951
$116 $348 $1800

XMAS COMICS #7
SECOND SERIES • DECEMBER 1952
$116 $348 $1800

Fawcett #1 issues with an endorsement visit by Captain Marvel.

What better way to introduce a new title or new character than with an introduction by The World's Mightiest Mortal.

Military men, a cowboy, an adventurer, funny animals and puppets were all welcomed to the Fawcett roster by the company linchpin, promising that fun and adventure lie within the comic pages.

CAPTAIN MIDNIGHT #1
SEPTEMBER 1942
$349 $1047 $6100

DON WINSLOW OF THE NAVY #1
FEBRUARY 1943
$142 $426 $2200

FAWCETT'S FUNNY ANIMALS #1
DECEMBER 1942
$71 $213 $1100

GEORGE PAL'S PUPPETOONS #1
DECEMBER 1945
$52 $156 $775

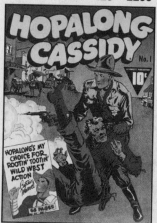

HOPALONG CASSIDY #1
FEBRUARY 1943
$200 $600 $3100

LANCE O'CASEY #1
SPRING 1946
$36 $108 $475

MASTER COMICS #50
MAY 1944
$55 $165 $850

WITH HOPPY THE MARVEL BUNNY **ANIMAL FAIR #1**
MARCH 1946
$36 $108 $475

OVERSTREET
ACCESS

Price your comics with Overstreet's proven value pricing system

On Overstreet Access, you can...

- Create Collections!
- Create Boxes Within Collections!
- View and Organize Your Collections!
- Import and Export Collections!
- Want List!
- Gap List!
- Find Retailers!

Here's what you get:

- Expanded Overstreet® Prices!
- Superior Collection Management Tools!
- Cover Scanning in the App!
- Import/Export Tools!
- 190,000 Variants Added!

Want to get 15% off an Annual membership to Overstreet Access?

Use this code to get 15% off Bronze, Silver, or Gold Annual Membership for Overstreet Access!

LOST24

Coupon expires December 31, 2024

Visit OverstreetAccess.com for more info

Mr. Mind and the Monster Society of Evil

Although he also illustrated the adventures of other characters, the late, great artist Charles Clarence (C.C.) Beck (June 8, 1910 – November 22, 1989) is best known for drawing Captain Marvel. He contributed this piece to The Overstreet Comic Book Price Guide #15 *(1985).*

"I was hooked as a youth," said Bernie McCarty, sports columnist, publisher, and longtime fan of comic books. He went on to say, in issue 5 of *Fawcett Collectors of America/Some Opinionated Bastards:*

Charles Clarence (C.C.) Beck
Photo by Jackie Estrada

"The most deliciously exciting moment of my youthful comic book reading career occurred in the spring of 1943 when I opened my copy of *Captain Marvel Adventures* #22 and saw a drawing of a movie screen at a kids' matinee. After all these years I remember the wording on the screen: 'A thrilling new serial, The Monster Society of Evil, starring Captain Marvel.'"

The serial which starred "the World's mightiest mortal" and featured "the World's wickedest worm" ran for two years and was an example of the kind of material in Fawcett's Captain Marvel stories which made them outstanding successes during the Golden Age of comics. Almost everyone today from the age of eight to about 80 has heard of Captain Marvel, the red-clad hero who was really Billy Batson, Boy Radio Reporter, in his off moments. Captain Marvel was not a full-grown man who had to put on or strip off a disguise before swinging into action as all the other characters of the day had to – he was a boy who changed to a mighty hero when danger threatened.

It was Billy Batson who usually got into trouble in the Fawcett stories, not Captain Marvel, although the "Big Red Cheese," as he was sometimes called, also found himself in some embarrassing situations now and then, too, for another feature of his per-

sonality which distinguished him from other heroes of the day was that he was vulnerable – and as a result, often very, very funny!

For example, in one installment of the serial Captain Marvel found himself being tickled into helplessness by the worm, Mr. Mind, who had crawled under his uniform. This sort of thing could never have happened to any other hero of the day, needless to say. They were all stern, godlike creatures who, when they weren't battling whole armies of enemies, were wont to stand around looking noble and heroic.

Each chapter of the serial ended with a cliffhanger, just as did the real movie serials of the old days. When Captain Marvel himself wasn't left hanging in deadly peril, Billy Batson was, or Mr. Mind was, or The Fate of the World was. Billy found himself frozen in ice, wrapped in a cocoon, in a cannibals' stew pot; in one installment Mr. Mind was dropped on his head and turned goody-goody as he suffered amnesia. What a horrible fate for a villain that was!

Although almost everyone today has heard of Captain Marvel, only those who grew up reading his stories in the '40s really understand his appeal. Captain Marvel was the reader himself – a 14-year-old boy who could change to a powerful adult when necessary. When his adult form was no longer needed, he could change back to a boy again by saying the magic word, Shazam. How many now middled aged men and women secretly whispered the magic word to themselves in those days, hoping that it would turn them into adults? And how many now find that they can almost turn back into children again by uttering the mystic word of power? One who does is Tom Long, artist, writer, and comics fan who says:

"Whenever I need to escape the mundane present,

CAPTAIN MARVEL ADVENTURES PRESENTS
THAT THRILLING SERIAL

MONSTER SOCIETY of EVIL

STARRING

CAPTAIN MARVEL

— CHAPTER 25 —

THE END OF MR. MIND!

CAST OF CHARACTERS

CAST OF CHARACTERS

MR. MIND — EVIL WORM MASTER-
MIND WHO FOR TWO YEARS HAS
ATTEMPTED TO CRUSH
CIVILIZATION!

CAPT. MARVEL — WORLD'S
MIGHTIEST MORTAL, WHO MUST
USE EVERY OUNCE OF HIS
POWERS TO STOP MR. MIND'S
HIDEOUS PLOTS!

UNDERSEA KINGD...
MIND ESCAPES IN...
...ING MEMBERS OF...

...ME NIGHT SET FOR...

BR...
THE PE...

WELL, WELL! IMAGINE MEETING YOU HERE, CAPTAIN MARVEL! HEH! HEH! HEH!

CAPT. MARVEL
IN
"BATTLE AT THE CHINA WALL"
68 PAGES IN FULL COLOR!

NOVEMBER

NO. 29

10¢

...E'S DEFEATED
...E AIR! HE'S WRECKED
...LABORATORIES!
...E TO GO TO NOW!
...SES!

...LL IS LOST!
THIS IS
THE END!

THERE! HE'S
STRAPPED
FIRMLY!

...DAILY VOICE
...R MIND DIES TO-
...HT AT ELEVEN

TICK! TICK!

...CONDS

I simply step into my library, pull out some of my old *Captain Marvel* comics, and – Shazam! Boom! It still works!"

Trina Robbins and many other cartoonists, including the late Don Newton, grew up reading Captain Marvel stories. Nelson Bridwell, Jim Steranko, and Alex Toth were fans of the Big Red Cheese. (The reader must not try to figure out the ages of these people; some of them may have first met the World's Mightiest Mortal when they picked up an old *Whiz* or *Captain Marvel Adventures* at a comic convention years after the magazines had disappeared from the stands.)

The late Otto binder, science fiction author and expert on space travel, explained the unique appeal of the serial in this way:

"I've always been amazed at the popularity of Mr. Mind. The volume of mail from the readers was enormous! The only way I can figure it out is that Mr. Mind was a surprising contrast to all the other villains – always big, brawny, devilish hulks – so that a tiny miserable worm, filled with more hate than all the other villains combined, simply tickled the readers' fancies."

Otto and the other scripters of Fawcett comics were mature, professional writers – not teenage cartoonists just out of high school or fumble-fingered typists assigned to supply words for lettering men to insert in drawings made by hack artists more used to doing retouching and pasteup work than to illustrating. Otto knew that great stories are not built around great heroes, but around great villains. Mr. Mind was one of the greatest.

The little worm, who had no arms nor legs, and whose voice was so weak that he had to speak through an amplifier hung around his neck, enlisted other villains in his Monster Society of Evil. In addition to various cartoon villains, he had Adolf Hitler and his Nazi henchmen helping him and three villainous Japanese scientists named Doctors Smashi, Hashi, and Peeyu performing at his bidding. (Nazis, we all knew in those days, were unable to function without strong, evil leaders.)

As horrible and monstrous as were the villains and their machinations in the serial, readers were never frightened by them any more than Billy or Captain Marvel were. The readers knew that it was all make believe and that everything would come out all right – if not in the next chapter or two, eventu-

ally. This was another feature that distinguished Captain Marvel stories from others; there was no attempt to horrify and brainwash the readers by showing ghouls, demented psychopathic murderers, sex-crazed drug addicts, and child molesters in stories for children. Neither was there an attempt to create heroes so insufferably noble and eternally indestructible that they became boring after a few issues. Captain Marvel and Mr. Mind kept things going for over two exciting, breathtaking years!

While Otto wrote all 25 chapters of The Monster Society of Evil, many different artists worked on the drawings. World War II was going on at the time and artists were leaving their drawing boards and entering the armed services in droves. It is almost impossible at this late date to identify just who did what in the drawings, as everything in those days was done anonymously. Some of the panels, as we can see when we look back at them today, were quite poorly drawn, it must be admitted. Once an artist (who shall remain unnamed) drew a Mr. Mind the size of a watermelon! His excuse? "He's so little nobody can see him, so I drew him bigger."

The cartoonists and writers of the '40s have been accused of warping the minds of their youthful readers. It is true that much of the male chauvinism, the superpatriotic Americanism, and the degrading treatment of minorities that was displayed in comics of nearly a half-century ago would not be acceptable today. Why? Because it would be too tame today. Today we have much more horrible things to show in our comics and on our television screens.

But humor, gentle and directed at our hero, not at others, we don't have. Silly, impossible situations drawn in cartoon style we don't have. Above all, we don't have grand villains like Hitler and his cohorts to pick on with impunity!

And no more worm villains, of course. Today, Mr. Mind would probably be declared an endangered species and we'd have pickets protesting and marching outside if we put him in an electric chair and fried him as we did in chapter 25 of the Monster Society of Evil serial back in the days when comics were comic, and everybody loved them.

Those were the days!

– C.C. Beck

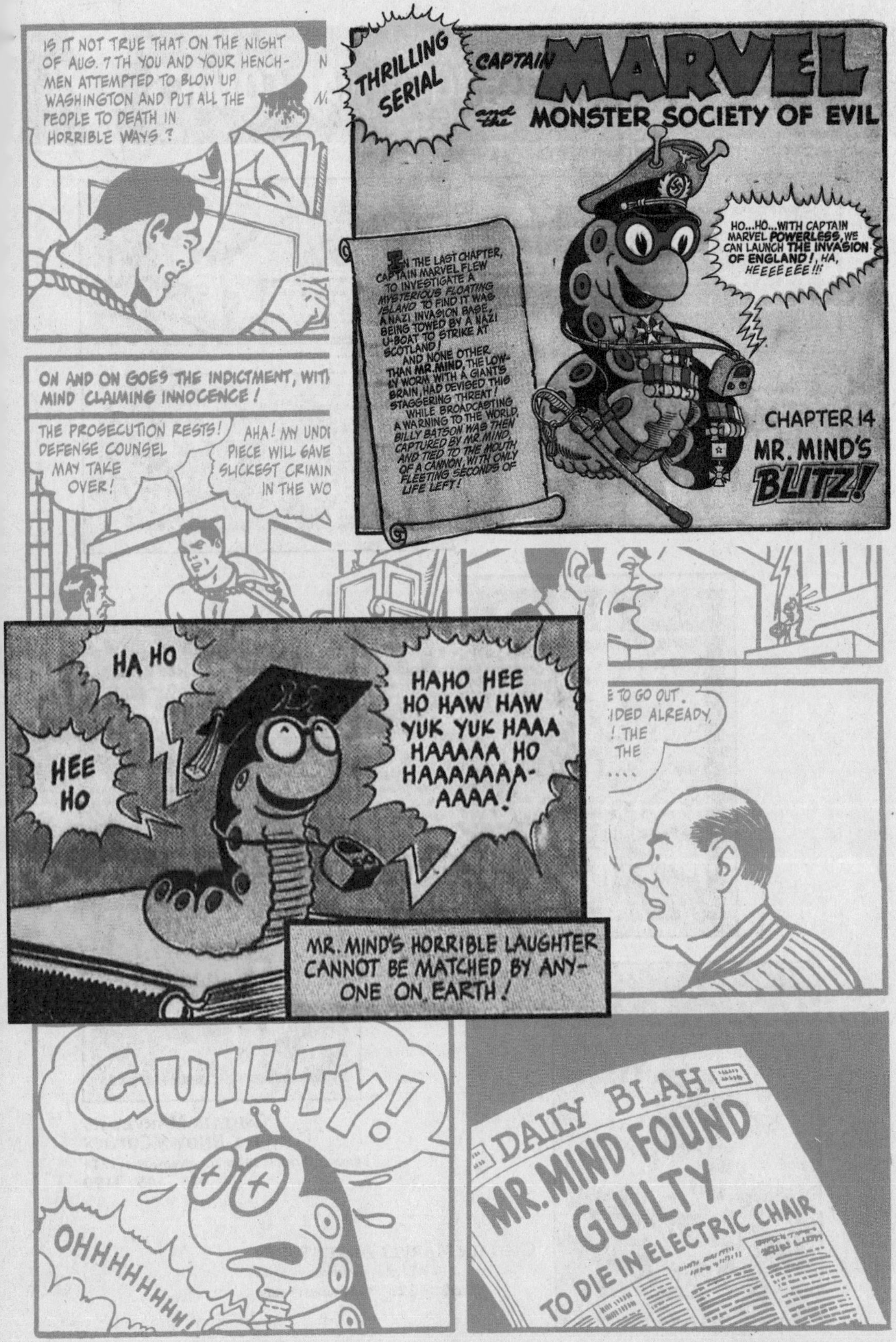

IS IT NOT TRUE THAT ON THE NIGHT OF AUG. 7TH YOU AND YOUR HENCHMEN ATTEMPTED TO BLOW UP WASHINGTON AND PUT ALL THE PEOPLE TO DEATH IN HORRIBLE WAYS ?
THRILLING SERIAL
CAPTAIN MARVEL and the MONSTER SOCIETY OF EVIL
IN THE LAST CHAPTER, CAPTAIN MARVEL FLEW TO INVESTIGATE A MYSTERIOUS FLOATING ISLAND TO FIND IT WAS A NAZI INVASION BASE, BEING TOWED BY A NAZI U-BOAT TO STRIKE AT SCOTLAND! AND NONE OTHER THAN MR. MIND, THE LOWLY WORM WITH A GIANTS BRAIN, HAD DEVISED THIS STAGGERING THREAT! WHILE BROADCASTING A WARNING TO THE WORLD, BILLY BATSON WAS THEN CAPTURED BY MR. MIND AND TIED TO THE MOUTH OF A CANNON, WITH ONLY FLEETING SECONDS OF LIFE LEFT!
HO...HO...WITH CAPTAIN MARVEL POWERLESS, WE CAN LAUNCH THE INVASION OF ENGLAND! HA, HEEEEEEE!!!
CHAPTER 14
MR. MIND'S BLITZ!
ON AND ON GOES THE INDICTMENT, WITH MIND CLAIMING INNOCENCE!
THE PROSECUTION RESTS! DEFENSE COUNSEL MAY TAKE OVER!
HA HO
HEE HO
HAHO HEE HO HAW HAW YUK YUK HAAA HAAAAA HO HAAAAAAA-AAAA!
MR. MIND'S HORRIBLE LAUGHTER CANNOT BE MATCHED BY ANYONE ON EARTH!
GUILTY!
OHHHHHHH!
DAILY BLAH
MR. MIND FOUND GUILTY
TO DIE IN ELECTRIC CHAIR

**CAPTAIN MARVEL ADVENTURES
BOND BREAD GIVEAWAYS**
1948 - 1950
$27 $81 $365

**CAPTAIN MARVEL ADVENTURES
WELL KNOWN COMICS**
Bestmaid/Samuel Lowe Co. giveaway • 1944
$20 $60 $260

**CAPTAIN MARVEL JR.
WELL KNOWN COMICS**
Bestmaid/Samuel Lowe Co. giveaway • 1944
$15 $45 $190

CAPTAIN MARVEL ADVENTURES
Wheaties giveaway • 1944
$65 $325 **NM DOESN'T EXIST**

**CAPTAIN MARVEL AND
THE LTS. OF SAFETY #1**
1950
$41 **$123** **$600**

**CAPTAIN MARVEL AND
THE LTS. OF SAFETY #2**
1950
$29 **$87** **$390**

**CAPTAIN MARVEL AND
THE LTS. OF SAFETY #3** 1951
$29 **$87** **$390**

**FAWCETT MINIATURES
CAPTAIN MARVEL**
1946
$14 **$42** **$140**

**FAWCETT MINIATURES
CAPTAIN MARVEL**
1946
$14 **$42** **$140**

**FAWCETT MINIATURES
CAPTAIN MARVEL JR.**
1946
$14 **$42** **$140**

WISCO/KLARER COMIC BOOK
1948
$26 **$78** **$350**

WHIZ COMICS
Wheaties giveaway • 1946
$83 **$415** **NM** DOESN'T EXIST

Captain Marvel Adventures #18 preliminary cover re-creation in graphite by C.C. Beck (c.1975).

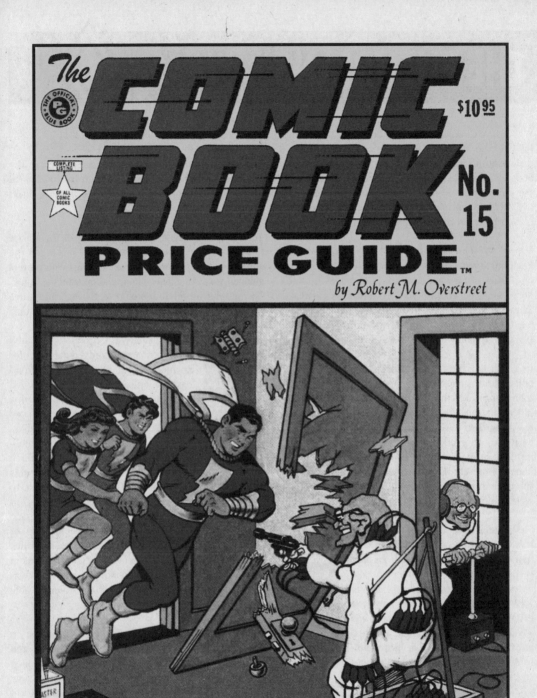

The Overstreet Comic Book Price Guide #15 (1985) featured this cover by C.C. Beck.

THE FUTURIANS

While Dave Cockrum had many fans prior to and after his work on Marvel's *X-Men*, it was his two stints on that title and his co-creation of Nightcrawler, Storm and Colossus that propelled him to superstardom in the ranks of comic book artists. Between the *X-Men* and DC's *Legion of Super-Heroes*, he had more than proven he could handle a team book.

Marvel Graphic Novel #9 (1983, subtitled The Futurians") was Cockrum's chance to play writer-artist on a team of his own creation. In its pages he introduced eight genetically modified individuals – Avatar, Vandervecken, Silkie, Werehawk, Silver Shadow, Mosquito, Sunswift, and Blackmane – all with incredible powers.

In the distant future, two warring factions stand against each other: The Inheritors and the Futurians. The Inheritors cause the sun to turn into a red giant, then travel in time to escape what they have done. Sending genetic markers back in time, the Futurians hope to prevent The Inheritors from succeeding by seeding normal humans with superpowers.

The graphic novel received three printings, so it clearly sold well, but Cockrum said he was lured away from Marvel by the promise of big money to take the series to Lodestone Publishing in 1985 (Lodestone was a sister company to Deluxe Comics, publisher of *Wally Wood's T.H.U.N.D.E.R. Agents*, also featured in this volume). That incarnation of *The Futurians* ended on a cliffhanger after only three issues.

In 1987, Eternity Comics (later part of Malibu) published a trade paperback collecting the three Lodestone issues and a fourth, previously unpublished issue of the series. That fourth issue would eventually see print as *The Futurians* #0 from Aardwolf Productions (1995).

Later, David S. Miller would publish the four-issue *Avatar of The Futurians* (2010), which was collected

as *Dave Cockrum's Futurians: Avatar* (2011).

The starts and stops limited what sustained impact The Futurians might have had. Cockrum explained as much inside the front cover of *Futurians* #0 from Aardwolf Productions:

The Futurians began as a graphic novel for Marvel (*Marvel Graphic Novel* #9), wherein I recounted the adventures of eight extraordinary humans with powers gained by way of genetic manipulation from the future. The graphic novel did pretty well, went into three printings, and a series was called for.

Unfortunately, I let myself be lured away from Marvel and did the series for an independent publisher who promised pie-in-the-sky money. If I'd stayed with Marvel, we might be publishing *Futurians* #250 or something by now. Instead, I went with the independent, occasionally called Lodestone Publications, and my run only lasted three issues. A fourth issue was finished; this book you hold in your hands. Due to the vagaries of publishing, however, it never saw print as an individual issue until now. It was collected together with the previous three issues into a limited-edition second graphic novel in 1987. That second graphic novel was short-printed and is next-to-impossible to find.

There has been renewed interest in *The Futurians* in recent months, and my friends at Aardwolf and I decided to reprint the "lost" fourth issue, now numbered 0 for this edition, to test the waters for a possible new series. If you bought the three Lodestone issues but never saw the second graphic novel (and I know there are lots of you out there), here's your chance to finish the story.

Writer Cliff Meth developed a Futurians screenplay which from time to time has attracted interest from Hollywood, but as of this writing fate of the characters and concepts remains in limbo.

FIRST PUBLICATION:
Marvel Graphic Novel #9
(Marvel, February 1984)

LAST PUBLICATION:
The Futurians #3
(Lodestone, December 1985)

REVIVAL(S):
The Futurians (Eternity, 1987, trade paperback includes previously unpublished *The Futurians* #4), *The Futurians* #0 (Aardwolf, black and white, first stand-alone publication of what would have been *Futurians* #4), *Avatar of the Futurians* #1-4 (David S. Miller, 2010), *Dave Cockrum's Futurians: Avatar* (David S. Miller, 2011)

Dave Cockrum specialty illustration of Avatar of the Futurians (undated).
Image courtesy of Hertiage Auctions.

MARVEL GRAPHIC NOVEL #9
1983
$2 **$6** **$14**

THE FUTURIANS #1
OCTOBER 1985
$4

THE FUTURIANS #2
NOVEMBER 1985
$4

THE FUTURIANS #3
DECEMBER 1985
$4

THE FUTURIANS
VOLUME 2 • 1987
$10

THE FUTURIANS #0
AUGUST 1995
$4

**AVATAR OF
THE FUTURIANS #1**
JULY 2010
$4

**AVATAR OF
THE FUTURIANS #2**
2010
$4

**AVATAR OF
THE FUTURIANS #3**
2010
$4

**AVATAR OF
THE FUTURIANS #4**
2010
$4

**DAVE COCKRUM'S
FUTURIANS: AVATAR**
2011
$20

Artist and DC Publisher Jim Lee's interpretation of Dave Cockrum's Futurians (2004).
Inscribed "From one of your biggest fans – thanks, Dave, for bringing to life whole new
worlds and whole new galaxies for us to play in." Image courtesy of Hertiage Auctions.

In addition to the more highly publicized Ultraverse and the creator-owned Bravura line, Malibu attempted to craft another universe out of three of their existing, non-licensed series.

"When the Ultraverse launched, marketing shifted heavy resources to promote it. I was afraid (and others were, too) that we might lose one or more of the titles that would become the Genesis line simply by them being lost in the crowd. We thought if we could connect them somehow, that would strengthen them together, and extend the publishing life," said Roland Mann, then an editor for Malibu.

"We had gotten to a point where we had a lot of different groupings of books. There was the Ultraverse, Bravura, the licensing books that were spearheaded by *Star Trek: Deep Space Nine*. And then we had these books that were essentially orphans, the standalones. They were the *Ex-Mutants, Protectors,* and my own *Dinosaurs For Hire.* They didn't seem to fit anywhere. Editor Roland Mann came up with the idea of combining them under one umbrella to hopefully give them all a sales boost in a market that was slowing rapidly for all publishers," said Tom Mason, who served as Malibu's Creative Director.

"The idea was probably mine because I edited all the titles involved. It had to be approved by Malibu's founders: Scott Mitchell Rosenberg, Tom Mason, Chris Ulm, and Dave Olbrich. *Ex-Mutants* and *The Protectors* were owned by Malibu, so we didn't have to seek approval from any of the creatives involved. "Essentially, aside from the Ultraverse, if it wasn't a licensed property, it became a Genesis book," Mann said.

So, unlike the Ultraverse, which was built from the ground up, Genesis was cobbled together with existing properties.

"The Ultraverse was carefully planned from the ground up. Chris Ulm led a large group of creators who were working together to create an integrated universe and tell stories that fit together to make a whole. And it took a year from the time Chris pitched the initial project until the first book came out. Just the first three months of that alone was doing the inhouse development work and signing up the writers who would become known as the Founders. If you're a developer, this is like planning a massive apartment complex, getting all the zoning and infrastructure in place and scheduling the equipment and ordering the lumber, Mason said.

"The Genesis stuff was three disparate universes already. R.A. Jones had created *The Protectors* with research assistance from Ron Goulart, and contributions from Roland and Martin Powell. It was a very traditional super-hero universe. *The Ex-Mutants* were based on the previous version of Ex-Mutants that had been reworked by Chris, Dave and me. Those characters existed in a post-apocalyptic universe with Hank Kanalz as the current writer. *Dinosaurs For Hire* existed in a modern day world where comic book characters were pop culture icons. So, putting them together was kind of a Dr. Frankenstein stitch up. To continue my lame building analogy, we had three houses in different parts of the country and wanted to somehow make them a neighborhood," he said.

The Genesis universe didn't last long. Ultimately, diminishing sales for the titles when compared to the Ultraverse.

"I recall once asking the marketing department about an ad/marketing plan for an upcoming title, and I was flat out told that there was no money for advertising the Genesis line anymore because those resources were going to promote the Ultraverse, which was selling stronger," Mann said. "That's when I knew before being told that the end wouldn't be long."

FIRST PUBLICATION:
Protectors #1
(September 1992)

LAST PUBLICATION:
Protectors #20
(May 1994)

REVIVAL(S):
None as the Genesis imprint. Marvel's acquisition of Malibu and their reluctance to use Ultraverse characters makes this even less likely. Dinosaurs For Hire remains the property of Tom Mason and could return.

Samuel Clarke Hawbaker's original art for the cover of *Protectors* #1 (1992).
Image courtesy of Heritage Auctions.

DINOSAURS FOR HIRE #1
FEBRUARY 1993
$4

DINOSAURS FOR HIRE #2
MARCH 1993
$4

DINOSAURS FOR HIRE #3
APRIL 1993
$4

DINOSAURS FOR HIRE #4
MAY 1993
$4

DINOSAURS FOR HIRE #5
JUNE 1993
$4

DINOSAURS FOR HIRE #6
JULY 1993
$4

DINOSAURS FOR HIRE #7
AUGUST 1993
$4

DINOSAURS FOR HIRE #8
SEPTEMBER 1993
$4

DINOSAURS FOR HIRE #8
POLYBAGGED VARIANT
SEPTEMBER 1993
$4

DINOSAURS FOR HIRE #9
OCTOBER 1993
$4

DINOSAURS FOR HIRE #10
NOVEMBER 1993
$4

DINOSAURS FOR HIRE #11
DECEMBER 1993
$4

DINOSAURS FOR HIRE #12
FEBRUARY 1994
$4

EX-MUTANTS #1
SEPTEMBER 1993
$4

EX-MUTANTS #2
OCTOBER 1993
$4

FERRET #1
ONE SHOT • 1992
$4

FERRET #1
MAY 1993
$4

FERRET #2
JUNE 1993
$4

FERRET #2
NEWSSTAND EDITION • JUNE 1993
$4

FERRET #3
JULY 1993
$4

FERRET #3
NEWSSTAND EDITION • JULY 1993
$4

FERRET #4
AUGUST 1993
$4

FERRET #4
NEWSSTAND EDITION • AUGUST 1993
$4

FERRET #5
SEPTEMBER 1993
$4

FERRET #5
POLYBAGGED • SEPTEMBER 1993
$4

FERRET #6
OCTOBER 1993
$4

FERRET #7
NOVEMBER 1993
$4

FERRET #8
DECEMBER 1993
$4

FERRET #9
JANUARY 1994
$4

FERRET #10
MARCH 1994
$4

GRAVESTONE #1
JULY 1993
$4

GRAVESTONE #2
JULY 1993
$4

GRAVESTONE #3
SEPTEMBER 1993
$4

GRAVESTONE #3
POLYBAGGED • SEPTEMBER 1993
$4

GRAVESTONE #4
OCTOBER 1993
$4

GRAVESTONE #5
NOVEMBER 1993
$4

GRAVESTONE #6
DECEMBER 1993
$4

GRAVESTONE #7
FEBRUARY 1994
$4

MAN OF WAR #1
APRIL 1993
$5

MAN OF WAR #1
NEWSSTAND EDITION • APRIL 1993
$4

MAN OF WAR #2
MAY 1993
$5

MAN OF WAR #2
NEWSSTAND EDITION • MAY 1993
$4

MAN OF WAR #3
JUNE 1993
$5

MAN OF WAR #3
NEWSSTAND EDITION • JUNE 1993
$4

MAN OF WAR #4
JULY 1993
$5

MAN OF WAR #4
NEWSSTAND EDITION • JULY 1993
$4

MAN OF WAR #5
AUGUST 1993
$5

MAN OF WAR #5
NEWSSTAND EDITION • AUGUST 1993
$4

MAN OF WAR #6
SEPTEMBER 1993
$5

MAN OF WAR #6
POLYBAGGED • SEPTEMBER 1993
$5

MAN OF WAR #7
OCTOBER 1993
$5

MAN OF WAR #8
FEBRUARY 1994
$5

PROTECTORS #1
SEPTEMBER 1992
$4

PROTECTORS #1
VARIANT COVER • SEPTEMBER 1992
$4

PROTECTORS #1
VARIANT COVER • SEPTEMBER 1992
$4

PROTECTORS #1
NEWSSTAND ED. • SEPTEMBER 1992
$4

PROTECTORS #2
OCTOBER 1992
$4

PROTECTORS #2
NEWSSTAND ED. • OCTOBER 1992
$4

PROTECTORS #3
NOVEMBER 1992
$4

PROTECTORS #3
NEWSSTAND ED. • NOVEMBER 1992
$4

PROTECTORS #4
DECEMBER 1992
$4

PROTECTORS #4
NEWSSTAND ED. • DECEMBER 1992
$4

PROTECTORS #5
JANUARY 1993
$4

PROTECTORS #5
POLYBAGGED • JANUARY 1993
$4

PROTECTORS #6
FEBRUARY 1993
$4

PROTECTORS #6
NEWSSTAND ED. • FEBRUARY 1993
$4

PROTECTORS #7
MARCH 1993
$4

PROTECTORS #7
NEWSSTAND ED. • MARCH 1993
$4

PROTECTORS #8
APRIL 1993
$4

PROTECTORS #8
NEWSSTAND ED. • APRIL 1993
$4

PROTECTORS #9
MAY 1993
$4

PROTECTORS #9
NEWSSTAND ED. • MAY 1993
$4

PROTECTORS #10
JUNE 1993
$4

PROTECTORS #10
NEWSSTAND ED. • JUNE 1993
$4

PROTECTORS #11
JULY 1993
$4

PROTECTORS #11
NEWSSTAND ED. • JULY 1993
$4

PROTECTORS #12
AUGUST 1993
$4

PROTECTORS #12
NEWSSTAND ED. • AUGUST 1993
$4

PROTECTORS #13
SEPTEMBER 1993
$4

PROTECTORS #14
OCTOBER 1993
$4

PROTECTORS #15
NOVEMBER 1993
$4

PROTECTORS #16
DECEMBER 1993
$4

PROTECTORS #17
JANUARY 1994
$4

PROTECTORS #18
FEBRUARY 1994
$4

PROTECTORS #19
MARCH 1994
$4

PROTECTORS #20
MAY 1994
$4

Part of Dean Zachary and Ken Branch's original art for the cover of
The Ferret #4 (1993). Image courtesy of Heritage Auctions.

Tom Mason • Dinosaurs for Hire

Tom Mason

Tom Mason was one of the founders of Malibu Comics, the founding editor of its creator-owned imprint, Bravura, and an original founder of their Ultraverse line. Since leaving comics, he's worked extensively as a writer and story editor in television. Along with fellow Malibu veteran Dan Danko, he has written or chaperoned 500 episodes of animated television, and they took home an Emmy in the process. He also he co-writes the Captain Awesome *books for Simon & Schuster under the pseudonym Stan Kirby, and serves as a consultant for Space Goat Publishing.*

Paralleling the early days of Malibu, Mason developed a creator-owned title called Dinosaurs For Hire, *which featured a trio of walking, talking, thinking dinosaurs who worked for the federal government and who packed what seemed like an inordinate amount of firepower in just about every situation. The original black and white series, later followed by one in full color, captured the imagination of our J.C. Vaughn well before he was ours, and actually helped set him on the path to Gemstone Publishing's door. Which is to say, you can blame Tom Mason and* Dinosaurs For Hire *for everything since.*

Overstreet: *Dinosaurs For Hire* is what put you on the map with me, Tom. What had you done up to that point?

Tom Mason (TM): I'd been around, but not where people would know me. I'd been a cartoonist and had my work published in *Playboy* and *Cosmopolitan*. I was an art director at Fantagraphics where I created the humor magazine *HONK!*, then I recreated it freelance for Jan Strnad's Mad Dog Graphics as *SPLAT!* When I left Fantagraphics, Dave Olbrich had called me to launch Malibu Comics with him, and that was being backed by Scott Rosenberg, who owned Sunrise Distribution.

And I was content for awhile to be just an office guy. My official title at Malibu back then was Creative Director, and I'm officially one of the four founders, and I was happy just making comics with Dave and Chris Ulm who was the Editor-In-Chief. Up until that time, I'd had no interest in writing comic books. Technically I was in the industry and had been for a few years, but I never saw my jobs as stepping stones to working for the Big Two, Marvel and DC. The two humor magazines I'd done I was just the editor. I wasn't writing for them or pushing my own stuff into the pages. I became a comic book writer by accident. When Scott Rosenberg made the decision to shut down his Eternity office in New York and move everything to the West Coast so that everything came out of Malibu, we picked up some Eternity titles that weren't finished yet. One of them was the last issue of a mini-series called *Battle To The Death*. It was written Marvel-style, so there was a plot and finished art, but no dialogue. And it was late and in danger of having its orders cancelled by the distributors. So Chris Ulm and I wrote the dialogue for it in a couple of days after the original writer declined. There are traces of the *Dinosaurs For Hire* sensibility all over that issue. But I started writing comics because there was one that urgently needed to get done, and I happened to be sitting in front of a computer.

After that, I wrote a couple of odd things – including two issues of *Solo Ex-Mutants*, an *Ex-Mutants* spin-off. Those issues have some humor, but are mostly played straight. And I discovered that I really liked this whole writing thing. Plus the company was bootstrapped and we weren't making big bucks by being on staff, so writing some stuff freelance became a way to pick up extra money.

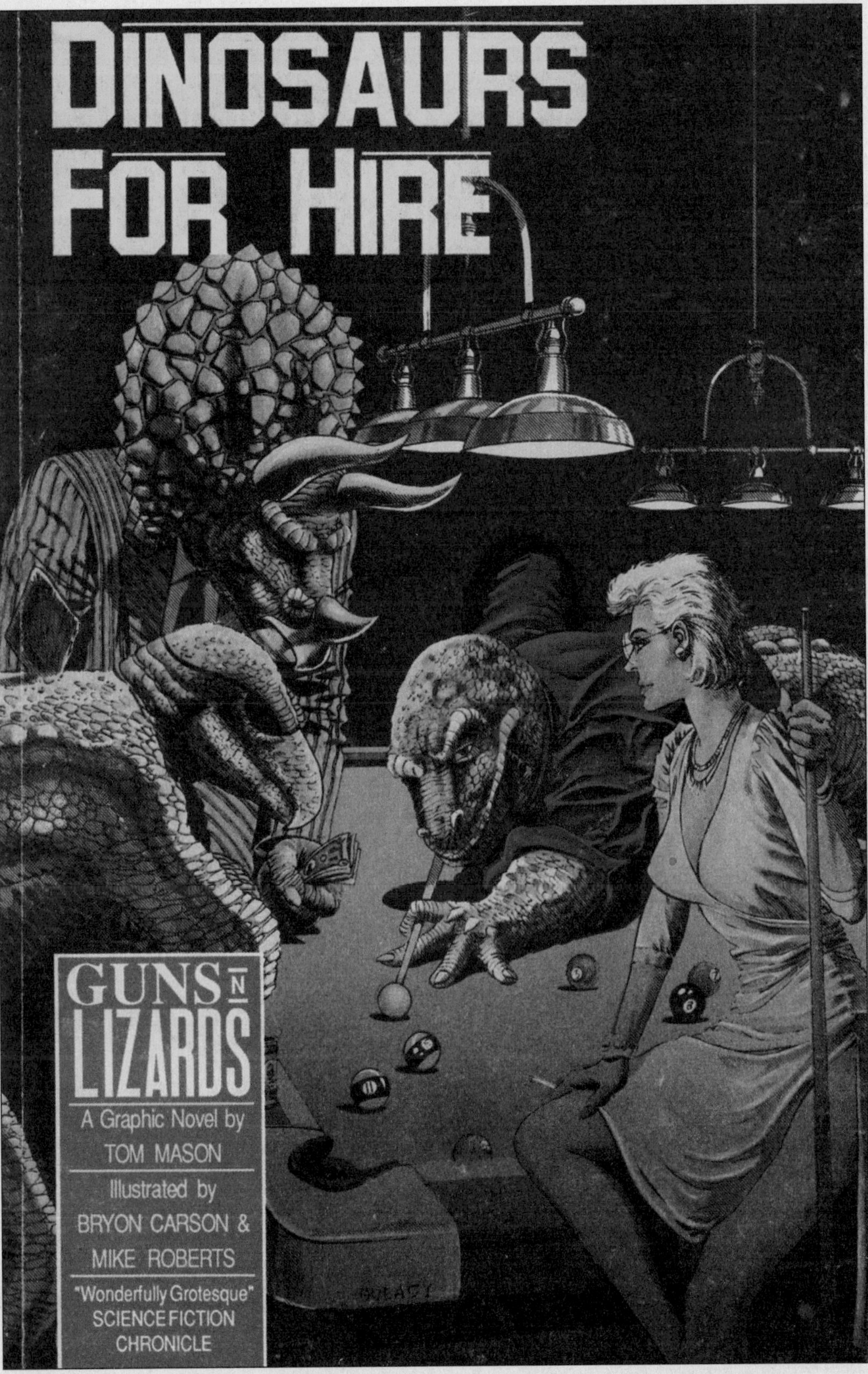
DINOSAURS FOR HIRE
GUNS N LIZARDS
A Graphic Novel by
TOM MASON
Illustrated by
BRYON CARSON &
MIKE ROBERTS
"Wonderfully Grotesque"
SCIENCE FICTION
CHRONICLE

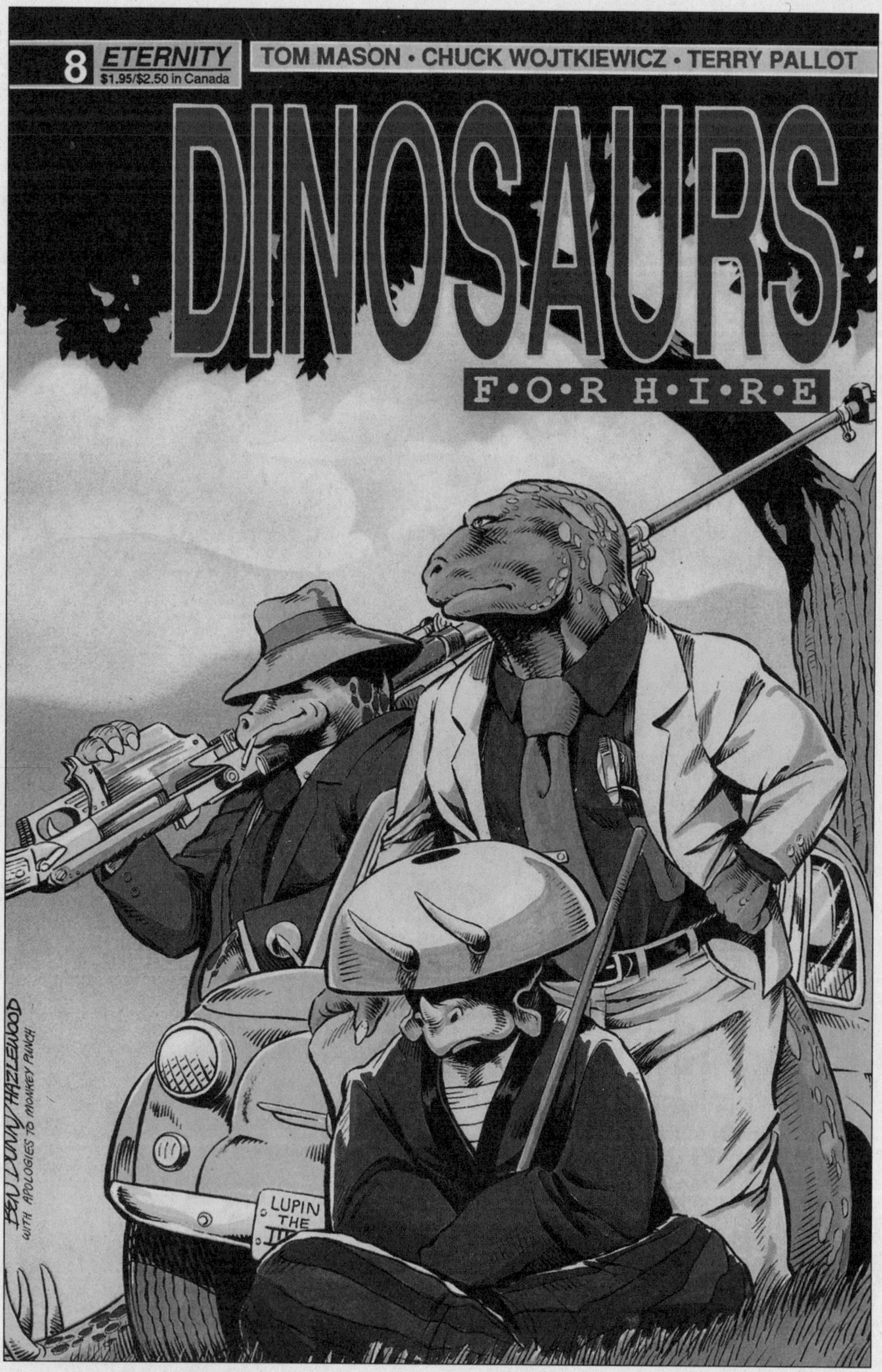
8
ETERNITY
$1.95/$2.50 in Canada
TOM MASON • CHUCK WOJTKIEWICZ • TERRY PALLOT
DINOSAURS
F•O•R H•I•R•E
BEN DUNN/HAZLEWOOD
WITH APOLOGIES TO MONKEY PUNCH
LUPIN
THE

Overstreet: I remember Eternity had published the *Ex-Mutants* comics by that point and also a trade paperback collection of Dave Cockrum's *The Futurians*. How did that all fit into Malibu? What was the plan?

TM: That's the craziest part of the whole story! Pre-Malibu Comics, Scott Rosenberg owned Sunrise, the southern California comic book distributor. He secretly financed four (yes, that's right) comic book companies with the idea that they would publish comics, he'd push them through his existing distribution channel at Sunrise, then sell individual copies by mail order through yet another company of his called Direct Comics. Having a distribution company that distributes books from multiple publishers, then expands to publishing its own books while also running a mail order division isn't a bad way to create a vertically-integrated company without many assets. Unfortunately, he did it in secret, and had been trying to manipulate the market to create "hot" comics that could be sold at higher prices post-publication, and it all went bad when the bubble of inflated high-priced "hot" comics burst. Sunrise was bankrupt and shut down leaving behind a trail of bad debt that hurt a lot of small publishers at the same time Malibu was launching.

Of his four original secret companies, Amazing and Wonder were run out of West Virginia by David Campiti, and Imperial and Eternity were run from Brooklyn by Brian Marshall. Imperial, Amazing and Wonder were closed down, and Campiti went on to his own company, Pied Piper (and later Innovation). *Ex-Mutants* had been created by David Lawrence and Ron Lim, and was published by Campiti through the Amazing imprint. But they lost control of the title in a bizarre dispute with Scott that I could never figure out – this had all happened just before I signed on to Malibu. The end result was that Scott ended up with *Ex-Mutants* being published through Eternity on the East Coast. Eternity still had some books that were selling well, but Scott wanted to move its operations to the West Coast so we inherited the Eternity books that were in the pipeline. That included *Ex-Mutants* and *The Futurians* hardcover and books like *Ninja* and *Yakuza*. Then because the Eternity name had a much, much higher brand recognition among retailers than Malibu Comics, we dropped the Malibu name as an imprint and carried on under the Eternity Comics name with Malibu as the parent company. Had enough yet? A lot of this is archived via *The Comics Journal's* website.

Getting back to the other part of your question, the original Malibu plan was created by Dave Olbrich who would be the publisher. He was working at Sunrise and he pitched Scott on creating a comic book company – at this time not knowing that Scott was already secretly backing his four other companies. The concept for Malibu at the time was not exactly revolutionary, but the stuff that Dave wanted to publish would be creator-owned black and white titles with the idea that while we wouldn't pay a lot of money upfront, we would pay, and pay on time, we'd publish them and the creators would retain all the media exploitation rights. And they'd get publishing rights back after their project had run its course. And except for the occasional glitches that were quickly resolved, we managed to pay on time or early for the bulk of the company's run – right up until the year leading up to Marvel buying the company. That last year was when we were running out of operating capital and started deferring payments.

Overstreet: What was the original spark for you when you came up with *Dinosaurs For Hire*?

TM: Jan Strnad (DC's *Sword Of The Atom*, *Dalgoda*) and I used to live in the same neighborhood in Hollywood. I was having lunch with him and a mutual friend of ours, Mike Valerio. This was before I joined Dave to launch Malibu. Jan was trying to find interesting books to put out through his own comic book company, Mad Dog Graphics. One of the ideas that was kicked around at lunch was the idea of Elvis Presley as a crimefighter (he had been famously "deputized" by President Nixon back in the 1970s and used to drive around at night pulling people over).

It was a ragged idea, and Mike agreed to write it, and it was going to be called *Elvis: Undercover*. But as fate would have it, Mike couldn't get a handle on it and passed. I picked it up, and though I'd never written a comic book before, Jan sat with me and gave me a master class in comic book writing. I owe him everything for that! I finished the script, Jan lined up artist Don Lomax, pages were done, *The Los Angeles Times* got wind of it and wrote a story about it. Then Jan got worried about getting sued by the Elvis estate and pulled the book. So I had a finished script laying around.

And that's what it did for awhile. Just sat in a drawer. But I subscribe to the old saying of "Never throw anything away." Shortly thereafter, Dave Olbrich got the backing for Malibu Comics and brought me onboard. We'd been up and running for several months and working on the schedule. We started kicking ideas around for new projects. I mentioned the script I'd done for *Elvis: Undercover* and Jan's concerns about publishing it. Dave suggested that I change Elvis to something else - how about a dinosaur, he said. It was his basic idea and he just threw it out there. I loved it, and went one better. I split the Elvis character into three distinct personalities and made them a trio of dinosaurs. And that became *Dinosaurs For Hire*. I went through the old script, chopped it up and added new stuff, and then we were off and running.

Overstreet: After you got the basic idea, what were your next few steps?

TM: I had to find an artist. I knew Bryon Carson because he'd done some other stuff for us earlier. He was a good artist and fun to work with, and he said he liked to draw dinosaurs. I sent him the script and he was on board. Then it was the usual publishing stuff – get a cover, press release, solicitation copy for the distributors, all that. More importantly, I also had to figure out the second issue. I'd never written a second script for *Elvis: Undercover*, so I didn't have a script I could crib from. I had to write a *Dinosaurs For Hire* script entirely from scratch.

Overstreet: How long did that second script take you to write? What hurdles did you face with it?

TM: It took the full month and then some. I think Bryon was waiting on me to get it done. *Elvis: Undercover* was basically a one-shot joke. It was never intended to be more than that. Rewriting that first script into *Dinosaurs For Hire*

©1991 Tom Mason

#1 was just that – rewriting. I hadn't done any preparatory work – no world-building, no character bios, no deep background, no origin. So there was nothing to base a second story on – I was winging it, trying to think it through, and write a script that wouldn't close off future story opportunities.

Overstreet: When did you think things were really beginning to come together for the property?

TM: I think the third issue of the original black and white series is when I started to figure things out. The first issue was a rewrite of the Elvis story. The second one was written in a hurry and picked up on a vampire tease from the first issue. The third one I had some time to think things through a bit and the cover by Scott Bieser really clarified it in my head. It was a good companion to Bryon's cover to the first issue. Put the two covers side-by-side and that's the series.

Overstreet: I think when you say "Scott Bieser really clarified it in my head" other writers will know what you mean, but could you explain that a bit?

TM: Scott did the guest cover for issue 3, and it was a pin-up style illustration of Professor Tyrell (the "Boss" of the dinosaurs), standing in front of the dinos, and everybody has a gun. It was a real "attitude" pose and it captured my vision perfectly. That's what the team was – confident, can-do, skilled, and the fact that it was dinosaurs led by a woman made it fun to me.

Overstreet: Since you guys had just started Malibu at the time, what was an average day like for you at that point, if there was such a thing?

TM: An average day? It would sort of go like this – Dave would get to the office first. I'd try to get there around 8:30. There wasn't any email in those days to worry about, so I'd spend the morning going over the upcoming business with Dave, figuring out what had to be done by the end of the day. And then FedEx and UPS would show up around 10, and that would take priority – it was going to be either scripts, pencils, inks or letters or cover coloring, and it would have to be logged in and shipped back out that day by 4:30 when they dropped by again to pick everything up. The afternoon would be spent trying to get ahead, find new projects, handle any problems that cropped up during the day, deal with any creator issues, the usual publishing stuff. During the course of each month, I'd still write the solicitation copy, write and design the print ads, and write and send out the press releases. And every Tuesday, we'd send completed books to the printer, so that meant

DINOSAURS
F·O·R·H·I·R·E

DINOSAURS RULE!

Created & Written by TOM MASON
Illustrated by Bryon Carson, Scott Bieser, Chuck Wojtkiewicz & Mike Roberts

designing all the text features, and paginating each issue, and dropping in the ads and stuff. We'd probably knock off around 7 PM. Chris and I would occasionally go out for dinner or a beer after work, and still be kicking around ideas. On evenings and weekends, I'd try to have a non-work life, but still do some writing.

Overstreet: Those kinds of periods are inherently hard to sustain over protracted periods, but they also tend to be fertile for the imagination. What were the best and worst parts of those days for you?

TM: The best part of it is that you're really in the middle of things. It's game on, and all of us, the four of us (Chris, Dave, Scott and me), were putting in crazy hours. But we were learning as we went, trying to build up a company and keep it going from month-to-month. We got to try a bunch of things, really experiment with marketing and promotional ideas, and the types of books we could publish. It was tiring, but very exciting, and very creative to have people to bounce loopy ideas off of and try to turn them into something practical. The worst part is you eventually just get tired and your brain shuts down. The last thing you want to see when that happens is a printed comic where the word balloon fell off somewhere between your desk and the printing press and nobody caught it. So you have to take a couple of days and detox.

Overstreet: If *DFH* #1 was largely a rewrite of *Elvis: Undercover*, was the humor in the first issue mostly intact from the earlier version?

TM: Very much so. Some of the jokes no longer worked, because they were Elvis-specific, but lot of the jokes did stay the same. Archie was basically the reworked Elvis, and Reese and Lorenzo were added as his buddies. Red was Elvis' main pal, Sonny, but he was called Red in both versions of the script and was always a little person. The love of guns, girls and snark was in both, and the overall attitude was similar. I still had the two government "handlers," Smith and Jones. I kept them from the original script, too.

I still have the original draft of the *Elvis: Undercover* #1 script. I've gone back to it and reworked it a little to update it and tighten up the jokes. I think it's still funny and different enough from *Dinosaurs For Hire* #1 and I'm trying to line up a publisher for it.

Overstreet: From the first page, it was clear that you were willing to make fun of just about anything or anyone, left, right or center, and that even though you weren't particularly vicious about it, you didn't seem to have too many sacred cows. Is that accurate? And how much of that is still reflected in your approach to humor?

TM: I love poking fun at pop culture, and celebrities and politicians and any sort of big powerful thing. And I'm unapologetic about it, too. I've pissed off a bunch of people who did think I was too vicious, but I won't walk back a joke because of that. They're just jokes. I do have a couple of sacred cows. There are subjects that I don't think are funny or are too serious and "messagey" or that I can't make funny so I avoid them. Everything else is fair game. I might have a character represent a certain point of view for the sake of the story, but my goal isn't to make a political point or to be seen as either liberal or conservative or anything else – I want to make fun, knockabout comics about dinosaurs with guns. My background is humor, but humor on its own doesn't sell, so being able to mix it with action made it appealing to me and gave me a broader audience. It also gave me a wider range of subjects to pick on. I can do funny stuff and wrap it around big dinosaurs shooting things repeatedly.

Overstreet: From the original series, I always remember the line "The three bullets I was saving for a Beatles reunion" seemed a bit harsh, but then you had a cover blurb, something like "Outraged Beatles Fan letter included" a few issues later, it actually made the original thing funnier. What sorts of other angry letters did you get?

TM: That was my early brush with angry fans. That was a lot of fun, and I actually had more fans in support of the joke – it was just the one Beatles fan who was incensed. But there were other incidents as well. When the first issue of the color series came out, I was asked to participate on a radio call-in show at the last minute, but they deliberately sandbagged me. There was a woman on the show (an outraged mother, not one of the hosts) and she was thoroughly pissed at me because it was her belief Dinosaurs were strictly for children and shouldn't be co-opted for "this kind of awful attempt at humor." She wanted me to walk back the comic, apologize for it and promise to keep dinosaurs as a child's plaything. When the hosts gave me my chance to respond, I said that she should be a better mother and more carefully scrutinize her child's reading material. The interview ended shortly after that.

The biggest criticism I got, oddly enough, was from inside Malibu Comics. Malibu's co-president

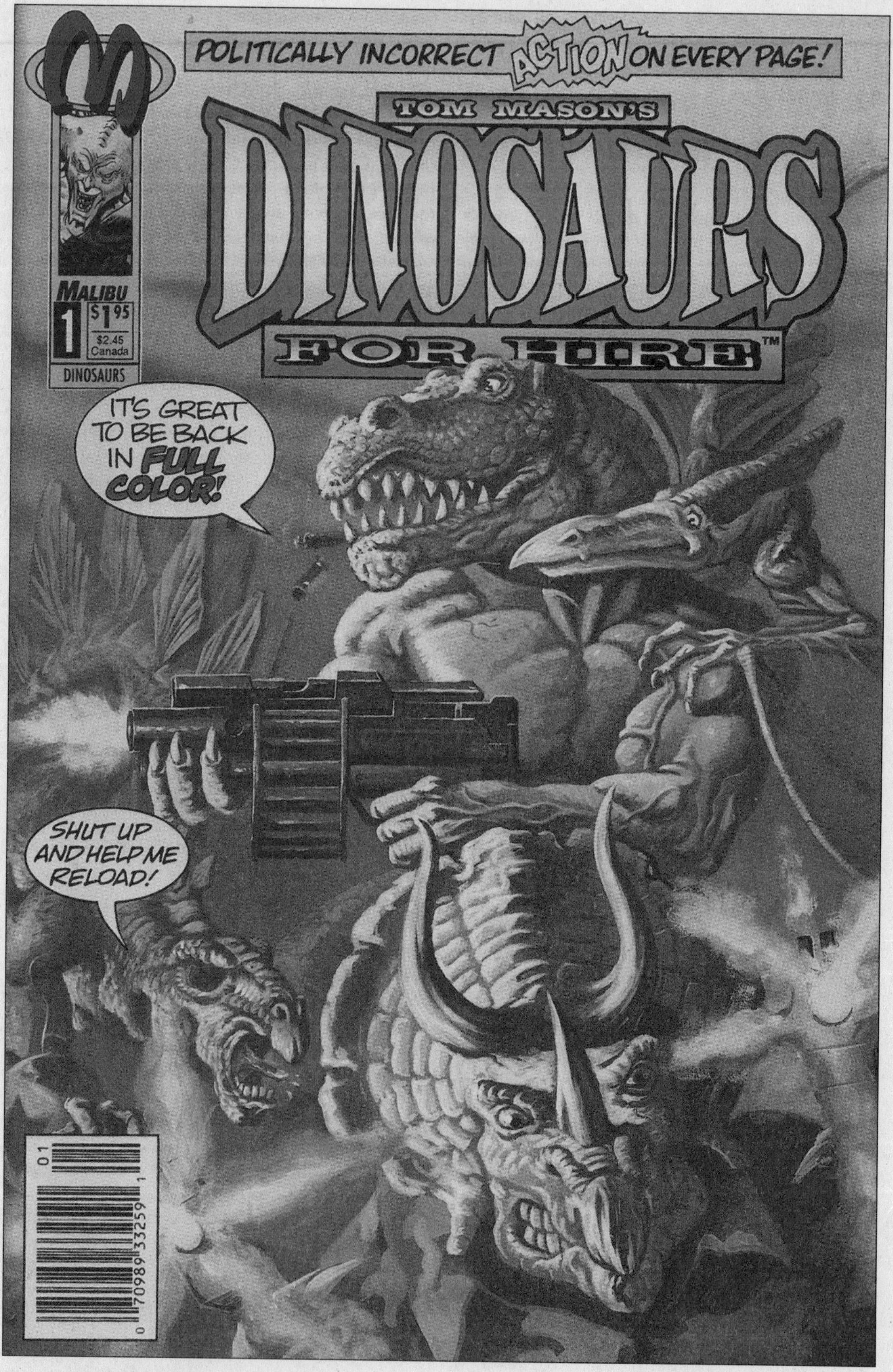
POLITICALLY INCORRECT ACTION ON EVERY PAGE!
TOM MASON'S
DINOSAURS
FOR HIRE™
MALIBU
1
$1.95
$2.45 Canada
DINOSAURS
IT'S GREAT TO BE BACK IN FULL COLOR!
SHUT UP AND HELP ME RELOAD!

Bob Jacob was furious with me over the first issue of the color comic. He had earlier merged his videogame company with Malibu and liked to throw his weight around, calling himself "the new sheriff in town." He drove over from his office after the first issue shipped and took me outside to scold me about the content – he hated it, didn't think it was funny, didn't like the art, didn't like the tone. What he wanted was a comic book that he could license into toys and stuff and what he got was an embarrassment to him. "I can't show this book to people!" he yelled at me. That was great. I enjoyed every second of that.

What got me was that he then accused me of pushing the issue through Malibu in secret – that somehow in front of everyone I had gone behind his back, behind everyone's back, to create the issue he hated without anyone overseeing it. I told him that was total bullshit – all of the material, including the press and promotion for the series, had gone through the proper channels, the script had been vetted by both Dave Olbrich and Chris Ulm before a panel was drawn, and that Chris, in his role as Editor-In-Chief at the company personally trafficked the book at each stage. Further to that, I reminded him that *Dinosaurs For Hire* was not a Malibu title, it was a creator-owned title that was published by Malibu. He snorted and stomped around like an angry leprechaun for a bit then finally said, "That's what's wrong with creator-owned comics!" Our relations were quite strained after that, and he was eventually forced out of the company - not by me, though but by the investors Worldwide Sports & Entertainment who came aboard after the launch of the Ultraverse.

Overstreet: How were the sales on the early issues?
TM: Pretty darn good actually. Each issue of the black and white series hovered around the 9,000 copy level which doesn't sound great, but was profitable for the company and the talent. Then when the color series launched it was doing around 90,000 for that first issue.

Overstreet: Other than the Eternity collection of *The Futurians*, I seem to remember that everything Eternity did was black and white. Is that correct? Was there any thought given to doing color material?
TM: Eternity had big plans to launch a color series back when the company was still operating out of New York in the pre-Malibu era. It was *Pirate Corp$* by Evan Dorkin. The first issue was done and colored and it went to the printer during the shift of Eternity from New York to California. It

was scheduled to debut at the San Diego Comic Con that year. When it came out, though, the color printing was awful. The cover was muddy and dark and it just ruined Dorkin's terrific art. There would be no second issue, and even though the coloring for that issue wasn't done by the Malibu half of the equation and we hadn't supervised the printing, we'd have to take the blame for it. And it would be a long time before we'd try color again. The expense and the risk were too great until we could find a way to do it right.

Overstreet: After you got up and running, and after you got a handle on the series with #3, what sort of challenges did you face with *Dinosaurs For Hire*?
TM: Keeping me on schedule was one, and finding the time to write an issue was two. I had to write them in my off time, when I was home. I would write for about a half hour every morning after I got up, and put in an hour or two in the evenings after work. I developed a trick to always stop in the middle of a scene and leave it unfinished so it was easier to get back into the next time I sat down. It was a bi-monthly book because of that schedule. I just couldn't write it any faster. A perk to being in the office was that I was also rewriting and forever tweaking the script – when I'd go over the pencils before sending it to the letterer, I'd punch up the dialogue and the jokes, and then do it again just before an issue went to the printer. I was never really done writing until the original art was in the envelope and off to the printer. Another difficulty was finding an artist who could stay on the book. Sales were okay on the black and white series, but the money still wasn't big enough to have someone stay on the book as a full-time gig, so I was doing stand-alone issues just in case.

Overstreet: Bryon Carson, who you've mentioned, penciled the first three issues and the fifth issue. Who else was involved with the original black and white series?
TM: Scott Bieser did an issue, Chuck Wojtkiewicz did several issues, Scott Benefiel did one, and Nigel Tully did the *Fall Classic*.

Overstreet: Which issue of the first run is your favorite and why?
TM: I have to play the weasel card. I love them all – not because of my writing because what writer loves their own writing unconditionally? Certainly not me. I just love seeing what each artist did to my scripts – how they took my words and then elevated them by bringing the script to life. It's a magical process to see it happen, and after I'd send out a

script, I'd be like a kid at Christmas waiting to see what the artist did with it, waiting for that package with the art to arrive. That's everything to me.

Overstreet: Why did the first series come to an end after nine issues?

TM: I was approaching some serious creative burnout and I just couldn't maintain the hours that I was putting in. Writing in the morning, going to work, then writing more in the evenings. It was just a lot. Issue #9 was a stand-alone issue that was essentially a fill-in by Scott Benefiel. Chuck had left for another gig, so if the series was to continue I had to find yet another artist to do #10 as I was writing it, and I was just too tired.

Overstreet: You mentioned that you started out as more of an editor-producer at first, and that you were pulled in multiple directions with your job as Creative Director. What sort of growth did you go through as a writer during that period?

TM: It was an incredibly fertile time because I was writing almost everything and writing constantly. During the day I was editing books, and in the evening I was writing my own scripts, and in between I was writing promotional copy, ad copy, letters pages, press releases, writing introductions for books, proofreading, conducting promotional interviews. It was everything. What I learned first was speed – writing very, very fast – and a great appreciation for computers. Without a computer to cut, paste, edit, repurpose I don't think I could've done any of it.

By actually working in comics and putting together comics, I was seeing how others wrote – reading a couple dozen scripts every month rubs off on you. I would pick up tips and tricks from other writers – structure, dialogue, staging, characterization – just by osmosis. But mostly, it's speed – get the first draft down completely and as quickly as possible and spend the rest of your time fixing it.

Writing is a very solitary craft – it's just you and the computer. But during the day I was surrounded by people and activity and I could bounce ideas off the room. We had an open office for a long time and Chris's and Dave's desks were within feet of my own. We were always hollering out "What about this?" or "How about that?"

Overstreet: What happened with the property in the interim between the end first series and its revival as the full color second series?

TM: It sat. I assumed that after the black and white

series was over, that the property was too, at least for awhile. I didn't really think about it again for a long time. There had been some movement to try to turn the comic book into a movie during its black-and-white days, and if I'd been smarter and known then what I know now, I would've stopped it all. The movie technology of the time didn't exist to make a real movie of the comic that anyone would want to see – so every conversation was about how to minimize the appearance of the dinosaurs to keep the budget down. I'd had a meeting with Jonathan Betuel, the guy who did *The Last Starfighter* and *My Science Project*. He was interested in optioning the comic, but I didn't think we were a good fit. It was eventually optioned by two goofballs who had no money and no track record, but they had optioned a couple of other comic books including *The Trouble With Girls*, and they were actually in the business, but in non-producing jobs.

I had one meeting with them after we signed a deal, and then they cut me loose. They had a script written that was just terrible and from a writer who hasn't done anything since. I had no input into it and they were shopping it around without me. The script thankfully went nowhere, but *Dinosaurs For Hire* ended up at Fox being developed as an animated series. And I had one meeting at Fox, and it was clear that they wanted a series that was much closer to *Teenage Mutant Ninja Turtles* with lots of slapstick hijinks and catchphrases that could take the world by storm. The meeting with me was basically a courtesy to see if I had any ideas for how they could dumb down the concept and make it kid-friendly for TV. Well, I didn't have any ideas for that direction. And fortunately the series never made it out of development, and the option lapsed. I was very lucky that nothing happened because I could've lost my comic during that time and in exchange gotten either a terrible movie or a worse cartoon show. That's the way Hollywood works and I knew that even at the time, and it still happened to me. I wasn't mad at anyone or even the generic "Hollywood," but I was very disappointed in myself. I got smarter after that, but only incrementally, of course.

The upshot is that after all of that, I was content to just keep the *Dinosaurs* on the shelf for awhile and do nothing with them. Nothing. During this downtime, however, Malibu Comics found a financial partner - the company merged with a local video game company called Acme Interactive. The new combined company had two distinct divisions

– Malibu Comics which would make comics, and Malibu Interactive that would continue to make video games. Acme (now Malibu Interactive) was run by Bob Jacob who was now co-president with Scott. Bob immediately announced how stupid he thought we – Chris Ulm, Dave Olbrich and me – were. From his POV, we had once been publishing Image Comics, then we "let" Image get away and go off and publish on their own. He thought we somehow, magically, should've made a deal that kept the Image titles with us once the creators left – we should've owned those titles. Well, that's not the deal we made with Image, and it's not a deal they would've signed. It's a complete misreading of the business and the deal. Bob would have none of that though. He obviously knew better.

So his mandate was that Malibu going-forward with his new guidance would be publishing fewer creator-owned titles and more company-owned projects. This was when Chris Ulm pitched the idea that would become the Ultraverse. But in the interim, Malibu didn't really have that many company-owned properties in its arsenal, and Bob was antsy to start licensing out. He had contacts at Sega, and all the other video game companies because of the work he'd been doing at Acme, and he got Sega to pick up *Ex-Mutants* for a video game, and sure enough they also wanted *Dinosaurs For Hire* as well. And one of the stipulations was that to support the game, everybody wanted the comic book back on the racks. And so, I dusted it off and was back in the prehistory business.

Overstreet: So, was that the origin of the Genesis line or imprint, or did that follow later?

TM: That followed later, after the second

series, the color one, was up and running. Malibu was breaking off into sub-imprints at the time. We had the Ultraverse books, the Bravura books, and all the licensed books. Suddenly, there were three books that didn't fit into any of those categories – *Ex-Mutants*, *Protectors* and *Dinosaurs For Hire*. Sales on them were just okay, less than the UV titles certainly. I forgot who came up with the idea of bunching them together, but it was mostly to increase sales and give them an identity of their own so they felt less like orphans. Roland Mann was the editor on all three, and he may have proposed it. I'm pretty sure he came up with the Genesis name. I agreed to go along with it because it felt like a way to keep my book going, even though it was a creator-owned book and the other two were company-owned. I also said I'd participate in the unifying crossover if I could make fun of it as it was happening, and then ignore it afterwards. In retrospect, I think I should've insisted that the title be moved over to the licensing group, but that might not've worked either.

Overstreet: For the second series, you added a fourth dinosaur. Was that driven by the video game or was it something you just wanted to do?

TM: That was something I wanted to do. When the series was greenlit for the new color run, Chris and I talked about what I could do with the concept to add something to it. I thought bringing in a flying dinosaur could add another dimension to the book – basically air support for whatever they got involved in.

Overstreet: Given that you'd had a lot of new experiences between the two series, did you change your approach to the property in any way for the second one or did it feel like you were just picking up where you left off?

TM: I talked it over with Chris and Dave, and we all felt that as a relaunch, I should do something a bit different, find a way to bring something new to the book. I put more thought into the writing, into the background of the characters, and their role in their universe. I tried to be a bit more "cerebral" about a book that's essentially about dinosaurs shooting stuff.

Overstreet: On the logo of the second series, it said "*Tom Mason's Dinosaurs For Hire*" rather than just "*Dinosaurs For Hire.*" Given what you said a bit earlier, was that a message to Bob Jacobs or was that just coincidence?

TM: It's so funny – I was happy making comics, and happy in the day job helping to launch the Ultraverse and later Bravura, but now there was my comic book, and a video game. I had a courtesy meeting with the video game people in Diamond Bar, California and they were really nice and open about what they were doing. We talked about the concept and the characters and the limitations of game technology at the time. The game was going to be a side-scrolling shooter and I was content to just let them run with it and check in periodically. But at the Malibu end, I was having trouble wading through the deal with Sega, the company that would actually publish the game. I kept thinking that because I was one of the founders of the company and one of the operational heads of it, that I should get some kind of favored-nations status, but every time something happened with *Dinosaurs For Hire*, I felt like I was getting Bill Fingered. I had been trying to figure out what my rights were and what was going on with the licensing. There's this terrible clause in most contracts that uses the phrase "best efforts" which means that no one will really do anything they're not required to do. I couldn't get a straight answer from Bob about how I'd be credited in the game, and my worry was that either I'd get no credit or that all credit would go to Malibu, like "based on a Malibu Comics title" or that I'd get a really tiny credit tucked away in the instruction manual. So since *DFH* was a creator-owned comic, I had the logo redesigned to incorporate my name in such a way that if someone wanted to strip it out they'd have to pay to redesign it. But the comic would be several issues into print by the time the game was out and it would mess up the branding if anyone did that. So I changed to logo to guarantee my own credit. A totally ego-driven FU.

Overstreet: What were the differences and similarities the second time around?

TM: Mainly the difference is that the writing process was a bit crazier. I would write full script, but with instructions to the artist – Mitch Byrd for the early relaunch issues – that he could mess around with it to help with the pacing. I always try to cram too many things into a page, and that makes the layouts unwieldy at times. When the pencils came back, I'd go through and do balloon

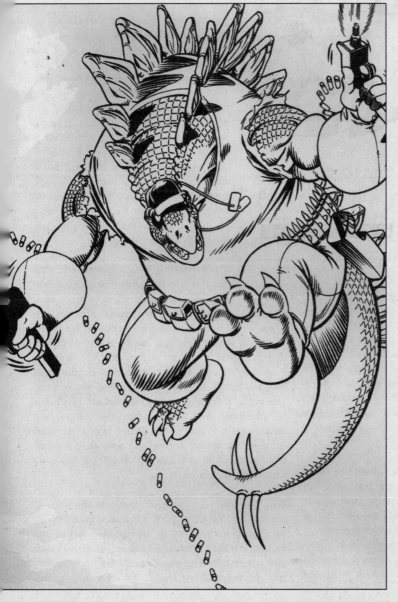

AND YOU THOUGHT THEY WERE EXTINCT!

THEY'RE BIG
THEY'RE BAD,
THEY PACK SERIOUS HEAT,
AND THEY WORK FOR THE
U.S. GOVERNMENT.

CREATED BY TOM MASON

DINOSAURS FOR HIRE™ trademark &
copyright © 1992 Tom Mason

DINOSAURS
F·O·R H·I·R·E ™

amazing to me. Artists make the work so much better, and I don't like to try to "control" them – here's my script, have at it. Everytime an issue came in, it was like Christmas for me.

Overstreet: You've written for a lot of different fields. How does that process compare to any of the others?

TM: It's still the same for me. Television and books actually take longer to get to the final result than comics do, but the process is the same. On TV shows that I've worked, I'm still writing and tweaking the script even as it's being recorded in the booth – if an actor has trouble with a line or something on the page sounds bad when it's said out loud, then I'm there to try to fix it. It's all that team stuff that you hear about – making comics and TV shows and books are all team efforts. It's just the size of the team that varies, and how you can manage the process to make something good. The big difference is the audience – I hardly ever hear from TV watchers or book readers, but I know how to find the comic book audience. They're online, and they show up at conventions, so I can interact with them and get that real "I love you!/You suck!" dynamic going.

Overstreet: What happened that the second series of *Dinosaurs For Hire* came to an end?

TM: This is where I made a strategic mistake, one of those live and learn deals. The cut-off for books at Malibu at that time was between 20,000-25,000, depending on a variety of factors. *DFH* (and *The Protectors* and *Ex-Mutants*) had been heading that way and based on projections the end was coming. The books were going away, and Roland was going to transition over to the Ultraverse where he'd already been editing a couple of books. So sales did it in. It seems outrageous now that a comic would be cancelled at sales of 20,000 copies, but it was a different industry then.

What I should've done was taken over the book as a packager and tried to take it somewhere else (or package it for Malibu) as an outside vendor, and looked at other options like going back to black and white and/or relaunching it. But the industry was collapsing at just around the same time, so any

placement for the letterer, and punch up the dialogue a bit, especially if Mitch added some fun stuff which he always did. Then when the lettering came back, I'd go through it again before sending it to the inker, and when it came back inked, I'd do a final pass on the dialogue. It's one of the benefits of having an inhouse lettering department and coloring department. They were all very patient with my selfish system, and I tried not to take advantage and just get changes made when they had gaps in their day.

Overstreet: Just a bit ago you described the "magical process" of comic book writing, waiting to see what the artist does with the script, and so on. For you is that something you still enjoy or is that something that fades naturally with experience?

TM: I still enjoy it. It's all good – you send something off to someone else, you hope it connects with them, and when the art comes back it's always

of those moves might not have succeeded. But I would've like to have tried.

Overstreet: With a given that you'll probably play the weasel card, again, can you pick out any particularly favorite issues from the second series?
TM: I won't weasel this time – the first issue of the second series. It had been quite a while since I written the guys, and I had a lot of stuff swirling around inside just dying to get out. That first issue is just an explosion of a billion thoughts, ideas, jokes and characters.

Overstreet: Was there anything with the series that you wanted to do but didn't get around to?
TM: Not really. I was always writing close to the wire just to get the current issue completed, so I wasn't thinking long-term and hadn't plotted out any spin-offs or side projects. There was one idea that always lurked around in the back of my head, but it was just an idea: a 4-issue series of solo issues, all #1s, starring each Dinosaur.

Overstreet: What is the property's status at this point?
TM: It's funny. It was in limbo for awhile. Malibu Comics had certain publishing rights, but I held all the media exploitation rights. As the second series ended, Malibu was up for sale. The company was partially owned then by the Malaysian billionaire businessman Ananda Krishnan, through an organization called Worldwide Sports & Entertainment (WSE) which was made up of some ex-Goldman Sachs suits. As the comic book market was crashing, they were anxious to get their money out before they lost it, so they were trying to force a sale or find investors to take their place. Dinosaurs For Hire's publishing contract was listing as one of the assets and I couldn't get it back. Then Malibu was sold to Marvel and my publishing contract went with it.

I tried to negotiate those rights back because Marvel had no other rights beyond publishing and they weren't interested in it. But I couldn't make it happen – they held firm. But there's also a clause in the contract that Malibu Publisher Dave Olbrich had added in years earlier – I don't remember the

Tom Mason back in Malibu days

exact wording, but it basically said that there couldn't be a *Dinosaurs For Hire* comic book without my direct participation and approval. So the property was just at a standstill until those rights lapsed. And I forgot all about it, until a friend of mine named J.C. Vaughn emailed me and said "I think that contract has expired now." And he was right. So I contacted Marvel and got the rights back. It was lucky too, because it was about a year before Disney bought them. If I'd waited, I'd have to deal with Disney legal instead of Marvel legal, and who knows how that would've gone?

That's where *Dinosaurs For Hire* is now – fully in my hands. And I've been working on some scripts for a possible relaunch.

Overstreet: Is there any time table for that or is it just as the opportunity presents itself?
TM: The opportunity has definitely presented itself. I'm just negotiating the deal points to see if we can make it happen. I'm hopeful! But making comics is a funny business, and there are lots of twists and turns getting something published.

Overstreet: What else are you working on at present?
TM: Dan and I wrapped up production on 52 episodes of an animated series called *Bat Pat* that should be out in late 2015 or early 2016. Dan and I are working on our 16th Captain Awesome book for Simon & Schuster. I'm doing some development work on an animated series that's going to Cannes in the fall, and I have a couple of pitches in at Space Goat for possible mini-series in 2016. And I've just started writing for a new show for Netflix – the series got a 20-episode commitment. Beyond that? It's anybody's guess.

MARVEL 2099

Marvel 2099 is a Marvel Comics imprint that presented a possible future of the Marvel universe set in the year 2099. In 1992, Stan Lee and John Byrne developed a series called *The Marvel World of Tomorrow* to explore the futuristic concept, but then it evolved into an entire line of comics. It was originally going to be Marvel 2093 (100 years after many of the books would launch) before landing at the slightly more distant Marvel 2099.

The imprint was set in a dystopian, high-tech world with North America ruled by mega-corporations like Alchemax and its private police force, the ominously named Public Eye. Early on, Marvel 2099 establishes that superheroes are no longer a part of the world, that many have become mythological or even religious figures, and that the present day (in the 1990s) was known as the Age of Heroes.

It started with four titles: *Spider-Man 2099*, *Ravage 2099*, *Doom 2099*, and *Punisher 2099*. The line began with Peter David and Rick Leonardi's *Spider-Man 2099* and geneticist Miguel O'Hara who unintentionally turns himself into the new Wall Crawler. In *Ravage 2099*, Lee and Paul Ryan introduced the newly created (rather than reimagined) character Paul-Phillip Ravage who was mutated by the future's pollutants. *Doom 2099* was created by John Francis Moore and Pat Broderick, starring Victor Von Doom as an antihero who materializes after having been missing for decades. Pat Mills, Tony Skinner, and Tom Morgan created Jack Gallows to carry on Frank Castle's work as *The Punisher 2099*.

Building on the success of the initial quartet of titles, Marvel 2099 soon expanded to feature more ongoing books. *2099 Unlimited* introduced Hulk 2099, and explored multiple characters within Marvel 2099, with contributions by Gerard Jones, Evan Skolnick, Chris Wozniak, and early work by Warren Ellis. John Francis Moore and Ron Lim led the *X-Men 2099* series with team members like Desert Ghost, Skullfire, Meanstreak, Bloodhawk, Metalhead, and others. *Ghost Rider 2099* by Len Kaminski

embraced cyberpunk with hacker Kenshiro Cochrane being killed and resurrected as the robot-controlling Ghost Rider. In *Hulk 2099*, Gerard Jones and Dwayne Turner introduced John Eisenhart as a studio executive who became the new gamma-altered Hulk. *Fantastic Four 2099* brought the original foursome to the future where it is questioned if they are the real team or a group of clones. A team of young mutants were featured in *X-Nation 2099*, created by Tom Peyer and Humberto Ramos.

When the novelty of the futuristic stories wore off and sales began to decline, Marvel started closing the chapter on Marvel 2099 by cancelling the titles and filtering surviving characters into one book: *2099: World of Tomorrow*. The imprint officially closed in '98 with the one-shot *2099: Manifest Destiny*. In the book Captain America is pulled from suspended animation, then he and Miguel O'Hara assemble a new team of Avengers with the 2099 heroes.

Though the line ended, it wasn't the last time that readers would see the characters of Marvel 2099, namely Miguel O'Hara. Spider-Man 2099 was featured in the *Captain Marvel* storyline "Future Tense." Robert Kirkman wrote a group of *Marvel Knights 2099* one-shots for the Marvel Knights imprint's 5th anniversary in 2004. The Exiles traveled to 2099 in their "World Tour" arc, in which Spider-Man 2099 joined the team and left with them.

The *Timestorm* miniseries was a crossover that saw the current Marvel characters meeting alternate versions of those in 2099. Spider-Man 2099 appeared in *The Superior Spider-Man*, then he led three more volumes of his own series. The characters of 2099 participated in the "Secret Wars" event and Wade Wilson's daughter Warda led the *Deadpool 2099* series. A series of one-shots commemorated Marvel 2099's 25th anniversary, starring Spider-Man, Fantastic Four, Doom, Punisher, and Venom of 2099.

– Amanda Sheriff

FIRST PUBLICATION:
Spider-Man 2099 Vol. 1 #1
(November 1992)

LAST PUBLICATION:
2099: Manifest Destiny
(March 1998)

REVIVAL(S):
Black Panther 2099 (2004), *Daredevil 2099* (2004), *Inhumans 2099* (2004), *Mutant 2099* (2004), *Punisher 2099 Vol. 2* (2004), *Spider-Man 2099 Vol. 2* (2014), *Spider-Man 2099 Vol. 3* (2015), *Secret Wars 2099* (2015), *Deadpool 2099* (2016), *2099 Alpha* (2020), *Conan 2099* (2020), *Fantastic Four 2099 Vol. 2* (2020), *Punisher 2099 Vol. 3* (2020), *2099 Omega* (2020), *Doom 2099 Vol. 2* (2020), *Ghost Rider 2099 Vol. 2* (2020), *Spider-Man 2099 Vol. 4* (2020), *Venom 2099* (2020).

Rick Leonardi and Al Williamson's original cover art for *Spider-Man 2099* #11 (1993).
Image courtesy of Heritage Auctions.

DOOM 2099 #1
FOIL EMBOSSED COVER
JANUARY 1993
$6

DOOM 2099 #1
FOIL EMBOSSED NEWSSTAND EDITION
JANUARY 1993
$6

DOOM 2099 #2
FEBRUARY 1993
$4

DOOM 2099 #3
MARCH 1993
$4

DOOM 2099 #4
APRIL 1993
$4

DOOM 2099 #5
MAY 1993
$4

DOOM 2099 #6
JUNE 1993
$4

DOOM 2099 #7
JULY 1993
$4

DOOM 2099 #8
AUGUST 1993
$4

DOOM 2099 #9
SEPTEMBER 1993
$4

DOOM 2099 #10
OCTOBER 1993
$4

DOOM 2099 #11
NOVEMBER 1993
$4

DOOM 2099 #12
DECEMBER 1993
$4

DOOM 2099 #13
JANUARY 1994
$4

DOOM 2099 #14
FEBRUARY 1994
$4

DOOM 2099 #15
MARCH 1994
$4

DOOM 2099 #16
APRIL 1994
$4

DOOM 2099 #17
MAY 1994
$4

DOOM 2099 #18
JUNE 1994
$4

DOOM 2099 #18
BAGGED WITH POSTER
JUNE 1994
$5

DOOM 2099 #19
JULY 1994
$4

DOOM 2099 #20
AUGUST 1994
$4

DOOM 2099 #21
SEPTEMBER 1994
$4

DOOM 2099 #22
OCTOBER 1994
$4

DOOM 2099 #23
NOVEMBER 1994
$4

DOOM 2099 #24
DECEMBER 1994
$4

DOOM 2099 #25
FOIL EMBOSSED COVER
JANUARY 1995
$6

DOOM 2099 #25
JANUARY 1994
$5

DOOM 2099 #26
FEBRUARY 1995
$4

DOOM 2099 #27
MARCH 1995
$4

DOOM 2099 #28
APRIL 1995
$4

DOOM 2099 #29
VARIANT WITH ACETATE OUTER COVER
MAY 1995
$5

DOOM 2099 #29
MAY 1995
$4

DOOM 2099 #30
JUNE 1995
$4

DOOM 2099 #31
JULY 1995
$4

DOOM 2099 #32
AUGUST 1995
$4

DOOM 2099 #33
SEPTEMBER 1995
$4

DOOM 2099 #34
OCTOBER 1995
$4

DOOM 2099 #35
NOVEMBER 1995
$4

DOOM 2099 #36
DECEMBER 1995
$4

DOOM 2099 #37
JANUARY 1996
$4

DOOM 2099 #38
FEBRUARY 1996
$4

DOOM 2099 #39
MARCH 1996
$4

DOOM 2099 #40
APRIL 1996
$4

DOOM 2099 #41
MAY 1996
$4

DOOM 2099 #42
JUNE 1996
$4

DOOM 2099 #43
JULY 1996
$4

DOOM 2099 #44
AUGUST 1996
$4

PUNISHER 2099 #1
FOIL EMBOSSED COVER
FEBRUARY 1993
$6

PUNISHER 2099 #1
FOIL EMBOSSED NEWSSTAND EDITION
FEBRUARY 1993
$6

PUNISHER 2099 #2
MARCH 1993
$4

PUNISHER 2099 #3
APRIL 1993
$4

PUNISHER 2099 #4
MAY 1993
$4

PUNISHER 2099 #5
JUNE 1993
$4

PUNISHER 2099 #6
JULY 1993
$4

PUNISHER 2099 #7
AUGUST 1993
$4

PUNISHER 2099 #8
SEPTEMBER 1993
$4

PUNISHER 2099 #9
OCTOBER 1993
$4

PUNISHER 2099 #10
NOVEMBER 1993
$4

PUNISHER 2099 #11
DECEMBER 1993
$4

PUNISHER 2099 #12
JANUARY 1994
$4

PUNISHER 2099 #13
FEBRUARY 1994
$4

PUNISHER 2099 #14
MARCH 1994
$4

PUNISHER 2099 #15
APRIL 1994
$4

PUNISHER 2099 #16
MAY 1994
$4

PUNISHER 2099 #17
JUNE 1994
$4

PUNISHER 2099 #18
JULY 1994
$4

PUNISHER 2099 #19
AUGUST 1994
$4

PUNISHER 2099 #20
SEPTEMBER 1994
$4

PUNISHER 2099 #21
OCTOBER 1994
$4

PUNISHER 2099 #22
NOVEMBER 1994
$4

PUNISHER 2099 #23
DECEMBER 1994
$4

PUNISHER 2099 #24
JANUARY 1995
$4

PUNISHER 2099 #25
FOIL EMBOSSED COVER
FEBRUARY 1995
$6

PUNISHER 2099 #25
FEBRUARY 1995
$5

PUNISHER 2099 #26
MARCH 1995
$4

PUNISHER 2099 #27
APRIL 1995
$4

PUNISHER 2099 #28
MAY 1995
$4

PUNISHER 2099 #29
JUNE 1995
$4

PUNISHER 2099 #30
JULY 1995
$4

PUNISHER 2099 #31
AUGUST 1995
$4

PUNISHER 2099 #32
SEPTEMBER 1995
$4

PUNISHER 2099 #33
OCTOBER 1995
$4

PUNISHER 2099 #34
NOVEMBER 1995
$4

RAVAGE 2099 #1
FOIL EMBOSSED COVER
DECEMBER 1992
$5

RAVAGE 2099 #1
FOIL EMBOSSED NEWSSTAND EDITION
DECEMBER 1992
$5

RAVAGE 2099 #2
JANUARY 1993
$4

RAVAGE 2099 #3
FEBRUARY 1993
$4

RAVAGE 2099 #4
MARCH 1993
$4

RAVAGE 2099 #5
APRIL 1993
$4

RAVAGE 2099 #6
MAY 1993
$4

RAVAGE 2099 #7
JUNE 1993
$4

RAVAGE 2099 #8
JULY 1993
$4

RAVAGE 2099 #9
AUGUST 1993
$4

RAVAGE 2099 #10
SEPTEMBER 1993
$4

RAVAGE 2099 #11
OCTOBER 1993
$4

RAVAGE 2099 #12
NOVEMBER 1993
$4

RAVAGE 2099 #13
DECEMBER 1993
$4

RAVAGE 2099 #14
JANUARY 1994
$4

RAVAGE 2099 #15
FEBRUARY 1994
$4

RAVAGE 2099 #16
MARCH 1994
$4

RAVAGE 2099 #17
APRIL 1994
$4

RAVAGE 2099 #18
MAY 1994
$4

RAVAGE 2099 #19
JUNE 1994
$4

RAVAGE 2099 #20
JULY 1994
$4

RAVAGE 2099 #21
AUGUST 1994
$4

RAVAGE 2099 #22
SEPTEMBER 1994
$4

RAVAGE 2099 #23
OCTOBER 1994
$4

RAVAGE 2099 #24
NOVEMBER 1994
$4

RAVAGE 2099 #25
FOIL EMBOSSED COVER
DECEMBER 1994
$6

RAVAGE 2099 #25
DECEMBER 1994
$5

RAVAGE 2099 #26
JANUARY 1995
$4

RAVAGE 2099 #27
FEBRUARY 1995
$4

RAVAGE 2099 #28
MARCH 1995
$4

RAVAGE 2099 #29
APRIL 1995
$4

RAVAGE 2099 #30
MAY 1995
$4

RAVAGE 2099 #31
JUNE 1995
$4

RAVAGE 2099 #32
JULY 1995
$4

RAVAGE 2099 #33
AUGUST 1995
$4

SPIDER-MAN 2099 #1
FOIL EMBOSSED COVER
NOVEMBER 1992
$1 $4 $10

SPIDER-MAN 2099 #1
FOIL EMBOSSED NEWSSTAND EDITION
NOVEMBER 1992
$1 $4 $10

SPIDER-MAN 2099 #2
DECEMBER 1992
$4

SPIDER-MAN 2099 #3
JANUARY 1993
$4

SPIDER-MAN 2099 #4
FEBRUARY 1993
$4

SPIDER-MAN 2099 #5
MARCH 1993
$4

SPIDER-MAN 2099 #6
APRIL 1993
$4

SPIDER-MAN 2099 #7
MAY 1993
$4

SPIDER-MAN 2099 #8
JUNE 1993
$4

SPIDER-MAN 2099 #9
JULY 1993
$4

SPIDER-MAN 2099 #10
AUGUST 1993
$4

SPIDER-MAN 2099 #11
SEPTEMBER 1993
$4

SPIDER-MAN 2099 #12
OCTOBER 1993
$4

SPIDER-MAN 2099 #13
NOVEMBER 1993
$5

SPIDER-MAN 2099 #14
DECEMBER 1993
$4

SPIDER-MAN 2099 #15
JANUARY 1994
$4

SPIDER-MAN 2099 #16
FEBRUARY 1994
$4

SPIDER-MAN 2099 #17
MARCH 1994
$4

SPIDER-MAN 2099 #18
APRIL 1994
$4

SPIDER-MAN 2099 #19
MAY 1994
$4

SPIDER-MAN 2099 #20
JUNE 1994
$4

SPIDER-MAN 2099 #21
JULY 1994
$4

SPIDER-MAN 2099 #22
AUGUST 1994
$4

SPIDER-MAN 2099 #23
SEPTEMBER 1994
$4

SPIDER-MAN 2099 #24
OCTOBER 1994
$4

SPIDER-MAN 2099 #25
FOIL EMBOSSED COVER
NOVEMBER 1994
$5

SPIDER-MAN 2099 #25
NOVEMBER 1994
$4

SPIDER-MAN 2099 #26
DECEMBER 1994
$4

SPIDER-MAN 2099 #27
JANUARY 1995
$4

SPIDER-MAN 2099 #28
FEBRUARY 1995
$4

SPIDER-MAN 2099 #29
MARCH 1995
$4

SPIDER-MAN 2099 #30
APRIL 1995
$4

SPIDER-MAN 2099 #31
MAY 1995
$4

SPIDER-MAN 2099 #32
JUNE 1995
$4

SPIDER-MAN 2099 #33
JULY 1995
$4

SPIDER-MAN 2099 #34
AUGUST 1995
$4

SPIDER-MAN 2099 #35
SEPTEMBER 1995
$5

SPIDER-MAN 2099 #35
VARIANT COVER
SEPTEMBER 1995
$5

SPIDER-MAN 2099 #36
OCTOBER 1995
$5

SPIDER-MAN 2099 #36
VARIANT COVER
OCTOBER 1995
$5

SPIDER-MAN 2099 #37
NOVEMBER 1995
$5

SPIDER-MAN 2099 #37
VARIANT COVER
NOVEMBER 1995
$5

SPIDER-MAN 2099 #38
DECEMBER 1995
$5

Spider-Man 2099 #38
Variant cover
December 1995
$5

Spider-Man 2099 #39
January 1996
$4

Spider-Man 2099 #40
February 1996
$4

Spider-Man 2099 #41
March 1996
$4

Spider-Man 2099 #42
April 1996
$4

Spider-Man 2099 #43
May 1996
$4

Spider-Man 2099 #44
June 1996
$4

Spider-Man 2099 #45
July 1996
$4

Spider-Man 2099 #46
August 1996
$4

**SPIDER-MAN 2099
ANNUAL #1**
1994
$5

**SPIDER-MAN 2099
SPECIAL #1**
1995
$5

**2099: WORLD OF
TOMORROW #1**
SEPTEMBER 1996
$4

**2099: WORLD OF
TOMORROW #2**
OCTOBER 1996
$4

**2099: WORLD OF
TOMORROW #3**
NOVEMBER 1996
$4

**2099: WORLD OF
TOMORROW #4**
DECEMBER 1996
$4

**2099: WORLD OF
TOMORROW #5**
JANUARY 1997
$4

**2099: WORLD OF
TOMORROW #6**
FEBRUARY 1997
$4

**2099: WORLD OF
TOMORROW #7**
MARCH 1997
$4

**2099: WORLD OF
TOMORROW #8**
APRIL 1997
$4

In 1990, Stan Lee announced "The Marvel World of Tomorrow," a concept exploring future versions of popular Marvel characters that he had been quietly developing during his years as Marvel's Hollywood brand ambassador. At the time, Lee also revealed that superstar artist John Byrne would be his collaborator on the project. Soon, however, creative differences between the two industry giants would result in the creation of two separate universes: Lee's popular 2099 imprint and Byrne's independently published graphic novel, *2112*, a prequel to his hit creator-owned series, *Next Men*.

It all began with a typically bombastic announcement in Lee's widely read Stan's Soapbox column in the August issue of *Marvel Age* magazine:

We'll soon be presenting another Marvel universe, a somewhat altered Marvel universe, a Marvel universe skewed to a different time, with different dangers, different powers, different dramas, in a world that will be known, now and forever, as – THE MARVEL WORLD OF TOMORROW! (...) Perhaps the most exciting part of the whole megillah is the fact that I'll be collaborating with JOLTIN' JOHNNY BYRNE, one of the brightest stars in the comics firmament, who's co-plotting and illustrating our very first issue! [1]

In a discussion of his *Next Men* series, John Byrne explains how their collaboration began. "In 1990," Byrne recalls, "Stan Lee contacted me and asked me if I would like to be 'editor-in-chief' of a whole new line he was going to create at Marvel – a line which would be set in Marvel's future, unconnected to the Marvel Universe as we knew it. As it happened, I had been giving some thought to a 'Futureverse' of my own, and, being flattered by Stan's offer, I suggested that what I had come up with (but at that time thought I had no place to develop) would fit the bill for his project." [2]

The plan at the time was for Lee to script, and for Byrne to plot and draw a 64-page pilot. Byrne's first thought was that if he didn't do it, somebody else would. "Call it ego," Byrne admits, "but I felt I was better qualified than most to project the future timelines of the universe with which I had been so intimately involved for so many years. So I took a number of different notions that had been percolating through my head for some time, and shuffled them into a package [to create a] logical extrapolation of Marvel's timeline." [3]

When John Byrne shared his initial ideas, however, Stan Lee had his own thoughts about how the project should take shape. According to Byrne, "When Stan saw the pilot pages, he asked for more specific [Marvel Universe] references. I'd tried to keep the thing 'clean,' so as not to turn the whole [Marvel Universe] into a Superboy story."

But Lee was looking for more of a connection to the existing Marvel Universe. "Stan thought we should at least hint at what had happened to some of the folk we knew from the present continuity," Byrne stated. [4]

To work in these additional story threads, Byrne added 12 additional pages and some bridging material to make them fit. But this relatively simple workaround proved insufficient for Stan Lee. "Unfortunately, things were not quite what I had been led to believe," Byrne said. [5]

Ultimately, due to the growing clash of visions, the highly anticipated Lee/Byrne collaboration was not to be. According to Paul Ryan, Byrne's replacement on the series (by then retitled *Ravage 2099*) the "creative differences" between Byrne and Lee had become apparent. "It didn't work out. John walked away." [6] Tom DeFalco, then Editor-in-Chief of Marvel Comics called Ryan, asking if he'd consider replacing John Byrne on Lee's series. "I said, 'Why don't you check with Stan first to make sure it's okay,' and Stan said, 'Why not?'" Ryan said. [7]

After Byrne's departure from the "World of Tomorrow" project, he was left with a completed 64-page graphic novel without a publisher. "I found myself in a position in which I could only

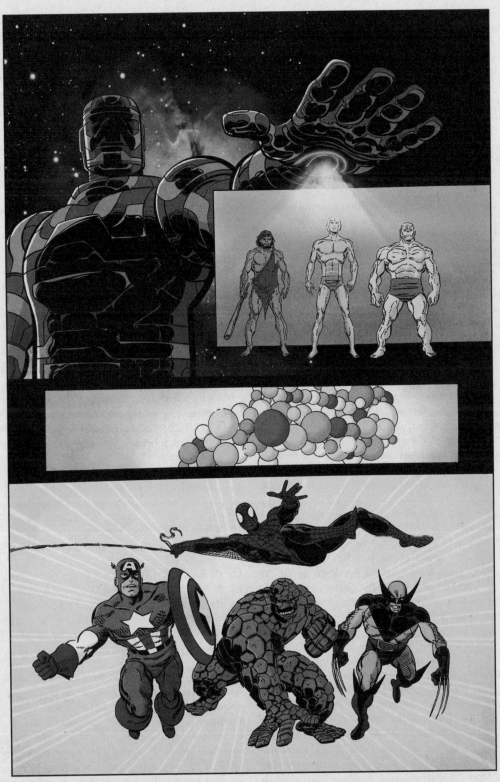

Unpublished original art by John Byrne newly colored by Rich Seetoo.
Image courtesy of J.C. Washburn.

maintain artistic integrity – pretentious term, but there you are – if I took back that part of the work that was exclusively mine, as distinguished from the elements [added] to make the story fit into Marvel continuity," Byrne said. [8] "Luckily, it was not a case of rewriting or redrawing, but simply of removing pages I had not wanted in there in the first place. I'd taken a set of concepts, bent them slightly to fit Stan's needs, and then had only to 'unbend' them to get back to my own original material." [9]

The problem, though, was that this left Byrne with some 64 pages of original material which, at that moment, had no home. "I'd received a tentative offer from DC Comics, one of their editors expressing an interest in publishing the work," Byrne recalls. "But I felt that what I really needed to do was go 'independent' with this. I needed to find a company that would be willing to publish the work, while allowing me to retain full rights to the property. As memory serves, it was my longtime friend and sometime collaborator, Roger Stern, who suggested I try Dark Horse." [10]

Byrne was hesitant to publish the book with DC. "That seemed vaguely scabrous somehow," he recalls. [11] So Byrne decided to follow Stern's advice and reached out to Dark Horse instead. "They accepted the proposal with open arms. I also pitched Next Men, which had been floating in my brain for a while, and which they also liked." [12] In his conversation with Bob Schreck, Special Projects Director at Dark Horse, Byrne initially "sort of tiptoed around the idea" of what he wanted to do. But "by the end of the conversation, I was tiptoeing no longer," Byrne said. He offered "World of Tomorrow" (now retitled 2112) to Dark Horse, and Schreck accepted the book. They were "cheerfully girding their loins for a confrontation with Marvel, which, happily, never came," Byrne said. [13]

Although Lee and Byrne would successfully reunite years later, their "World of Tomorrow" collaboration would bear little resemblance to the 2099 series that ultimately saw print. Despite Byrne having left with his own portion of "The Marvel World of Tomorrow" concept, Marvel still wanted to pursue the commercial potential of a line of comics set in a futuristic Marvel superhero universe. In his book, Marvel Comics: The Untold Story, Sean Howe outlines how Marvel envisioned this new direction. "With pressure to beat 1991's astronomical sales figures," Tom DeFalco

and Marvel's editorial staff 'focused on its big launches,'" Howe writes. "A discarded Stan Lee/John Byrne project about Marvel characters in the year 2099 was retooled into an entire new line of comics: futuristic versions of Spider-Man, The Punisher, and Doctor Doom provided plenty of collectible product." [14] While John Byrne's 2112/Next Men universe lasted 45 issues, and is still regarded by many as his most fully realized work.

– J.C. Washburn

Bibliography

1 Lee, Stan. Marvel Age Magazine #91. Marvel Comics, August 1990.
2 John Byrne, "FAQ: Next Men," ByrneRobotics.com, https://www.byrne-robotics.com/FAQ/listing.asp?ID=15.
3 Byrne, John. Forward, John Byrne's Next Men: Book One. Dark Horse Comics, January 1996.
4 Byrne, "FAQ: Next Men."
5 Byrne, Forward, John Byrne's Next Men: Book One.
6 Victor Cardigan, "Ravage 2099: An Interview with Artist Paul Ryan," Doom2099.com, https://www.doom2099.com/25/february_ravage/paul_ryan_interview.html.
7 Cardigan, "An Interview with Artist Paul Ryan."
8 Byrne, Forward, John Byrne's Next Men: Book One.
9 Byrne, "FAQ: Next Men."
10 Byrne, Forward, John Byrne's Next Men: Book One.
11 Byrne, "FAQ: Next Men."
12 Byrne, "FAQ: Next Men."
13 Byrne, Forward, John Byrne's Next Men: Book One.
14 Howe, Sean. Marvel Comics: The Untold Story. Harper Perennial, October 2013.

J.C. Washburn is an American writer, historian, and critic in the field of comics. He is a longtime journalist in New England, and has been the founder, moderator, and a major contributor for more than a dozen online comic book communities totaling over 50,000 members, since 2015. He is also a lifelong comic book aficionado, with a special interest in the Bronze Age and Modern Age, a period covering roughly 1970 to the present.

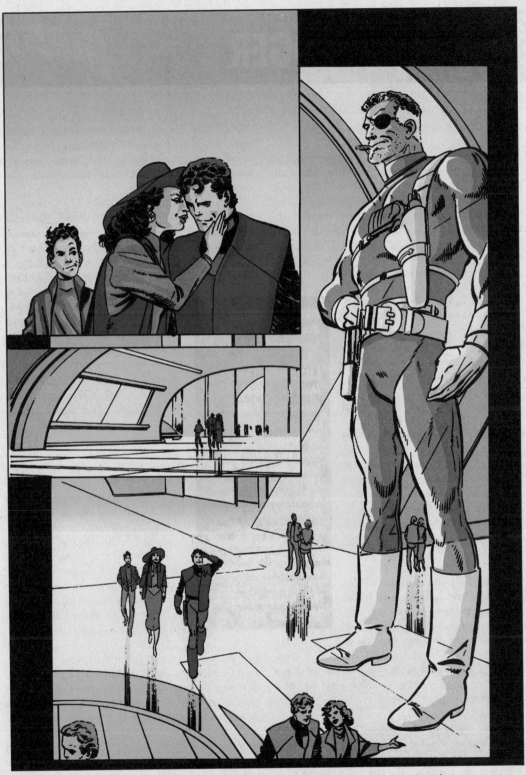

Unpublished original art by John Byrne newly colored by Matt Web.
Image courtesy of J.C. Washburn.

It started, as these things do, when Mike Baron met Steve Rude in Madison, Wisconsin.

"I was working at an insurance company when an editor friend phoned me and said there was a guy trying to sell them his art and I ought to take a look. I arranged to meet Dude on the steps of the Student Union. He opened his portfolio right there on the steps and I gave up my dream of drawing. I asked Steve what he wanted to do. "I want to do comics, but I can't write. What do you want to do?" And thus, we began to work together," Baron said.

Initially set in the year 2481, Horatio Hellpop's considerable powers as Nexus come from an alien entity known as the Merk, who demands Nexus hunt down and kill mass murderers that come to Hellpop in dreams.

With writing inspirations that included Carl Barks, John D. MacDonald, and Philip Jose Farmer, Baron's stories of Nexus contained everything from serious science fiction to action-adventure, and from spiritual searching to moments of whimsy. Rude's art style was a match for the eclectic nature of Baron's script, showcasing strong, fluid linework and the same versatile range as the stories.

Nexus Vol. 1 #1 was the first of three black and white magazine-sized issues at Capital Comics. It was the first publication from the new imprint of Capital City Distribution. After those issues, Baron, Rude, and Capital launched a color comics line that would include both *Nexus* Vol. 2 and a new Mike Baron creation, *The Badger* (as well as a third, unrelated title, *Whisper*).

The 1980s world of *The Badger*, Norbert Sykes, a Vietnam veteran who lives with centuries-old a Druid weather wizard, and the future depicted in *Nexus* were centuries apart, but the characters would meet for the first time in *Nexus* #6, which left thing on a cliffhanger when Capital ended their comic book line.

FIRST PUBLICATION:
Nexus Vol. 1 #1 (Capital Comics, January 1981)

LAST PUBLICATION:
Nexus Vol. 2 #6 (Capital Comics, March 1984)

REVIVAL(S):
Nexus Vol. 2 #7 – 80 (First Comics, April 1985 – May 1991), *Nexus: The Origin, Nexus: Alien Justice, Nexus: The Wages of Sin, Nexus: Executioner's Song, Nexus: God Con, Nexus: Nightmare in Blue* (Dark Horse, December 1992 – October 1997), *Nexus* #99-102 (Rude Dude Productions, July 2007 – June 2009)

First Comics stepped in, picking up with *Nexus* #7 and *Badger* #5, and both series enjoyed healthy runs. When First stopped publishing, Nexus survived again by moving to Dark Horse, where it moved to a series of mini-series format rather than continuous numbering.

In *Nexus: Executioner's* Song #1, though Baron and Rude made a nod toward the original numbering; After Nexus Volume 2 #80 at First, and *Nexus: The Origin, Nexus: Alien Justice, Nexus: The Wages of Sin, Nexus: Executioner's Song, Nexus: God Con, Nexus: Nightmare in Blue* mini-series – and what we now call "ghost numbering," Steve Rude's Rude Dude venture took over publishing *Nexus:Space Opera*, also known as *Nexus* #99-102. This numbering did not include crossovers with Madman or Magnus, Robot Fighter or *Nexus the Liberator*, since neither Baron nor Rude were involved with that mini-series.

Badger has moved to Image, then IDW, and back to First Comics over the years. Both title characters have been featured in novels by Baron, original graphic novels, archival editions and more. Nexus had multiple spin-offs including one-shots for supporting characters Clonezone and Mezz, multiple mini-series with Nexus compatriot Judah Maccabee, *Hammer of God*, as well as a reprint series, *Nexus Legends*.

In addition to crossovers in the pages of Nexus, First Comics had the characters interact with other characters they published in the five-issue mini-series *Crossroads* (see *The Overstreet Comic Book Price Guide to Lost Universes* #1, pages 158-159).

In recent times, both Baron (*Nexus: Nefarious*) and Rude (*Nexus: The Coming of Gourmando*) have published independent adventures of the character. As we go to press, each has Nexus projects forthcoming.

Steve Rude's original art for *Nexus* #1 Page 21 (1983).
Image courtesy of Heritage Auctions.

THE BADGER #1
1983
$2 $6 $15

THE BADGER #2
1983
$4

THE BADGER #3
1984
$4

THE BADGER #4
APRIL 1984
$4

THE BADGER #5
MAY 1985
$4

THE BADGER #6
JULY 1985
$4

THE BADGER #7
SEPTEMBER 1985
$4

THE BADGER #8
NOVEMBER 1985
$4

THE BADGER #9
JANUARY 1986
$4

THE BADGER #10
MARCH 1986
$4

THE BADGER #11
MAY 1986
$4

THE BADGER #12
JUNE 1986
$4

THE BADGER #13
JULY 1986
$4

THE BADGER #14
AUGUST 1986
$4

THE BADGER #15
SEPTEMBER 1986
$4

THE BADGER #16
OCTOBER 1986
$4

THE BADGER #17
NOVEMBER 1986
$4

THE BADGER #18
DECEMBER 1986
$4

THE BADGER #19
JANUARY 1987
$4

THE BADGER #20
FEBRUARY 1987
$4

THE BADGER #21
MARCH 1987
$4

THE BADGER #22
APRIL 1987
$4

THE BADGER #23
MAY 1987
$4

THE BADGER #24
JUNE 1987
$4

THE BADGER #25
JULY 1987
$4

THE BADGER #26
AUGUST 1987
$4

THE BADGER #27
SEPTEMBER 1987
$4

THE BADGER #28
OCTOBER 1987
$4

THE BADGER #29
NOVEMBER 1987
$4

THE BADGER #30
DECEMBER 1987
$4

THE BADGER #31
JANUARY 1988
$4

THE BADGER #32
FEBRUARY 1988
$4

THE BADGER #33
MARCH 1988
$4

THE BADGER #34
APRIL 1988
$4

THE BADGER #35
MAY 1988
$4

THE BADGER #36
JUNE 1988
$4

THE BADGER #37
JULY 1988
$4

THE BADGER #38
AUGUST 1988
$4

THE BADGER #39
SEPTEMBER 1988
$4

THE BADGER #40
OCTOBER 1988
$4

THE BADGER #41
NOVEMBER 1988
$4

THE BADGER #42
DECEMBER 1988
$4

THE BADGER #43
JANUARY 1989
$4

THE BADGER #44
FEBRUARY 1989
$4

THE BADGER #45
MARCH 1989
$4

THE BADGER #46
APRIL 1989
$4

THE BADGER #47
MAY 1989
$4

THE BADGER #48
JUNE 1989
$4

THE BADGER #49
JULY 1989
$4

THE BADGER #50
AUGUST 1989
$5

THE BADGER #51
SEPTEMBER 1989
$4

THE BADGER #52
OCTOBER 1989
$4

THE BADGER #53
NOVEMBER 1989
$4

THE BADGER #54
DECEMBER 1989
$4

THE BADGER #55
JANUARY 1990
$4

THE BADGER #56
FEBRUARY 1990
$4

THE BADGER #57
MARCH 1990
$4

THE BADGER #58
APRIL 1990
$4

THE BADGER #59
MAY 1990
$4

THE BADGER #60
JUNE 1990
$4

THE BADGER #61
JULY 1990
$4

THE BADGER #62
AUGUST 1990
$4

THE BADGER #63
SEPTEMBER 1990
$4

THE BADGER #64
OCTOBER 1990
$4

THE BADGER #65
NOVEMBER 1990
$4

THE BADGER #66
DECEMBER 1990
$4

THE BADGER #67
JANUARY 1991
$4

THE BADGER #68
FEBRUARY 1991
$4

THE BADGER #69
MARCH 1991
$4

THE BADGER #70
APRIL 1991
$4

BADGER BEDLAM #1
ALSO LABELED VOLUME 2 #1
SPRING 1991
$5

BADGER GOES BERZERK #1
SEPTEMBER 1989
$4

BADGER GOES BERZERK #2
OCTOBER 1989
$4

BADGER GOES BERZERK #3
NOVEMBER 1989
$4

BADGER GOES BERZERK #4
DECEMBER 1989
$4

**BADGER:
SHATTERED MIRROR #1**
JULY 1994
$4

**BADGER:
SHATTERED MIRROR #2**
AUGUST 1994
$4

**BADGER:
SHATTERED MIRROR #3**
SEPTEMBER 1994
$4

**BADGER:
SHATTERED MIRROR #4**
OCTOBER 1994
$4

**BADGER: ZEN POP
FUNNY-ANIMAL VERSION #1**
JULY 1994
$4

**BADGER: ZEN POP
FUNNY-ANIMAL VERSION #2**
JULY 1994
$4

**THE BADGER VOL. 3 #1
(#78)**
MAY 1997
$4

**THE BADGER VOL. 3 #2
(#79)**
JUNE 1997
$4

**THE BADGER VOL. 3 #3
(#80)**
JULY 1997
$4

**THE BADGER VOL. 3 #4
(#81)**
AUGUST 1997
$4

**THE BADGER VOL. 3 #5
(#82)**
SEPTEMBER 1997
$4

**THE BADGER VOL. 3 #6
(#83)**
OCTOBER 1997
$4

**THE BADGER VOL. 3 #7
(#84)**
NOVEMBER 1997
$4

**THE BADGER VOL. 3 #8
(#85)**
DECEMBER 1997
$4

**THE BADGER VOL. 3 #9
(#86)**
JANUARY 1998
$4

THE BADGER VOL. 3 #10 (#87)
FEBRUARY 1998
$4

THE BADGER VOL. 3 #11 (#88)
MARCH 1998
$4

THE BADGER #1
FEBRUARY 2016
$4

THE BADGER #1
VARIANT COVER
FEBRUARY 2016
$4

THE BADGER #2
MARCH 2016
$4

THE BADGER #2
VARIANT COVER
MARCH 2016
$4

THE BADGER #3
APRIL 2016
$4

THE BADGER #3
VARIANT COVER
APRIL 2016
$4

THE BADGER #4
MAY 2016
$4

THE BADGER #4
VARIANT COVER
MAY 2016
$4

THE BADGER #5
JUNE 2016
$4

THE BADGER #5
VARIANT COVER
JUNE 2016
$4

COYOTE #14
SEPTEMBER 1985
$6

**FIRST COMICS
GRAPHIC NOVEL #19**
1987
$12

**FIRST COMICS
GRAPHIC NOVEL #4**
1985
$15

NEXUS #1
MAGAZINE • JANUARY 1981
$4 $12 $50

NEXUS #2
MAGAZINE • JUNE 1982
$3 $9 $25

NEXUS #3
MAGAZINE • OCTOBER 1994
$2 $6 $16

NEXUS VOL. 2 #1
MAY 1983
$2 $6 $15

NEXUS VOL. 2 #2
JULY 1983
$3

NEXUS VOL. 2 #3
SEPTEMBER 1983
$3

NEXUS VOL. 2 #4
NOVEMBER 1983
$3

NEXUS VOL. 2 #5
JANUARY 1984
$3

NEXUS VOL. 2 #6
MAY 1984
$3

NEXUS VOL. 2 #7
APRIL 1985
$3

NEXUS VOL. 2 #8
MAY 1985
$3

NEXUS VOL. 2 #9
JUNE 1985
$3

NEXUS VOL. 2 #10
JULY 1985
$3

NEXUS VOL. 2 #11
AUGUST 1985
$3

NEXUS VOL. 2 #12
SEPTEMBER 1985
$3

NEXUS VOL. 2 #13
OCTOBER 1985
$3

NEXUS VOL. 2 #14
NOVEMBER 1985
$3

NEXUS VOL. 2 #15
DECEMBER 1985
$3

NEXUS VOL. 2 #16
JANUARY 1986
$3

NEXUS VOL. 2 #17
FEBRUARY 1986
$3

NEXUS VOL. 2 #18
MARCH 1986
$3

NEXUS VOL. 2 #19
APRIL 1986
$3

NEXUS VOL. 2 #20
MAY 1986
$3

NEXUS VOL. 2 #21
JUNE 1986
$3

NEXUS VOL. 2 #22
JULY 1986
$3

NEXUS VOL. 2 #23
AUGUST 1986
$3

NEXUS VOL. 2 #24
SEPTEMBER 1986
$3

NEXUS VOL. 2 #25
OCTOBER 1986
$3

NEXUS VOL. 2 #26
NOVEMBER 1986
$3

NEXUS VOL. 2 #27
DECEMBER 1986
$3

NEXUS VOL. 2 #28
JANUARY 1987
$3

NEXUS VOL. 2 #29
FEBRUARY 1987
$3

NEXUS VOL. 2 #30
MARCH 1987
$3

NEXUS VOL. 2 #31
APRIL 1987
$3

NEXUS VOL. 2 #32
MAY 1987
$3

NEXUS VOL. 2 #33
JUNE 1987
$3

NEXUS VOL. 2 #34
JULY 1987
$3

NEXUS VOL. 2 #35
AUGUST 1987
$3

NEXUS VOL. 2 #36
SEPTEMBER 1987
$3

NEXUS VOL. 2 #37
OCTOBER 1987
$3

NEXUS VOL. 2 #38
NOVEMBER 1987
$3

NEXUS VOL. 2 #39
DECEMBER 1987
$3

NEXUS VOL. 2 #40
JANUARY 1988
$3

NEXUS VOL. 2 #41
FEBRUARY 1988
$3

NEXUS VOL. 2 #42
MARCH 1988
$3

NEXUS VOL. 2 #43
APRIL 1988
$3

NEXUS VOL. 2 #44
MAY 1988
$3

NEXUS VOL. 2 #45
JUNE 1988
$3

NEXUS VOL. 2 #46
JULY 1988
$3

NEXUS VOL. 2 #47
AUGUST 1988
$3

NEXUS VOL. 2 #48
SEPTEMBER 1988
$3

NEXUS VOL. 2 #49
OCTOBER 1988
$3

NEXUS VOL. 2 #50
NOVEMBER 1988
$4

NEXUS VOL. 2 #51
DECEMBER 1988
$3

NEXUS VOL. 2 #52
JANUARY 1989
$3

NEXUS VOL. 2 #53
FEBRUARY 1989
$3

NEXUS VOL. 2 #54
MARCH 1989
$3

NEXUS VOL. 2 #55
APRIL 1989
$3

NEXUS VOL. 2 #56
MAY 1989
$3

NEXUS VOL. 2 #57
JUNE 1989
$3

NEXUS VOL. 2 #58
JULY 1989
$3

NEXUS VOL. 2 #59
AUGUST 1989
$3

NEXUS VOL. 2 #60
SEPTEMBER 1989
$3

NEXUS VOL. 2 #61
OCTOBER 1989
$3

NEXUS VOL. 2 #62
NOVEMBER 1989
$3

NEXUS VOL. 2 #63
DECEMBER 1989
$3

NEXUS VOL. 2 #64
JANUARY 1990
$3

NEXUS VOL. 2 #65
FEBRUARY 1990
$3

NEXUS VOL. 2 #66
MARCH 1990
$3

NEXUS VOL. 2 #67
APRIL 1990
$3

NEXUS VOL. 2 #68
MAY 1990
$3

NEXUS VOL. 2 #69
JUNE 1990
$3

NEXUS VOL. 2 #70
JULY 1990
$3

NEXUS VOL. 2 #71
AUGUST 1990
$3

NEXUS VOL. 2 #72
SEPTEMBER 1990
$3

NEXUS VOL. 2 #73
OCTOBER 1990
$3

NEXUS VOL. 2 #74
NOVEMBER 1990
$3

NEXUS VOL. 2 #75
DECEMBER 1990
$3

NEXUS VOL. 2 #76
JANUARY 1991
$3

NEXUS VOL. 2 #77
FEBRUARY 1991
$3

NEXUS VOL. 2 #78
MARCH 1991
$3

NEXUS VOL. 2 #79
APRIL 1991
$3

NEXUS VOL. 2 #80
MAY 1991
$3

NEXUS: THE LIBERATOR #1
(#81) • AUGUST 1992
$4

NEXUS: THE LIBERATOR #2
(#82) • SEPTEMBER 1992
$4

NEXUS: THE LIBERATOR #3
(#83) • OCTOBER 1992
$4

NEXUS: THE LIBERATOR #4
(#84) • NOVEMBER 1992
$4

**NEXUS: THE WAGES OF SIN
#1**
(#85) • MARCH 1995
$4

**NEXUS: THE WAGES OF SIN
#2**
(#86) • APRIL 1995
$4

**NEXUS: THE WAGES OF SIN
#3**
(#87) • MAY 1995
$4

**NEXUS: THE WAGES OF SIN
#4**
(#88) • JUNE 1995
$4

**NEXUS: EXECUTIONER'S
SONG #1**
(#89) • JUNE 1996
$4

**NEXUS: EXECUTIONER'S
SONG #2**
(#90) • JULY 1996
$4

NEXUS: EXECUTIONER'S SONG #3

(#91) • AUGUST 1996

$4

NEXUS: EXECUTIONER'S SONG #4

(#92) • SEPTEMBER 1996

$4

NEXUS: GOD CON #1

(#93) • APRIL 1997

$4

NEXUS: GOD CON #2

(#94) • MAY 1997

$4

NEXUS: NIGHTMARE IN BLUE #1

(#95) • JULY 1997

$4

NEXUS: NIGHTMARE IN BLUE #2

(#96) • AUGUST 1997

$4

NEXUS: NIGHTMARE IN BLUE #3

(#97) • SEPTEMBER 1997

$4

NEXUS: NIGHTMARE IN BLUE #4

(#98) • OCTOBER 1997

$4

NEXUS VOL. 2 #99

JULY 2007

$3

NEXUS VOL. 2 #100
JANUARY 2008
$5

NEXUS VOL. 2 #101/102
JUNE 2009
$5

CLONEZONE SPECIAL #1
MAY 1989
$4

HAMMER OF GOD #1
FEBRUARY 1990
$4

HAMMER OF GOD #2
MARCH 1990
$4

HAMMER OF GOD #3
APRIL 1990
$4

HAMMER OF GOD #4
MAY 1990
$4

HAMMER OF GOD: BUTCH #1
MAY 1994
$4

HAMMER OF GOD: BUTCH #2
JULY 1994
$4

HAMMER OF GOD: BUTCH #3
AUGUST 1994
$4

HAMMER OF GOD: PENTATHALON #1
JANUARY 1994
$4

HAMMER OF GOD: SWORD OF JUSTICE #1
FEBRUARY 1991
$4

HAMMER OF GOD: SWORD OF JUSTICE #2
MARCH 1991
$4

MADMAN COMICS BOOGALOO
JUNE 1999
$9

MEZZ: GALACTIC TOUR 2494 #1
MAY 1994
$4

MAGNUS ROBOT FIGHTER/ NEXUS #1 PREVIEW
JANUARY 1994
$4

MAGNUS ROBOT FIGHTER/NEXUS #1
MARCH 1994
$4

MAGNUS ROBOT FIGHTER/NEXUS #2
APRIL 1994
$4

THE NEXT NEXUS #1
JANUARY 1989
$4

THE NEXT NEXUS #2
FEBRUARY 1989
$4

THE NEXT NEXUS #3
MARCH 1989
$4

THE NEXT NEXUS #4
APRIL 1989
$4

NEXUS: ALIEN JUSTICE #1
DECEMBER 1992
$4

NEXUS: ALIEN JUSTICE #2
JANUARY 1993
$4

NEXUS: ALIEN JUSTICE #3
FEBRUARY 1993
$4

NEXUS FREE COMIC BOOK DAY 2007
MAY 2007
$4

NEXUS GREATEST HITS #1
AUGUST 2007
$4

NEXUS LEGENDS #1
MAY 1989
$4

NEXUS LEGENDS #2
JUNE 1989
$4

NEXUS LEGENDS #3
JULY 1989
$4

NEXUS LEGENDS #4
AUGUST 1989
$4

NEXUS LEGENDS #5
SEPTEMBER 1989
$4

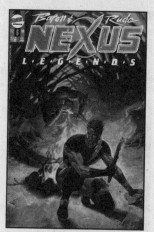

NEXUS LEGENDS #6
OCTOBER 1989
$4

NEXUS LEGENDS #7
NOVEMBER 1989
$4

NEXUS LEGENDS #8
DECEMBER 1989
$4

NEXUS LEGENDS #9
JANUARY 1990
$4

NEXUS LEGENDS #10
FEBRUARY 1990
$4

NEXUS LEGENDS #11
MARCH 1990
$4

NEXUS LEGENDS #12
APRIL 1990
$4

NEXUS LEGENDS #13
MAY 1990
$4

NEXUS LEGENDS #14
JUNE 1990
$4

NEXUS LEGENDS #15
JULY 1990
$4

NEXUS LEGENDS #16
AUGUST 1990
$4

NEXUS LEGENDS #17
SEPTEMBER 1990
$4

NEXUS LEGENDS #18
OCTOBER 1990
$4

NEXUS LEGENDS #19
NOVEMBER 1990
$4

NEXUS LEGENDS #20
DECEMBER 1990
$4

NEXUS LEGENDS #21
JANUARY 1991
$4

NEXUS LEGENDS #22
FEBRUARY 1991
$4

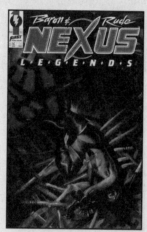

NEXUS LEGENDS #23
MARCH 1991
$4

NEXUS MEETS MADMAN
JANUARY 1996
$4

NEXUS: NEFARIOUS
HARDCOVER • 2023
$18

NEXUS: THE ORIGIN
JULY 1996
$4

NEXUS: THE ORIGIN
NOVEMBER 2007
$4

Steve Rude and Eric Shanower's *Nexus* #16 splash page 1 original art (1986).
Image courtesy of Heritage Auctions.

In 1981, Capital City Distribution, a Wisconsin-based comic book distributor, began publishing comics under the name Capital Comics. Their schedule was fraught with problems, but over three years, they had published three titles: *Nexus* (two series totaling nine issues), *Badger* (four issues), and *Whisper* (two issues).

Nexus, the first of their titles, was created by writer Mike Baron and penciler Steve Rude in 1981, was a sci-fi superhero comic set 500 years in the future. *Badger*,

created by Baron with art by Jeffrey Butler, centered on titular superhero/vigilante who suffered from "multiple personalities disorder." *Whisper* was written by Steven Grant with art by Rich Larson and told the story of American Ninja Alexis Devlin.

"We were just in the right place at the right time. A friend cued us in that they wanted to publish their own books, so I got in touch and arranged to meet them," Baron said. "We showed the finished Nexus pages to them at the Student

Union, again. The Union is a Madison institution," he said.

All of the series showed promise, but Capital decided to pull the plug on their publishing venture in 1984. Almost immediately, other publishers were interested in picking up the titles. One stood out.

"First Comics was located near one of Capital's satellite distribution locations in Evanston, Illinois, and I heard about the line folding pretty early," said Mike Gold, the editorial director and co-founder of First Comics.

"Mike Baron was a regular at our Chicago Minicons, a somewhat monthly reduction of the Chicago Comicon, and he came down to promote *Nexus* and, later, *Badger*. In fact, he wore a Badger costume, lending credence to The Badger being an autobiographical interpretation of a rather extreme sort. So, I was in love with both series, and *Whisper*, only two issues old, was the cherry on top of the cake. [Capital Comics'] Rich Bruning doesn't get the credit he deserves for being the original editor of those books," he said.

Gold said it was a "no brainer."

"These were three of the best comics being published by anybody at that moment in time. Fans liked them, retailers liked them, and we liked them. When we built First Comics, I had a very rigid publishing plan about what types of material we would publish and the order in which we would publish them. It was part of our business plan, part of our financing prospectus, and coincidentally, we had

just completed these commitments. The Capital books fit in like a glove (this was pre-OJ). I would have been an idiot *not* to have pursued them," he said.

There were other publishers interested – Baron sites Eclipse among them – but First became the front runner.

When it came time for the final negotiations and purchase, Gold to Madison with First Comics publisher Rick Obidiah. The meeting was in the offices of Capital City Distribution, which were in a building that faced the Wisconsin Capitol building.

"We were negotiating at Rich's office in Madison Wisconsin, a lovely town that had been home to our publisher Rick Obadiah. The office space overlooked the Wisconsin state capital building; this location is critical to the moment. Sitting around the conference table were Capital owners Milton Griepp and John Davis, Rich Bruning, Mike Baron, Rick Obadiah and myself. We worked things out for Nexus and Badger and Mike was there to represent the creators' interests, but when it came to Whisper, Milton was reluctant to include that in the deal. I explained why that was important to both First Comics from a promotional point of view and to the Whisper property itself as it would have been orphaned. Milt didn't agree and we went back and forth as one often does in such negotiations. As we did, Mike started getting frustrated," Gold said.

As the conversation and attention in the room focused on the acquisition, Griepp realized that the folks from First Comics

were expecting that the purchase would include Whisper.

It seemed as in an impasse had been reached.

"Milt turned to Rich and asked him if my arguments made any sense to him. Rich, bless his heart, said 'Well, yes, they do.' Milt held his ground, as did I. I can be stubborn — these days I only do that when I'm on the clock, but back then I regarded it as an art form," he said.

It was at this point that Baron, who has always been known as someone with strong opinions, began to get frustrated with the bottleneck.

"Mike ran out of patience. He walked over to the window — remember, we were across from the state capital building — and he lifted open that window. He lowered himself out of that window and declared he was going to just hang on by his hands until we reached a deal or until he fell," he said.

"Milton's back was to that window and, without looking, he just shook his head and said 'Well, if you feel that way about it...' and we closed. Mike pulled himself up and back into the office; yes, he was that strong. Rick looked at me in confusion as if to say 'Ummm, what the hell are we doing here?'" Gold said.

"But we all had our deal. John and Milton went on to take us on a tour of their distribution catacombs, and I'm sure lunch

was involved as I fondly recall having a long discussion about music with John. Rick and I drove back to Evanston, Mike went back to his house (a great place in the Madison suburbs that seemed to have been designed by The Road Runner) and we got back to making funny books," he said. "And, evidently, a legend."

Nexus, *Badger*, and *Whisper* – and various spin-offs – enjoyed healthy runs at First. *Nexus* went onto Dark Horse, *Badger* has had a few incarnations, and *Whisper's* presently being revived. As an editor who once recruited them for a company, what does Gold think the selling points are of each of them today?

"First of all, no pun intended, each has a legacy. That's very important in the comics racket, then as now. Second, each was a great concept and had been well-executed. I don't think any of those three concepts are the least bit dated although *Whisper* might be more accessible today than it was originally. It's really good stuff, and Steven remains one of our better writers. *Nexus*, of course, never went away. *The Badger* comes and goes and I'm sure he'll be back, but I don't think Mike is dressing up as the guy any longer. He probably still fits in the costume," Gold said.

– Bob Harrison with additional reporting by J.C. Vaughn

Bob Harrison is a collector, commentator, and comics historian, whose work can be found regularly on PopCultureSquad.com. This is his first Overstreet contribution.

Timothy Truman's SCOUT

From the pages of *Starslayer*, Grimjack and his graphic novel *Time Beavers* onward through his career, writer-artist Timothy Truman has offered readers hard-boiled action and no small amount of grit. It was at Eclipse that Truman created what is perhaps his signature title, *Scout*. And while Eclipse as a whole was clearly a non-universe, *Scout* and its spin-offs describe a single coherent reality.

"I'd always been interested in Native American culture when I was growing up. My great-grandmother on my father's side was a full-blooded Cherokee, and I'm sure that played a part in it. In college, the interest intensified, and I started reading a lot of scholarly studies and histories about various Native American tribes. Finally, my wife Beth purchased a big, thick book by a historian named Arthur Haley called *Apaches: A Culture and History Portrait* and gave it to me for my birthday. That book really set the scene for coming up with *Scout*. I became intensely interested in Apache culture. It was the Reagan era, so, as an unrepentant leftist, I saw things going on around me that concerned me quite a bit. So, I speculated about what might happen if these things were allowed to progress and eventually pictured this bleak future where America had basically become an impoverished third-world nation. It seemed to me that the only person who might have any sort of hope of existing in such a future would be someone with these old school traditional Apache cultural ideals that I was reading about. So, before I knew it, the whole scenario for the Scout series appeared," Truman said.

"The story takes place in the near future in a sort of ravaged, impoverished, dystopian United States. The country has split off into various smaller states or governments, the main one being centered in the American Southwest, called New America. The star of the series is an Apache named Emanuel Santana who is AWOL from a special Army training program. Scout learns, or at least thinks, that he is the reincarnation of the mythical Apache hero, Child of Water, and that it's his mission to destroy the Four Monsters of Apache legend. The monsters have taken the form of four businessmen and statesmen aligned with acting President, Jerry Grail – himself a former pro-wrestler. The reader never knows whether or not the Monsters are real or just a figment of Santana's imagination," he said.

Scout #1 (September 1985) kicked off the original series, which ran 24 issues and concluded in October 1987. *Swords of Texas* #1 kicked off a four-issue mini-series that same month, and *New America* #1 launched another four-issue mini-series the following month. 1987 also saw the release of the *Scout Handbook*. *Scout: War Shaman* #1 (March 1988) launched a 16-issue run that concluded in December 1989.

"The second series, *Scout: War Shaman*, takes place about a decade or so after the first series, chronologically, during which time Scout married and had two small children, Tahzey and Victorio. After his wife dies, he and the boys set out on a trek across the southwest. Most people were really taken with the second series, the fact that you have this outlaw who has been branded a terrorist by the government, who is on the run and must worry about the welfare and safety of his two small children. In what was a pretty dramatic step for the time, at the end of the series, Scout dies. One boy, Tahzey, is adopted by one of Santana's allies, a militant missionary named Rev. Sanddog Yuma. However, the fate of the youngest boy, Victorio, is uncertain. When we last see him, he's very much alone, hiding in some rocks. Keeping his fate uncertain was a deliberate move on my part, as readers will hopefully discover in *Scout: Marauder*," Truman said.

- Scott Braden

FIRST PUBLICATION:
Scout #1
(September 1985)

LAST PUBLICATION:
Scout: War Shaman #16
(December 1989)

REVIVAL(S):
Scout: Marauder
graphic novel (TBD).

Timothy Truman's original art for *Scout* #8 Page 2 (1986).
Image courtesy of Heritage Auctions.

SCOUT #1
SEPTEMBER 1985
$4

SCOUT #2
NOVEMBER 1985
$4

SCOUT #3
JANUARY 1986
$4

SCOUT #4
FEBRUARY 1986
$4

SCOUT #5
MARCH 1986
$4

SCOUT #6
APRIL 1986
$4

SCOUT #7
MAY 1986
$4

SCOUT #8
JUNE 1986
$4

SCOUT #9
JULY 1986
$4

SCOUT #10
AUGUST 1986
$4

SCOUT #11
SEPTEMBER 1986
$4

SCOUT #12
OCTOBER 1986
$4

SCOUT #13
NOVEMBER 1986
$4

SCOUT #14
DECEMBER 1986
$4

SCOUT #15
JANUARY 1987
$4

SCOUT #16
FEBRUARY 1987
$5

SCOUT #17
MARCH 1987
$4

SCOUT #18
APRIL 1987
$4

SCOUT #19
MAY 1987
$5

SCOUT #20
JUNE 1987
$4

SCOUT #21
JULY 1987
$4

SCOUT #22
AUGUST 1987
$4

SCOUT #23
AUGUST 1987
$4

SCOUT #24
OCTOBER 1987
$4

SCOUT HANDBOOK #1
AUGUST 1987
$4

SWORDS OF TEXAS #1
OCTOBER 1987
$4

SWORDS OF TEXAS #2
NOVEMBER 1987
$4

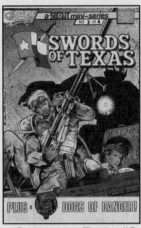

SWORDS OF TEXAS #3
JANUARY 1988
$4

SWORDS OF TEXAS #4
MARCH 1988
$4

NEW AMERICA #1
NOVEMBER 1987
$4

NEW AMERICA #2
DECEMBER 1987
$4

NEW AMERICA #3
JANUARY 1988
$4

NEW AMERICA #4
FEBRUARY 1988
$4

SCOUT: WAR SHAMAN #1
MARCH 1988
$4

SCOUT: WAR SHAMAN #2
MAY 1988
$4

SCOUT: WAR SHAMAN #3
JUNE 1988
$4

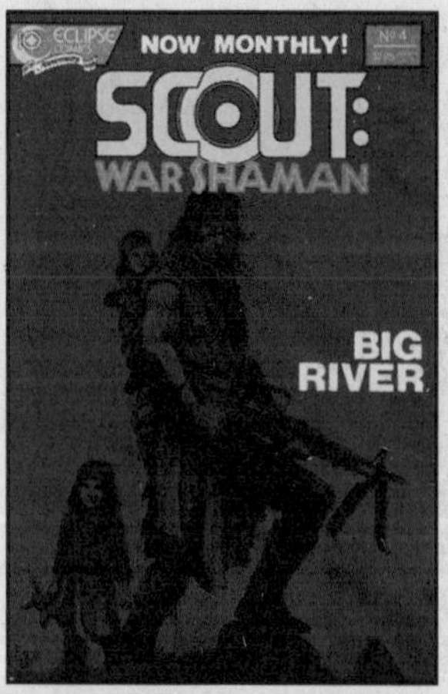
ECLIPSE
NOW MONTHLY!
Nº 4
SCOUT:
WAR SHAMAN
BIG RIVER

SCOUT: WAR SHAMAN #4
JULY 1988
$4

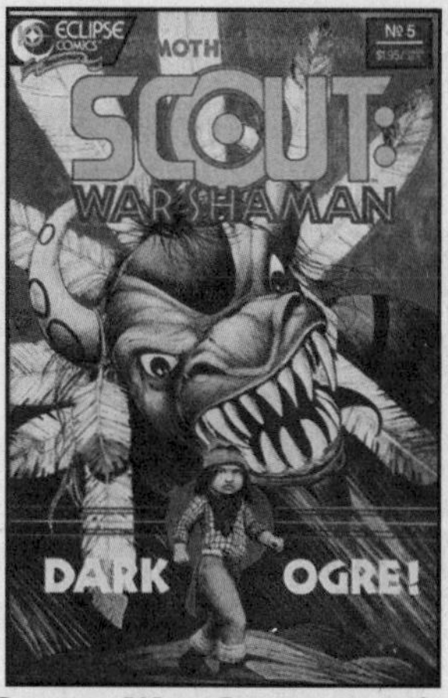
ECLIPSE COMICS
Nº 5
SCOUT:
WAR SHAMAN
DARK OGRE!

SCOUT: WAR SHAMAN #5
AUGUST 1988
$4

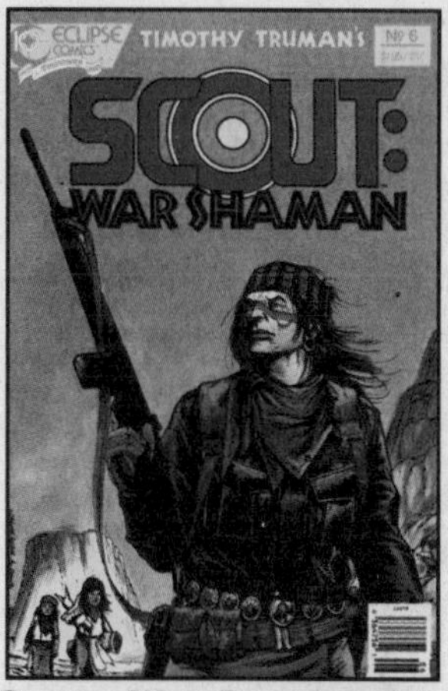
ECLIPSE COMICS
TIMOTHY TRUMAN'S
Nº 6
SCOUT:
WAR SHAMAN

SCOUT: WAR SHAMAN #6
SEPTEMBER 1988
$4

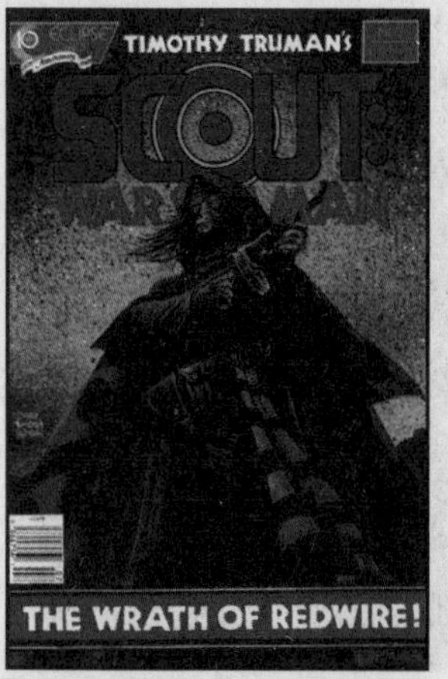
TIMOTHY TRUMAN'S
SCOUT:
THE WRATH OF REDWIRE!

SCOUT: WAR SHAMAN #7
OCTOBER 1988
$4

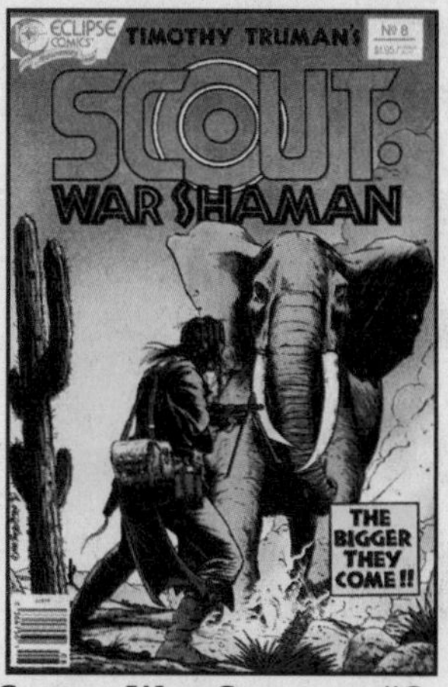
ECLIPSE COMICS
TIMOTHY TRUMAN'S
Nº 8
SCOUT:
WAR SHAMAN
THE BIGGER THEY COME!!

SCOUT: WAR SHAMAN #8
DECEMBER 1988
$4

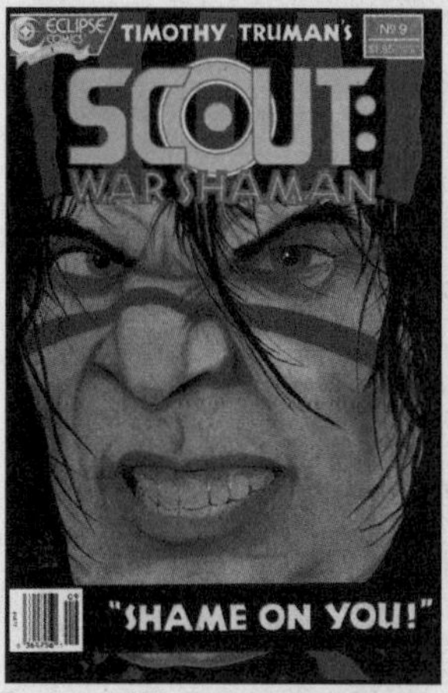
ECLIPSE
TIMOTHY TRUMAN'S
Nº 9
SCOUT:
WAR SHAMAN
"SHAME ON YOU!"

SCOUT: WAR SHAMAN #9
JANUARY 1989
$4

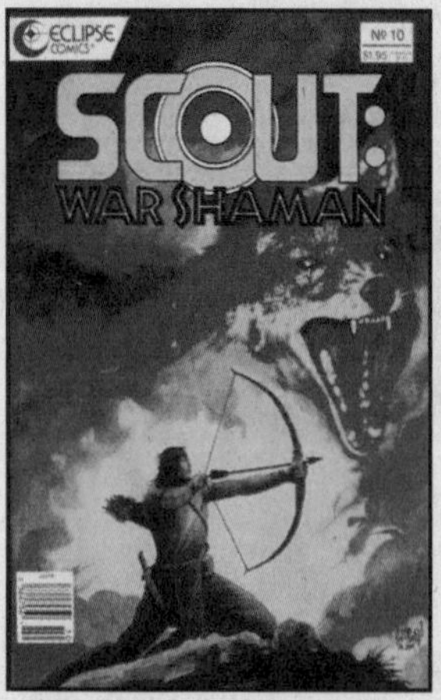
ECLIPSE COMICS
Nº 10
SCOUT:
WAR SHAMAN

SCOUT: WAR SHAMAN #10
FEBRUARY 1989
$4

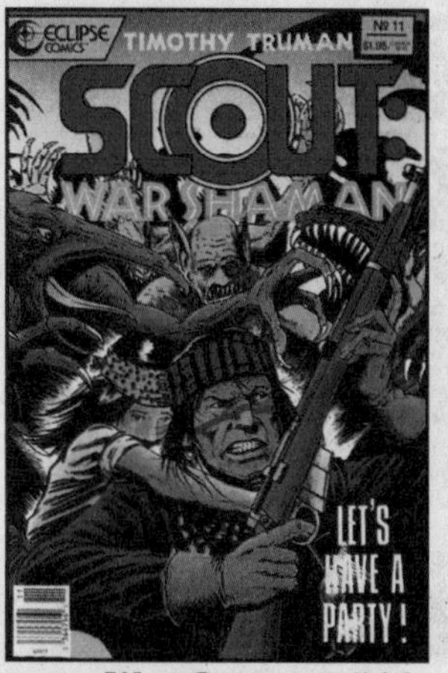
ECLIPSE
TIMOTHY TRUMAN
Nº 11
SCOUT
LET'S HAVE A PARTY!

SCOUT: WAR SHAMAN #11
MARCH 1989
$4

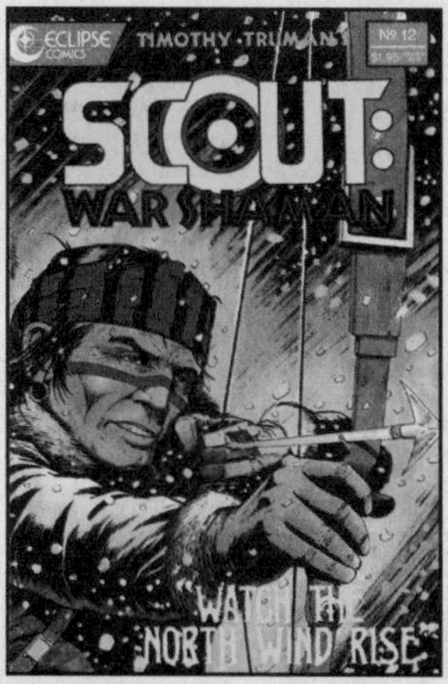
ECLIPSE COMICS
TIMOTHY TRUMAN'S
Nº 12
SCOUT:
WAR SHAMAN
NORTH WIND RISE

SCOUT: WAR SHAMAN #12
MARCH 1989
$4

SCOUT: WAR SHAMAN #13
APRIL 1989
$4

SCOUT: WAR SHAMAN #14
JUNE 1989
$4

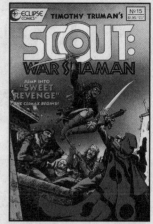

SCOUT: WAR SHAMAN #15
AUGUST 1989
$4

SCOUT: WAR SHAMAN #16
DECEMBER 1989
$4

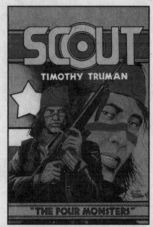

SCOUT: THE FOUR MONSTERS
ECLIPSE GRAPHIC ALBUM SERIES #19
1988
SC $15   HC $35

SCOUT: MOUNT FIRE
1989
SC $15

From Timothy Truman's original art for the cover of Scout #18 (1987).
Image courtesy of Heritage Auctions.

LOST UNIVERSES

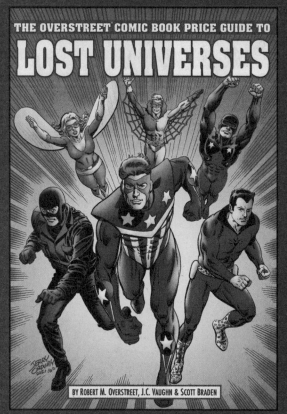

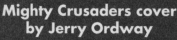

**Mighty Crusaders cover
by Jerry Ordway**

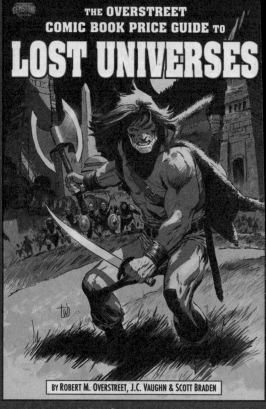

**Ironjaw cover
by Lee Weeks**

In-depth looks at the original Milestone and Valiant to
Tower's T.H.U.N.D.E.R. Agents and Charlton's superheroes,
and from Topps' Kirbyverse and the MLJ/Archie heroes to
Malibu's Ultraverse and Marvel's New Universe, this full-color
book dives deep into Atlas-Seaboard, Comics Greatest World,
Defiant, Future Comics, Triumphant and more.

NOW ON SALE

 GEMSTONE PUBLISHING

WWW.GEMSTONEPUB.COM

The Shadow at Archie?

Who knows what evil lurks in the hearts of editors...The Shadow knows!

The mere mention of his name invokes many things: the classic radio show whose catch phrase, "Who knows what evil lurks in the hearts of men – The Shadow knows!" remains firmly ingrained in the American consciousness; the original magazine pulps, enthralling millions before the advent of comic books; the merchandising spawned by the radio series; the movie serials and featurettes of the 1940s; and the various comic book adaptations – from the original Street & Smith editions to the Marvel, Dark Horse and, of course, celebrated Mike Kaluta DC issues! Not to mention his encounters with Batman! Like all great literary figures, however, The Shadow has a little known skeleton in his closet –from August 1964 until September 1965, his course was charted by the good folks at... are you ready... Archie Comics!

When you first pick up the Archie Comics' version of *The Shadow* #1 (August 1964), the cover deceives you into thinking that this will be just like the classic Street & Smith *Shadow* comics of the Golden Age. The slouched hat, the dark cloak and his distinctive nose are clearly in view. Then you turn to the first page. In a story entitled "The Shadow vs. the RXG Spymaster," we see Lamont Cranston as the Shadow – no hat, a bright blue cloak, and blonde hair astonishing us all right off the bat with the awesome power of... ventriloquism! That's right – he throws his

voice! To change into his secret identity, he does nothing more than put on glasses and remove his cape! Amazingly, this is all it takes to project the mystery man described as "America's top secret agent," in the "US Secret Service!" Also on hand are secretary Margo Lane and chauffeur Shrevy. The plot involves the classic, evil Shadow villain Shiwan Khan trying to steal plans for a "new, experimental Cold War" theme. Despite this trite story, we are treated to a James Bond-esque scene in which Cranston, trapped in his own limo, gleefully informs his would be assassin that his Rolls is equipped with a "dual set of controls," enabling him to control the car from the back seat and to knockout the driver with an electrical charge. In the backup story, "The Eyes of the Tiger," the Shadow tackles some common thugs attempting an insurance scam by holding a penlight under his face so that he appears ghostlike. The crooks think he is a tiger (!), and the Shadow takes advantage of their fear to knock them out. The issue is written by Bob Bernstein with art by John Rosenberger.

As if the incongruities of the Archie version weren't evident in issue 1 the cover to *The Shadow* #2 (September 1964), leaves no doubt. No, you're not seeing things: hurtling across the cover is the Shadow – decked out in a... (gulp)... superhero costume! A sign of things to come, for the stories inside portray him as he appeared in issue 1. "Shiwan Khan's Murderous Master Plan" opens with Lamont and Shrevy, on

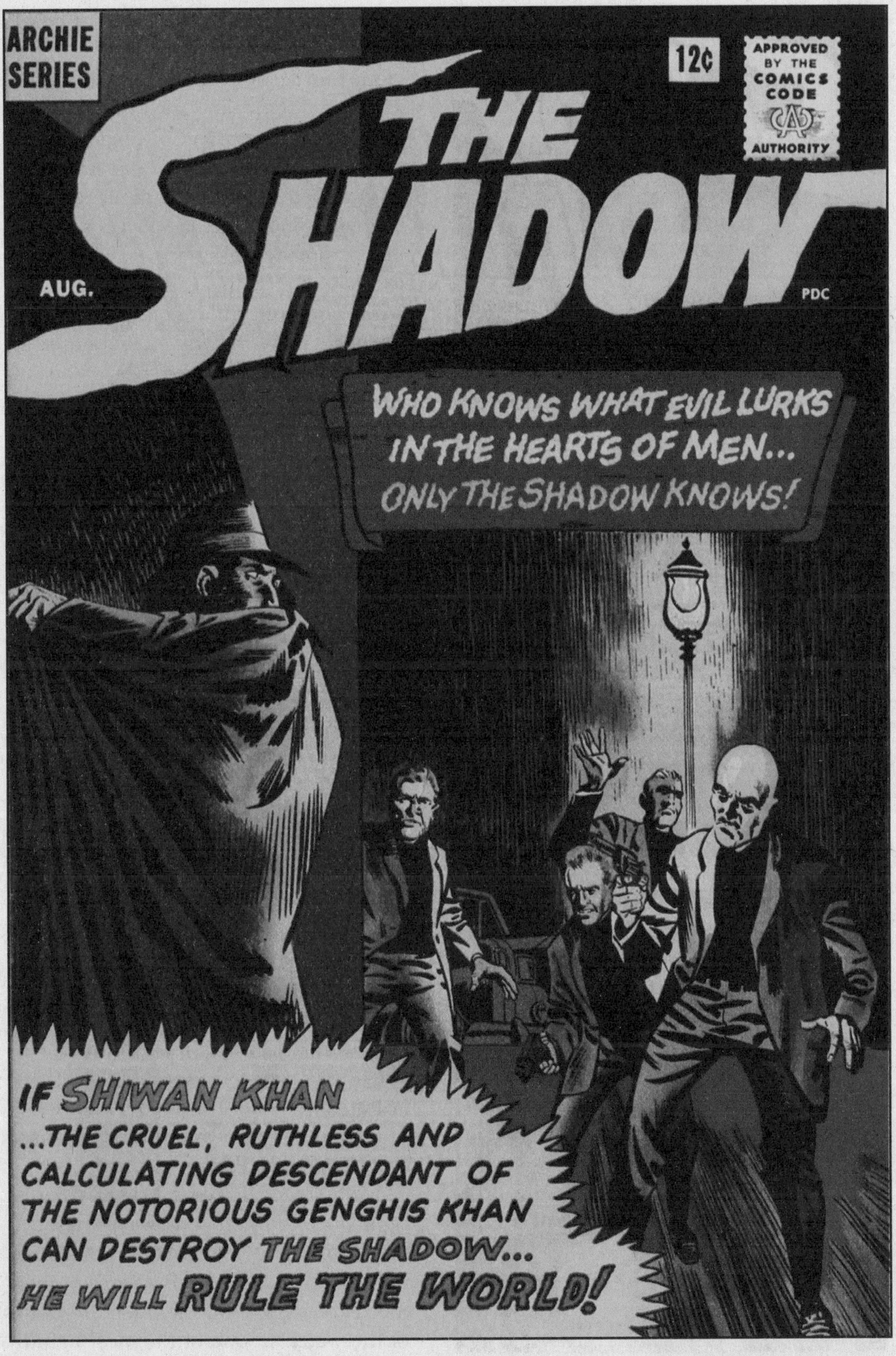
ARCHIE SERIES
12¢
APPROVED BY THE COMICS CODE AUTHORITY
THE SHADOW
AUG.
PDC
WHO KNOWS WHAT EVIL LURKS IN THE HEARTS OF MEN... ONLY THE SHADOW KNOWS!
IF SHIWAN KHAN ...THE CRUEL, RUTHLESS AND CALCULATING DESCENDANT OF THE NOTORIOUS GENGHIS KHAN CAN DESTROY THE SHADOW... HE WILL RULE THE WORLD!

their way to China via jet, almost being blown out of the sky by a "mushroom cloud that accompanies an atomic bomb explosion." Once in China, the Shadow uses "mass hypnosis" on some soldiers, mesmerizing them into believing they are trapped behind bars. This constant use of hypnosis actually makes things less dramatic, like Superman's total invincibility in the old days. In fact, when captured by a femme fatale spy, he once more resorts to hypnosis to have her turn on her boss, Shiwan Khan. Once again, the script is by Bob Bernstein with art by John Rosenberger. The backup finds the legendary Paul Reinman rendering a Bernstein script, "Margo Lanes Honeymoon." Wishing Lamont would show some interest in her, Margo slumbers and dreams of their "honeymoon" – a honeymoon spent avoiding assassins! Like all the "teaser" Superman comics through the years where Supes "almost" bought the farm (many of which were also "dream" sequences), this issue should have the same collectability.

The real fun, however, starts in *The Shadow* #3 (November 1964) featuring the "superhero" Shadow of the previous issue's cover! This all-Bernstein/Reinman issue features "Shiwan Khan's House of Horrors" – a whirlwind adventure of the most implausible kind! Lamont, now sporting jet black hair, is on the trail of Khan (who else?) and his men, who have kidnapped Margo. Unfortunately, Khan has brainwash Shrevy to drive off the "uncompleted Narrows bridge" (that's right, New Yorkers – it wasn't always there)! As they plummet, the Shadow re-hypnotizes Shrevy by staring into the rearview mirror, then gets him out of the water. In one of the most befuddling sequences ever, the Shadow goes undercover in Chinatown by donning a large Mardi Gras-like mask worn over his own mask which he's already wearing! Never mind the fact that he's still wearing his costume! This story catapults the Shadow all over the map from Chinatown to the World's Fair, recalling classic '50s *Batman* (paid homage to in the *Mask of the Phantasm* animated movie). Khan pulls out all the stops in this story – sharks, lions, tanks, etc. As so eloquently put by the observant Shadow, "Great Guns – this was all a macabre plot to trap me!" Don't leave now, his dialogue gets better, "Six sharks in the pool! Six bullets in my automatic! I'd better not miss!" "The Princess of Death" tries to prove Lamont and the Shadow are one and the same in a backup tail which we've read before (and will no doubt again). This issue also begins one page strips of the Joe Simon and Jack Kirby character, the Fly, which run to issue 7.

None of the previous issues could have prepared readers for the villain of *The Shadow* #4 (January 1965): "The Diabolical Dr. Demon," Hitler's evil scientist, has come out of hiding to "finish Der Fuhrer's work." Only two men can keep him from ruling the world – our hero, of course, and Dr. Demon's only competitor, the irrepressible Shiwan Khan (does this guy ever learn?!). In this Bernstein and Reinman outing, just to make sure we're aware of who the bad guy is, we are told that "If Hitler had listened to Dr. Demon, Germany might have won the war!" Jeepers – thank goodness for Schickelgruber's momentary deafness! There is an unnerving sequence where the Doc traps both the Shadow and Khan in a furnace, but thankfully the Doc jumps to his

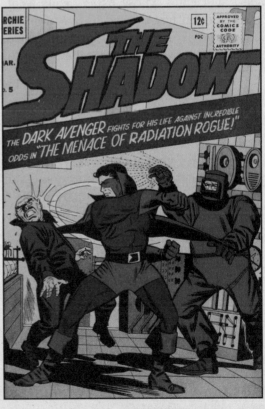

own death. Seemingly in keeping with the theme of intolerance, "The Human Bomb," title character of the backup story, looks like a KKK grandmaster with dynamite strapped to his white cloak. Margo and Shrevy (who really should know better) read Lamont's mail and learn of threats from a mad bomber. They plan to stop him. Lamont hears their scheme over the intercom, and when the mad bomber arrives, hypnotizes them into thinking that they acted alone in saving him, even though he used his own "Shadow" powers.

From the silliest villain names file, *The Shadow* #5 (March 1965) brings us, "The Menace of Radiation Rogue," as well as the scripting talents of Jerry Siegel! A Shiwan Khan dupe who Reinman renders in a red radiation suit, he looks like he's ready to date Ma Hunkel, the original Red Tornado! (The Siegel and Reinman creative team remains on board until the final issue.) Once a scientist whose experiments went awry and left him doused in radiation, he concocts a serum that will keep him alive for the next few days. He has the power to transfer the deadly radiation to others. At one point, he even manages to get ahold of the Shadow, spouting this classic dialogue while contaminating him, "Now you know why I'm called Radiation Rogue! You probably thought it was a vainglorious, meaningless name, but now you know better, eh?" The amazingly anticlimactic ending has the Shadow brainwash (*yawn*) Radiation Rogue into turning on Shiwan Khan.

"The Incredible Alliance of Shiwan Khan and Attila the Hunter," from *The Shadow* #6 (May 1965), finds Khan teaming up with another villain of infamous descent – just as Shiwan is related to Genghis Khan, so, too is Attila related to his namesake (I keep waiting for Chucky Manson Jr. to show up)! This story is notable for such classic Khan dialogue as his description of Attila, "a handsome, hard faced Asiatic who fights like a demon!" as well as his self-description, "I am a skilled practitioner in the black art of skullduggery, bar none!" Another multi-locales tale, from the waters of the New England coast to the Cranston Museum of Art to Terror Island! As if two supervillains weren't enough, one of Khan's henchman disguises himself as the Shadow and tries to kill him. He retreats when he realizes that, without the Shadow, Khan would no longer need his services and would probably execute him!

The Shadow #7 (July 1965) will live in infamy as the issue in which the Archie editors outdid themselves. It wasn't enough that they stuck the classic mystery man in a superhero suit – in this issue, he acquires a "belt buckle power beam" and (I'm not making this up) "multi-action Shadow gun," enabling him to shoot "weakness gas" and "electric blasts!" "The Shadow Battles the Brute," however, is a classic even without these new gadgets! Shiwan Khan encourages his stooges to duke it out in an all-encompassing slugfest. The last guy standing gets to be zapped with a "growth ray (good thing he wasn't wearing a pacemaker)! The newly huge thug, a bald guy the size of the Kingpin and wearing Plastic Man's red, laced shirt and goggles is sent out to pillage the world. The Shadow tries to hypnotize him, but can't penetrate the goggles. This leads to a battle on the estate of "Cyrus Galloway, rich explorer," whose mementos, including live crocodiles, proliferate his property. The Shadow lures the Brute into an elephant trap, which he soon escapes from. The Shadow then breaks the Brute's goggles with a "supersonic note" from a "special whistle," hoping now to hypnotize him, however, he's also "wearing shatterproof contact lenses that screen out hypnotism." Eventually, Khan double-crosses the Brute by not giving him his cut of the action! The Brute turns good and saves Margo, sacrificing himself by jumping in her place as a stone gargoyle statue is about to crush her. This roller coaster of a comic is augmented by great bad dialogue from the Shadow and the Brute: "There's nothing I Khan... I mean can... do to prevent it!" says the Shadow at one point; while the Brute pontificates, "Of course I have a terrible temper, smash things, rob and steal and am as treacherous as an eel! Outside of that, I am quite likable! And handsome, too... see?" A caption sums it all up best: "Remember that in the Archie series of slambang, surprise-a-second comics, anything

can happen, and usually does!" This is truly an amazing issue!

"The Game of Death" in *The Shadow* #8 (September 1965) finishes off the series with a standard one-hero-vs.-all-his-villain story. A rich guy employs various villains to kill the Shadow, and the one who succeeds will be given the honor of unmasking him. They include Attila the Hunter, the "insidious" Elasto (a new villain who – you'll never guess – stretches), the "diabolical" Dimensionoid (an alien who can transform himself into "any number of geometrical monsters," and whose only motivation is that he has to kill the Shadow as part of initiation into a "cabal of Ultra-villains" on his planet), and two baddies who perished in previous issues: Dr. Demon and Radiation Rogue. No reasons are given for their resurrections. The Shadow prevails in this by the numbers entry, however, his method of defeating Elasto is quite ingenious: he tricks him

into stretching into the ionosphere, where the "extreme lack of oxygen" makes him blackout. In the end, the Shadow psyches out the rich dude – taunting that he can't go through with killing him. Instead of whisking him off to justice, the Shadow implores him to "see a psychiatrist!" The series also included text stories which actually were more faithful to the character.

The Archie version of the Shadow is quite an enigma in the history of comics. Yet, for many reasons, I feel that it is quite collectible: certainly, it is the first time Archie licensed a property from an outside source (and one with an established track record to boot); it is definitely a product of its times, what with all the Cold War paranoia; it features some of the hokiest and most rapid fire dialogue since dragnet; the involvement of Siegel and Reinman; and of course it takes an established character and turns his world upside down! Who knows what lunacy lurks in the back issue boxes?!?

– Paul Castiglia

Paul Castiglia has written comics for publishers including Archie, DC, Dark Horse, and others. His work includes *Archie's Weird Mysteries*, *Teenage Mutant Ninja Turtles*, *Sonic the Hedgehog*, and more. He is the editor/historian of the Archie Americana vintage collections, and co-author/editor of the comics history book, *The MLJ Companion*. His latest comics projects include writing the *A.C.I.D.* series based on the toy line from Chap Mei, and the upcoming *Robot Monster Comics in 3D* graphic novel that he's editing and co-writing. He's also an animation scriptwriter for *Thomas & Friends Adventures* (Mattel) and *Cocoa Talk* (Minno). As a film historian, Castiglia speaks at vintage screenings and is the author of the upcoming book, *Scared Silly* covering classic horror-comedy movies like Abbott & Costello Meet Frankenstein.

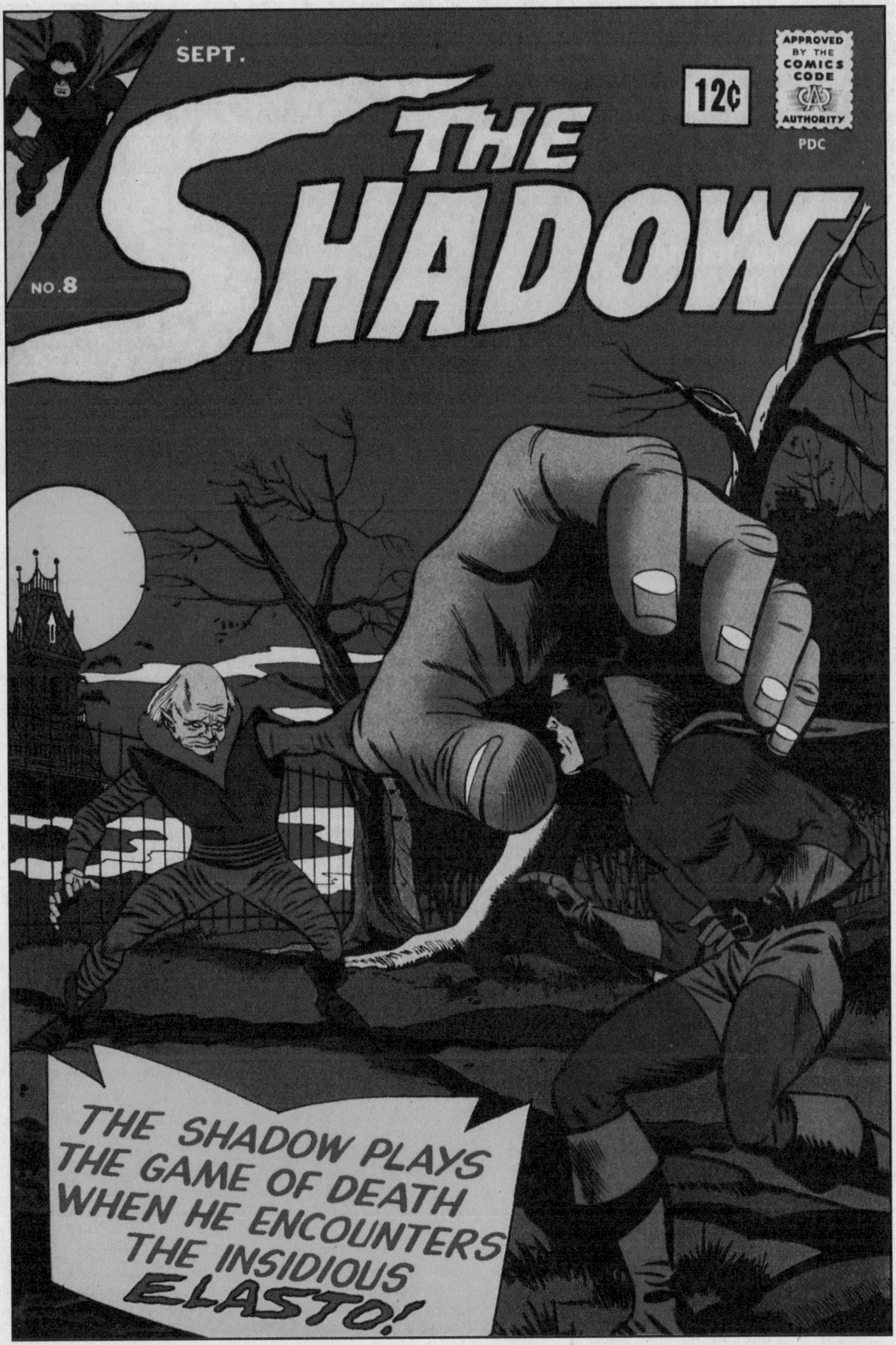
SEPT.
12¢
APPROVED BY THE COMICS CODE AUTHORITY
PDC
THE SHADOW
NO.8
THE SHADOW PLAYS THE GAME OF DEATH WHEN HE ENCOUNTERS THE INSIDIOUS ELASTO!

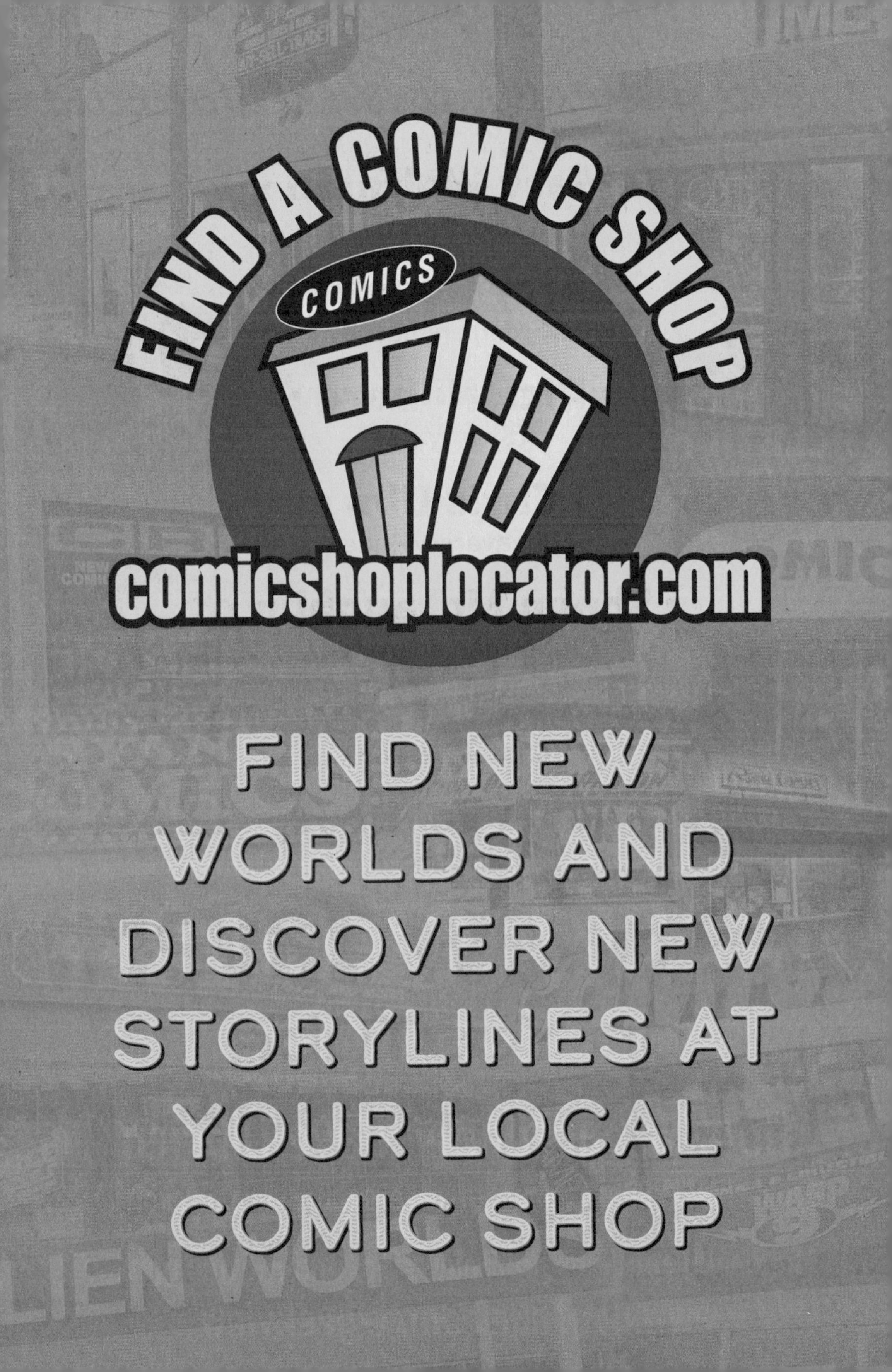
FIND A COMIC SHOP
COMICS
comicshoplocator.com
FIND NEW WORLDS AND DISCOVER NEW STORYLINES AT YOUR LOCAL COMIC SHOP

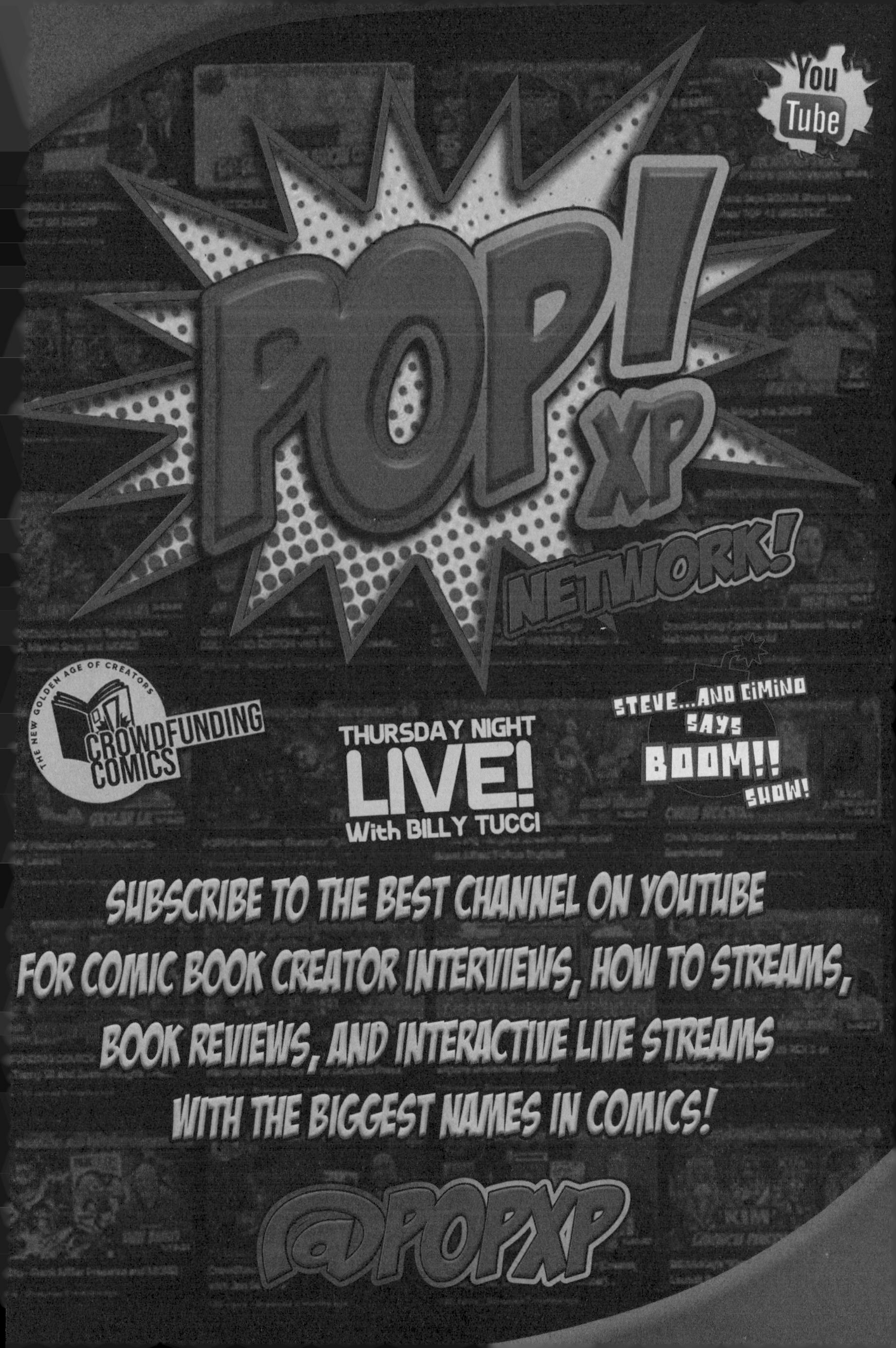

POP! XP NETWORK!
You Tube
THE NEW GOLDEN AGE OF CREATORS
CROWDFUNDING COMICS
THURSDAY NIGHT LIVE! With BILLY TUCCI
STEVE...AND CIMINO SAYS BOOM!! SHOW!
SUBSCRIBE TO THE BEST CHANNEL ON YOUTUBE FOR COMIC BOOK CREATOR INTERVIEWS, HOW TO STREAMS, BOOK REVIEWS, AND INTERACTIVE LIVE STREAMS WITH THE BIGGEST NAMES IN COMICS!
@POPXP

OVERSTREET

THE WAR REPORT:
A Pause in the Action

The War Report has been a vital part of <u>The Overstreet Comic Book Price Guide</u> for more than a decade now. It has served as an excellent example of how experts in one niche of our hobby can come together to increase awareness of their specialty, and in turn see its appeal to the broader comic book audience increase significantly.

We often wonder why fans of Disney comics, Archie, Dell's Four Color, original Valiant, Romance, or others haven't banded together in similar fashion to get the word out. The invitation stands open.

This fall, we'll turn our attention to <u>The Overstreet Comic Book Price Guide To War Comics</u>, a specialty publication set for next fall. Much like <u>The Overstreet Comic Book Price Guide To Lost Universes</u>.

It will spotlight the histories of the major titles, showcase some key original art, and illuminate the collecting habits of some of the masters of this historic area of collecting.

We hope you'll join us!

- The Overstreet Team

Every comic listed is pictured!

Key series spotlights!

Collector profiles!

Key original art!

Behind-the-scenes info!

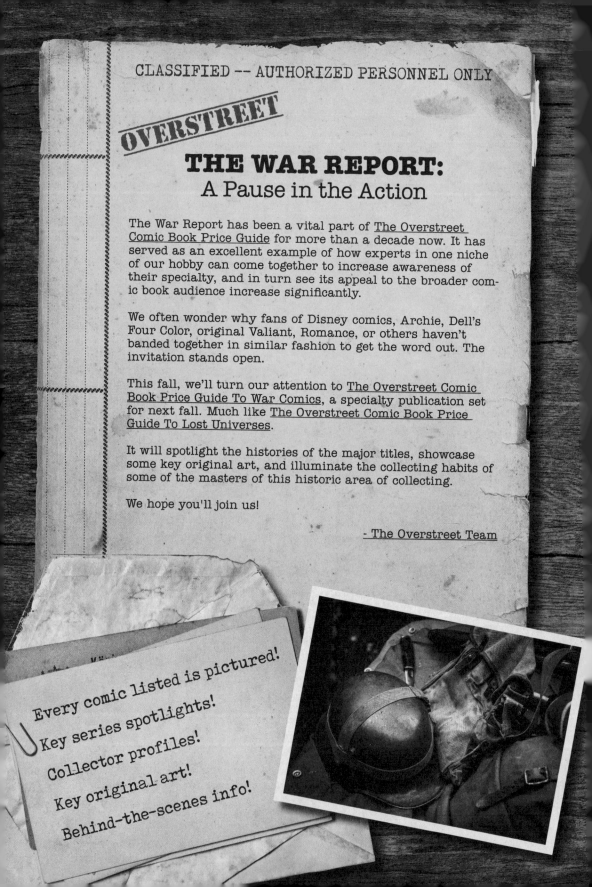

THE OVERSTREET COMIC BOOK PRICE GUIDE TO

WAR COMICS

by Robert M. Overstreet

RUSS HEATH

COMING FALL 2025!

OVERSTREET
ACCESS

Price your comics with Overstreet's proven value pricing system

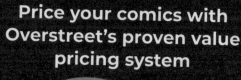

On Overstreet Access, you can...

- Create Collections!
- Create Boxes Within Collections!
- View and Organize Your Collections!
- Import and Export Collections!
- Want List!
- Gap List!
- Find Retailers!

Here's what you get:

- Expanded Overstreet® Prices!
- Superior Collection Management Tools!
- Cover Scanning in the App!
- Import/Export Tools!
- 190,000 Variants Added!

Want to get 15% off an Annual membership to Overstreet Access?

Visit OverstreetAccess.com for more info

"WHETHER YOU FIND A COMIC SHOP ON *FREE COMIC BOOK DAY* OR ANY OTHER DAY, IT CAN BE THE START OF A PHENOMENAL RELATIONSHIP."

BIG DEAL COMICS

NEW COMICS EVERY WEDNESDAY

WELCOME!

AND WHETHER YOU LIKE *SUPERHEROES* OR *CRIME* COMICS, *WAR* STORIES OR *SCIENCE FICTION*, YOU CAN FIND *ALL* OF THOSE AND *MORE* AT YOUR COMIC SHOP.

WHEN ESTABLISHING A *RELATIONSHIP* WITH A COMIC BOOK *RETAILER*, WHAT SHOULD A *CUSTOMER* LOOK FOR?

FOR *STARTERS*, A RETAILER OR DEALER SHOULD GIVE YOU A *GOOD IMPRESSION*. ARE THEY GOOD WITH CUSTOMERS?

DO THEY SHOW YOU A *POSITIVE* ATTITUDE? DO THEY GET YOUR *PASSION* FOR COLLECTING?

BEYOND FIRST IMPRESSIONS, IT'S IMPORTANT TO FIND DEALERS WHO ARE *TRUSTWORTHY*.

DO THE *RESEARCH*! ASK OTHER COLLECTORS FOR *RECOMMENDATIONS*.

COLLECTORS SHOULD BUILD A *RAPPORT* WITH THE RETAILERS WHO CAN HELP FIND THE ISSUES YOU *NEED* OR *WANT* RATHER THAN JUST OFFERING *GENERIC* RECOMMENDATIONS.

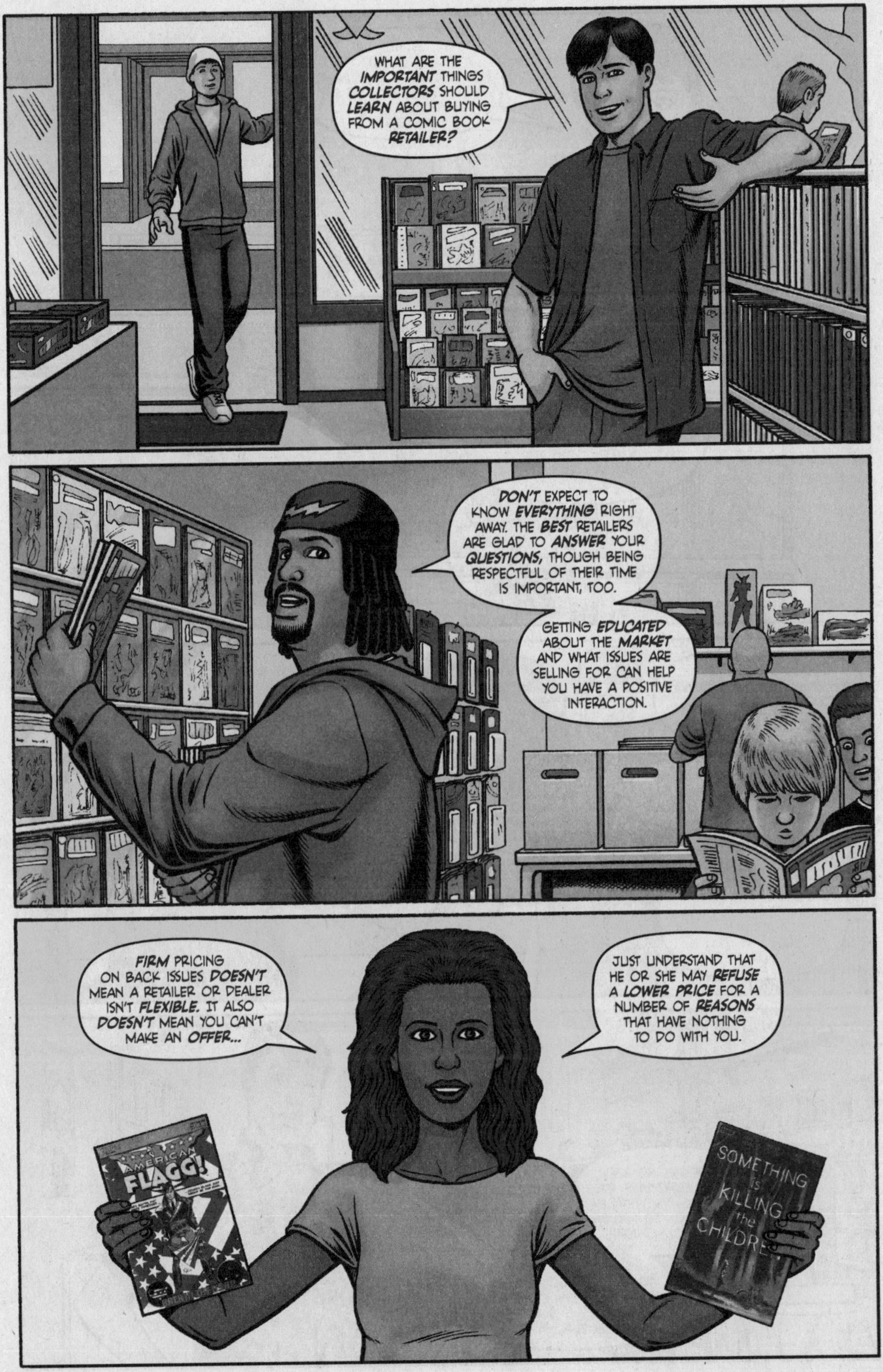
WHAT ARE THE IMPORTANT THINGS COLLECTORS SHOULD LEARN ABOUT BUYING FROM A COMIC BOOK RETAILER?
DON'T EXPECT TO KNOW EVERYTHING RIGHT AWAY. THE BEST RETAILERS ARE GLAD TO ANSWER YOUR QUESTIONS, THOUGH BEING RESPECTFUL OF THEIR TIME IS IMPORTANT, TOO.
GETTING EDUCATED ABOUT THE MARKET AND WHAT ISSUES ARE SELLING FOR CAN HELP YOU HAVE A POSITIVE INTERACTION.
FIRM PRICING ON BACK ISSUES DOESN'T MEAN A RETAILER OR DEALER ISN'T FLEXIBLE. IT ALSO DOESN'T MEAN YOU CAN'T MAKE AN OFFER...
JUST UNDERSTAND THAT HE OR SHE MAY REFUSE A LOWER PRICE FOR A NUMBER OF REASONS THAT HAVE NOTHING TO DO WITH YOU.
AMERICAN FLAGG!
SOMETHING is KILLING the CHILDRE

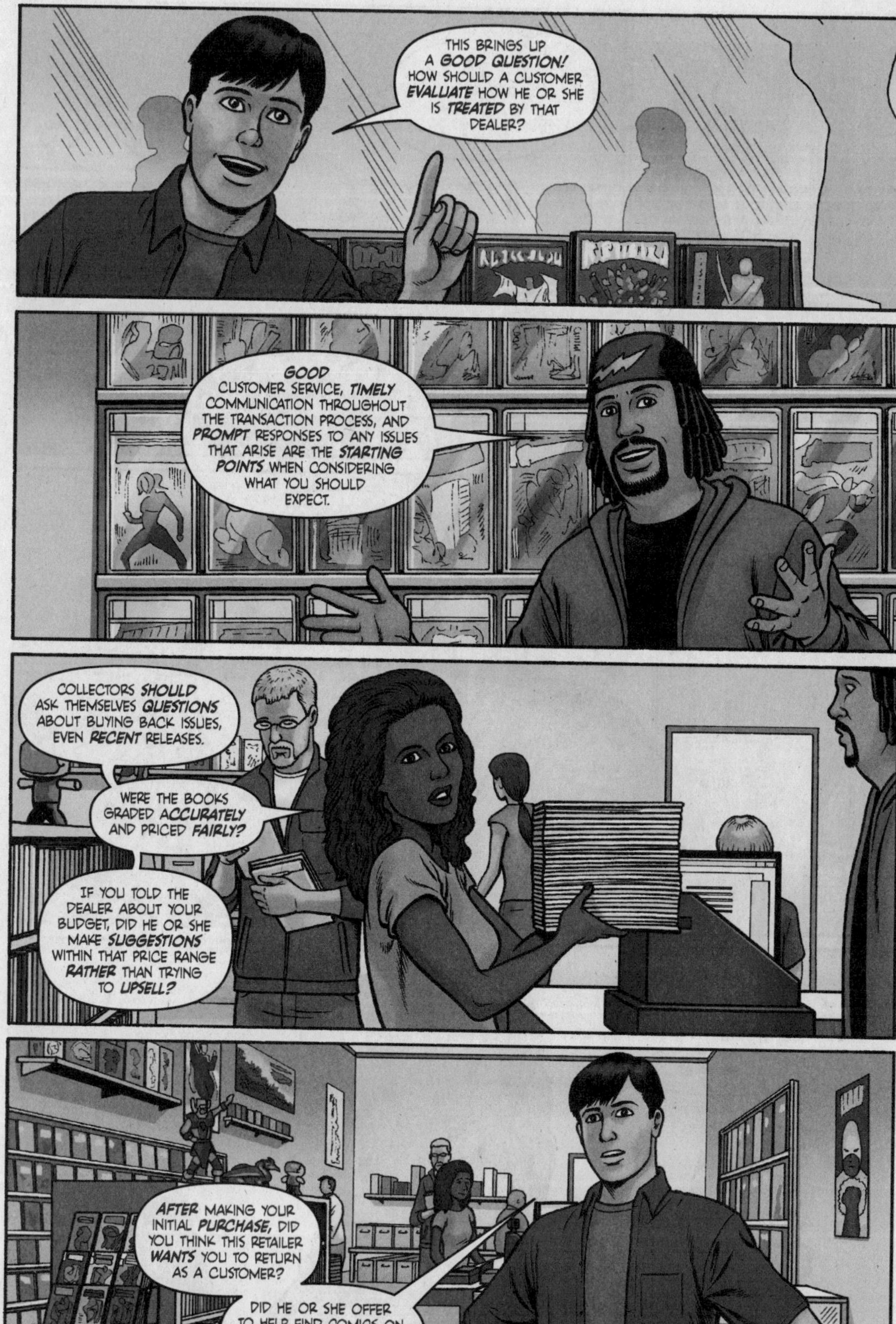
THIS BRINGS UP A GOOD QUESTION! HOW SHOULD A CUSTOMER EVALUATE HOW HE OR SHE IS TREATED BY THAT DEALER?
GOOD CUSTOMER SERVICE, TIMELY COMMUNICATION THROUGHOUT THE TRANSACTION PROCESS, AND PROMPT RESPONSES TO ANY ISSUES THAT ARISE ARE THE STARTING POINTS WHEN CONSIDERING WHAT YOU SHOULD EXPECT.
COLLECTORS SHOULD ASK THEMSELVES QUESTIONS ABOUT BUYING BACK ISSUES, EVEN RECENT RELEASES.
WERE THE BOOKS GRADED ACCURATELY AND PRICED FAIRLY?
IF YOU TOLD THE DEALER ABOUT YOUR BUDGET, DID HE OR SHE MAKE SUGGESTIONS WITHIN THAT PRICE RANGE RATHER THAN TRYING TO UPSELL?
AFTER MAKING YOUR INITIAL PURCHASE, DID YOU THINK THIS RETAILER WANTS YOU TO RETURN AS A CUSTOMER?
DID HE OR SHE OFFER TO HELP FIND COMICS ON YOUR WANT LIST OR MAKE SUGGESTIONS BASED ON YOUR PURCHASE?

GOOD POINTS! ON THE OTHER HAND, WHAT ARE SOME OF THE MOST COMMON *RED FLAGS* THAT SHOULD MAKE A COLLECTOR CAUTIOUS?

INACCURATE GRADING AND *INFLATED* PRICES FOR SURE...

SOMETIMES *HIGH PRICES* ARE COUPLED WITH *"DISCOUNTS"* TO MAKE YOU THINK YOU'RE GETTING A DEAL WHEN YOU AREN'T.

EACH SITUATION HAS TO BE EVALUATED ON ITS OWN, BUT...

DISORGANIZATION (THOUGH I HAVE SOME BAD DAYS ON THAT SCORE MYSELF)...

POOR COMMUNICATION, AND *NEGATIVE* OR DISMISSIVE *ATTITUDE*...

AND IF THE SPACE IS *OVERLY CROWDED* OR CREATES A NEGATIVE SHOPPING *EXPERIENCE*...

IF THE DEALER IS *PUSHY, AGGRESSIVE,* OR *PRESSES* YOU FOR A QUICK DECISION, IT COULD MEAN THAT IT'S EITHER A *BAD DEAL*...

"OR THEY *AREN'T* CONCERNED WITH CREATING *GOOD RELATIONSHIPS* AND *REPEAT CUSTOMERS*."

BRAND X COMICS

CLOSED

"SINCE ANY BUSINESS *RELATIONSHIP* IS A *TWO-WAY* STREET, THIS *ISN'T* ALL ON RETAILERS. WHAT CAN *CUSTOMERS* DO TO *FOSTER* GOOD RELATIONSHIPS WITH DEALERS?"

COMMUNICATION AND *COURTESY* ARE THE *BACKBONE* OF BUILDING A GOOD RELATIONSHIP WITH *ANYONE,* AND THAT INCLUDES GUYS LIKE ME.

IF A DEALER HAS FOUND A BOOK ON YOUR *WANT LIST* THAT YOU ALREADY PURCHASED ELSEWHERE, GIVE IT CONSIDERATION AS A *POTENTIAL UPGRADE.*

DON'T *BRAG* TO A RETAILER ABOUT FINDING BOOKS AT A *LOWER PRICE* ELSEWHERE, INSULT THE PRICES, OR OFFER *SIGNIFICANTLY* LESS THAN ASKING PRICE OF A BACK ISSUE.

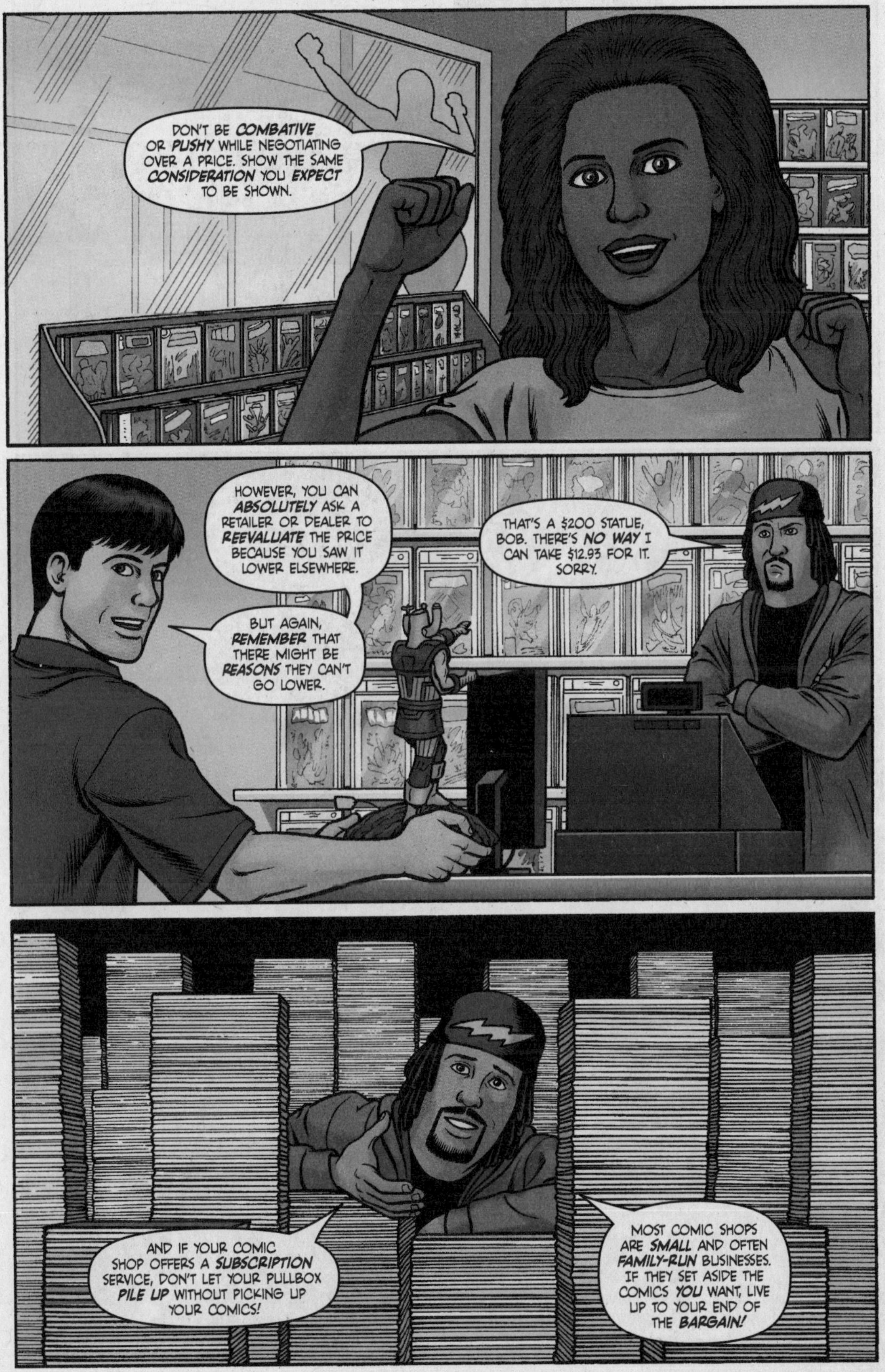
DON'T BE COMBATIVE OR PUSHY WHILE NEGOTIATING OVER A PRICE. SHOW THE SAME CONSIDERATION YOU EXPECT TO BE SHOWN.
HOWEVER, YOU CAN ABSOLUTELY ASK A RETAILER OR DEALER TO REEVALUATE THE PRICE BECAUSE YOU SAW IT LOWER ELSEWHERE.
BUT AGAIN, REMEMBER THAT THERE MIGHT BE REASONS THEY CAN'T GO LOWER.
THAT'S A $200 STATUE, BOB. THERE'S NO WAY I CAN TAKE $12.93 FOR IT. SORRY.
AND IF YOUR COMIC SHOP OFFERS A SUBSCRIPTION SERVICE, DON'T LET YOUR PULLBOX PILE UP WITHOUT PICKING UP YOUR COMICS!
MOST COMIC SHOPS ARE SMALL AND OFTEN FAMILY-RUN BUSINESSES. IF THEY SET ASIDE THE COMICS YOU WANT, LIVE UP TO YOUR END OF THE BARGAIN!

IT'S PROBABLY *OBVIOUS* FROM THE STORE WHERE YOU PICKED UP *THIS* ISSUE, BUT MOST COMIC SHOPS CARRY WAY MORE THAN JUST COMICS.

STATUES, ACTION FIGURES, POSTERS, T-SHIRTS, AND EVEN *ORIGINAL* COMIC ART...

THOSE ARE *JUST A FEW* OF THE GREAT CATEGORIES YOU CAN FIND WHEN YOU BUILD A *STRONG RELATIONSHIP* WITH THE RIGHT RETAILER!

AND WHILE I'M *NOT* NAMING ANY NAMES, THE STORE WHERE YOU GOT THIS COMIC *COULD* VERY WELL BE THE *PERFECT* PLACE TO GROW YOUR COLLECTION!

REMEMBER: COLLECT WHAT YOU LOVE, AND HAVE *FUN* DOING IT!

Script by J.C. VAUGHN & AMANDA SHERIFF
Story by J.C. VAUGHN
Illustrated by BRENDON & BRIAN FRAIM
Colored by Hi-Fi's BRIAN MILLER
Lettered by MINDY LOPKIN
Edited by MARK HUESMAN

WHETHER YOUR COMICS ARE *INCREDIBLY RARE* OR THE *LATEST RELEASES* FRESH OFF THE RACK AT YOUR *LOCAL COMIC SHOP*...

CAREFUL STORAGE IS ONE OF THE KEY ELEMENTS IN *PROTECTING* YOUR COLLECTION FROM THE *DANGERS* OF *LIGHT, HEAT,* AND *HUMIDITY.*

WHEN HANDLING COMICS, ALWAYS *WASH*...

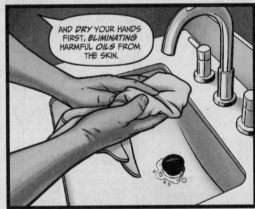

AND *DRY* YOUR HANDS FIRST, *ELIMINATING* HARMFUL *OILS* FROM THE SKIN.

"START ON A *CLEAN, UNOBSTRUCTED* SURFACE, WITH NO FOOD OR DRINK PRESENT."

Story by J.C. VAUGHN   Script by J.C. VAUGHN & MARK HUESMAN   Art by GENE GONZALES
Colored by Hi-Fi's BRIAN MILLER   Lettered by MINDY LOPKIN   Edited by AMANDA SHERIFF

LET'S PAUSE HERE FOR JUST A MOMENT TO DISCUSS THE *DIFFERENT TYPES* OF BAGS AND BOARDS. THERE ARE *MANY* FROM WHICH TO CHOOSE.

AMONG THE THINGS YOU SHOULD *CONSIDER* IN ADDITION TO THE *COST* OF THE PRODUCTS IS THE *AMOUNT* OF *TIME* YOU'LL BE LEAVING YOUR COMICS IN THEM.

FOR INSTANCE, IF YOU'RE USING *MYLAR* AND *ACID-FREE* BACKING BOARDS, YOUR COMICS CAN BE STORED IN THESE WITHOUT ANY NEGATIVE EFFECT IN *PERPETUITY*.

MORE *COMMON* BAGS AND *BOARDS* ARE PERFECT FOR A NUMBER OF YEARS, PARTICULARLY WHEN STORED IN THE *RIGHT CONDITIONS*, BUT THEY ARE *NOT A PERMANENT* SOLUTION.

OKAY, LET'S GET *BACK* TO THE *PROCESS*.

"PLACE THE COMIC (FRONT *COVER SIDE UP*) ON A STIFF, ACID-FREE CARDBOARD BACKING BOARD, ONE THAT IS *SLIGHTLY LARGER* THAN THE COMIC."

"THIS WILL HELP TO PREVENT BENDING AND CRACKING."

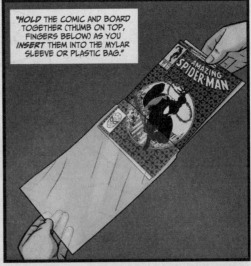

"*HOLD* THE COMIC AND BOARD TOGETHER (THUMB ON TOP, FINGERS BELOW) AS YOU *INSERT* THEM INTO THE MYLAR SLEEVE OR PLASTIC BAG."

"*WATCH* FOR ANY *TEARS* ON THE SIDES OF THE COMIC SO THEY DON'T GET *SNAGGED* ON THE BAG OPENING."

"MAKE *SURE* NO AREAS HAVE *FOLDED* OVER WHEN THE COMIC WAS *INSERTED*."

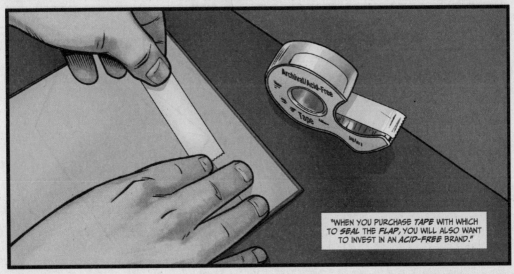

"WHEN YOU PURCHASE *TAPE* WITH WHICH TO *SEAL* THE *FLAP*, YOU WILL ALSO WANT TO INVEST IN AN *ACID-FREE* BRAND."

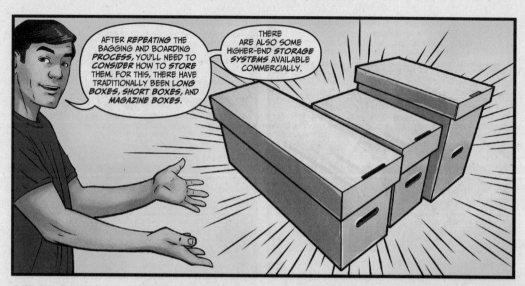

AFTER *REPEATING* THE BAGGING AND BOARDING *PROCESS*, YOU'LL NEED TO *CONSIDER* HOW TO *STORE* THEM. FOR THIS, THERE HAVE TRADITIONALLY BEEN LONG *BOXES*, SHORT *BOXES*, AND *MAGAZINE BOXES*.

THERE ARE ALSO SOME HIGHER-END *STORAGE* SYSTEMS AVAILABLE COMMERCIALLY.

"STORING YOUR COMICS IN *CARDBOARD BOXES* PROVIDES *PROTECTION* FROM *LIGHT*, *HEAT*, AND *HUMIDITY*..."

"THOUGH YOU SHOULD *ALWAYS* BE *AWARE* OF THE *HUMIDITY* WHEREVER YOUR BOXES ARE STORED. THESE BOXES SHOULD ALSO BE *ACID-FREE*."

"THE STANDARD COMIC *SHORT BOX* CAN HOLD ABOUT *100-150* COMICS."

"A LONG BOX CAN HOLD *ABOUT 300 COMICS.*"

"*DON'T* FORCE A COMIC INTO A *TIGHT BOX...*"

SINCE THIS MAY *DAMAGE* THE COMICS ON EITHER SIDE OF THE ONE YOU'RE *FORCING* IN.

"BE SURE TO DOUBLE-CHECK YOUR DIMENSIONS AS WELL! FORCING GOLDEN AGE OR SILVER AGE ISSUES INTO BOXES SPECIFIED FOR MODERN SIZES WILL NOT ONLY DAMAGE THE COMICS..."

IN SUCH A SITUATION IT'S ALSO MORE THAN LIKELY THE LID OF THE BOX WILL ALSO IMPACT THE COMICS.

"WHAT'S MORE AN OBSTRUCTED LID INVITES EASY EXPOSURE TO POLLUTANTS, VERMIN AND BUGS!"

C'MON, GUYS!

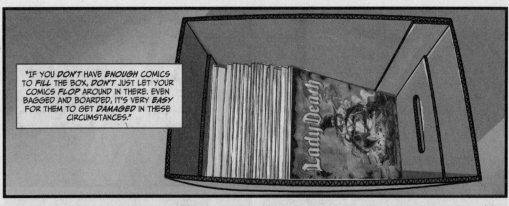

"IF YOU *DON'T* HAVE *ENOUGH* COMICS TO *FILL* THE BOX, *DON'T* JUST LET YOUR COMICS *FLOP* AROUND IN THERE. EVEN BAGGED AND BOARDED, IT'S VERY *EASY* FOR THEM TO GET *DAMAGED* IN THESE CIRCUMSTANCES."

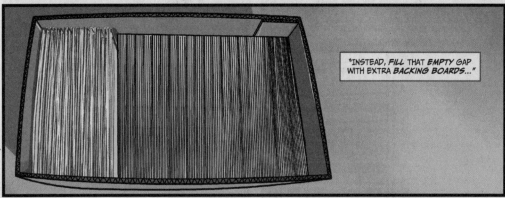

"INSTEAD, *FILL* THAT *EMPTY* GAP WITH EXTRA *BACKING BOARDS*..."

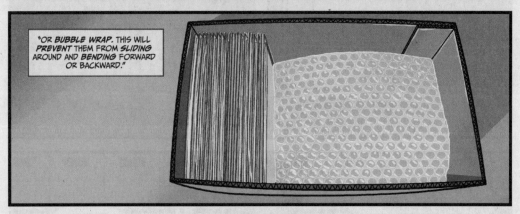

"OR *BUBBLE WRAP.* THIS WILL *PREVENT* THEM FROM *SLIDING* AROUND AND *BENDING* FORWARD OR BACKWARD."

SILICA GEL PACKS CAN *GREATLY* AID IN *REDUCING* THE EFFECTS OF *HUMIDITY* WHEN YOU PLACE THE PACKS IN YOUR COMIC BOXES.

BOXES SHOULD BE STORED *VERTICALLY* IN COOL, *DRY,* DARK ENVIRONMENTS.

"STACKING THE BOXES ON *SHELVING* IS *PREFERABLE* TO STACKING THE BOXES ON EACH OTHER, WHEN THIS IS *POSSIBLE.*"

"IF YOUR SHELVING IS LOCATED *NEAR WATER* PIPES, YOU CAN *CONSIDER COVERING* THE SHELVING UNITS WITH *PLASTIC SHEETS.* REGARDLESS OF THE THREAT, ALWAYS BE *AWARE* OF THE *POTENTIAL DANGERS* TO YOUR COMICS!"

THANKS FOR CONSIDERING THESE STEPS TO *PROTECT* YOUR *COLLECTION.* PROTECTING YOUR COMICS AND HELPING THEM LAST IS THE *FIRST STEP* IN SERIOUS COLLECTING.

SEE YOU AT A *COMIC SHOP* SOON!

Preservation & Storage of Comic Books

By William M. Cole P.E.

Comic Book collecting today is for both fun and profit. Yet, the comic book you thought was going to increase in value year after year has suddenly turned yellow after only three months and is now worthless. What happened? What could have been done to prevent the yellowing? This article will discuss how paper is made. What materials are best suited for long-term storage and the guidelines for proper preservation.

HOW PAPER IS MADE

Paper generally has plant fibers that have been reduced to a pulp, suspended in water and then matted into sheets. The fibers in turn consist largely of cellulose, a strong, lightweight and somewhat durable material; cotton is an example of almost pure cellulose fiber. Although cotton and other kinds of fiber have been used in paper making over the years, most paper products today are made from wood pulp.

Wood pulps come in two basic varieties: groundwood and chemical wood. In the first process, whole logs are shredded and mechanically beaten. In the second, the fibers are prepared by digesting wood chips in chemical cookers. Because groundwood is the cheaper of the two, it is the primary component in such inexpensive papers as newsprint, which is used in many newspapers, comic books and paperbacks. Chemically purified pulps are used in more expensive applications, such as stationery and some magazines and hardcover books.

Since groundwood pulp is made from whole wood fiber, the resulting paper does not consist of pure cellulose. As much as one third of its content may consist of non cellulose materials such as lignin, a complex woody acid. In chemical pulps, however, the lignin and other impurities are removed during the cooking process.

DETERIORATION OF PAPER

The primary causes of paper deterioration are oxidation and acid hydrolysis. Oxidation attacks cellulose molecules with oxygen from the air, causing darkening and increased acidity. In addition, the lignin in groundwood paper breaks down quickly under the influence of oxygen and ultraviolet light. Light induced oxidation of lignin is what turns newspapers yellow after a few days' exposure to sunlight. (Light can also cause some printing inks to fade.)

In acid hydrolysis, the cellulose fibers are cut by a reaction involving heat and acids, resulting in paper that turns brown and brittle. The sources of acidity include lignin itself, air pollution, and

reaction by products from the oxidation of paper. Another major source is alum, which is often used with rosin to prepare the paper surface for accepting printing inks. Alum eventually releases sulfuric acid in paper.

Acidity and alkalinity are measured in units of pH, with 0 the most acidic and 14 the most alkaline. (Neutral pH is 7.0) Because the scale is based on powers of 10, a pH of 4.5 is actually 200 times more acidic than a pH of 6.5. Fresh newsprint typically carries a pH of 4.5 or less, while older more deteriorated paper on the verge of crumbling, may run as low as pH 3.0. Although some modern papers are made acid free, most paper collectibles are acidic and need special treatment to lengthen their lives. Other factors which contribute to the destruction of paper include extremes of temperature and humidity, insects, rodents, mold and improper handling and storage.

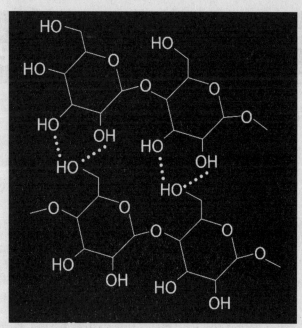

GUIDELINES FOR PRESERVATION

First and foremost, keep your paper collectibles cool, dark and dry. Store books and other items in an unheated room, if possible, and regularly monitor the humidity. Excess heat and humidity should be controlled with an air conditioner and a dehumidifier. Storage materials such as envelopes, sleeves and boxes, should be of ARCHIVAL QUALITY only to prevent contamination of their contents.

MYLAR® According to the US Library of Congress, the preferred material for preserving valuable documents is uncoated archival quality polyester film, such as Mylar® type D or equivalent material such as Melinex® 516. Mylar® is an exceptionally strong transparent film that resists moisture, pollutants, oils and acids. With a life expectancy of hundreds of years, Mylar® will outlast most other plastics. In addition, the brilliance and clarity of Mylar® enhances the appearance of any paper collectible. (Mylar® is a registered trademark of DuPont Teijin films. Their brands of archival quality polyester films are Mylar® type D and Melinex® 516 of which they are exclusive manufacturers.)

POLYETHYLENE AND POLYPROPYLENE

For years collectors have stored their movie posters, comic books, baseball cards and other collectibles in polyethylene bags, PVC sheets and plastic wraps. Although such products may be useful in keeping away dirt, grease and vermin, many plastic sleeves contain plasticizers and other additives which can migrate into paper and cause premature aging. Both polyethylene and polypropylene contain solvents and additives in their manufacture to assure clarity and increase the flexibility in the plastic. Polyethylene when uncoated without any solvents is a good moisture barrier but has a high gas transmission rate, and eventually shrinks and loses its shape under warmer conditions.

In recent years polypropylene bags have been sold under the guise of being archivally sound. This is far from the truth. Only uncoated and untreated material is suitable for archival protection. Currently, the only way to seal polypropylene is to add a substance called PVDC (Polyvinyl Dichloride which is a relative of PVC) to allow the material to be heat sealed. Therefore, once you add the harmful additive, the sleeve now becomes non-archival and should not be used for long term storage.

ACID FREE BOARDS AND BOXES

Because ordinary cardboard is itself acidic, storage in cardboard boxes may be hazardous to your collection, and is a leading cause of premature deterioration of comic collections. For proper storage, only acid free boards that meet the US Government's MINIMUM requirements are acceptable. These requirements have been defined as boards having a 3% calcium carbonate buffer throughout and a minimum pH of 8.5. Anything less will hasten your collection's destruction. While many advertisers claim that their boards are "acid free at time of manufacture," they are in reality only spray coated with an alkaline substance making them acid free for only a very short time. Boards termed "acid free at time of manufacture" do not offer sufficient protection or storage for anything other than short-term. True acid free boards have been impregnated with a calcium buffer resulting in an acid free, alkaline pH content of 8.5 throughout.

DEACIDIFICATION

Another way to extend the longevity of your collectibles is to deacidify them before storage.

Deacidifying sprays and solutions are now available for home use. By impregnating the paper with an alkaline reserve, you can neutralize existing acids and inhibit oxidation, future acidity and staining due to certain fungi. However it is best left to the professionals to deacidify your comic books. Deacidification with proper storage conditions will add centuries to the lifetime of paper.

In summary, we recommend the following guidelines for the maximum protection of your collectibles: Deacidify the paper; store in Mylar® sleeves with acid free boards and cartons; and keep the collection cool, dry and dark. Periodic inspections and pH and humidity tests are also recommended. By following these simple guidelines you can be assured of a comic book collection that not only will increase in value, but will also last for many years to come.

Bill Cole manufactured collectors supplies for over 50 years and was the owner of Bill Cole Enterprises, Inc. of East Wareham, MA. Mr. Cole is a retired Army Officer and is also the author of numerous articles on preservation. He currently is a "Professional Comic Book Grader". Questions or comments may be directed to him at bcole@bcemylar.com. His website is www.bcemylar.com.

Grading Definitions

When grading a comic book, common sense must be employed. The overall eye appeal and beauty of the comic book must be taken into account along with its technical flaws to arrive at the appropriate grade.

10.0 GEM MINT (GM): This is an exceptional example of a given book - the best ever seen. The slightest bindery defects and/or printing flaws may be seen only upon very close inspection. The overall look is "as if it has never been handled or released for purchase." Only the slightest bindery or printing defects are allowed, and these would be imperceptible on first viewing. No bindery tears. Cover is flat with no surface wear. Inks are bright with high reflectivity. Well centered and firmly secured to interior pages. Corners are cut square and sharp. No creases. No dates or stamped markings allowed. No soiling, staining or other discoloration. Spine is tight and flat. No spine roll or split allowed. Staples must be original, centered and clean with no rust. No staple tears or stress lines. Paper is white, supple and fresh. No hint of acidity in the odor of the newsprint. No interior autographs or owner signatures. Centerfold is firmly secure. No interior tears.

9.9 MINT (MT): Near perfect in every way. Only subtle bindery or printing defects are allowed. No bindery tears. Cover is flat with no surface wear. Inks are bright with high reflectivity. Generally well centered and firmly secured to interior pages. Corners are cut square and sharp. No creases. Small, inconspicuous, lightly penciled, stamped or inked arrival dates are acceptable as long as they are in an unobtrusive location. No soil-ing, staining or other discoloration. Spine is tight and flat. No spine roll or split allowed. Staples must be original, generally centered and clean with no rust. No staple tears or stress lines. Paper is white, supple and fresh. No hint of acidity in the odor of the newsprint. Centerfold is firmly secure. No interior tears.

9.8 NEAR MINT/MINT (NM/MT): Nearly perfect in every way with only minor imperfections that keep it from the next higher grade. Only subtle bindery or printing defects are allowed. No bindery tears. Cover is flat with no surface wear. Inks are bright with high reflectivity. Generally well centered and firmly secured to interior pages. Corners are cut square and sharp. No creases. Small, inconspicuous, lightly penciled, stamped or inked arrival dates are acceptable as long as they are in an unobtrusive location. No soiling, staining or other discoloration. Spine is tight and flat. No spine roll or split allowed. Staples must be original, generally centered and clean with no rust. No staple tears or stress lines. Paper is off-white to white, supple and fresh. No hint of acidity in the odor of the newsprint. Centerfold is firmly secure. Only the slightest interior tears are allowed.

9.6 NEAR MINT+ (NM+): Nearly perfect with a minor additional virtue or virtues that raise it from Near Mint. The overall look is "as if it was just purchased and read once or twice." Only subtle bindery or printing defects are allowed. No bindery tears are allowed, although on Golden Age books bindery tears of up to 1/8" have been noted. Cover is flat with no surface wear. Inks are bright with high reflectivity. Well centered and firmly secured to interior pages. One corner may be almost imperceptibly blunted, but still almost sharp and cut square. Almost imperceptible indentations are permissible, but no creases, bends, or color break. Small, inconspicuous, lightly penciled, stamped or inked arrival dates are acceptable as long as they are in an unobtrusive location. No soiling, staining or other discoloration. Spine is tight and flat. No spine roll or split allowed. Staples must be original, generally centered, with only the slightest discoloration. No staple tears, stress lines, or rust migration. Paper is off-white, supple and fresh. No hint of acidity in the odor of the newsprint. Centerfold is firmly secure. Only the slightest interior tears are allowed.

9.4 NEAR MINT (NM): Nearly perfect with only minor imperfections that keep it from the next higher grade. Minor feathering that does not distract from the overall beauty of an otherwise higher grade copy is acceptable for this grade. The overall look is "as if it was just purchased and read once or twice." Subtle bindery defects are allowed. Bindery tears must be less than 1/16" on Silver Age and later books, although on Golden Age books bindery tears of up to 1/4" have been noted. Cover is flat with no surface wear. Inks are bright with high reflectivity. Generally well centered and secured to interior pages. Corners are cut square and sharp with ever-so-slight blunting permitted. A 1/16" bend is permitted with no color break. No creases. Small, inconspicuous, lightly penciled, stamped or inked arrival dates are acceptable as long as they are in an unobtrusive location. No soiling, staining or other discoloration apart from slight foxing. Spine is tight and flat. No spine roll or split allowed. Staples are generally centered; may have slight discoloration. No staple tears are allowed; almost no stress lines. No rust migration. In rare cases, a comic was not stapled at the bindery and therefore has a missing staple; this is not con-

sidered a defect. Any staple can be replaced on books up to Fine, but only vintage staples can be used on books from Very Fine to Near Mint. Mint books must have original staples. Paper is cream to off-white, supple and fresh. No hint of acidity in the odor of the newsprint. Centerfold is secure. Slight interior tears are allowed.

9.2 NEAR MINT– (NM–): Nearly perfect with only a minor additional defect or defects that keep it from Near Mint. A limited number of minor bindery defects are allowed. A light, barely noticeable water stain or minor foxing that does not distract from the beauty of the book is acceptable for this grade. Cover is flat with no surface wear. Inks are bright with only the slightest dimming of reflectivity. Generally well centered and secured to interior pages. Corners are cut square and sharp with ever-so-slight blunting permitted. A 1/16"-1/8" bend is permitted with no color break. No creases. Small, inconspicuous, lightly penciled, stamped or inked arrival dates are acceptable as long as they are in an unobtrusive location. No soiling, staining or other discoloration apart from slight foxing. Spine is tight and flat. No spine roll or split allowed. Staples may show some discoloration. No staple tears are allowed; almost no stress lines. No rust migration. In rare cases, a comic was not stapled at the bindery and therefore has a missing staple; this is not considered a defect. Any staple can be replaced on books up to Fine, but only vintage staples can be used on books from Very Fine to Near Mint. Mint books must have original staples. Paper is cream to off-white, supple and fresh. No hint of acidity in the odor of the newsprint. Centerfold is secure. Slight interior tears are allowed.

9.0 VERY FINE/NEAR MINT (VF/ NM): Nearly perfect with outstanding eye appeal. A limited number of bindery defects are allowed. Almost flat cover with almost imperceptible wear. Inks are bright with slightly diminished reflectivity. An 1/8" bend is allowed if color is not broken. Corners are cut square and sharp with ever-so-slight blunting permitted but no creases. Several lightly penciled, stamped or inked arrival dates are acceptable. No obvious soiling, staining or other discoloration, except for very minor foxing. Spine is tight and flat. No spine roll or split allowed. Staples may show some discoloration. Only the slightest staple tears are allowed. A very minor accumulation of stress lines may be present if they are nearly imperceptible. No rust migration. In rare cases, a comic was not stapled at the bindery and therefore has a missing staple; this is not considered a defect. Any staple can be replaced on books up to Fine, but only vintage staples can be used on books from Very Fine to Near Mint. Mint books must have original staples. Paper is cream to off-white and supple. No hint of acidity in the odor of the newsprint. Centerfold is secure. Very minor interior tears may be present.

8.5 VERY FINE+ (VF+): Fits the criteria for Very Fine but with an additional virtue or small accumulation of virtues that improves the book's appearance by a perceptible amount.

8.0 VERY FINE (VF): An excellent copy with outstanding eye appeal. Sharp, bright and clean with supple pages. A comic book in this grade has the appearance of having been carefully handled. A limited accumulation of minor bindery defects is allowed. Cover is relatively flat with minimal surface wear beginning to show, possibly including some minute wear at corners. Inks are generally bright with moderate to high reflectivity. A 1/4" crease is acceptable if color is not broken. Stamped or inked arrival dates may be present. No obvious soiling, staining or other discoloration, except for minor foxing. Spine is almost flat

with no roll. Possible minor color break allowed. Staples may show some discoloration. Very slight staple tears and a few almost very minor to minor stress lines may be present. No rust migration. In rare cases, a comic was not stapled at the bindery and therefore has a missing staple; this is not considered a defect. Any staple can be replaced on books up to Fine, but only vintage staples can be used on books from Very Fine to Near Mint. Mint books must have original staples. Paper is tan to cream and supple. No hint of acidity in the odor of the newsprint. Centerfold is mostly secure. Minor interior tears at the margin may be present.

7.5 VERY FINE– (VF–): Fits the criteria for Very Fine but with an additional defect or small accumulation of defects that detracts from the book's appearance by a perceptible amount.

7.0   FINE/VERY FINE (FN/VF): An above-average copy that shows minor wear but is still relatively flat and clean with outstanding eye appeal. A small accumulation of minor bindery defects is allowed. Minor cover wear beginning to show with interior yellowing or tanning allowed, possibly including minor creases. Corners may be blunted or abraded. Inks are generally bright with a moderate reduction in reflectivity. Stamped or inked arrival dates may be present. No obvious soiling, staining or other discoloration, except for minor foxing. The slightest spine roll may be present, as well as a possible moderate color break. Staples may show some discoloration. Slight staple tears and a slight accumulation of light stress lines may be present. Slight rust migration. In rare cases, a comic was not stapled at the bindery and therefore has a missing staple; this is not considered a defect. Any staple can be replaced on books up to Fine, but only vintage staples can be used on books from Very Fine to Near Mint. Mint books must have original staples. Paper is tan to cream, but not brown. No hint of acidity in the odor of the newsprint. Centerfold is mostly secure. Minor interior tears at the margin may be present.

6.5 FINE+ (FN+): Fits the criteria for Fine but with an additional virtue or small accumulation of virtues that improves the book's appearance by a perceptible amount.

6.0 FINE (FN): An above-average copy that shows minor wear but is still relatively flat and clean with no significant creasing or other serious defects. Eye appeal is somewhat reduced because of slight surface wear and the accumulation of small defects, especially on the spine and edges. A FINE condition comic book appears to have been read a few times and has been handled with moderate care. Some accumulation of minor bindery defects is allowed. Minor cover wear apparent, with minor to moderate creases. Inks show a major reduction in reflectivity. Blunted or abraded corners are more common, as is minor staining, soiling, discoloration, and/or foxing. Stamped or inked arrival dates may be present. A minor spine roll is allowed. There can also be a 1/4" spine split or severe color break. Staples show minor discoloration. Minor staple tears and an accumulation of stress lines may be present, as well as minor rust migration. In rare cases, a comic was not stapled at the bindery and therefore has a missing staple; this is not considered a defect. Any staple can be replaced on books up to Fine, but only vintage staples can be used on books from Very Fine to Near Mint. Mint books must have original staples. Paper is brown to tan and fairly supple with no signs of brittleness. No hint of acidity in the odor of the newsprint. Minor interior tears at the margin may be present. Centerfold may be loose but not detached.

5.5 FINE– (FN–): Fits the criteria for Fine but with an additional defect or small accumulation of defects that detracts from the book's appearance by a perceptible amount.

5.0 VERY GOOD/FINE (VG/FN): An above-average but well-used comic book. A comic in this grade shows some moderate wear; eye appeal is somewhat reduced because of the accumulation of defects. Still a desirable copy that has been handled with some care. An accumulation of bindery defects is allowed. Minor to moderate cover wear apparent, with minor to moderate creases and/or dimples. Inks have major to extreme reduction in reflectivity. Blunted or abraded corners are increasingly common, as is minor to moderate staining, discoloration, and/or foxing. Stamped or inked arrival dates may be present. A minor to moderate spine roll is allowed. A spine split of up to 1/2" may be present. Staples show minor discoloration. A slight accumulation of minor staple tears and an accumulation of minor stress lines may also be present, as well as minor rust migration. In rare cases, a comic was not stapled at the bindery and therefore has a missing staple; this is not considered a defect. Any staple can be replaced on books up to Fine, but only vintage staples can be used on books from Very Fine to Near Mint. Mint books must have original staples. Paper is brown to tan with no signs of brittleness. May have the faintest trace of an acidic odor. Centerfold may be loose but not detached. Minor tears may also be present.

4.5 VERY GOOD+ (VG+): Fits the criteria for Very Good but with an additional virtue or small accumulation of virtues that improves the book's appearance by a perceptible amount.

4.0 VERY GOOD (VG): The average used comic book. A comic in this grade shows some significant moderate wear, but still has not accumulated enough total defects to reduce eye appeal to the point that it is not a desirable copy. Cover shows moderate to significant wear, and may be loose but not completely detached. Moderate to extreme reduction in reflectivity. Can have an accumulation of creases or dimples. Corners may be blunted or abraded. Store stamps, name stamps, arrival dates, initials, etc. have no effect on this grade. Some discoloration, fading, foxing, and even minor soiling is allowed. As much as a 1/4" triangle can be missing out of the corner or edge; a missing 1/8" square is also acceptable. Only minor unobtrusive tape and other amateur repair allowed on otherwise high grade copies. Moderate spine roll may be present and/or a 1" spine split. Staples discolored. Minor to moderate staple tears and stress lines may be present, as well as some rust migration. Paper is brown but not brittle. A minor acidic odor can be detectable. Minor to moderate tears may be present. Centerfold may be loose or detached at one staple.

3.5 VERY GOOD– (VG–): Fits the criteria for Very Good but with an additional defect or small accumulation of defects that detracts from the book's appearance by a perceptible amount.

3.0 GOOD/VERY GOOD (GD/VG): A used comic book showing some substantial wear. Cover shows significant wear, and may be loose or even detached at one staple. Cover reflectivity is very low. Can have a book-length crease and/or dimples. Corners may be blunted or even rounded. Discoloration, fading, foxing, and even minor to moderate soiling is allowed. A triangle from 1/4" to 1/2" can be missing out of the corner or edge; a missing 1/8" to 1/4" square is also acceptable. Tape and other amateur repair may be present. Moderate spine roll likely. May have a spine split of anywhere from 1" to 1-1/2". Staples may be rusted or replaced. Minor to moderate staple tears and moderate stress lines may be present, as well as some rust migration. Pa-

per is brown but not brittle. Centerfold may be loose or detached at one staple. Minor to moderate interior tears may be present.

2.5 GOOD+ (GD+): Fits the criteria for Good but with an additional virtue or small accumulation of virtues that improves the book's appearance by a perceptible amount.

2.0 GOOD (GD): Shows substantial wear; often considered a "reading copy." Cover shows significant wear and may even be detached. Cover reflectivity is low and in some cases completely absent. Book-length creases and dimples may be present. Rounded corners are more common. Moderate soiling, staining, discoloration and foxing may be present. The largest piece allowed missing from the front or back cover is usually a 1/2" triangle or a 1/4" square, although some Silver Age books such as 1960s Marvels have had the price corner box clipped from the top left front cover and may be considered Good if they would otherwise have graded higher. Tape and other forms of amateur repair are common in Silver Age and older books. Spine roll is likely. May have up to a 2" spine split. Staples may be degraded, replaced or missing. Moderate staple tears and stress lines may be present, as well as rust migration. Paper is brown but not brittle. Centerfold may be loose or detached. Moderate interior tears may be present.

1.8 GOOD– (GD–): Fits the criteria for Good but with an additional defect or small accumulation of defects that detracts from the book's appearance by a perceptible amount.

1.5 FAIR/GOOD (FR/GD): A comic showing substantial to heavy wear. A copy in this grade still has all pages and covers, although there may be pieces missing up to and including missing coupons and/or Marvel Value Stamps that do not impact the story. Books in this grade are commonly creased, scuffed, abraded, soiled, and possibly unattractive, but still generally readable. Cover shows considerable wear and may be detached. Nearly no reflectivity to no reflectivity remaining. Store stamp, name stamp, arrival date and initials are permitted. Book-length creases, tears and folds may be present. Rounded corners are increasingly common. Soiling, staining, discoloration and foxing is generally present. Up to 1/10 of the back cover may be missing. Tape and other forms of amateur repair are increasingly common in Silver Age and older books. Spine roll is common. May have a spine split between 2" and 2/3 the length of the book. Staples may be degraded, replaced or missing. Staple tears and stress lines are common, as well as rust migration. Paper is brown and may show brittleness around the edges. Acidic odor may be present. Centerfold may be loose or detached. Interior tears are common.

1.0 FAIR (FR): A copy in this grade shows heavy wear. Some collectors consider this the lowest collectible grade because comic books in lesser condition are usually incomplete and/or brittle. Comics in this grade are usually soiled, faded, ragged and possibly unattractive. This is the last grade in which a comic remains generally readable. Cover may be detached, and inks have lost all reflectivity. Creases, tears and/or folds are prevalent. Corners are commonly rounded or absent. Soiling and staining is present. Books in this condition generally have all pages and most of the covers, although there may be up to 1/4 of the front cover missing or no back cover, but not both. Tape and other forms of amateur repair are more common. Spine roll is more common; spine split can extend up to 2/3 the length of the book. Staples may be missing or show rust and discoloration. An accumulation of staple tears and stress lines may be present, as well as rust migration. Paper is brown and may show brittleness around the edges but not in the central portion of the pages. Acidic odor may be present. Accumulation of interior tears. Chunks may be missing. The centerfold may be missing if readability is generally preserved (although there may be difficulty). Coupons may be cut.

0.5 POOR (PR): Most comic books in this grade have been sufficiently degraded to the point where there is little or no collector value; they are easily identified by a complete absence of eye appeal. Comics in this grade are brittle almost to the point of turning to dust with a touch, and are usually incomplete. Extreme cover fading may render the cover almost indiscernible. May have extremely severe stains, mildew or heavy cover abrasion to the point that some cover inks are indistinct/absent. Covers may be detached with large chunks missing. Can have extremely ragged edges and extensive creasing. Corners are rounded or virtually absent. Covers may have been defaced with paints, varnishes, glues, oil, indelible markers or dyes, and may have suffered heavy water damage. Can also have extensive amateur repairs such as laminated covers. Extreme spine roll present; can have extremely ragged spines or a complete, book-length split. Staples can be missing or show extreme rust and discoloration. Extensive staple tears and stress lines may be present, as well as extreme rust migration. Paper exhibits moderate to severe brittleness (where the comic book literally falls apart when examined). Extreme acidic odor may be present. Extensive interior tears. Multiple pages, including the centerfold, may be missing that affect readability. Coupons may be cut.

0.3 INCOMPLETE (INC): Books that are coverless, but are otherwise complete, or covers missing their interiors.

0.1 INCOMPLETE (INC): Coverless copies that have incomplete interiors, wraps or single pages will receive a grade of .1 as will just front covers or just back covers.

(10.0)   GEM MINT   (GM)

GRADE DESCRIPTION:
This is an exceptional example of a given book - the best ever seen. The slightest bindery defects and/or printing flaws may be seen only upon very close inspection.

The overall look is "as if it has never been handled or released for purchase."

BINDERY/PRINTING DEFECTS - Only the slightest bindery or printing defects are allowed, and these would be imperceptible on first viewing. No bindery tears.

COVER/EXTERIOR - Flat with no surface wear. Inks are bright with high reflectivity. Well centered and firmly secured to interior pages. Corners are cut square and sharp. No creases. No dates or stamped markings allowed. No soiling, staining or other discoloration.

SPINE - Tight and flat. No spine roll or split allowed.

STAPLES - Must be original, centered and clean with no rust. No staple tears or stress lines.

PAPER/INTERIOR - Paper is white, supple and fresh. No hint of acidity in the odor of the newsprint. No interior autographs or owner signatures. Centerfold is firmly secure. No interior tears.

Collectors should thoroughly examine any book listed as 10.0. These books should also be carefully scrutinized for restoration.

BINDERY/PRINTING

only the slightest,
most imperceptible defects

COVER INKS/GLOSS

bright with high reflectivity

COVER WEAR

flat, no wear,
well centered, secure

COVER CREASES

none allowed

SOILING, STAINING

none allowed

DATES/STAMPS

none allowed

SPINE ROLL

tight and flat, no roll

SPINE SPLIT

none allowed

STAPLES

original, centered, clean

STAPLE TEARS

none allowed

RUST MIGRATION

none allowed

STRESS LINES

none allowed

CORNERS

sharp, square, no creases

CENTERFOLD

firmly secure

INTERIOR TEARS

none allowed

PAPER QUALITY/COLOR

white, supple and fresh

ACID ODOR

none allowed

MISSING PIECES

none allowed

AMATEUR REPAIRS

none allowed

COUPON CUT

none allowed

READABILITY

preserved

MINT

GRADE DESCRIPTION:
Near perfect in every way.

The overall look is "as if it was just purchased."

BINDERY DEFECTS - Only subtle bindery or printing defects are allowed. No bindery tears.

COVER/EXTERIOR - Flat with no surface wear. Inks are bright with high reflectivity and minimal fading. Generally well centered and firmly secured to interior pages. Corners are cut square and sharp. No creases. Small, inconspicuous, lightly penciled, stamped or inked arrival dates are acceptable as long as they are in an unobtrusive location. No soiling, staining or other discoloration.

SPINE - Tight and flat. No spine roll or split allowed.

STAPLES - Must be original, generally centered and clean with no rust. No staple tears or stress lines.

PAPER/INTERIOR - Paper is white, supple and fresh. No hint of acidity in the odor of the newsprint. Centerfold is firmly secure. No interior tears.

Comics published before 1970 in MINT condition are extremely scarce.

BINDERY/PRINTING

only subtle defects,
no bindery tears

COVER INKS/GLOSS

bright with high reflectivity

COVER WEAR

flat, no wear,
well centered, secure

COVER CREASES

none allowed

SOILING, STAINING

none allowed

DATES/STAMPS

small, inconspicuous
dates/initials allowed

SPINE ROLL

tight and flat, no roll

SPINE SPLIT

none allowed

STAPLES

original, clean,
generally centered

STAPLE TEARS

none allowed

RUST MIGRATION

none allowed

STRESS LINES

none allowed

CORNERS

sharp, square, no creases

CENTERFOLD

firmly secure

INTERIOR TEARS

none allowed

PAPER QUALITY/COLOR

white, supple and fresh

ACID ODOR

none allowed

MISSING PIECES

none allowed

AMATEUR REPAIRS

none allowed

COUPON CUT

none allowed

READABILITY

preserved

(9.8) NEAR MINT / MINT (NM/MT)

GRADE DESCRIPTION:
Nearly perfect in every way with only minor imperfections that keep it from the next higher grade.

The overall look is "as if it was just purchased."

BINDERY DEFECTS - Only subtle bindery or printing defects are allowed. No bindery tears.

COVER/EXTERIOR - Flat with no surface wear. Inks are bright with high reflectivity and minimal fading. Generally well centered and firmly secured to interior pages. Corners are cut square and sharp. No creases. Small, inconspicuous, lightly penciled, stamped or inked arrival dates are acceptable as long as they are in an unobtrusive location. No soiling, staining or other discoloration.

SPINE - Tight and flat. No spine roll or split allowed.

STAPLES - Must be original, generally centered and clean with no rust. No staple tears or stress lines.

PAPER/INTERIOR - Paper is off-white to white, supple and fresh. No hint of acidity in the odor of the newsprint. Centerfold is firmly secure. Only the slightest interior tears are allowed.

BINDERY/PRINTING
only subtle, no bindery tears

COVER INKS/GLOSS
bright with high reflectivity

COVER WEAR
flat, no wear, well centered

COVER CREASES
none allowed

SOILING, STAINING
none allowed

DATES/STAMPS
small, inconspicuous
dates/initials allowed

SPINE ROLL
tight and flat, no roll

SPINE SPLIT
none allowed

STAPLES
original, clean,
generally centered

STAPLE TEARS
none allowed

RUST MIGRATION
none allowed

STRESS LINES
none allowed

CORNERS
sharp, square, no creases

CENTERFOLD
firmly secure

INTERIOR TEARS
slightest tears allowed

PAPER QUALITY/COLOR
off-white to white, supple and fresh

ACID ODOR
none allowed

MISSING PIECES
none allowed

AMATEUR REPAIRS
none allowed

COUPON CUT
none allowed

READABILITY
preserved

GRADE DESCRIPTION:

Nearly perfect with a minor additional virtue or virtues that raise it from Near Mint. The overall look is "as if it was just purchased and read once or twice."

BINDERY DEFECTS - Only subtle bindery or printing defects are allowed. No bindery tears are allowed, although on Golden Age books bindery tears of up to 1/8" have been noted.

COVER/EXTERIOR - Flat with no surface wear. Inks are bright with high reflectivity. Well centered and firmly secured to interior pages. One corner may be almost imperceptibly blunted, but still almost sharp and cut square. Almost imperceptible indentations are permissible, but no creases, bends, or color break. Small, inconspicuous, lightly penciled, stamped or inked arrival dates are acceptable as long as they are in an unobtrusive location. No soiling, staining or other discoloration.

SPINE - Tight and flat. No spine roll or split allowed.

STAPLES - Must be original, generally centered, with only the slightest discoloration. No staple tears, stress lines, or rust migration.

PAPER/INTERIOR - Paper is off-white, supple and fresh. No hint of acidity in the odor of the newsprint. Centerfold is firmly secure. Only the slightest interior tears are allowed.

BINDERY/PRINTING

only subtle, no tears on Silver Age
and later, 1/8" on Golden Age

COVER INKS/GLOSS

bright with high reflectivity

COVER WEAR

flat, no wear, well centered

COVER CREASES

almost imperceptible indentations
allowed

SOILING, STAINING

none allowed

DATES/STAMPS

small, inconspicuous
dates/initials allowed

SPINE ROLL

tight and flat, no roll

SPINE SPLIT

none allowed

STAPLES

original, generally cen-
tered, slight discoloration

STAPLE TEARS

none allowed

RUST MIGRATION

none allowed

STRESS LINES

none allowed

CORNERS

almost sharp, one imperceptible
blunted corner allowed

CENTERFOLD

firmly secure

INTERIOR TEARS

slightest tears allowed

PAPER QUALITY/COLOR

off-white, supple and fresh

ACID ODOR

none allowed

MISSING PIECES

none allowed

AMATEUR REPAIRS

none allowed

COUPON CUT

none allowed

READABILITY

preserved

GRADE DESCRIPTION:

Nearly perfect with only minor imperfections that keep it from the next higher grade. Minor feathering that does not distract from the overall beauty of an otherwise higher grade copy is acceptable for this grade. The overall look is "as if it was just purchased and read once or twice."

BINDERY DEFECTS - Subtle defects are allowed. Bindery tears must be less than 1/16" on Silver Age and later books, although on Golden Age books bindery tears of up to 1/4" have been noted.

COVER/EXTERIOR - Flat with no surface wear. Inks are bright with high reflectivity. Generally well centered and secured to interior pages. Corners are cut square and sharp with ever-so-slight blunting permitted. A 1/16" bend is permitted with no color break. No creases. Small, inconspicuous, lightly penciled, stamped or inked arrival dates are acceptable as long as they are in an unobtrusive location. No soiling, staining or other discoloration apart from slight foxing.

SPINE - Tight and flat. No spine roll or split allowed.

STAPLES - Generally centered; may have slight discoloration. No staple tears are allowed; almost no stress lines. No rust migration. In rare cases, a comic was not stapled at the bindery and therefore has a missing staple; this is not considered a defect. Any staple can be replaced on books up to Fine, but only vintage staples can be used on books from Very Fine to Near Mint. Mint books must have original staples.

PAPER/INTERIOR - Paper is cream to off-white, supple and fresh. No hint of acidity in the odor of the newsprint. Centerfold is secure. Slight interior tears are allowed.

Comics published before 1970 in NEAR MINT condition are scarce. This grade is commonly viewed by the average collector as the best grade obtainable.

Collectors should thoroughly examine these books for restoration, particularly in the case of pre-1965 books. Expensive and key books listed as being in "high grade" frequently have some restoration. In most cases, restoration performed on otherwise NEAR MINT books will reduce the grade. A VERY FINE comic book cannot be transformed into a NEAR MINT comic book through restoration.

BINDERY/PRINTING

subtle, tears up to 1/16" on Silver Age and later, 1/4" on Golden Age

COVER INKS/GLOSS

bright with high reflectivity

COVER WEAR

flat, no wear, generally centered, secure

COVER CREASES

1/16" bend with no color break allowed

SOILING, STAINING

none allowed except for slight foxing

DATES/STAMPS

small, inconspicuous dates/initials allowed

SPINE ROLL

tight and flat, no roll

SPINE SPLIT

none allowed

STAPLES

generally centered, slight discoloration

STAPLE TEARS

none allowed

RUST MIGRATION

none allowed

STRESS LINES

almost no lines

CORNERS

ever-so-slight blunting, no creases

CENTERFOLD

secure

INTERIOR TEARS

slight tears allowed

PAPER QUALITY/COLOR

cream/off-white, supple and fresh

ACID ODOR

none allowed

MISSING PIECES

none allowed

AMATEUR REPAIRS

none allowed

COUPON CUT

none allowed

READABILITY

preserved

(9.2)   NEAR MINT-   (NM–)

GRADE DESCRIPTION:

Nearly perfect with only a minor additional defect or defects that keep it from Near Mint. The overall look is "as if it was just purchased and read once or twice."

BINDERY DEFECTS - A limited number of minor defects are allowed.

COVER/EXTERIOR - Flat with no surface wear. Inks are bright with only the slightest dimming of reflectivity. Generally well centered and secured to interior pages. Corners are cut square and sharp with ever-so-slight blunting permitted. A 1/16-1/8" bend is permitted with no color break. No creases. Small, inconspicuous, lightly penciled, stamped or inked arrival dates are acceptable as long as they are in an unobtrusive location. No soiling, staining or other discoloration apart from slight foxing.

SPINE - Tight and flat. No spine roll or split allowed.

STAPLES - May show some discoloration. No staple tears are allowed; almost no stress lines. No rust migration. In rare cases, a comic was not stapled at the bindery and therefore has a missing staple; this is not considered a defect. Any staple can be replaced on books up to Fine, but only vintage staples can be used on books from Very Fine to Near Mint. Mint books must have original staples.

PAPER/INTERIOR - Paper is off-white to cream, supple and fresh. No hint of acidity in the odor of the newsprint. Centerfold is secure. Slight interior tears are allowed. A light, barely noticeable water stain or minor foxing that does not distract from the beauty of the book is acceptable for this grade.

BINDERY/PRINTING
limited number of
minor defects

COVER INKS/GLOSS
bright with slightest
dimming of reflectivity

COVER WEAR
flat, no wear, generally centered,
secure

COVER CREASES
1/16-1/8" bend with no color
break allowed

SOILING, STAINING
none allowed except for
slight foxing

DATES/STAMPS
small, inconspicuous
dates/initials allowed

SPINE ROLL
tight and flat, no roll

SPINE SPLIT
none allowed

STAPLES
some discoloration

STAPLE TEARS
none allowed

RUST MIGRATION
none allowed

STRESS LINES
almost no lines

CORNERS
ever-so-slight blunting, no creases

CENTERFOLD
secure

INTERIOR TEARS
slight tears allowed

PAPER QUALITY/COLOR
cream to off-white,
supple and fresh

ACID ODOR
none allowed

MISSING PIECES
none allowed

AMATEUR REPAIRS
none allowed

COUPON CUT
none allowed

READABILITY
preserved

(9.0) VERY FINE / NEAR MINT (VF/NM)

GRADE DESCRIPTION:
Nearly perfect with outstanding eye appeal. The overall look is "as if it was just purchased and read a few times."

BINDERY DEFECTS - A limited number of defects are allowed.

COVER/EXTERIOR - Almost flat with almost imperceptible wear. Inks are bright with slightly diminished reflectivity. An 1/8" bend is allowed if color is not broken. Corners are cut square and sharp with ever-so-slight blunting permitted but no creases. Several lightly penciled, stamped or inked arrival dates are acceptable. No obvious soiling, staining or other discoloration, except for very minor foxing.

SPINE - Tight and flat. No spine roll or split allowed.

STAPLES - Staples may show some discoloration. Only the slightest staple tears are allowed. A very minor accumulation of stress lines may be present if they are nearly imperceptible. No rust migration. In rare cases, a comic was not stapled at the bindery and therefore has a missing staple; this is not considered a defect. Any staple can be replaced on books up to Fine, but only vintage staples can be used on books from Very Fine to Near Mint. Mint books must have original staples.

PAPER/INTERIOR - Paper is cream to off-white and supple. No hint of acidity in the odor of the newsprint. Centerfold is secure. Very minor interior tears may be present.

Collectors should thoroughly examine any such book for restoration, particularly in the case of pre-1965 books. This is a crucial grade that is often misused when a book actually falls in either Very Fine or Near Mint.

BINDERY/PRINTING

limited number of defects

COVER INKS/GLOSS

bright with slightly
diminished reflectivity

COVER WEAR

almost flat, imperceptible wear

COVER CREASES

1/8" bend with no
color break allowed

SOILING, STAINING

very minor foxing

DATES/STAMPS

several dates, stamps,
and/or initials allowed

SPINE ROLL

tight and flat, no roll

SPINE SPLIT

none allowed

STAPLES

some discoloration
allowed

STAPLE TEARS

only the slightest
tears allowed

RUST MIGRATION

none allowed

STRESS LINES

very minor accumulation of
nearly imperceptible lines

CORNERS

no creases

CENTERFOLD

secure

INTERIOR TEARS

very minor tears allowed

PAPER QUALITY/COLOR

cream/off-white, supple

ACID ODOR

none allowed

MISSING PIECES

none allowed

AMATEUR REPAIRS

none allowed

COUPON CUT

none allowed

READABILITY

preserved

GRADE DESCRIPTION:

An almost near perfect copy with outstanding eye appeal. Sharp, bright and clean with supple pages. A comic book in this grade has the appear-ance of having been carefully handled.

BINDERY DEFECTS - A limited accumulation of minor defects is allowed. One or two more than the Very Fine/Near Mint grade.

COVER/EXTERIOR - Almost flat with slight surface wear, possibly including some wear at one of the corners. Inks are generally bright with high reflectivity. A 1/8" – 1/4" bend is acceptable if color is not broken. Accumulation of several lightly penciled, stamped or inked arrival dates may be present. No obvious soiling, staining or other discoloration, except for very minor foxing.

SPINE - Almost flat with no roll. Very minor color break allowed.

STAPLES - Staples may show some discoloration. Very slight staple tears and an accumulation of very minor lines may be present. No rust migration. In rare cases, a comic is not stapled at the bindery and therefore has a missing staple; this is not considered a defect. Any staple can be replaced on books up to Fine, but only vintage staples can be used on books from Very Fine to Near Mint. Mint books must have original staples.

PAPER/INTERIOR: Paper is cream and supple. Centerfold is mostly secure. Very minor interior tears may be present.

NOTE: Certain defects are allowed if other defects are not present.

BINDERY/PRINTING

very limited accumulation of minor defects

COVER INKS/GLOSS

generally bright with moderate to high reflectivity

COVER WEAR

Almost flat with minimal wear

COVER CREASES

1/8" - 1/4" bend with no color break allowed

SOILING, STAINING

very minor foxing

DATES/STAMPS

accumulation of several dates, initials, and store stamps allowed

SPINE ROLL

almost completely flat with no roll

SPINE SPLIT

very minor color break allowed

STAPLES

some discoloration allowed

STAPLE TEARS

only the slightest tears allowed

RUST MIGRATION

none allowed

STRESS LINES

accumulation of very minor lines allowed

CORNERS

no creases, very minute wear allowed

CENTERFOLD

mostly secure

INTERIOR TEARS

very minor tears in margin allowed

PAPER QUALITY/COLOR

cream, supple

ACID ODOR

none allowed

MISSING PIECES

none allowed

AMATEUR REPAIRS

none allowed

COUPON CUT

none allowed

READABILITY

preserved

GRADE DESCRIPTION:

An excellent copy with outstanding eye appeal. Sharp, bright and clean with supple pages. A comic book in this grade has the appearance of having been carefully handled.

BINDERY DEFECTS - A limited accumulation of minor defects is allowed.

COVER/EXTERIOR - Relatively flat with minimal surface wear beginning to show, possibly including some minute wear at corners. Inks are generally bright with moderate to high reflectivity. A 1/4" crease is acceptable if color is not broken. Stamped or inked arrival dates may be present. No obvious soiling, staining or other discoloration, except for minor foxing.

SPINE - Almost flat with no roll. Possible minor color break allowed.

STAPLES - Staples may show some discoloration. Very slight staple tears and a few almost very minor to minor stress lines may be present. No rust migration. In rare cases, a comic was not stapled at the bindery and therefore has a missing staple; this is not considered a defect. Any staple can be replaced on books up to Fine, but only vintage staples can be used on books from Very Fine to Near Mint. Mint books must have original staples.

PAPER/INTERIOR - Paper is tan to cream and supple. No hint of acidity in the odor of the newsprint. Centerfold is mostly secure. Minor interior tears at the margin may be present.

NOTE: Certain defects are allowed if other defects are not present.

BINDERY/PRINTING

limited accumulation of
minor defects

COVER INKS/GLOSS

generally bright with moderate to
high reflectivity

COVER WEAR

relatively flat with minimal wear

COVER CREASES

1/4" bend with no color break
allowed

SOILING, STAINING

minor foxing

DATES/STAMPS

dates, initials, and
store stamps allowed

SPINE ROLL

almost completely flat

SPINE SPLIT

minor color break allowed

STAPLES

some discoloration
allowed

STAPLE TEARS

very slight
tears allowed

RUST MIGRATION

none allowed

STRESS LINES

very minor to minor lines allowed

CORNERS

minute wear allowed

CENTERFOLD

mostly secure

INTERIOR TEARS

minor tears in margin allowed

PAPER QUALITY/COLOR

tan to cream, supple

ACID ODOR

none allowed

MISSING PIECES

none allowed

AMATEUR REPAIRS

none allowed

COUPON CUT

none allowed

READABILITY

preserved

(7.5) **VERY FINE –** (VF–)

GRADE DESCRIPTION:
An above average copy that shows very minor wear but is still relatively flat and clean with outstanding eye appeal. A copy with slightly more wear than a Very Fine copy. Sharp, bright and clean with supple pages. A comic book in this grade has the appearance of having been carefully handled.

BINDERY DEFECTS - A slight accumulation of minor defects is allowed.

COVER/EXTERIOR - Mostly flat with minimal surface wear beginning to show, with slight yellowing or tanning allowed, possibly including some wear at corners. Inks are generally bright with slight to moderate reflectivity. 1/4" to 1/2" bend with very slight color break allowed. Stamped or inked arrival dates may be present. Minor foxing may be present

SPINE - Nearly flat with a possible minor to moderate color break allowed.

STAPLES - Some discoloration allowed. Accumulation of slight staple tears and a few minor stress lines may be present. Slight rust migration allowed. In rare cases, a comic is not stapled at the bindery and therefore has a missing staple; this is not considered a defect. Any staple can be replaced on books up to Fine, but only vintage staples can be used on books from Very Fine to Near Mint. Mint books must have original staples.

PAPER/INTERIOR: Paper is light tan to cream and supple. Centerfold is mostly secure. Minor interior tears in margins may be present.

NOTE: Certain defects are allowed if other defects are not present.

BINDERY/PRINTING

limited accumulation of
minor defects

COVER INKS/GLOSS

generally bright with slight to
moderate reflectivity

COVER WEAR

mostly flat with yellowing or
tanning, minimal wear

COVER CREASES

1/4" - 1/2" bend with very slight
color break allowed

SOILING, STAINING

minor foxing

DATES/STAMPS

dates, initials, and
store stamps allowed

SPINE ROLL

nearly flat

SPINE SPLIT

minor to moderate color break
allowed

STAPLES

some discoloration
allowed

STAPLE TEARS

accumulation of
slight tears allowed

RUST MIGRATION

slight migration allowed

STRESS LINES

a few minor lines allowed

CORNERS

slight wear, blunting or abrading
allowed

CENTERFOLD

mostly secure

INTERIOR TEARS

minor tears in margin allowed

PAPER QUALITY/COLOR

tan to cream, supple

ACID ODOR

none allowed

MISSING PIECES

none allowed

AMATEUR REPAIRS

none allowed

COUPON CUT

none allowed

READABILITY

preserved

(7.0) FINE/VERY FINE (F/VF)

GRADE DESCRIPTION:
An above-average copy that shows minor wear but is still relatively flat and clean with outstanding eye appeal. A comic book in this grade appears to have been read a few times and has been handled with care.

BINDERY DEFECTS - A small accumulation of minor defects is allowed.

COVER/EXTERIOR - Minor wear beginning to show, with interior yellowing or tanning allowed, possibly including minor creases. Corners may be blunted or abraded. Inks are generally bright with a moderate reduction in reflectivity. Stamped or inked arrival dates may be present. No obvious soiling, staining or other discoloration, except for minor foxing.

SPINE - The slightest roll may be present, as well as a possible moderate color break.

STAPLES - Staples may show some discoloration. Slight staple tears and a small accumulation of light stress lines may be present. Slight rust migration. In rare cases, a comic was not stapled at the bindery and therefore has a missing staple; this is not considered a defect. Any staple can be replaced on books up to Fine, but only vintage staples can be used on books from Very Fine to Near Mint. Mint books must have original staples.

PAPER/INTERIOR - Paper is tan to cream, but not brown. No hint of acidity in the odor of the newsprint. Centerfold is mostly secure. Minor interior tears at the margin may be present.

NOTE: Certain defects are allowed if other defects are not present.

BINDERY/PRINTING

small accumulation of
minor defects

COVER INKS/GLOSS

moderate reduction in reflectivity

COVER WEAR

minimal wear, interior yellowing
or tanning allowed

COVER CREASES

minor creases allowed

SOILING, STAINING

minor foxing

DATES/STAMPS

dates, initials, and
store stamps allowed

SPINE ROLL

slightest roll allowed

SPINE SPLIT

moderate color break allowed

STAPLES

some discoloration
allowed

STAPLE TEARS

slight tears
allowed

RUST MIGRATION

slight migration
allowed

STRESS LINES

small accumulation of
light lines

CORNERS

may be blunted or abraded

CENTERFOLD

mostly secure

INTERIOR TEARS

minor tears in margin allowed

PAPER QUALITY/COLOR

tan to cream, not brown

ACID ODOR

none allowed

MISSING PIECES

none allowed

AMATEUR REPAIRS

none allowed

COUPON CUT

none allowed

READABILITY

preserved

FINE +

GRADE DESCRIPTION:

An above-average copy that shows minor wear but is still relatively flat and clean with no significant creasing or other serious defects. Eye appeal is slightly reduced because of light surface wear and the accumulation of small defects, especially on the spine and edges.

A FINE + comic book appears to have been read a few times and has been handled with moderate care.

BINDERY DEFECTS - Small to moderate accumulation of minor defects is allowed. One or two more than the Fine/Very Fine grade.

COVER/EXTERIOR - Minimal to minor wear beginning to show, possibly including some wear at corners. Inks show a moderate to major reduction in reflectivity. Blunted or abraded corners are beginning to appear. Minor accumulation of creases are apparent. Stamped or inked arrival dates may be present. Slight discoloration, staining or foxing.

SPINE - Slight to minor spine roll is allowed. There can also be a 1/8" spine split or color break at spine.

STAPLES - Staples show some discoloration. Slight to minor staple tears and a slight accumulation of minor stress lines may be present. Slight to minor rust migration. In rare cases, a comic is not stapled at the bindery and therefore has a missing staple; this is not considered a defect. Any staple can be replaced on books up to Fine, but only vintage staples can be used on books from Very Fine to Near Mint. Mint books must have original staples.

PAPER/INTERIOR: Paper is light tan to cream, not brown. Centerfold may be slightly loose. Minor interior tears at the margin may be present.

NOTE: Certain defects are allowed if other defects are not present.

BINDERY/PRINTING

small to moderate accumulation
of minor defects

COVER INKS/GLOSS

moderate to major reduction in
reflectivity

COVER WEAR

minimal to minor wear

COVER CREASES

minor accumulation of creases

SOILING, STAINING

slight discoloration, staining,
and/or foxing

DATES/STAMPS

dates/initials/stamps allowed

SPINE ROLL

slight to minor roll allowed

SPINE SPLIT

up to 1/8" split or severe
color break allowed

STAPLES

some discoloration
allowed

STAPLE TEARS

slight to minor tears
allowed

RUST MIGRATION

slight to minor migration
allowed

STRESS LINES

accumulation of minor slight lines

CORNERS

may be blunted or abraded

CENTERFOLD

slightly loose

INTERIOR TEARS

minor tears in margin

PAPER QUALITY/COLOR

tan to cream, not brown

ACID ODOR

none allowed

MISSING PIECES

none allowed

AMATEUR REPAIRS

none allowed

COUPON CUT

none allowed

READABILITY

preserved

(6.0) FINE (FN)

GRADE DESCRIPTION:

An above-average copy that shows minor wear but is still relatively flat and clean with no significant creasing or other serious defects. Eye appeal is somewhat reduced because of slight surface wear and the accumulation of small defects, especially on the spine and edges. A FINE condition comic book appears to have been read a few times and has been handled with moderate care.

BINDERY DEFECTS - Some accumulation of minor defects is allowed.

COVER/EXTERIOR - Minor wear apparent, with minor to moderate creases. Inks show a significant reduction in reflectivity. Blunted corners are more common, as is minor staining, soiling, discoloration, and/or foxing. Stamped or inked arrival dates may be present.

SPINE - A minor spine roll is allowed. There can also be a 1/4" spine split or severe color break.

STAPLES - Staples may show minor discoloration. Minor staple tears and a few slight stress lines may be present, as well as minor rust migration. In rare cases, a comic was not stapled at the bindery and therefore has a missing staple; this is not considered a defect. Any staple can be replaced on books up to Fine, but only vintage staples can be used on books from Very Fine to Near Mint. Mint books must have original staples.

PAPER/INTERIOR - Paper is brown to tan and fairly supple with no signs of brittleness. No hint of acidity in the odor of the newsprint. Minor interior tears at the margin may be present. Centerfold may be loose but not detached.

FINE has historically been the most difficult grade to identify. It is the highest grade which allows a wide range of defects to occur.

NOTE: Certain defects are allowed if other defects are not present.

BINDERY/PRINTING
some accumulation of
minor defects

COVER INKS/GLOSS
major reduction in reflectivity

COVER WEAR
minor wear

COVER CREASES
minor to moderate creases

SOILING, STAINING
minor discoloration, staining,
and/or foxing

DATES/STAMPS
dates/initials/stamps allowed

SPINE ROLL
minor roll allowed

SPINE SPLIT
up to 1/4" split or severe
color break allowed

STAPLES
minor discoloration
allowed

STAPLE TEARS
minor tears
allowed

RUST MIGRATION
minor migration
allowed

STRESS LINES
accumulation of minor lines

CORNERS
blunting or abrasion
more common

CENTERFOLD
loose, not detached

INTERIOR TEARS
minor tears in margin

PAPER QUALITY/COLOR
brown to tan, supple, not brittle

ACID ODOR
none allowed

MISSING PIECES
none allowed

AMATEUR REPAIRS
none allowed

COUPON CUT
none allowed

READABILITY
preserved

GRADE DESCRIPTION:

An average to above average copy that shows moderate wear. Eye appeal is somewhat reduced because of the accumulation of defects. Still a desirable copy that has been handled with some care.

BINDERY DEFECTS - A moderate accumulation of defects allowed.

COVER/EXTERIOR - Minor surface wear showing, with heightened yellowing or tanning allowed; wear at corners more common. Inks show major reduction in reflectivity. Minor to moderate creases with slight dimpling. Stamped or inked arrival dates allowed. Minor accumulation of discoloration, staining or foxing may be present.

SPINE - A minor spine role is allowed. Spine can have a 1/4" - 1/2" split or color break at spine.

STAPLES - Staples show discoloration. Minor staple tears and an accumulation of stress lines may be present as well as minor rust migration. In rare cases, a comic is not stapled at the bindery and therefore has a missing staple; this is not considered a defect. Any staple can be replaced on books up to Fine, but only vintage staples can be used on books from Very Fine to Near Mint. Mint books must have original staples.

PAPER/INTERIOR: Paper is brown to tan and fairly supple with no signs of brittleness. Centerfold is loose, but not detatched. Minor interior tears may be present.

NOTE: Certain defects are allowed if other defects are not present.

BINDERY/PRINTING

moderate accumulation
of defects

COVER INKS/GLOSS

major reduction in reflectivity

COVER WEAR

minor wear with heightened
yellowing or tanning

COVER CREASES

minor to moderate creases with
slight dimpling

SOILING, STAINING

minor accumulation of discoloration, staining, and/or foxing

DATES/STAMPS

dates/initials/stamps allowed

SPINE ROLL

minor roll allowed

SPINE SPLIT

up to 1/4" - 1/2" split or
color break allowed

STAPLES

some discoloration
allowed

STAPLE TEARS

minor tears
allowed

RUST MIGRATION

minor migration
allowed

STRESS LINES

accumulation of minor lines

CORNERS

blunting or abrasion
more common

CENTERFOLD

loose, not detached

INTERIOR TEARS

minor tears

PAPER QUALITY/COLOR

brown to tan, supple, not brittle

ACID ODOR

none allowed

MISSING PIECES

none allowed

AMATEUR REPAIRS

none allowed

COUPON CUT

none allowed

READABILITY

preserved

(5.0) VERY GOOD/ FINE (VG/FN)

GRADE DESCRIPTION:
An above-average but well-used comic book. A comic in this grade shows some moderate wear; eye appeal is somewhat reduced because of the accumulation of defects. Still a desirable copy that has been handled with some care.

BINDERY DEFECTS - An accumulation of defects is allowed.

COVER/EXTERIOR - Minor to moderate wear apparent, with minor to moderate creases and/or dimples. Inks have major to extreme reduction in reflectivity. Blunted or abraded corners are increasingly common, as is minor to moderate staining, discoloration, and/or foxing. Stamped or inked arrival dates may be present.

SPINE - A minor to moderate spine roll is allowed. A spine split of up to 1/2" may be present.

STAPLES - Staples may show minor discoloration. A slight accumulation of minor staple tears and an accumulation of minor stress lines may also be present, as well as minor rust migration. In rare cases, a comic was not stapled at the bindery and therefore has a missing staple; this is not considered a defect. Any staple can be replaced on books up to Fine, but only vintage staples can be used on books from Very Fine to Near Mint. Mint books must have original staples.

PAPER/INTERIOR - Paper is brown to tan with no signs of brittleness. May have the faintest trace of an acidic odor. Centerfold may be loose but not detached. Minor interior tears may also be present.

NOTE: Certain defects are allowed if other defects are not present.

BINDERY/PRINTING

accumulation of defects

COVER INKS/GLOSS

major to extreme reduction in reflectivity

COVER WEAR

minor to moderate wear

COVER CREASES

minor to moderate creases and dimples

SOILING, STAINING

minor to moderate discoloration, staining, and/or foxing

DATES/STAMPS

dates/initials/stamps allowed

SPINE ROLL

minor to moderate roll

SPINE SPLIT

up to 1/2" split

STAPLES

minor discoloration

STAPLE TEARS

slight accumulation of minor tears

RUST MIGRATION

minor migration

STRESS LINES

accumulation of minor lines

CORNERS

blunting or abrasion increasingly common

CENTERFOLD

loose, not detached

INTERIOR TEARS

minor tears

PAPER QUALITY/COLOR

brown to tan, supple, not brittle

ACID ODOR

may have the faintest odor

MISSING PIECES

none allowed

AMATEUR REPAIRS

none allowed

COUPON CUT

none allowed

READABILITY

preserved

(4.5) VERY GOOD + (VG+)

GRADE DESCRIPTION:

An average comic book with less wear and defects than one in Very Good. A comic in this grade shows some moderate wear, but still has enough eye appeal to be a desirable copy.

COVER/EXTERIOR - Cover shows moderate wear, and may be loose but not completely detached. Major to extreme reduction in reflectivity. Can have moderate accumulation of creases or dimples. Corners may be blunted or abraded. Store stamps, name stamps, arrival dates, initials, etc. have no effect on this grade. Moderate discoloration, fading, and/or foxing. As much as 1/8" triangle can be missing out of the corner or edge; a missing 1/16" square is also acceptable. Only minor amateur repair allowed on otherwise high grade copies.

SPINE - Minor to moderate roll may be present and a 1/2"- 1" spine split/color break.

STAPLES - Staples discolored. Accumulation of minor staple tears and stress lines may be present, as well as rust migration.

PAPER/INTERIOR: Paper is brown to tan, supple but not brittle. A minor acidic odor can be detectable. Minor tears throughout book may be present. Centerfold may be loose or detached at one staple. Comics in this condition are still desirable and collectable. The best known copies of some pre-1965 books are in this grade range.

NOTE: Certain defects are allowed if other defects are not present.

BINDERY/PRINTING

do not affect grade

COVER INKS/GLOSS

major to extreme reduction
in reflectivity

COVER WEAR

moderate wear,
may be loose

COVER CREASES

minor to moderate accumulation
of creases or dimples

SOILING, STAINING

moderate accumulation of
discoloration, fading, foxing,
even minor soiling

DATES/STAMPS

do not affect grade

SPINE ROLL

minor to moderate roll

SPINE SPLIT

1/2" to 1" split

STAPLES

minor to major
discoloration

STAPLE TEARS

accumulation of
minor tears

RUST MIGRATION

minor to moderate
migration

STRESS LINES

minor accumulation of lines

CORNERS

blunting or abrasion
increasingly common

CENTERFOLD

loose or detached at one staple

INTERIOR TEARS

minor throughout book

PAPER QUALITY/COLOR

brown to tan, supple, not brittle

ACID ODOR

very minor odor

MISSING PIECES

1/8" triangle, 1/16" square

AMATEUR REPAIRS

very minor repairs on otherwise
high grade

COUPON CUT

none allowed

READABILITY

preserved

(4.0) VERY GOOD (VG)

GRADE DESCRIPTION:

The average used comic book. A comic in this grade shows some significant moderate wear, but still has not accumulated enough total defects to reduce eye appeal to the point that it is not a desirable copy.

COVER/EXTERIOR - Cover shows moderate to significant wear, and may be loose but not completely detached. Moderate to extreme reduction in reflectivity. Can have an accumulation of creases or dimples. Corners may be blunted. or abraded. Store stamps, name stamps, arrival dates, initials, etc. have no effect on this grade. Some discoloration, fading, foxing, and even minor soiling is allowed. As much as a 1/4" triangle can be missing out of the corner or edge; a missing 1/8" square is also acceptable. Only minor unobtrusive tape and other amateur repair allowed on otherwise high grade copies.

SPINE - Moderate roll may be present and/or a 1" spine split.

STAPLES - Staples discolored. Minor to moderate staple tears and stress lines may be present, as well as some rust migration.

PAPER/INTERIOR - Paper is brown but not brittle. A minor acidic odor can be detectable. Minor to moderate interior tears may be present. Centerfold may be loose or detached at one staple.

Comics in this condition are still desirable and collectable. The best known copies of some pre-1965 books are in VG condition.

There are significant differences between this grade and GOOD; over-grading sometimes occurs.

NOTE: Certain defects are allowed if other defects are not present.

BINDERY/PRINTING
do not affect grade

COVER INKS/GLOSS
major to extreme reduction in reflectivity

COVER WEAR
moderate to significant wear, may be loose

COVER CREASES
accumulation of creases or dimples

SOILING, STAINING
some discoloration, fading, foxing, even minor soiling

DATES/STAMPS
do not affect grade

SPINE ROLL
moderate roll

SPINE SPLIT
up to 1" split

STAPLES
discolored

STAPLE TEARS
minor to moderate tears

RUST MIGRATION
some migration

STRESS LINES
minor to moderate lines

CORNERS
blunted or abraded corners

CENTERFOLD
loose or detached at one staple

INTERIOR TEARS
minor to moderate tears

PAPER QUALITY/COLOR
brown, not brittle

ACID ODOR
minor odor

MISSING PIECES
1/4" triangle, 1/8" square

AMATEUR REPAIRS
minor repairs on otherwise high grade

COUPON CUT
none allowed

READABILITY
preserved

(3.5) VERY GOOD – (VG–)

GRADE DESCRIPTION:
An average comic book with more wear and defects than one in Very Good. A comic in this grade shows some significant moderate wear, but still has not accumulated enough total defects to reduce eye appeal to the point that it is not a desirable copy.

COVER/EXTERIOR - Cover shows moderate to significant wear, and may be loose and almost completely detached. Major to extreme reduction in reflectivity. Moderate accumulation of creases or dimples. Corners may be blunted or abraded. Store stamps, name stamps, arrival dates, initials, etc. have no effect on this grade. Accumulation of discoloration, fading, foxing, and even minor soiling is allowed. As much as 1/4" triangle can be missing out of the corner or edge; a missing 1/8" square is also acceptable. Only minor amateur repair allowed on otherwise high grade copies.

SPINE - Moderate roll and a 1" spine split with possible color break.

STAPLES - Staples discolored. Minor to moderate staple tears and stress lines may be present, as well as some rust migration.

PAPER/INTERIOR: Paper is brown but not brittle. A minor acidic odor can be detectable. Minor to moderate interior tears may be present. Centerfold may be loose or detached at one staple. Comics in this condition are still desirable and collectable. The best known copies of some pre-1965 books are in this grade range.

NOTE: Certain defects are allowed if other defects are not present.

BINDERY/PRINTING

do not affect grade

COVER INKS/GLOSS

major to extreme reduction
in reflectivity

COVER WEAR

significant wear,
may be loose or detached at staple

COVER CREASES

moderate accumulation of creases
or dimples

SOILING, STAINING

accumulation of discoloration,
fading, foxing, even minor soiling

DATES/STAMPS

do not affect grade

SPINE ROLL

moderate roll

SPINE SPLIT

up to 1" split with possible
color break

STAPLES

discolored; one may be
missing or replaced

STAPLE TEARS

minor to moderate
tears

RUST MIGRATION

some migration

STRESS LINES

minor to moderate lines

CORNERS

blunted or abraded corners

CENTERFOLD

loose or detached at one staple

INTERIOR TEARS

minor to moderate tears

PAPER QUALITY/COLOR

brown, not brittle

ACID ODOR

minor odor

MISSING PIECES

1/4" triangle, 1/8" square

AMATEUR REPAIRS

minor repairs on otherwise
high grade

COUPON CUT

none allowed

READABILITY

preserved

(3.0) GOOD / VERY GOOD (GD/VG)

GRADE DESCRIPTION:
A used comic book showing some substantial wear. A copy in this grade has all pages and covers, although there may be small pieces missing. Still a reasonably desirable copy and completely readable.

COVER/EXTERIOR - Cover shows significant wear, and may be loose or even detached at one staple. Cover reflectivity is very low. Can have a book-length crease and/or minor dimples. Corners may be blunted, abraded or even rounded. Store stamps, name stamps, arrival dates, initials, etc. have no effect on this grade. An accumulation of discoloration, fading, foxing, and even minor to moderate soiling is allowed. A triangle from 1/4" to 1/2" can be missing out of the corner or edge; a missing 1/8" to 1/4" square is also acceptable. Tape and other amateur repair may be present.

SPINE - Moderate roll likely. May have a spine split of anywhere from 1" to 1-1/2".

STAPLES - Staples may be rusted or replaced. Minor to moderate staple tears and moderate stress lines may be present, as well as some rust migration.

PAPER/INTERIOR - Paper is brown but not brittle. A minor to moderate acidic odor can be detectable. Centerfold may be loose or detached at one staple. Minor to moderate interior tears may be present.

NOTE: Certain defects are allowed if other defects are not present.

BINDERY/PRINTING

do not affect grade

COVER INKS/GLOSS

very low reflectivity

COVER WEAR

significant wear, loose,
may be detached at one staple

COVER CREASES

book-length creases,
minor dimples

SOILING, STAINING

accumulation of discoloration,
fading, foxing,
minor to moderate soiling

DATES/STAMPS

do not affect grade

SPINE ROLL

moderate roll likely

SPINE SPLIT

up to 1-1/2" split

STAPLES

rusted or replaced

STAPLE TEARS

minor to moderate
tears

RUST MIGRATION

some migration

STRESS LINES

moderate lines

CORNERS

blunted or abraded,
may be slightly rounded

CENTERFOLD

loose or detached at one staple

INTERIOR TEARS

minor to moderate tears

PAPER QUALITY/COLOR

brown, not brittle

ACID ODOR

minor to moderate odor

MISSING PIECES

1/4" to 1/2" triangle,
1/8" to 1/4" square

AMATEUR REPAIRS

may be present

COUPON CUT

none allowed

READABILITY

preserved

(2.5) GOOD + (GD+)

GRADE DESCRIPTION:
This grade shows substantial wear but less than a good copy. Comics in this grade have all pages and covers, although there may be small pieces missing. Books in this grade are commonly creased, scuffed, abraded, soiled, but still completely readable.

COVER/EXTERIOR - Cover shows significant wear and may even be loose or partially detached. Nearly none to no reflectivity. Store stamp, name stamp, arrival date and initials are permitted. Near book-length creases and dimples may be present. Blunted, abraded or slightly rounded corners are common. Moderate soiling, staining, discoloration and foxing may be present. The largest piece allowed missing from the front or back cover is usually 1/2" triangle or a 1/4" square. Tape and other forms of amateur repair are common in Silver Age and older books.

SPINE - Moderate roll is likely. May have up to an 1-1/2" split with accumulation of color breaks.

STAPLES - Staples may be rusted or replaced. Moderated staple tears and stress lines may be present, as well as some rust migration.

PAPER/INTERIOR: Paper brown but not brittle. A minor to moderate acidic odor may be present. Centerfold may be loose or detached. Moderate interior tears may be present.

A comic book in Good+ condition can have a moderate to large accumulation of defects but still preserves readability with all coupons still intact.

NOTE: Certain defects are allowed if other defects are not present.

BINDERY/PRINTING

do not affect grade

COVER INKS/GLOSS

nearly no reflectivity
to no reflectivity

COVER WEAR

significant wear,
loose or detached at staples

COVER CREASES

book-length creases
with minor dimples

SOILING, STAINING

accumulation of discoloration,
fading, foxing,
or moderate soiling

DATES/STAMPS

do not affect grade

SPINE ROLL

moderate roll likely

SPINE SPLIT

up to 1-1/2" split with
accumulation of color breaks

STAPLES

rusted or replaced

STAPLE TEARS

moderate tears

RUST MIGRATION

some migration

STRESS LINES

moderate lines

CORNERS

bluunted, abraded or slightly
rounded corners

CENTERFOLD

loose or detached

INTERIOR TEARS

moderate tears

PAPER QUALITY/COLOR

brown, not brittle

ACID ODOR

minor to moderate odor

MISSING PIECES

1/4" - 1/2" triangle,
1/8" - 1/4" square

AMATEUR REPAIRS

may be present

COUPON CUT

none allowed

READABILITY

preserved

(2.0)   GOOD   (GD)

GRADE DESCRIPTION:

This grade shows substantial wear; often considered a "reading copy." Comics in this grade have all pages and covers, although there may be small pieces missing. Books in this grade are commonly creased, scuffed, abraded, soiled, but still completely readable.

COVER/EXTERIOR - Cover shows significant wear and may even be detached. Nearly no reflectivity to no reflectivity. Store stamp, name stamp, arrival date and initials are permitted. Book-length creases and dimples may be present. Rounded corners are more common. Moderate soiling, staining, discoloration and foxing may be present. The largest piece allowed missing from the front or back cover is usually a 1/2" triangle or a 1/4" square, although some Silver Age books such as 1960s Marvels have had the price corner box clipped from the top left front cover and may be considered Good if they would otherwise have graded higher. Tape and other forms of amateur repair are common in Silver Age and older books.

SPINE - Definite roll likely. May have up to a 2" spine split.

STAPLES - Staples may be degraded, replaced or missing. Moderate staple tears and stress lines are common, as well as rust migration.

PAPER/INTERIOR - Paper is brown but not brittle. A moderate acidic odor may be present. Centerfold may be loose or detached. Moderate interior tears may be present.

Some of the most collectable comic books are rarely found in better than GOOD condition. Most collectors consider this the lowest collectable grade because comic books in lesser condition are often incomplete and/or brittle. Traditionally, collectors have sometimes found it difficult to differentiate this grade from the next lower grade, FAIR. This task can be simplified if one remembers that a comic book in GOOD condition can have a moderate to large accumulation of defects but still preserves readability.

NOTE: Certain defects are allowed if other defects are not present.

BINDERY/PRINTING

do not affect grade

COVER INKS/GLOSS

nearly no reflectivity to
no reflectivity

COVER WEAR

significant wear,
may be detached

COVER CREASES

book-length creases with minor to
moderate creases, dimples

SOILING, STAINING

discoloration, fading, foxing,
or moderate soiling

DATES/STAMPS

do not affect grade

SPINE ROLL

roll likely

SPINE SPLIT

up to 2" split

STAPLES

degraded, replaced
or missing

STAPLE TEARS

moderate tears

RUST MIGRATION

may have migration

STRESS LINES

lines are common

CORNERS

rounded corners more common

CENTERFOLD

loose or detached

INTERIOR TEARS

moderate tears

PAPER QUALITY/COLOR

brown, not brittle

ACID ODOR

moderate odor

MISSING PIECES

1/2" triangle, 1/4" square

AMATEUR REPAIRS

common in Silver Age and older

COUPON CUT

none allowed

READABILITY

preserved

GRADE DESCRIPTION:

A comic showing substantial to heavy wear. A copy in this grade still has all pages and covers, although there may be pieces missing. Books in this grade are commonly creased, scuffed, abraded, soiled, and possibly unattractive, but still readable.

COVER/EXTERIOR - Cover shows significant to considerable wear and may even be detached. Nearly none to no reflectivity. Store stamp, name stamp, arrival date and initials are permitted. Book-length creases and major dimpling may be present. Blunted, abraded or rounded corners are common. Significant discoloration, staining, foxing and soiling may be present. Up to 1/2" triangle or a 1/4" square of the back cover may be missing. Tape and other forms of amateur repair are very common in Silver Age and older books, although tape should never be used in comic book repair.

SPINE - Roll is more likely. May have spine split up to 2" with major color breaks.

STAPLES - Staples may be degraded, replaced or missing. An accumulation of staple tears and stress lines are common, as well as rust migration.

PAPER/INTERIOR: Paper is brown and may be beginning to show very slight brittleness around the edges. Acidic odor may be present. Centerfold may be loose or detached. Moderate interior tears are common. Tape and other forms of amateur repair are very common in Silver Age and older books, although tape should never be used in comic book repair.

A comic book in Good– condition can have a large accumulation of defects and is generally readable. All coupons are still intact.

NOTE: Certain defects are allowed if other defects are not present.

BINDERY/PRINTING do not affect grade	**COVER INKS/GLOSS** nearly no reflectivity to no reflectivity
COVER WEAR signifcant considerable wear, may be detached	**COVER CREASES** creases, tears, and folds; major dimpling
SOILING, STAINING significant discoloration, fading, foxing and soiling	**DATES/STAMPS** do not affect grade
SPINE ROLL roll more likely	**SPINE SPLIT** up to 2" split with major color breaks

STAPLES degraded, replaced, one missing	**STAPLE TEARS** accumulation of moderate tears	**RUST MIGRATION** may have migration

STRESS LINES lines are common	**CORNERS** rounded corners common
CENTERFOLD loose or detached	**INTERIOR TEARS** moderate tears
PAPER QUALITY/COLOR brown, very slight brittleness	**ACID ODOR** moderate odor
MISSING PIECES up to 1/2" triangle, 1/4" square	**AMATEUR REPAIRS** very common in Silver Age and older
COUPON CUT none allowed	**READABILITY** generally preserved

(1.5) FAIR / GOOD (FR/GD)

GRADE DESCRIPTION:
A comic showing substantial to heavy wear. A copy in this grade still has all pages and covers, although there may be pieces missing up to and including missing coupons and/or Marvel Value Stamps that do not impact the story. Books in this grade are commonly creased, scuffed, abraded, soiled, and possibly unattractive, but still generally readable.

COVER/EXTERIOR - Cover shows considerable wear and may be detached. Nearly no reflectivity to no reflectivity remaining. Store stamp, name stamp, arrival date and initials are permitted. Book-length creases, tears and folds may be present. Rounded corners are increasingly common. Soiling, staining, discoloration and foxing is generally present. Up to 1/10 of the back cover may be missing. Tape and other forms of amateur repair are increasingly common in Silver Age and older books.

SPINE - Roll is common. May have a spine split between 2" and 2/3 the length of the book.

STAPLES - Staples may be degraded, replaced or missing. Staple tears and stress lines are common, as well as rust migration.

PAPER/INTERIOR - Paper is brown and may show brittleness around the edges. Acidic odor may be present. Centerfold may be loose or detached. Interior tears are common.

NOTE: Certain defects are allowed if other defects are not present.

BINDERY/PRINTING

do not affect grade

COVER INKS/GLOSS

nearly no reflectivity
to no reflectivity

COVER WEAR

considerable wear,
may be detached

COVER CREASES

creases, tears, and folds

SOILING, STAINING

generally present

DATES/STAMPS

do not affect grade

SPINE ROLL

roll common

SPINE SPLIT

between 2" and 2/3 length

STAPLES

degraded, replaced,
one missing

STAPLE TEARS

tears are common

RUST MIGRATION

may have migration

STRESS LINES

lines are common

CORNERS

rounded corners
very common

CENTERFOLD

loose or detached

INTERIOR TEARS

tears are common

PAPER QUALITY/COLOR

brown, edges show brittleness

ACID ODOR

odor present

MISSING PIECES

up to 1/10 of the
back cover missing

AMATEUR REPAIRS

increasingly common in
Silver Age and older

COUPON CUT

none allowed

READABILITY

generally preserved

GRADE DESCRIPTION:

A copy in this grade shows heavy wear. Some collectors consider this the lowest collectible grade because comic books in lesser condition are usually incomplete and/or brittle. Comics in this grade are usually soiled, faded, ragged and possibly unattractive. This is the last grade in which a comic remains generally readable.

COVER/EXTERIOR - Cover may be detached, and inks have lost all reflectivity. Creases, tears and/or folds are prevalent. Corners are commonly rounded or absent. Soiling and staining is present. Books in this condition generally have all pages and most of the covers, although there may be up to 1/4 of the front cover missing or no back cover, but not both. Tape and other forms of amateur repair are more common.

SPINE - Spine roll is more common; spine split can extend up to 2/3 the length of the book.

STAPLES - Staples may be missing or show rust and discoloration. An accumulation of staple tears and stress lines may be present, as well as rust migration.

PAPER/INTERIOR - Paper is brown and may show brittleness around the edges but not in the central portion of the pages. Acidic odor may be present. Accumulation of interior tears. Chunks may be missing. The centerfold may be missing if readability is generally preserved (although there may be difficulty). Coupons may be cut.

Demand for comics in this grade from the 1930s through the 1960s is high, but FR books should be examined for brittleness. Some POOR condition books have missing pages replaced with pages from a different issue or title to give the appearance of a FAIR book.

BINDERY/PRINTING	COVER INKS/GLOSS
do not affect grade	no reflectivity

COVER WEAR	COVER CREASES
may be detached	creases, tears and folds

SOILING, STAINING	DATES/STAMPS
present	do not affect grade

SPINE ROLL	SPINE SPLIT
roll more common	up to 2/3 length

STAPLES	STAPLE TEARS	RUST MIGRATION
may be missing	accumulation of tears	may have migration

STRESS LINES	CORNERS
accumulation of lines	rounded or absent

CENTERFOLD	INTERIOR TEARS
may be missing	accumulation of tears

PAPER QUALITY/COLOR	ACID ODOR
brown, edges show brittleness	odor present

MISSING PIECES	AMATEUR REPAIRS
up to 1/4 front cover or entire back cover, and/or chunks	more common

COUPON CUT	READABILITY
coupon may be cut	generally preserved to difficulty

GRADE DESCRIPTION:
Most comic books in this grade have been sufficiently degraded to the point where there is little or no collector value; they are easily identified by a complete absence of eye appeal. Comics in this grade are brittle almost to the point of turning to dust with a touch, and are usually incomplete.

COVER/EXTERIOR - Extreme fading may render the cover almost indiscernible. May have extremely severe stains, mildew or heavy cover abrasion to the point that some cover inks are indistinct/absent. Covers may be detached with large chunks missing. Can have extremely ragged edges and extensive creasing. Corners are rounded or virtually absent. Covers may have been defaced with paints, varnishes, glues, oil, indelible markers or dyes, and may have suffered heavy water damage. Can also have extensive amateur repairs such as laminated covers.

SPINE - Extreme roll present; can have extremely ragged spines or a complete, book-length split.

STAPLES - Staples can be missing or show extreme rust and discoloration. Extensive staple tears and stress lines may be present, as well as extreme rust migration.

PAPER/INTERIOR - Paper exhibits moderate to severe brittleness (where the comic book literally falls apart when examined). Extreme acidic odor may be present. Extensive interior tears. Multiple pages, including the centerfold, may be missing that affect readability. Coupons may be cut.

BINDERY/PRINTING

do not affect grade

COVER INKS/GLOSS

extreme fading

COVER WEAR

detached with chunks missing

COVER CREASES

extreme creases, ragged edges

SOILING, STAINING

extreme soiling, staining
and discoloration

DATES/STAMPS

do not affect grade

SPINE ROLL

extreme roll

SPINE SPLIT

extremely ragged or
completely split

STAPLES

missing or extremely
rusted, discolored

STAPLE TEARS

extensive tears

RUST MIGRATION

extreme migration

STRESS LINES

many lines

CORNERS

rounded or absent

CENTERFOLD

may be missing

INTERIOR TEARS

extensive tears

PAPER QUALITY/COLOR

moderate to severe brittleness

ACID ODOR

extreme odor

MISSING PIECES

large chunks of front cover and
back cover, and/or interior

AMATEUR REPAIRS

extensive repairs

COUPON CUT

coupon(s) may be cut

READABILITY

multiple pages missing

GRADE DESCRIPTION:

These designations are only used for the purpose of authentication. Numerous collectors and comic fans will purchase coverless comics to either read or to obtain a filler copy of a book for their collection.

Books that are coverless, but are otherwise complete, will receive a grade of 0.3, as will covers missing their interiors.

Copies in this designation typically will in most cases be beyond collectability to the majority of the hobby.

Detective Comics #27,
May 1939.
© DC Comics.
Coverless.

GRADE DESCRIPTION:
These designations are only used for the purpose of authentication. Numerous collectors and comic fans will purchase coverless comics to either read or to obtain a filler copy of a book for their collection.

Coverless copies that have incomplete interiors, wraps or single pages will receive a grade of 0.1, as will just front covers or just back covers.

Copies in this designation typically will in most cases be beyond collectability to the majority of the hobby.

Rare key comics and incomplete pages i.e. centerfolds are considered to be valuable by the collecting community for either restoration purposes or for individuals who just wish to own a piece of comic history.

Action Comics #1, June 1938.
© DC Comics.
Partial front cover only.